Changing Sky

Also by TR FISCHER

Colorado Tempest Series:

Prey For Me - Book One

Sierra Chronicles:

A Man Around The House - Book One

TR FISCHER

Changing Sky

For Basia,
Happy reading,

Renaissance
PRESS

To the men and women serving as medics in the United States armed services who put their lives on the line that others may live.

CHAPTER ONE

Spring, senior year of high school

LYING IN THE GRASS, SKYLAR tucked her arms behind her head and stared up at the clouds. The Colorado sun baked her skin as she lay on the thick carpet of green in Denver's Washington Park. "That one looks like a bear."

"It looks like a blob." Joe laughed and ruffled her hair.

"Cut it out." She batted his hand, pointed toward the mountains. "Over there, dummy."

"Have you been smoking something, Sky?" His hand flopped on the grass touching hers but neither one pulled away.

"Hey, that looks like a goose with three little goslings," she gestured toward a cluster of clouds to the north.

"It does." They fell quiet a moment.

Cars passing on Downing Street filled the silence. But they'd have been fine without that. They were used to quiet between them. It was never awkward with Joe the way it was with other people. Where you struggled to bridge the gap, to put words in the air, your heart speeding up, your breath coming quick and shallow as the silence stretched.

Joe squeezed her hand. "It's morphing into a caterpillar." He rolled on his side, putting him closer than just a friend. "Are you coming to my game tonight? Coach Hill says there's gonna be a scout from the Giants to watch me and Alex." He rolled a baseball in one hand, tracing the red stitching with his fingertips. He probably did that in his sleep.

Skylar bent her knees, her bare feet flat on the soft grass, toes curling and straightening, loving the feel of it. "I have a science test to study for. I have to get an A."

"You're wasting your time. McGuire hardly ever gives A's." Abel McGuire was the oldest and strictest science teacher at South High School.

"I've gotten an A on everything so far." Skylar knew she sounded cocky. And she wasn't sorry. Even though she probably should be. How many times had her mother told her arrogance was unbecoming? Who used words like unbecoming anymore?

"You're the teacher's pest." Joe rolled the baseball up her forearm.

"Pet," Skylar corrected, nudging his leg with her foot.

"No ... pest." He laughed. "He's probably giving you A's to get you off his back. Everyone knows you make your teachers work too hard. I've heard they have staff meetings about you that run late into the night."

"Funny." Joe could joke all he wanted. Skylar had goals. A plan. Every year of her life was mapped out until she was thirty. There would be four years of college. Two of grad school. Marriage to Mr. Right somewhere between age twenty-six and twenty-eight, give or take. No kids until after the big three-o. "If my grades drop at all, I'll lose my scholarship and I can kiss college goodbye." Though she focused on the clouds, she felt his eyes boring into the side of her head, willing her to look at him. But she knew if she did, she would kiss him.

His gaze moved lower like a heat-seeking missile. In all the years of her secret on-and-off crushes on Joe, he'd never shown any interest beyond being pals. Hanging out at the park, going for walks, riding bikes—and of course—playing baseball. Considering that she'd had breasts and hips since ninth grade, she didn't understand his recent change of heart.

Skylar was dying to know what it would be like to kiss him but was too embarrassed to let on, taking comfort in the knowledge that she got to be with him on a regular basis. If they crossed that line and things didn't work out, where would she be? And if things did work out, it would make parting for college too painful. "Stop staring."

"I can't help it." His voice sounded different now; soft and low, brimming with some unnamed emotion. He tucked a stray lock of her hair behind her ear, sending a pleasant sensation rushing through her. "You're my girl, Skylar."

"I'm not anyone's girl." A relationship didn't fit into the plan. Not now, anyway. Why had she met him so early? She wished for a cosmic pause button that would zoom them out four or five years.

"I get first dibs."

"You can't call shotgun on a girl, Joey." Skylar shot him a pointed look.

"I just did." His gold-flecked green eyes softened, melting her insides. He set the ball down, rested his hand on her hip. "And no one but you has called me Joey since fourth grade."

The two had been best friends for most of that time. But now Joe wanted more. He'd been asking her out every week for a month and she was out of excuses. And willpower. Skylar released a slow breath, wanting—and not wanting—to give in. "You'll always be Joey to me," she said softly.

"And you'll always be my girl." Joe kissed her lightly, as though testing her resolve. The feel of his lips on hers made Skylar's heart race. She couldn't help that her hand cupped the back of his head, pulling him in again. He was a lot better at this than she'd expected. Every time she thought she was driving, he'd take the wheel and steer them to a hotter place. When she finally drew back, he flashed a broad smile. "I knew it."

"What?" Her cheeks heated.

"You want me as much as I want you."

Even though he was right, Skylar flashed her eyes at him. Then she heard her mom's voice inside her head, reminding her that guys were trouble. Especially when they thought you belonged to them. How many times had Georgie said it? But Joe was always so sweet. Even when she pushed him away. Why did she do that? A pang of guilt snaked through her.

But moving from friendship would complicate things. Unless he was drafted early, they'd both be in college at least four years. Her financial limitations meant she had no choice but to stay in Colorado, but Joe had full-ride baseball scholarship offers from a number of Texas and California schools. And if he ended up in the pros, it wouldn't matter where he lived. He would be pitching in a different city every few days and they would hardly see each other.

Joe lifted one brow, a question in his gaze. It was cruel to leave him hanging. Skylar swallowed her fears. "I'll be there tonight." She touched his cheek and kissed him again. A tsunami of warmth swirled outward from her core. Why had she fought it so long? "Good luck."

Joe's eyes lit. "Thanks. I'll give you a ride home after." He helped her to her feet.

CHAPTER TWO

Eight years later …

SKYLAR SILENCED HER ALARM clock and stared at the popcorn ceiling for several seconds before tossing the covers aside and dragging herself out of bed. Freeway noise, cheerful birdsong and the sound of a dog barking drifted in through the open window. She thought of the honeysuckle that grew on the trellis outside the bedroom at Joe's place. How its sweetness wafted in on the breeze. Someone else was enjoying it now. She straightened the covers and placed the throw pillows in a neat row against the headboard. After a hearty breakfast of eggs, home fries and toast with grape jelly, she headed to work.

When she locked her car she blew out a breath, bracing for the next twenty minutes. Once she was out on her route the day was relatively easy. It was what happened beforehand that caused her stomach to swirl unpleasantly. Slinging her backpack over one shoulder, she entered the large metal building. Thick red beams arced upward from the sides of the warehouse, connecting with an even bigger one in the center of the ceiling. Smaller joists ran perpendicular to them supporting the roof.

A group of guys in brown uniforms huddled in the open area between the neat row of matching brown trucks backed up to the concrete dock. One of them glanced over and made a joke she couldn't decipher, eliciting loud guffaws that echoed through the open space. She knew the joke might not be about her, but that didn't quell her anxiety. As she strode to the small finished area that held the offices and restrooms, she kept her shoulders back and lifted her chin.

Inside the restroom, she changed into her brown work shorts and shirt. The shorts were too big at the waist and snug around her hips and backside. Barely manageable, given how much she had to move around. The shirt was worse. Her manager had promised to order a bigger size but it hadn't come in yet. Skylar leaned against the stall door and fastened the buttons.

The first time she'd tried it on, she thought she'd been given a man's shirt. But the label said different. Apparently, the uniform designer had never seen a woman with curves. The thick cotton fabric hugged her breasts, gapping open between the buttons at her bust line. She made a frustrated noise in her throat and dug in her pack for the safety pin she'd put there the night before. She worked the tip through the thick fabric, pinning the gap closed. Totally lame, but there was nothing for it.

Skylar exited the stall and stared at her reflection in the large rectangular mirror that hung over a row of stainless steel sinks. After pulling her hair into a knot, she gently pressed the soft puffy tissue around her eyes. No one here knew it wasn't normal because she'd looked like this since she started a few days earlier. "This isn't forever," she murmured, trying to convince herself.

She left the safety of the bathroom and moved through the open bay. Her job was physically demanding, but nothing like how she'd spent the last three years, responsible for so many. As a teacher, she'd been busy all day and taken work home with her more often than not. This job boiled down to efficient use of one's time and following protocol. Beating trains to their crossings and outsmarting traffic lights. Good customer service. Right now, it was all she could handle.

Skylar tossed her backpack into her truck and joined a group that was beginning to stretch. Of the eighty-three employees at the delivery hub, she was one of six women. She scanned for Porter and moved to the farthest point away from him, staying to the outside of the bunch to avoid being ogled from behind. Friendly jokes floated up as everyone stretched, preparing for eight hours of lifting and driving.

The August heat began early in the day and got worse by the hour. A few of the guys already stunk, forcing Skylar to breathe through her mouth so she wouldn't gag. Fortunately, none of them would be riding along. At least Bill knew how to shower and put on deodorant. And he wasn't the ogling type.

Someone nearby said, "We should start a pool for when Skylar pops a button and we'll get a look at what she's hiding in there. Five bucks says it happens this week." A few more chimed in with bets for which day.

Skylar kept her face impassive, avoiding eye contact with the men around her. She extended her right leg and pulled up on the toe, stretching her hamstring. Her hope was that after she proved herself, this kind of treatment would abate. In her current emotional state, she wasn't sure how long she could tolerate it.

When she leaned sideways to stretch her lats, the fabric over her breasts pulled taut. She pictured the safety pin holding her shirt together bursting from the pressure. The buttons would likely follow suit and someone would gather his money and gloat.

"Sky may be a gutter hire, but she's sure fun to watch." This came from a man she hadn't met. One of Porter's pals.

Skylar clenched her teeth. The official term was *street hire*, a pejorative in the minds of some. The union only allowed one of five new hires to come off the street. The rest had to come from union ranks. Not everyone was averse to her presence. In fact, most of the guys were midway between polite and friendly. But the few bad apples made it their mission to disrupt any positive interactions, so she'd stopped putting her energy there.

"True, but that's not why she's here. She's supposed to be able to empty and fill that truck every day. I give her one week on her own before she goes cryin' to management about how it's too hard." This came from Porter, the sound of his voice so close, it raised the hairs on the back of her neck. Apparently, he'd spotted her and slithered over like the snake that he was.

Skylar spun to face him, jamming her hand in the pocket that held her utility knife. His cold blue eyes followed, narrowing slightly. He crossed his arms over his puffed-out chest. She stared him down, unwilling to add words to the mix. Her dad had taught her to take on all comers without blinking—especially men who underestimated her. But her father's methods weren't her style, though she did keep them tucked away. An ace up her sleeve if she needed it.

"That route belongs to me." Porter stalked to his truck.

Skylar wiped her moist palms on the back of her shorts and headed to her truck where Bill perched on the rear bumper. She set aside her emotional armor. "Hey, Bill. Just think, at this time tomorrow, you could be playing golf." She was his final trainee before he retired.

He laughed. "Don't know about that, but I definitely won't be here. We all set?"

"Yes. I'll try to make your last day a good one." Skylar checked that the rear bulkhead door was latched before climbing in. Bill joined her, taking the passenger seat.

"Okay, Sky, you should have your first twenty or so stops in your head and be planning your trace." Bill referred to the path Skylar would take on her route. "Eventually, you'll know exactly where you'll be at a given moment. You've got software and the GPS, but you'll do better if you put it on your hard drive." He touched a finger to the side of his head. "The technology gets the streets and the traffic, but not the dogs or the school buses. Or the special requests."

In the rear, three stainless steel shelves ran the length of the side walls, each angled slightly upward in front to keep boxes from falling off. Skylar walked down the aisle where the air carried a mix of cardboard and diesel fuel, making sure the packages were in the order of their drop locations and looking for anything big that would get in the way. Bill had taught her to get any large boxes out early to make room for pickups and maneuvering in the narrow space. Satisfied, she took her seat and started the motor.

Bill buckled in. "A nine hour day becomes a twelve hour day if you don't bang out the first two just right." He opened a can of soda and placed it on the dash.

"What are you doing?" asked Skylar.

"Today you're gonna learn how to drive without throwing your load." He grinned, eyes twinkling.

The day before, she'd taken a turn too fast and a few boxes ended up on the floor.

"Not a drop of that comes out of the can."

Skylar sucked in an exaggerated breath and straight-armed the steering wheel. "Okay, Obi-Wan."

Bill shook his head, a humorous look on his face.

The next-day-air packages always came first. She made quick work of them, slipping in several other deliveries along the way. Getting there even one minute after ten-thirty entitled the customer to a full refund. Skylar approached a light on a busy street.

"Move to the right lane so you don't get boxed in. It's not bad now but it often is down here, especially before and after a Rockies game."

She cringed inwardly at the thought of driving by Coors Field, where the Colorado Rockies played baseball. So many memories. The regular season ended in just a few weeks. "What's the best route?" She pictured Joe on the mound. Left knee raised near his elbow, eyes aimed over his shoulder, shaded by the brim of his cap. The wind-up. Lightning release. Every ounce of energy focused on launching the baseball—which consisted of a piece of cork bound by a mile of string, all of it covered in horse or cow hide—just inside the strike zone. He'd had an eighty-seven mile per hour fastball his last season in high school. That was how she liked to remember him. Before his life mimicked that pitch.

"This way." Bill pointed to an adjacent alley and explained how to avoid getting blocked in by other delivery trucks.

Later that morning, she pulled in behind an art gallery in Lodo— the nickname for lower downtown, Denver. She glanced at the full soda can. "Are you going to let that go to waste? I think I have this down."

Bill raised a brow. "That can is gonna sit there all day. Besides, my wife won't let me drink that stuff."

Skylar made a show of looking around as she placed her dolly outside. "Is she hiding somewhere?"

He chuckled. "You've got a lot of spunk, Sky. I think you might make it."

"That's good. I always wanted to be a cardboard therapist," she lied.

"It's probably better than the other kind. You won't get fat wrangling boxes. I like to say we're occupational athletes."

She huffed as she hauled a large box down the metal steps to the dolly. "That's a fair assessment." Being constantly on the go was the reason she'd taken the job. No time for wallowing.

When Skylar returned, Bill had a thoughtful look on his face. "I saw your resume. What are you doing working here?"

She sat down and fastened her seatbelt. Eyes straight ahead. "Marking time."

"Mmm. The strong, silent type."

Skylar shrugged. Strong? Not so much. She thought about the month she'd lost. Gone. A black hole. The only clear memory was waking up in a hotel room wearing nothing but a gold watch on her wrist. Its large face and wide band told her it belonged to a man. For some reason, she recalled every detail—a small diamond on the bezel near each digit and a gold crown in place of the number twelve. Someone had been in the bathroom taking a shower and she'd panicked when she couldn't remember who it was. She'd slipped the watch off and tossed it on the pillow before tugging on her clothes. When the shower turned off, she'd grabbed her purse and fled with her shoes in her hand.

Skylar was relieved when Bill didn't probe further. She didn't want to be the thing he remembered on his last day. The one mind-blowing story that stood out after twenty-three years. She slowed for her next stop.

"Do you mind if I go in so I can say goodbye to Enrique?"

"Not at all." She didn't remember that name from the previous day.

Bill hopped out and Skylar backed in near the office of The Bloody Knuckles Garage, a motorcycle repair shop. Every time she backed into a parking space, her thoughts went to her father. Even when they were off duty, cops liked to park facing out so they could leave in a hurry. Though he'd retired and now worked as a private investigator, he still parked that way.

There were three boxes on this drop, but Skylar only saw two. A more careful search netted the third wedged near the wall. She stacked them all on the dolly and wheeled it inside.

"Enrique, this is Skylar," Bill said enthusiastically, the moment she'd cleared the door.

A man behind the counter got to his feet. Not the same sandy blond who'd been there the day before. This guy had dark hair, even darker eyes. His yesterday morning shadow was split by a brilliant smile that probably got him whatever he wanted whenever he wanted it. Gorgeous.

Suddenly the smile fell away and his golden-brown face darkened like the sky in a sudden summer storm. Skylar's steps faltered at the onslaught of black emotion that emanated from this man. She blinked, filled her lungs, struggling to make sense of it. Unsure what to do and fearful she might actually turn tail and sprint out the door, she planted her feet and glanced at Bill. His face fell, his eyes signaling a silent apology. A set-up gone south?

Enrique said nothing.

Remembering she had a job to do, Skylar slipped on her I-can-handle-this mask and maneuvered the dolly toward the counter. Apparently, Bill didn't know Enrique as well as he thought. He was too nice a man to have done this otherwise. As she scanned the boxes, she silently repeated what she'd said to her reflection hours before. This wasn't forever. Just until she caught her balance. Found her feet. She passed the scanner to Enrique for his signature.

On the wall behind him hung the calendar she'd noticed the day before. The one with a naked woman leaning back on a Harley. It was certainly what one would expect in a place like this. But even with the post-it-note covering the model's bare necessities, she wanted to tear it down and throw it away. Instead, she reasoned with herself. The woman hadn't been forced to do it. Most likely, she'd been paid very well. Skylar would have to learn to shut up and keep a straight face in places like this. Every job had its hazards.

"Any pick-ups today?"

He grunted something that sounded like yes and scribbled his name on the small screen.

Skylar slacked one hip and lifted a brow. "So, yes? Is that what you said?"

His eyes, now hooded beneath a forest of dark lashes, seemed to telegraph that he didn't appreciate clear communication. Perhaps it was just that it came from a fully clothed woman. "Yes," he said coolly.

Skylar wanted to clap and congratulate him for enunciating properly. But he looked to be about thirty, rather than eight, which was how he behaved. Knowing she would have to come here often, it wouldn't be wise to stir the pot any more. "Okay." She grabbed hold of the dolly.

"Andy usually handles the shipping." He thumbed toward an open door that led to a large bay filled with motorcycles, four-wheelers, snow mobiles and other machines one could ride.

Thank God. Skylar gave a slight nod. "I met him yesterday." Andy didn't act like he ate storm clouds for breakfast. How could anyone run a successful service business with such a sour attitude?

CHAPTER THREE

ENRIQUE WATCHED THE NEW delivery driver return to her truck. Her long tan legs quickly ate up the distance and a thick blond knot bobbed high on the back of her head. The boxy brown uniform did a poor job camouflaging the kind of curves most guys dreamed about. He wondered how she hauled boxes that weighed more than she appeared to herself.

Bill said she was better than any other trainee he'd worked with. A quick study. Thing was, Enrique was a quick study too. And it had taken him a quarter of a second to see she looked a lot like his ex-wife. His colossal mistake. Except Kendra wouldn't be caught dead dressed like that.

Enrique rubbed his chin. The idea of Kendra being caught dead had a certain appeal, but he moved on from that thought. "Andy."

His mechanic appeared in the doorway. "Yeah?"

"We got a new delivery driver."

"I met her yesterday." Andy grinned, stood a little taller. "Ya know, she sort of reminds me of Kendra."

Enrique glowered. "I want you to deal with her."

"This afternoon? I've got to finish the—"

"Every afternoon. And every morning." It would complicate things, but Enrique was determined to avoid her.

Andy shrugged. "Fine by me, but it will set me back time-wise."

Enrique watched the brown truck leave the lot and the shop cat meowed. "Pipe down. You'll get fed soon enough." He released a sigh that came out more like a growl. "C'mere, cat." The gray ball of fluff followed him to the back room, where he leapt onto the cot, purring loudly. "Hey. That's my bed." Enrique set the cat on the floor and filled his bowl with kibble. The cat approached slowly with his tail up, twitching at the tip. The phone rang and Enrique went to answer it.

"*Eh, primo*, it's Manny. Got any extra work this week?" Manny was his cousin, his *primo*. He'd worked on things like lawn mowers but he wasn't trained on pleasure machines. Someone who dropped thirty grand on a Harley didn't want just anyone looking under the hood, so to speak. Unfortunately, his uncle hadn't taken that into consideration when he was running the place.

Enrique closed his eyes and leaned back in his chair. "No. We've only got warranty work right now. Has to be done by certified techs. I'll text you if I get something you can do."

Manny sighed.

"*Lo siento*, Manny." And he *was* sorry. Manny was more like a best friend than a cousin. Plus, he had three kids and a fourth on the way. Sometimes his income didn't cover all their expenses.

"Who's gonna know?"

Enrique shifted uncomfortably. "Me." *I like to sleep at night.* Though he hadn't done enough of that for the last six months. He spent most evenings working in the shop since he lost more than half of each day running errands, ordering parts and dealing with customers who were in no hurry to pick up their machines.

"*Tio* Armando promised me work."

Their uncle had passed six months earlier, leaving the shop to Enrique, who had worked alongside him each summer since his early teens, until he enlisted in the army at nineteen. Problem was, the shop was hemorrhaging money. Enrique was too. Thanks to Kendra, who never met a purse or a pair of shoes she could live without. "Manny, I don't know what to tell you. I have no clue how *Tio* paid the bills around here. The finances are a mess. I'll show you the books if you want. I had to drop twenty-five grand on equipment last month. And we need a lot more if we're gonna get the good-paying work. I think I can get things turned around but it's not gonna be easy." If his family weren't counting on him, he'd have shut the place down and sold the building, the only real asset. Enrique liked a challenge but after six months, he was beginning to run out of steam.

"It's cool. It's just that Irena's after me to get our credit card paid off before Christmas."

At least that was four months away. Enrique ran a hand over his unshaven face. He hadn't shaved this morning. The delivery driver seemed to have noticed. Her eyes had taken him in, a softness there. But he'd shut her down quickly. He ignored that niggling feeling inside, like his mother poking his ribs with a sneaky finger when he'd been rude.

Skylar parked across the street from the motorcycle shop and read the sign in front of the business. "Smile and Relax Therapy?" She threw Bill a dubious look.

"Yep. Exactly what you think it is. Massage with a happy ending. And who knows what else? You need to be careful here, Sky. Keep your eyes open and check your mirrors before you get out. I've seen some real sleaze bags coming and going. Don't let your guard down."

Skylar tightened her jaw. "I'll go in by myself. I don't want them to think I need a chaperone." She checked that her knife was in her pocket and walked to the rear of the truck.

As she carried the package to the building, she took in her surroundings; what kind of cars and how many were parked in the lot, the location of each window and door. It was as if her father were a miniature cartoon character sitting on her shoulder. *Pay attention to details, Sky. You never know what's gonna matter later.* She exhaled. Why hadn't he warned her about Enrique? And why did her skin prickle?

A tall blond man on his way out made no effort to disguise a full-body scan as he held the door for her. "Thanks," Skylar gritted as she passed, because good manners were automatic. To her right was a shabby waiting area with a mid-grade brown leather sofa and a water dispenser with cone-shaped paper cups. What was the point of a cup one couldn't set down? She made her way to a counter along the opposite wall and set the box down.

A dark-haired woman emerged from a hall to the left. A clingy red dress belted around her waist exposed more of her meaty thighs than the world should have to see. Zebra-print heels completed the ensemble. "I'll take care of that." Her raspy voice indicated a heavy smoking habit.

Skylar scanned the box.

"You new?" The woman arched a perfectly shaped brow, flashing a sensual smile that made Skylar's skin crawl.

"I am. My name is Skylar." Rather than shake the woman's hand, Skylar held out the scanner.

"I'm Glenda. The good witch." She winked and signed the small screen.

Skylar quashed an eye roll. "Any pickups today?"

"We never have pickups." The good witch gave a throaty laugh. "Well, not that kind."

Thank God. "Okay." In several long strides, Skylar escaped. As she pulled out of the drive, she watched a man making his way up the steps. Big and bald with rolls of jiggling fat. "Geez. I feel bad for whoever has to touch him. Just standing in there for a minute made me want to take a shower." She had no clue why Porter would want this route. Then again ... he'd probably go for the good witch, him being such a warlock.

Bill ran a hand through his thinning gray hair. "I hear ya. They're always offering me a special deal. I s'pose you won't need to worry about that."

The afternoon was busy but uneventful. The cure for what ailed her. At the end of her route, Skylar drove to the warehouse. She backed her truck into the dock and the two of them exited.

"Not a drop spilled. Nicely done, Sky." Bill tossed the full soda into a trashcan. "You coming to my party?" He indicated a folding table that had been erected in the un-walled break room. Men were milling about, joking and sipping from red Solo cups.

Skylar reached into her backpack. Tried to think what to say. She'd heard about the party but had no interest in hanging out with the guys, not knowing who had her on their hate list. "I don't think so. But I brought something for you." She pulled out an envelope and passed it to Bill.

"You did? Thank you." He stopped to open it and Skylar waited. It was a gift card for a restaurant where Bill said he'd always wanted to take his wife. He eyed her. "This is very generous, Sky. I'm not sure I deserve it. We've only known each other—"

"Of course you do. You mentioned your anniversary is next month.

I hope it's enough for a night to remember." That thought brought a sharp pang of sadness. Skylar gave him a quick hug. "Good luck. And thanks." Not allowed to wear her uniform outside of work, she made a beeline for the restroom.

When she was back in her street clothes, she peeked out the door. Everyone at the party was toasting Bill. She hurried quietly along the office wall, barely suppressing the urge to jump when she rounded the corner and spotted Porter blocking her path. He held a plate with a piece of uneaten cake. Skylar sucked in a breath and sidestepped him.

"I brought you a peace offering." He kept pace with her as she moved toward the exit. "What's your hurry?"

Skylar glanced over. "I have to be somewhere."

With each step, Porter moved closer to her side, effectively steering her closer to the wall. "You're not much of a team player, are you, Sky?"

She stopped walking and Porter got out ahead several strides before he figured it out. He turned. She'd pulled her knife from her pocket and he stood mute as she flicked it open and pretended to clean a fingernail. Knowing full well it was a felony to threaten someone with a knife, she didn't look up or say anything. If the tremor she felt in her middle made its way to her hands, she'd slice her finger. After a moment, she closed the knife and slipped it into her pocket. "I don't like cake. But thanks for thinking of me, Porter." His name came out hard. She brought her eyes to his and jerked her chin.

He got out of the way.

She felt him watching her, hating her, on her way to the door.

CHAPTER FOUR

May, senior year of high school

SKYLAR THRUMMED HER FINGERS on the library table. Someone pulled out the chair beside her and she glanced over.

Joe bumped her shoulder with his hip. "Hey."

Skylar smiled. "Hi."

He leaned close and kissed her. The only thing in the world that was better than chocolate.

"Are you lost? You know this is the library, right?" She scooted her chair to make room for him.

"Ha ha." He pulled a book from his backpack and set it on the table. "Your mom said I'd find you here."

"Did she have to draw you a map?"

He smirked. "I've been here before. Once."

Skylar snorted and took a moment to stretch. "For story time when you were three?"

"Why didn't you answer my texts?"

She waved at her books. "I turn off my cell when I study."

"I need a favor. I'm failing trig."

"Is this your way of asking me to help you?"

"Yeah." His hand slid under her hair, caressing her neck. "But I was thinking of a trade."

Skylar tapped her pencil on the table. "A trade? What do you have that I want?" *Besides ... everything?*

He spread his hands, indicating himself.

She rolled her eyes and went back to her book. He'd read her mind, but she wasn't going to admit it. Especially here.

Joe sagged in his chair. "Coach says I'm off the roster beginning next week if I don't bring my grade up. Will you help me?"

Skylar relented and gave him a squeeze. "Of course I will. It will give us an excuse to see each other more often." Her mother was not happy they'd begun dating and limited their time together. Most likely, she'd make an exception for tutoring.

They spent the next two hours getting Joe up to speed for an upcoming test. A librarian came over. "Time to go, Skylar. We need to lock up."

"Are you on a first name basis with all the librarians?" Joe asked, shaking his head in wonder.

Skylar laughed. "Pretty much."

"I'll drive you home," Joe said, as they gathered their things.

"It's nice out. I can walk." The last place Skylar wanted to be— well, should be—was Joe's car. That was where she always lost herself with him. Every block with his hand on her shoulder or touching her hair, was like a fast-forward button. Who knew friendship could turn into this? She cared so deeply about him that it scared her. He'd be leaving Colorado in August and she wasn't sure how she'd survive.

"Come on." He grabbed her hand. "My girl isn't walking alone in the dark."

"It might actually be safer than riding in your car." She laced their fingers.

He laughed.

CHAPTER FIVE

ENRIQUE GLANCED UP FROM his desk. The delivery driver was petting the cat, who had recently decided the front counter was his favorite spot at this time of day. A coincidence? Not likely. He ended his call and got to his feet. "I'll get Andy."

"What's his name?"

Enrique frowned, confused. "Andy?"

Her light-brown eyes sparkled with humor. "The cat." She lifted him into her arms and he began purring when she worked her fingers behind his ears. Enrique stared, dumbfounded. In the four months since Enrique had rescued him from the dumpster in the alley, the cat had never let anyone hold him. The smile that blossomed lit her whole face. She made a soft murmur of pleasure when the cat nudged her chin, causing a layer of ice to melt in the glacier encasing Enrique's heart. "He's a sweet little guy."

Enrique snapped out of his trance. "He doesn't have a name. Andy!"

"Be there in a minute."

"No name? What do you call him?" She frowned.

"Cat." Enrique tried to think what to say to get out of there. She was a big girl and could wait by herself.

"Cat." She repeated flatly, like she didn't believe him. Her gaze probed his, as if scanning for signs of a soul.

No. Enrique refused to let himself be drawn in. He needed to rebuild the ice. It was his only protection from this mesmerizing woman. The best way to shake off a woman was to act like a jerk. "Well, sometimes when I'm feeling adventurous, I call him Shop Cat." He used a sarcastic tone.

"You must lead a very exciting life." His plan worked because this came out with an edge. All traces of humor left her face and she looked away. Enrique felt a sting of regret. She set the cat on the counter and scanned the packages. "I can't wait any longer." She held out the gadget and he went over and scribbled his name. While he did so, she leaned and petted the cat's head. "Don't take it personally, Shop Cat. Some humans are just grumpy like that. Most of the time they have a good reason." She shot a pointed look at Enrique, as if he were an exception. He passed her the scanner.

"Hey. Sorry. I was … busy." Andy skidded in, freshly shaved. For the first time in—ever. "How are ya?"

She gave a half-smile. "Hi, Andy."

Enrique escaped down the hall, slipping into the room where he slept. He hunkered near the door like his mom used to when she wanted to hear what was going on but was too proud to let it be known. *Metiche*. He was a rat. What was wrong with him?

"Did I do something to upset your boss?" she asked. "Am I parking in the wrong place or something?"

"What do you mean?" Andy asked.

"It seems like he's always upset with me." The hurt in her voice made Enrique wish he could see her expression. He exhaled. It wasn't her fault who she looked like.

"No. He just … no," Andy said. "Did you know Enrique rescued this cat from the dumpster? He was skin and bones a few months ago."

Enrique looked at the floor, grateful he could trust Andy not to air his dirty laundry. He supposed it shouldn't surprise him—they were army brothers. Had been on the same Afghanistan tour a few years before. Still, it bothered him that she thought he was angry with her. Time to get out of the pit.

"And he really has no name?" She sounded skeptical.

Andy cleared his throat. "Yeah. We just call him Cat."

Vamos vamos. "Come on, come on," Enrique whispered, swirling his hand in a get-on-with-it motion. There was paperwork to do. Errands to run. Parts to order.

"Any pickups today?" To his great relief, she sounded farther away. The front door opened.

"No. I guess I'll see ya tomorrow." Andy sounded disappointed.

After the front door closed, Enrique returned to his post at the computer. The cat meowed by the door as the brown truck left.

"She's hot. And she's really nice. No idea why you don't like her, but I totally owe you." A wide grin split Andy's face and his chest puffed out. "I think she's into me."

"No problem," Enrique said, not meaning it and not knowing why. With the shop on a greased slide to death, the last thing he needed was a distraction. It would take all his focus and a financial miracle to revive it. That issue aside, he'd just demonstrated he was in no place to pursue anything with the opposite sex.

That evening, Skylar opened the gate to a front yard near Washington Park and slipped inside. Spencer, a two-year-old yellow lab danced merrily in front of her. Though she was by no means a professional, after a few weeks of trying a technique she'd learned online, he'd finally stopped jumping up on her. "Spencer, sit." He did, tail wagging wildly when he spotted the leash. "Good dog. Ready for a walk?" She scratched his head and hooked the lead to his collar. "Let's go." They went toward the park. Skylar wanted to jog, but work had bled her dry. The evening walks were becoming a challenge but they were better than sitting home alone where she might take a nose dive into a bottle of booze.

It had begun when a neighbor needed someone to walk his dog while he was in the hospital. When she discovered how much it helped her state of mind, she'd asked if he knew others who needed their dogs walked. Now she kept busy most every night. Keeping company with a dog was a one-way thing. It was safe and even fun, most of the time.

Accustomed to the lackluster landscaping outside her apartment complex, Skylar felt entranced walking along the uneven sidewalk beneath the large trees. Before long, the leaves would change color and the neighborhood would erupt in bright pinks and oranges. In her mind, she could smell the musty drying leaves and hear them crackle beneath her feet.

Though she knew it was foolish, she went straight instead of turning right at the corner. Spencer sniffed eagerly along fences and at the base of every tree, marking each one. They came to the corner and Skylar eyed a large house across the street. The two-story blond brick Craftsman style home, ensconced in its black wrought-iron fence stared back at her, faithfully keeping her secret. Three boys were out in the yard. She allowed Spencer to explore a bush while she watched them kicking a soccer ball. Two of them crashed into each other and dropped to the grass with a squeal of delight. Crushing sadness stole her smile before it had a chance to fully form.

Her gaze shifted to the front gate where clusters of pink and peach roses cheerfully welcomed any who entered. Further down were bunches of Russian sage, a row of friendly giants with soft purple fronds that danced in the breeze. She resisted the urge to go smell the roses. Perhaps on the way back if she waited till dark. Spencer tugged the leash, pulling her from her reverie. "Sorry, buddy." They got moving again.

Wash Park was alive with people—joggers with earbuds or chatting in pairs, people walking dogs, others laying in the grass reading books and checking their cell phones. A group of teens played lacrosse. Skylar barely scooted out of the way in time as two little girls raced past on their bikes. She stopped beneath the sprawling maple where Joe had kissed her that first time. Her pulse quickened, as did her breath. She skimmed her fingertips along her forearm, remembering the feel of his baseball as if it had happened only moments before. A few rapid blinks kept her eyes from overflowing. Why did she torture herself? Nothing she did now would bring him back. Reliving those moments only lengthened the suspended animation her soul floated in. But the feelings they evoked were like a drug. And she was a junkie.

"Is your dog friendly?"

Skylar turned, the memory suddenly dissipating as though she'd turned off the TV. "Uh. Yes." A tall, well-built guy in gray plaid shorts and a white T-shirt came up next to her. He held a springer spaniel back as it strained against its leash, focused on Spencer.

"Who is this?" She extended her palm toward the spaniel.

"Bugsy Malone." He smiled. "I see you here a lot." Ignoring her, the dog made a beeline for Spencer. In seconds the two were tangled in their leads. "Easy, Bugs." The man grabbed the dog's collar and let go of the leash. "Do you mind pulling that through while I hold him? Sorry. I'm not very good with him."

"No problem." Skylar untangled the leashes.

"You're so good with the dogs. Is this what you do for a living?" he asked.

"No."

"I'm Chad." He reached out.

"Skylar." She shook his hand briefly. "Well, have a nice walk." She stepped back. Raised her hand in farewell.

"You, too." Disappointment flickered in his eyes. He couldn't know she was doing him a favor.

After making the rounds and letting Spencer greet most of the canines in the park, Skylar headed back. Having gotten his fill of exercise, the dog walked slowly, which was fine with her because exhaustion was nipping at her heels.

It was near dusk, so she crossed to the same side of the street as the big Craftsman house on the corner. Its straight square chimney stretched skyward. The oak front door with its leaded upper window beckoned her. The sweet-scented roses begged her to linger. She had every right to stop, even to pick some. But she kept walking. Laughter drifted from the backyard. Skylar paused briefly when a female voice called the children inside, grieving her dream of being that woman.

A squirrel chattered haughtily from a tree. Spencer's ears perked and he growled at it. "Come on. Let's get you home." The timeless war between dogs and squirrels. Clear. Simple. Her spirits lifted as the squirrel waved its fluffy tail like the flag of a matador and emitted a loud rebuke at the dog for having the audacity to breathe the same air.

After returning Spencer to his yard, Skylar plodded to her car. Her cell rang, a number not in her contacts. "Hello?"

"Skylar?"

"Yes."

"It's Alex."

Skylar tipped her head back and closed her eyes. After ignoring his calls and texts for several months, she'd known it was only a matter of time before he tracked her down. But hearing his voice made her heart clench. "Hi."

"How are you?" He lacked his usual confident tone.

"I'm surviving." She sagged against her car door. "You got a new number."

"I did." Alex cleared his throat. "I've been trying to find you. But I guess you know that. I've texted you a hundred times. I almost gave up. You just ... disappeared. What's going on? Where have you been? I called the school and they wouldn't tell me anything."

The desperation in his tone caused a fresh seed of guilt to sprout. "I took a leave of absence from work. I couldn't —" Her voice cut out. Skylar unlocked her car and climbed in.

"No one's been able to reach you. I stopped by your apartment and found out you moved." There was splashing and laughter in the background. He must be near a hotel pool. Or something like that. It was women, not children she heard. Alex never seemed to get his fill.

His life had gone on. Her guilt quickly morphed to defensiveness. "It's a free country."

"It's been over five months, Skylar. I thought maybe you'd ..." She knew the rest—*killed yourself.* He sighed. "Can I see you? I'll be in town for a few days starting tomorrow."

Skylar fastened her seatbelt. "I know." Despite everything, she couldn't help following the game schedules. Reading the stats. His performance had taken a hit, but he was still in the starting line-up. After the series in Philly, the Rockies were playing at home for most of the week. Alex played short stop.

"How about a late dinner tomorrow? Are you free?"

Skylar started her car. "I can't."

"The next day?"

"Alex, this isn't a scheduling conflict. I'm trying to get my head together."

"It's me, Sky. I don't care if you're messed up." The background noise stopped, as though he'd gone indoors for some privacy.

Her stomach burned. "I can't. I'm sorry." After all that had happened, the idea of going out in public with Alex Kelly was a non-starter. As was having him come to her crappy apartment. He'd sic the dogs on her. The two-footed ones. And the pity machine would start up again.

"It would be better if you said you had plans. But you've always been a lousy liar," he said quietly.

He had no clue what a lousy person she could be. She'd only recently learned it herself. She leaned her head against the window, massaging her neck with her free hand. "I'm not ready to see you. Don't take it personally. I'm not ready to see anyone."

"Sky, you gotta give me somethin'." His voice cracked.

A tear slid down her cheek. "I don't have anything to give."

Alex sighed and she pictured him running a hand through his hair and replacing his cap in that way of his. "I'm gonna keep trying. You better not ignore my calls now that you know my new number."

Skylar gave a weak laugh. "If you stalk me, I'll send my dad after you."

"He doesn't have a badge anymore."

"Being a PI makes him more of a threat. No pesky civil rights to worry about." Remembering an errand she had to do, she put her car in drive.

Alex chuckled, but it sounded forced. "He scares me."

"He scares everybody. I need to let you go, Alex. I work in the morning and I have something to do."

"Work? You told me you were on a leave of absence."

Skylar palmed her forehead. Keeping secrets was a new thing. "It's just something to keep me busy until I get through this." Though she still wondered if it were possible.

"But you're not gonna tell me where?" He sounded hurt.

"I'll call you." Skylar signaled and pulled into the street.

"No, you won't."

"I need some space right now."

"Sky?"

"Yeah?"

"Are you …?" Alex trailed off. Unusual. She'd never known him to concern himself with the consequences of voicing his true thoughts.

Skylar pulled onto Downing Street. "I'm sober, if that's what you're asking." Once more, she felt defensive. "You know what that was about, Alex. And you're the last person who should judge." This was one of the reasons she'd stopped answering calls. Her shocking string of firsts during June had caused even Alex Kelly to stop and stare.

"I'm not judging you. I miss you. I just want to see you. To know you're alright." There was a softness in his tone she'd never heard.

Skylar refused to fill the silence with a lie. She was light years from alright.

"Take care of yourself, Sky."

"I'm trying."

CHAPTER SIX

ENRIQUE SLIPPED INTO THE shop the moment he spotted the brown delivery truck. "Andy, she's here." Hoping it would provide some level of insulation, he'd made it a point not to remember the driver's name. Every time she spoke, he wanted to smile. That pretty face and the way she moved made him want other things. Exactly what got him in trouble before. Kendra's allure had shut down his brain.

"All done." Andy called, several minutes later.

After checking to make sure the coast was clear, Enrique returned to his desk. He was about to sit down when he spotted a large plastic jar on the counter. It had some sort of sign on the front. Andy snickered on his way out. Enrique picked the thing up and spun it around. *Name my cat and win a free oil change! All entries due by September 30th.* A basket containing a few short pencils and a stack of small pieces of paper sat nearby. *Quién se cree que es?* Who did she think she was? The lid had a wide slit and Enrique spotted a folded piece of paper inside. He glanced over his shoulder to make sure Andy wasn't watching and pried the lid off. The paper read, *Son of Grumpy.* He laughed in spite of himself.

So she wasn't just pretty. And strong. And hardworking.

"She's right, you know. You are grumpy." Andy suddenly materialized next to him. "If you were an old man or had a terminal illness, I'd give you a pass. It's been way too long since you had a woman."

"Get back to work." Enrique scowled and waved Andy off. "And you have no idea how long it's been."

Andy choked on a laugh. "The women across the street don't count."

Enrique slammed the door behind Andy. He stared as she parked at Smile & Relax. Watched her haul packages up the front steps. *Suficiente. Enough.* Time to get back to work. Enrique headed out to the secure lot where he stored machines that were awaiting parts. He made a list of the ones he wanted to get to in the next several days.

Andy opened the door. "You have a phone call."

Enrique headed back in, taking the handset from Andy. "Hello."

"Enrique, I'm so glad I caught you! You haven't answered my texts." Kendra sounded like they'd never split up. Like she'd never twisted a knife in his heart. She'd been texting him, begging for help with her bills.

He should have warned Andy not to answer calls from her number. "I can't help you, Kendra."

"You have to," she whined.

"No, I don't. Read the divorce decree. I'm paying off debts you racked up while I was at war. While you were sleeping with what's-his-name."

"His name is Randall. I was lonely, Enrique. You can't expect—"

His heart flooded with rage. "No," he ground out, cutting her off "*you* can't expect. Don't call me again. And don't text me. I'm sleeping on a damn cot at my shop so I can pay off my half and be done with it." In the span of twelve months, she'd spent all his income along with her own and racked up fifteen grand on credit cards. Though not a single charge had been his, the moronic judge had made them divide the debts equally. "We were going to buy a home and start a family."

"I'm sorry." Suddenly, she sounded small. Contrite.

"Too late."

She sniffed. "Randall left me. I'm all alone."

Enrique looked at the ceiling. "What a surprise. The money is gone and so is he."

"What am I going to do?"

He stifled the first thing that came to mind because it was a physical impossibility. And he didn't speak to women that way. "I've got work to do. Have a nice life." Despite his urge to launch it through the plate glass window in front, Enrique set the phone on the counter. During his tour in Afghanistan, he'd imagined every detail of their future while he ate and breathed sand and worked seven days a week for twelve straight months. A home of their own. A family. Instead, he was on the brink of becoming another homeless veteran.

It was simple. He'd chosen poorly. Style—and sex—over substance. A mistake he would not repeat.

His gaze slid to the plastic jar. At least *that* woman worked for a living. And she'd taken the time to do ... whatever this was. Thoughtful or funny? She drove a truck and hauled boxes all day. No acrylic nails or flouncy clothing. Though he was certain she'd look damn good in the latter.

CHAPTER SEVEN

LATER THAT WEEK, ENRIQUE was on hold with a parts distributor when the delivery driver showed up. Since Andy was pushing a deadline on a warranty job, he figured he'd leave him alone. Without speaking, she scanned the packages and handed him the gadget to sign. Guilt pricked again. She must still think he was angry with her. It would be easy enough to clear it up, but what after that? He needed the wall he'd erected between them because she had some sort of tractor beam that seemed capable of overpowering his good sense. He passed the scanner back.

"Is Andy around?" She wiped sweat from her temple and rubbed her wrist on her shorts.

"He's tied up." Enrique put his call on speaker so he wouldn't have to keep holding the phone. "What's up?"

She eyed him warily. "You could save some money on shipping. If you're interested."

Who wouldn't want to save money? Of course, that wasn't the real question. The real question was why he acted in a way that made her wary around him. The answer: he needed to maintain his distance. Everything about her drew him in. Like a moth to a flame. Being burned once was enough. The deflector shield had to stay up. But this wasn't personal. It was business. "Of course I'm interested."

Her shoulders lowered a notch. "I noticed you're using the overnight option for a lot of your packages when they would get there the next day even if you used regular ground." She glanced at her watch. "I have to go. Check our website. There's an address look-up feature. Everything in zone one will get there in one day unless there's a big weather event." She moved her dolly toward the door. "Anything this afternoon?"

He scanned the clipboard on his desk. "No."

As was his habit, Enrique gazed after her. She jogged to her truck and lugged the dolly inside. A moment later, she returned, jerked the front door open, leaned her head in. "Is the owner of the blue Honda in here?" There was a sharp edge to her words.

"No." He stood. "Are you blocked in?"

"I do not have time for this today." She hurried away.

Enrique would have helped, but the hold music stopped and someone came on the line. "Mr. Avalos, I'm sorry for the wait." While the woman gave him the information he'd waited for, he watched the driver stalk in front of her truck again. She yanked a blue car door open and leaned inside. Enrique could hardly believe it when she pushed the car into the street, one hand on the wheel, the other on the door frame, her legs churning slowly. When it was out of the way, she leaned in again, slammed the door and took off. Seconds later, a man sprinted out of Smile & Relax to where the car sat. He yelled after her and lifted a hand in a single finger salute. Enrique laughed and added *fiery* to the list of things he liked about her.

Liked? No. Admired. Respected. He did not like her.

He glanced at the *Name My Cat* jar and saw a new piece of paper inside. Each day he catalogued the entries, surprised at how he'd been drawn in. They were very creative. Everyone wanted to meet the cat, even hard-crusted bikers emblazoned with tattoos.

Enrique pulled the note from the jar: *Handsome*. The same handwriting as *Son of Grumpy*. How had she slipped it in? As if he'd been paged, the cat meandered into the room. "C'mere cat." The cat gave a diffident look. "Okay, how about Handsome? Come here, Handsome." The cat came close and purred, wending around Enrique's ankles. "You gotta be kidding me." Another laugh wrung from his chest. It felt good. Really good. "So you're a sucker for flattery?"

"Meow."

"Me, too," he admitted, hating the chink in his armor. Needing a distraction, he went to check the cat's food bowl. When he returned to his desk, he logged onto the delivery company site and found out he'd save hundreds a month if he followed her advice.

That evening, Skylar and Munchkin, a nine-month-old black and white harlequin Great Dane, entered Railyard Dog Park. "Okay, Munchkin. It's manners we're after. I want you to learn to make friends." He was a giant scaredy-dog who needed some serious socialization. For that reason, she kept him on his lead. A black lab puppy bounded up, happily wagging her tail. Munchkin growled a warning. "This is a friend, Munchkin." Skylar scratched him behind the ears and he quieted. "Good boy." She slipped him a treat and his hackles settled. Then he began sniffing the pup. After several more meet-and-greets, Munchkin had calmed and even seemed to enjoy meeting other dogs.

The owner of the black lab walked over, a smile on his chiseled face. "Are you filming a reality show?"

Skylar lifted a brow. Gave a half-smile. "Do you see any cameras?"

He chuckled. "Well, you clearly know what you're doing. Do you know about house training?"

"In theory."

"Theory?" He shot her a confused look.

"I'm not a dog owner. I just do this for … fun." Partly true.

"Seriously?" His gaze traveled the length of her. When he saw he'd been caught, he cleared his throat and brought his eyes to her face.

"You have to be committed for it to work."

He nodded. "I'm there."

"Get a cheap package of hot dogs and cut them into tiny bits."

"I've been told table food is bad for dogs."

"And I've been told carpet cleaning is expensive and doesn't always get rid of the odor. Then there's the temptation to murder your dog."

He shrugged. "Fair enough. Continue."

She explained the process. "I've had two friends tell me it worked. But you have to be focused. An accident will really set you back."

"Gotcha." He pulled out a cell phone and she guessed he was going to ask her for her number.

"Good luck." She waved. "Let's go, Munchkin."

"Munchkin?" He called, with a laugh.

Skylar pretended not to hear. "What is this? Happy hour at the dog park?" she muttered.

After she'd dropped Munchkin at home, she headed to her apartment where she showered and dried her hair as she did every work night. It felt wonderful to slough off the layers of sweat. She slipped into one of the over sized T-shirts she'd pilfered from Joe and stared out the garden-level window. The sun dipped behind the mountains, turning the sky pink, then orange, and finally a dusky purple until the mountains were only a silhouette of dark peaks and valleys. Skylar crawled into bed.

May, senior year of high school

A car honked outside. "Skylar, I told Joe to come to the door," Georgie said with an edge.

The doorbell rang as soon as she'd spoken. Skylar laughed. "He's just yanking your chain." She let him in.

"Hey, Mrs. Biondi." Joe didn't bother hiding his grin. Skylar was emboldened by his nonchalance around Georgie. He was never disrespectful, he just didn't let her get to him the way Skylar did. But that was changing. With Joe's encouragement, she'd learned to let Georgie's words roll off her more easily.

"Very funny, Joe. You do that again and I won't let her go." Georgie had one hand on her hip, chin lifted, lips a tight line.

"Sorry." Joe tugged Skylar by the hand. "Ready?"

"Yep." They went out and she climbed into Joe's car. He closed her door and she waved at her mom who stood like a marble statue in the front window. Georgie only shook her head before walking away. Earlier that day, she'd spent twenty minutes trying to convince Skylar that "this thing with Joe" was a bad idea. A heartbreak waiting to happen. Athletes were notoriously unfaithful. Worse than cops, which was the bar by which Georgie measured every male failing. They constantly traveled. Hosted wild parties. And don't get her started on the countless women they bedded. What about STD's? Georgie insisted that signing autographs and letting sycophants fawn over them corrupted even the good ones. Skylar wasn't sure how her mom knew all that since she'd never known any athletes besides Joe and a few of his high school teammates. But she'd been smart enough not to argue the point.

"Where are we going?" Skylar asked, when Joe got in the car.

"Ice cream. Then ..." he gave her a look. Hopeful, mischievous.

Skylar gave him a teasing smile. "Ice cream sounds good." But as soon as they rounded the corner, Joe pulled to the curb and they spent several minutes getting reacquainted at close range. His baseball team was in the throes of the state championship and they'd hardly seen each other outside their tutoring sessions. Skylar still wasn't over how it felt to be kissed by him. Together, they were like a bed of hot coals, each kiss like air from a bellows. "I hope you're not on a budget, Joey. I'm gonna need more than one scoop to cool me down." Skylar ran her fingers down the lines of his face, feeling his stubble.

"Sorry. I should have shaved. I was in a hurry. Coach kept us long and I didn't want to be late picking you up, so I only had time to shower."

"I like it." She traced the line of his mouth with the pad of her index finger. His full lips were soft, a deeper hue from their kisses, as she imagined hers were.

Suddenly, his face fell and his eyes shone with sadness. "I don't know how I'm gonna live without you, Sky."

"I know." Skylar released him and straightened in her seat. "Let's go before you make me cry." She switched on the radio.

They went to their favorite ice cream shop and ate at a table outside. "You could come with me." Joe held Skylar's hand in both of his.

He'd been working up to this, dropping hints about how things might be if they lived in the same place. "Joey, I can barely afford in-state tuition with my scholarships and grants, plus a part-time job." She stared at the table. How would their relationship survive with a thousand miles between them? But if she went with him, she might miss the opportunity to attend college. Her mother was proof of how difficult it was to do it later in life. She'd never failed to let Skylar know how hard it was to raise a child while going to school and juggling two low-paying jobs. *Without an education, you're a dependent. You either put up with bad behavior or you live in poverty like us. Every man knows this.* And life had been a challenge after her parents divorced. Skylar knew her dad did his part financially, but there never seemed to be enough money for anything beyond food and rent. As soon as she was old enough, Skylar babysat to earn money for clothes.

Joe lifted her chin. "I know what your mom has been saying to you. I can tell by the way she talks to me. How she looks at me. You know I'm not like that, Sky."

She chewed her lip. "I do. But we're so young. We might not feel the same way after—"

He shook his head, put his fist on his chest. "I will. I love you. And it's not just a feeling. It's a decision. I want you, Skylar. Forever."

His eyes were earnest. And Skylar knew he meant every word. But he was only human. There would be no shortage of beautiful coeds who'd chase after a good-looking baseball player with hopes of a career in the majors. He might tire of her with all her stupid hang-ups, her strong opinions.

"Stop it," he said.

"What?"

"Cutting me down in your head. Trying to figure out how to avoid getting hurt." He dropped her hand. "If you don't want to come, that's fine. We can try the long distance thing. But if you question how I feel about you, whether I'll see other girls just because I know how to throw a ball and swing a bat, then let's end things right now. I'm not your dad." Joe's eyes darkened.

Skylar blinked. "I'm sorry, Joey. I trust you. I'm just … I don't know how to get past all that crap."

"Well, you better figure it out, Sky, because baseball is the only game I play." He stood and moved behind her to help her up. Apparently they were leaving.

The ride home was shrouded in a heavy cloak of silence. And Joe kept his hands to himself. When he parked in front of her house, she quickly opened her door. He touched her arm. "Wait. I'm sorry. That came off really bad. Skylar, I just want us to be who we are. I know we're young, but what we have is real. We can't let other people screw it up."

Her eyes filled. How many times had her father spoken harshly and never apologized? She'd fantasized about finding a man who was different. And here was Joe doing exactly what she wanted without her ever having mentioned it. But her father's boorish behavior and her mother's seething resentment and bitter forecasts clouded her mind. Was it possible to be different? To have something different than what you saw all your life?

Joe's eyes searched hers. "I love you. You're the only girl I want." His fingers moved softly at the nape of her neck. "I have to know you feel the same way about me."

"I need to think." Skylar practically ran to the front door.

CHAPTER EIGHT

MIA PUSHED AWAY MEMORIES of what happened when Camden came into her bedroom at the foster home the night before. She twisted a strand of her long, dark hair and stared anxiously out the school bus window. All day long she'd felt sick thinking about what awaited her tonight. When school let out, she'd sneaked onto this bus instead of her own. There were only four other kids on board now. None of the earlier stops had felt right, so she'd stayed where she was, sitting several seats behind the girl named Kinsey, who'd invited her to join other third-graders in a game during recess. The bus slowed and Kinsey grabbed her backpack and slid to the edge of the seat, prompting Mia to do the same. The stop sign on the side of the bus went out and the brakes squeaked as it slowed.

"See you guys tomorrow," said the driver as they filed out. Mia tried to hide behind an older boy, but the driver stopped her as she passed. "Hold on a sec." He handed her a piece of paper. "Have your mom fill this out and sign it before tomorrow."

"Okay." She grabbed it and hurried down the steps. The other kids raced toward a trailer park and she stared after them. Kinsey laughed and ran alongside a boy who looked to be her big brother. Unsure what to do now that she'd left the safe haven of the school bus, Mia started their direction, stopping short when she saw the old man.

He waved at her from one of those chairs you could fold up and take places. He had something in his mouth, a long stick-looking thing. Smoke curled from the big end and coiled from his mouth after he sucked on it. His trailer was a bright shade of green, making it stand out from all the rest. An old blue truck was parked in the driveway nearby, one of the doors an ugly gray color.

The kids rounded the corner, horsing around. The old man waved again. "Come say hello, honey." It was a hot day but a cold feeling crept up her legs and she hurried the other direction.

A few classmates at school had cell phones. She'd thought about stealing one so she could call her dad and find out what happened. Then he'd come get her and they'd go back to the motel. It wasn't as good as the place they'd lived near the Smiley Branch Library, but they'd done okay. He wasn't sick anymore and they sometimes had money for pizza. But stealing was wrong. He'd made her promise to never do that so she wouldn't end up in jail like her mom.

Mia glanced around. There were no houses here. Just a building with a high fence in front that protected lots of motorcycles and other stuff. Across from there was a place called Smile and Relax Therapy. She wandered that way, not completely sure about that last word, but the first three sounded pretty good. Her dad always told her to relax and things would work out.

A big dog barked from behind the fence near the motorcycles, startling Mia. It didn't look like he could get out so she gave all of herself to looking at the other place. Daddy always said to do that—to give all of herself and she'd do just fine. That burning feeling came in her stomach at the thought of him. Where had he gone? Maybe he got hurt at work and was all alone in some hospital. Mia blinked away tears so she could see clearly. She'd just turned to go up the sidewalk toward the smile place when a man came out.

He smiled a fake kind of smile. "Hey, cutie. How was school today?" His long legs brought him close really fast and her heart began to pound. She stepped back when he reached out to touch her hair. "What's wrong, sugar?" He pulled a set of keys from his pocket. A long blond ponytail snaked down his back. He was taller and a lot bigger than her dad. "Are you lost? Do you need a ride home?" He tilted his head toward a beat up green car. "Come on."

Mia fled, her hair flying behind her like a dark cape, her backpack bouncing around on her shoulders. He called out, offering to help and she ignored him. She also ignored the snarling dog running inside the fence. Somehow she'd crossed the street without even looking. The dog had big teeth, black eyes and a short stubby tail. When she was far enough away that he finally shut up, she slowed to a walk. Her breath came fast and her legs were on fire. A look over her shoulder confirmed the man hadn't followed. She went to the corner where the sign read *Colfax Ave*. Three rows of cars sped past on each side of the street and there was no light for crossing.

Mia turned around. A red brick building sat on the corner with a sign sticking out above the entrance. *Grady's*. The other side of the building had *Karaoke Every Tuesday Night* painted in enormous red letters atop a white rectangle. She walked over and peeked through the glass. There were only a few people inside so she opened the front door and went in.

It smelled good and her stomach made a loud noise. Before her dad disappeared, she always had a snack after school before starting her homework. Mrs. D kept a lot of great snacks at the foster home. She'd shown them to Mia after the social worker had dropped her off the day before. They'd made Mia's mouth water at the time since she'd had nothing to eat for twenty-four hours. Her daddy hadn't come home from work the morning before. Hadn't cashed his check and bought food like he did every Saturday. The manager had found her alone in the motel room when it was time to pay the rent the next day. But even if she had to go hungry again, Mia would never go back to Mrs. D's house because Camden was there. He said he wasn't a foster child so he could do whatever he wanted.

"Come on in." A smiling woman with a pencil tucked behind her ear and a pad of paper in her hand waved Mia in. "Just one?"

Mia nodded and glanced around. Tables with fake wood grain tops made up rows like desks in a classroom. The ones in the middle of the room were square shaped and had chairs. Those along the walls were rectangles with cushy black benches. The place was clean and the music wasn't loud, so she'd be able to think. "I'm waiting for my dad to pick me up. Could I start my homework?" She looked outside, pretending to check for his car. Thing was, her dad didn't own a car. Besides stealing, Daddy said lying was wrong. And she'd done a lot of that today.

"Of course. I'll put you over here where it's quiet." The woman, whose nametag read Sydney, led her to a booth in the back. "Tell me what your daddy looks like and I'll keep an eye out."

She'd never had to describe him before. They shared the same dark hair and green eyes. Having lied to the woman made Mia feel nervous, so all she said was, "He looks like me but his hair is like that guy's." She pointed to a man in a red T-shirt who sat on a stool in front of a long counter. He glanced over and smiled at Mia.

"Got it." The woman went away.

Mia unzipped her backpack. Even if she couldn't get anything done in this place with the food smelling so good and her being so hungry, she figured she should at least pretend. As had happened often the past few days, worry about her dad brought fresh tears to her eyes. She took a napkin from the dispenser and wiped them away. Then she scrunched it up and stuck it in her pack so Sydney wouldn't ask her to pay for it.

James and the Giant Peach didn't look so bad. When her new teacher gave her the book, she'd explained that the class was on chapter seven. She'd asked Mia how long she thought it would take to get caught up and her eyes got big when Mia said she'd be caught up tomorrow. Reading was her favorite thing in all the world. She opened the book and began chapter one, finding she didn't have to pretend after all.

Even though no one told her to, every time she came to a word she didn't know, she wrote it down in her notebook so she could look it up later. *James and the Giant Peach* had a lot of interesting words. Today, she did more than just write down the ones that stood out.

Nuisance. Being hungry is a nuisance. Especially when you don't have money for food.

Ramshackle. "Ramshackle. Ramshackle," she whispered, trying it out.

Desolate. It sounded familiar, but she couldn't remember for sure. Something kind of sad.

Hideous. What it felt like when Camden touched me.

Luminous. Something to do with light. Or the moon?

Seething. Angry?

The story made her forget everything else and by the time she realized she needed to use the bathroom, she was already on chapter six, where the peach was becoming enormous. When she got back to her table, the man in the red shirt was sitting there. It wasn't only his hair that made him look like her dad; he was the same size—tall and thin. Mia stood still, not sure what to do. She eyed her belongings. There was no way to reach them from where she stood.

"Thought you might be hungry." Smiling, he pushed a plate mounded with French fries and a sandwich across the table. Mia's stomach growled again.

CHAPTER NINE

THE NEXT MORNING MIA awoke to a loud female voice. Bailey shushed whoever it was. Mia sat up, rubbed her eyes and looked around his room. Her backpack was still next to the mattress, which sat on the floor, her clothes folded neatly beside it. A shiny black dresser stood next to the door and there were posters of cars and naked women on the walls. Her dad wouldn't like that at all. In the corner, a laundry bin overflowed with T-shirts and jeans. Next to that was some sort of glass thing that was round like a ball on the bottom then straightened out. Something shaped like a straw stuck out of the ball. Like some weird kind of vase. When she'd asked about it the night before, Bailey ordered her not to touch it. That made her curious, so she'd sneaked over after he went out. It stunk and she wasn't even tempted to touch it.

Mia yawned. The night before, she'd stayed awake as long as she could, fearful he might break his promise and come in during the night. She'd sneaked an empty liquor bottle from atop the dresser and hidden it under the covers so she could hit him if he got in her bed. She still hurt from what Camden had done the night before. But every time she started to think about it, she made herself stop. It was better to forget.

The bathroom was just down the hall and Mia needed to go. She got to her feet and the large T-shirt Bailey had loaned her draped to her knees. As quickly as she could, she changed into yesterday's clothes. Then she placed the bottle back on the dresser in the exact same spot, taking a moment to read the label; *The World's Finest Bourbon. Jim Beam. Kentucky Straight Bourbon Whiskey.* Except for an occasional beer, her dad didn't drink. When she'd asked why, he'd said it made him do stupid things. But he refused to answer any more questions about it.

Mia crept to the door and peered out. The woman stood near the kitchen, both hands on her hips. It was Sydney from the restaurant. "Bailey, what the hell? Are you a perv? The cops are gonna come looking for her." She moved to where Mia could no longer see her.

"Sydney, chill out. Her dad didn't show. I wasn't gonna leave her alone."

"What an idiot. You're still on probation. Did she sleep in your room?"

Bailey pushed a shock of brown hair away from his eyes. "Yes. But I —"

Sydney said a word that Mia's dad would have swatted her backside for saying. "Here's the stuff you wanted. Don't ask me for anything else." She thrust a bag into his hands. "I'm out of here. I am not gonna get mixed up in this. Two months in jail was enough for me." A door slammed and the walls shook.

Mia sneaked down the hall, locking the bathroom door behind her. She wanted to shower, but after what Sydney had said she was afraid to take off her clothes. While she used the toilet and washed her face, she tried to think what to do. The paper the bus driver gave her had a schedule on the back. The school bus would be by before long, so she had to get to the trailer park. It wasn't far, but she didn't think she could remember the way. And she needed to call her dad. What had happened to him? Everything from the past few days flew around like a tornado in her head, making her want to cry. But she held it inside. There was a knock on the door and she opened it.

Bailey stood in the hall wearing a different pair of jeans and a clean shirt. "You hungry?" He smiled like everything was fine. And maybe it was. Maybe Sydney was wrong. He'd been nice to her the whole time at the restaurant. And last night, he'd slept on the couch letting her have his room. Acting more like a dad than a perv.

She nodded.

"I had Sydney get you some clothes. See if they fit and we'll have something to eat." He passed her a bag.

So far, he'd kept all of his promises. Her dad said a man's word was only good if he followed through and did what he said. If that was true, Bailey wasn't a perv. Camden was. No doubt about that. He'd come into her room and climbed into her bed, saying he knew she'd be scared all alone in a new place. When she'd argued with him, he told her to shut up and put his hands all over her. He even put his fingers inside her, telling her it would feel good. But it hurt. When she'd cried, he'd squeezed a hand on her throat, threatening even worse if she told. After she'd nodded her head in agreement, he'd taken his hand away. Not being able to breathe was the scariest thing ever. Especially with Camden's frightening blue eyes drilling into hers and his sweaty body pressing against her.

"Come out when you're ready." Bailey's words pulled her from the bitter memory and he went toward the kitchen.

Hoping she wasn't making a mistake by trusting him, Mia closed and locked the bathroom door. She emptied the bag. It had been a long time since she'd had new clothes. Real ones that weren't from the Goodwill store. Before she undressed, she put her ear to the door and heard sounds coming from the kitchen. She quickly changed into a new pair of panties, a shirt and some shorts. They all matched, giving her a good feeling when she looked in the mirror. Uncertain what to do with her dirty clothes, she stuffed them in the empty bag and took everything to Bailey's room.

Mia stacked the new things on the floor, hiding the underwear beneath everything else. The dirty clothes stayed in the bag, which she placed next to the bed. Her stomach growled on the way to the kitchen.

"Thank you for the clothes."

"Sure." Bailey shrugged, eyeing her over the rim of his coffee cup.

Just like her dad always did. For some reason, that made her realize he hadn't asked her the kinds of questions she'd expected at the restaurant yesterday. The kind the police had asked after the motel manager found her. Like where were her parents and what were their names? Bailey had picked up her book and asked about it. Then they'd talked about other books. When the restaurant was closing, instead of calling her on the lie about her dad coming to get her, he'd offered for her to stay at his place. But he hadn't touched her or made her feel scared. Something inside said it wasn't a good idea to be here. But if she went back to Mrs. D's, she knew Camden wouldn't leave her alone.

It was all so confusing.

"Do you like cereal? I have cornflakes."

"Cereal isn't good for you. It's made from extruded grains and there's no nutrition." She'd learned that when a woman came to speak at the library. She was the only kid who went in to listen. It made her feel good the way Bailey's eyes got wide after she said it. Like she was smarter than he expected.

He laughed and opened the refrigerator, which was way bigger than the one they'd had at the motel. She guessed it would hold three weeks worth of food. "How about eggs?"

"Okay. But I have to walk to the bus in ten minutes, so we need to hurry. And I need you to draw me a map to the trailer park." She was used to eating breakfast and getting ready for school without any help. Her dad worked all night and didn't get home until right before she left. Mia thought of that paper the bus driver had given her. Maybe Bailey would sign Mrs. D's name. Or maybe she could fake it. Another lie. Mia sighed.

Something like a shadow came into Bailey's eyes. "Mia, I have to go to work. You'll have to come with me."

She marched to his room and grabbed her backpack, stuffing the clothing inside. Then she hurried toward the front door.

Bailey got in her way and put his hands on her shoulders. "Mia, let's eat and we'll talk about school."

Her heart thudded in her throat. It felt like a boa constrictor was squeezing her chest. "I can't miss school." But she suddenly feared much worse than that.

"It'll be okay." Bailey turned the lock and spun her toward the kitchen. When she stopped pushing against him, he let go. "How do you like your eggs?"

Mia eyed the locked door. She should try to get out, but she was so hungry. "Sometimes I like them scrambled with vegetables like kale and bell peppers. But I hate onions." Why did she keep lying? It was as if her tongue had a mind of its own. There was no way to cook eggs in the motel.

"Sorry, Mia, I only have eggs. Maybe I can get some—what did you call it? That first thing?"

"Kale?"

"Yeah. Maybe I can get some later. You can go with me and help me find it."

She nodded. Easy. All she'd have to do is read the signs in the vegetable section to find kale since she knew how to spell it.

Once the eggs were cooked, Bailey placed them in two bowls and got forks from a drawer near the dishwasher. "Mia, you can't go to school today."

She stared at her food. "Why not?"

"I have to work soon and I don't know which school you go to. Maybe tomorrow." He pointed at her plate with his fork. "Eat up."

When they were done, Mia began cleaning up. *Being down on your luck doesn't mean you have to be lazy*, her dad liked to say. They'd been down on their luck ever since she could remember. Last year, after they finally got a nice place to live—a small two-bedroom apartment off the back of a house near the Smiley Branch Library—daddy got sick and his job let him go. Mia had spent the whole summer there reading books, getting online to learn about things, and making friends with the people that worked there.

"It's time to go, Mia. We'll do the dishes later." Bailey picked up her backpack and went toward the door.

She hurried to catch up. "I'll carry it."

"What's in here?" He unzipped it and yanked out the clothes, tossing them on the sofa. "You won't need these." He zipped it again.

Mia swallowed. Reached out for it.

"I got it, Mia." Once they were outside, he locked the door and slung her backpack over his shoulder. She kept her eyes on it as they went down the stairs. Every footstep made a thump followed by a small echo in the stairwell. The chipped blue metal railing felt cold to the touch. Bailey stopped all the sudden and Mia accidentally ran into him. He glanced down at her, one finger pressed to his lips. A woman was coming up the lower set of stairs. Mia thought about calling out for help. But she still wasn't sure if she needed it. At least she had food and a safe place to sleep. If she made Bailey angry, where would she be? After the lady went into an apartment on the second floor, they started moving again.

Bailey grabbed her hand when they got to the bottom, holding on tight, like he was afraid she might try to run off. But he had her backpack. And where would she go? They walked close behind a line of cars. Mia didn't remember the parking lot being so big the night before.

When they got to his car, she glanced around. All the buildings looked exactly alike. Bailey opened the car door and waited while she got in. "Buckle up, Mia." He tossed her backpack in the back seat and climbed in on the other side. Her stomach got tight. Bailey smiled. "It's okay, Mia."

But it was never okay when someone kept saying your name like that.

CHAPTER TEN

IT WAS ONLY FIVE blocks from Bailey's apartment to where he worked. Mia memorized the route so she could walk to the bus the next day. After parking near Smile and Relax Therapy, he came and opened her door, trapping her hand in his again and keeping her backpack out of her reach. Maybe if she cooperated, he would let her go to school tomorrow. "What's therapy?" she asked.

Bailey unlocked the front door. "Something that makes you feel better." After they went inside, he gave her the backpack. "Here you go, Mia."

She wondered if she'd see the creepy guy who offered her a ride home the day before. The thought made her stomach whirl.

He guided her past a sofa and a counter and into the first room in the hallway. "I've got work to do. You can stay in here. Keep yourself busy." The door closed with a click. She froze for a moment, fearing he'd locked her inside. Then she turned the knob and her heart fluttered happily when it opened.

Bailey had his cell phone to his ear. "Braden, I've got someone I'd like you to meet." He scowled when he spotted Mia. "Hang on a sec." He set the phone on the counter. "What's up, Mia?"

"Nothing." Mia closed the door and leaned against it. She heard Bailey talking on the phone again but couldn't make out his words. After she stopped shaking, she went to the window. There was a driveway right below the window, a large tree on the other side cast shadows across it. Just then, a motor revved and the school bus full of children drove by. She put her hand on the window and watched it go.

Mia searched the room for a phone, but didn't fine one. She'd seen one out by Bailey in addition to his cell phone. If she called her dad, he would come get her. If he didn't answer, she could call 911. Only that would bring the police and they'd probably take her back to Mrs. D's house. She'd get in trouble for running away.

Mia crept to the door and turned the knob again. Bailey looked over. The cheerful sparkle in his eyes that had made her trust him was gone now. She made her hands into tight balls, causing her fingernails to cut into her palms. Why had she been so stupid? You had to be smart to get into medical school. Besides finding her dad, there was nothing Mia wanted more than to become a doctor. She looked Bailey in the eye. "I want to call my dad. He'll come get me."

Bailey's chair creaked when he got up and came over to her. "Sure, Mia. But let me do it. You won't be able to give him directions. What's his number?" He held a cordless phone.

She told him and he pushed some buttons. "What's his name?"

"Marcus Garcia."

Bailey nodded. "Marcus?" He flashed a broad smile and her heart sped up. "Hi. My name is Bailey. Mia is here with me and she wants you to come get her." After a moment, Bailey's face fell. "What? You're in jail? For how long?" A pause. "Of course I'll watch over her." He hung up and set the phone down. He came over to her, looking sad. "Mia, your dad got in trouble. He's in jail."

Mia stared at the phone, barely able to breathe. Just like her mom. Her dad had promised never to do anything bad after they came to Denver. Her stomach felt like it was on fire. Bailey got down on one knee and pulled her against him. She didn't like it and tried to push away but he was too strong. "Mia, it's okay. I'll take care of you." He patted her head and smoothed a hand down her hair. Finally, he released her and got to his feet.

She folded her arms and imagined herself washing away his touch. Then she thought of her father. What had he done? He'd gone to work Friday night just like every other night. She'd helped him make a lunch to eat on his break. He was happy because he'd just gotten a raise. Why would he do something wrong? Every unanswered question brought more to her mind. One thing she knew was that people who went to jail had to be there for a certain length of time. It was called a sentence. Her mom had a mandatory fifteen-year sentence. That meant she couldn't get out early even if she was good. But she was never good. Mia finally found her voice. "How long will he be in jail?"

"Nine months." Bailey glanced away as he said it.

The whole school year? Mia blinked. Bailey wouldn't look at her now and it made her feel angry. "I want to talk to him." She moved toward the phone.

"He had to go, Mia. Maybe we can try calling again tomorrow." The front door opened and Bailey whirled that direction.

Loud footsteps sounded on the wood floor as a man walked in. His black hair was all shiny and stuck up in short points on his head. He was much bigger than Bailey and his eyes looked like polished gray stones surrounded by long black lashes. They squinted from Bailey to Mia, then back. Then they opened wide and he smiled, more scary than friendly. "Who is this little darlin'?" He came close and she backed up until she ran into the wall. He took her chin in his hand, turning her head one way, then the other.

"Dev, when did you get back?" Bailey's voice wobbled and he edged closer to her.

Dev released her and stepped away. "What difference does it make?"

"I thought you were gone till the end of the month." Bailey glanced down at her, a fearful look in his eyes. "Mia, how about you get back to your homework?" He pushed her back into the room off the hall.

She hid just inside the open door.

"Who the hell is she?" Dev whispered. "And what's she doing here?"

Bailey cleared his throat. "She's my niece. My sister's out of town." Bailey's chair creaked again. "Hey, I'm almost done with that project you emailed about. You wanna take a look?"

Heavy footsteps again. "How old is she?"

Mia grabbed a notebook from her backpack and hurried out. "Uncle Bailey, will you help me?"

"Uh, sure, Mia." Bailey stood and Dev's face got hard. He opened his mouth as if he were going to speak, but the phone rang. Bailey held up one finger. "Smile and Relax Therapy." He jerked his head and she moved back to the room, lurking in the doorway. "Sure. Just a sec." His face suddenly gray, Bailey pushed a button on the phone. "It's Braden. Do you want me to—"

"Put him through to my office." Dev hurried down the hall. Mia wondered why Bailey looked sick.

Bailey ushered her into the other room. "Good job, Mia." His smile faded quickly. "Mia, you've gotta stay in here." She wanted to scream at him for saying her name so much. He rubbed her shoulders and she forced herself not push him away. Dev scared her more than Bailey so she had to stay on his good side. "You can get in big trouble for not going to school—"

"But I told you—"

"Shh. I know. If anyone asks, tell them you're home-schooled. That way you won't end up in jail, too."

There were too many things out of place for her to think clearly. "Okay." Mia went to the sofa and pulled *James and the Giant Peach* from her backpack.

CHAPTER ELEVEN

SKYLAR GRITTED HER TEETH as she waited to exit the warehouse parking lot behind Porter. There was no traffic, but he didn't pull into the street. He was probably expecting her to lay on the horn. So she didn't. She'd successfully avoided him for days. This must be his revenge. After a minute, he went left and she went right. When she spotted his maniacal grin in his side mirror, she barely resisted flipping him off. "Grow up," she muttered, then headed across town to drop off five large boxes at a residence. When she arrived, she loaded two on the dolly and went to the door.

"It's about time!" A compact woman with short graying hair and heavy eye makeup opened the door, a dour look on her round face. "I expected this furniture last week. My husband is out of town. I have no idea how I'll get it assembled before my family arrives."

Skylar scanned the boxes. "Would you like me to bring them inside?"

"Of course I would." The woman rolled her eyes.

"Okay." The woman held the storm door open as Skylar passed through. She slid the boxes onto the carpet in the front room and turned to get the others.

"I need them upstairs."

Skylar took a deep breath. "I'm sorry, but I can't do that. Company policy." Not to mention her own. Crabby folks didn't get anything extra. Except a certain hot Latino who took in orphaned cats. What was it about Enrique that made her break all her rules? As she wrangled the other boxes, Skylar pondered the question. His smile, as rare as a white tiger, made her all stupid. And like someone on safari, she'd do just about anything for another sighting. She knocked and peered through the glass, irked that she had to do so.

"Yes?" Mrs. Crab opened the door as if she weren't expecting anyone.

"Do you mind holding the door?"

"I'm not going to do your job for you."

Skylar pasted on a smile. "No problem." She locked the wheels on the dolly, reached up and set the thing that made the door stay open. After getting everything inside, she held out the scanner for the woman to sign.

"I really need these taken upstairs." She held out a twenty-dollar bill. "Would this help?"

Do pigs fly? "I'm sorry, but money's not the issue."

"Thanks a lot." She scribbled her name with a huff.

Back at ya. "Have a nice day, ma'am." Skylar released the door on her way out, amazed she'd managed to hold her tongue. The drop had set her back thirty minutes and there were at least twenty more overnight packages to be delivered. She mapped it out in her head. The Rockies had an early game so she'd have to be creative in the route she took. There was no time to think of Joe or Alex, which meant this job was serving its purpose.

Her plan worked … until the last package. Skylar sneaked the wrong way down an alley, nearly colliding with another truck. She backed up and made just enough space for the other guy to pass. He flipped her the bird. "Yeah, yeah." It was ten thirty-two when she jogged into the business.

"Looks like I'll get a credit on this one." The balding proprietor smirked.

"Looks like you will. Sorry I'm late." While he signed for it, Skylar worried about how her manager would react.

"I'm not complaining." He gave a gap-toothed grin.

It was nearly eleven when Skylar arrived at The Bloody Knuckles Garage. As she backed in, she saw Enrique come out the front door of Smile & Relax and trot down the sidewalk. She felt a sharp pang of disappointment. But businesses like that likely had all manner of customers. He was right across the street so they probably gave him the same deal they'd offered Bill. She sighed. He sure didn't seem like a guy who needed to pay for pleasure, but what did she know? She cut off the mental repartee. It was no business of hers what Enrique did, whom he did it with, or whether he paid for it. Before grabbing the boxes, she stuffed a dog biscuit in her pocket. "Monty, no bark," she said to the lot dog, who *did* have a name. He quieted to a whine and ran along the fence as she made her way toward the door. "Be right back, buddy."

Andy held the door. "Hey, Sky."

"Hi. We need to make this quick. I'm running behind."

"Sure." He grabbed the boxes, holding each for her to scan. "You free for lunch?"

Skylar surprised herself when she said, "If you can wait till one. I'll meet you at Grady's." She was tired of eating alone. And lunch with Andy seemed a safe bet. No history to contend with. No guilt to mask.

"Really?" His brows raised, hopefully.

"Just lunch, Andy. As friends."

He grinned. "We gotta start somewhere."

Enrique slipped in and went past without a word, probably embarrassed that she'd seen him.

Skylar grinned at Andy and pointed at his chest. "We are not starting anything." She hurried outside. "Sit, Monty." After he obeyed, she gave him the treat. "Sorry, buddy, I have to go." He wagged his thanks. Rather than move her truck, she grabbed the only box for Smile & Relax and jogged across the street. Skylar groaned when she saw there was no one working the front desk. "Hello?" She knocked lightly on the first door she came to. A young girl opened it, a wary look on her face.

Skylar offered a smile. "Hi. Do you know where Bailey is?"

The girl shrugged. "He's back there. Getting therapy." She pointed down the hall but did not venture out.

She looked to be eight or nine. What on earth was she doing here? Skylar got that feeling in her gut. The one that was like an alarm and meant she had to figure out what the emergency was and what to do about it. She carried the box to the counter, keeping her distance so she wouldn't frighten the child. "Are you off school today?" she said in a casual tone.

Fear sparked in the girl's luminous green eyes. She twisted a long strand of dark brown hair. "I was supposed to go. Bailey said to tell people I'm—I can't remember. But I wanted to go."

"Is Bailey your dad?" Skylar glanced around, hoping no one was within earshot.

The girl shook her head. "My daddy is—" A door opened down the hall and the girl vanished behind the door, closing it noiselessly.

"Hey. Sorry. I was ..." Bailey trailed off. But it was obvious what he'd been doing. His skin was flushed. He casually tucked in his shirt and buckled his belt as though it was normal to do this in front of a virtual stranger.

Skylar wanted to throw up. Apparently, Smile & Relax Therapy had a wide range of options in their benefits package. The question of what a child was doing here clanged like a gong in her head. "I'm in a hurry. Can you sign for this?"

"Sure." He did so. "And we'll have a pick-up this afternoon."

"Okay." Skylar left. "Smile and relax," she muttered. "Right." Her hand went to her churning gut. When she neared her truck, she spotted Enrique inside the secure lot petting Monty.

"You bring treats for the dog. Why not the cat?" He sounded even more grouchy than usual.

Skylar stopped hard and faced him, intending to give him a tongue-lashing. After the hellish morning, she'd reached her tipping point. His broad smile told her he was only kidding and her anger instantly melted. Oh, he was handsome. She lamented that he was a customer across the street. "One thing at a time. How about you start by giving the poor cat a name?"

"I've read the names you put in. Are you really talking about the cat?" His dark eyes probed hers. She could get lost in them.

She laughed and climbed in her truck. "I think he's one fine looking cat. Especially when he smiles." That got her another light-up-his-face grin. Enough to last her all day.

At ten after one, she slid into the booth across from Andy, who was dressed in shorts and a T-shirt, rather than the dark blue coveralls she was accustomed to seeing him in. "Sorry I'm late." How many times would she say that today?

He passed her a menu. "I thought maybe you were gonna stand me up."

"This isn't a date. But I wouldn't do that." She took a long drink of water. "I've been running behind all day. Thanks for waiting." She pressed a napkin to her lips.

"No problem. Why don't you just work through lunch to get caught up?"

"Can't. Big brother's watching. I'm required to take a one-hour lunch. We've got a GPS tracking system that rivals the NSA."

"Seriously?" He gaped at her.

"Oh yeah. It keeps track of how long I'm at each stop, exactly where the truck is at a given moment. If I get behind more than say forty-five minutes on the day from what the software estimates, my boss can pore over the data and see if I stopped anywhere I shouldn't have."

"I'd hate that."

"It's not usually a problem if I work hard, but sometimes too many things go wrong." She glanced at her menu. "What's good here?"

"Everything."

They ordered and Skylar leaned back in her seat. "I'm beat." She rubbed her neck. "How are things at the shop?"

He shrugged. "Busy. Like always."

"Do you work more than forty hours if things get behind?" Skylar unwrapped the napkin from around her silverware.

"Not often. Enrique has family that he brings in for stuff. Plus, he works late a lot. It's a pretty complicated juggling act."

"What do you mean?"

"He inherited the shop from his uncle and he's trying to bring it into the new millennium. If he can pull it off, I think maybe his next feat will be walking on water. His uncle was a good mechanic, but the equipment is outdated and he wasn't a numbers guy. The finances were a big mess."

"How long have you been there?" Skylar asked.

"Six months. That's when Enrique took over." Andy told her about the other places he'd worked and why he preferred working for Enrique. Andy seemed happy. Apparently Enrique reserved his dark side for her. She wished she knew why.

The waitress brought their food. "I'm starving." Skylar took a big bite of her sandwich.

"Are you seeing anyone?" Andy asked.

Since her mouth was full, she flashed her eyes at him. After she swallowed, she said, "You don't mess around."

"Well?"

She laughed. "No. You?"

"Not yet." He smirked.

"I told you—"

"I can't help it, Skylar." He touched her hand and she quickly withdrew it.

"I'm offline."

Andy eyed her as he dipped a fry in ketchup. "Bad break-up?"

She sighed. Maybe this wasn't such a good idea. "Something like that."

"You wanna talk about it?" His features softened.

"No." She took a bite of dill pickle. "Tell me about you. Why aren't you taken?"

He spread his hands. "I know, right? Why can't women see what a catch I am?" His hot gaze told her he'd meant the comment for just one woman.

"Andy."

He curled his fingers and eyed them. "Maybe it has something to do with having grease under my fingernails. I guess I'm lazy."

"Yeah?" Skylar wasn't sure where he was going with this, but she wasn't about to placate him. She'd made plenty of mistakes, but she'd never sucked up or said things she didn't mean just to make someone feel better. And she wouldn't start now.

"I only started shaving every day after you showed up." He gave an embarrassed smile.

His honesty was endearing, making her smile. "Well, you have to start somewhere."

"So ... it doesn't seem like you're interested in me."

"Geez, Andy. Maybe you should learn how to finesse things." Skylar moved her plate aside and looked him in the eye. "The truth is, I'm digging my way out of a hole right now."

"What hole?"

The waitress reappeared with a pitcher of water and refilled their glasses. "Thank you," said Skylar, grateful for the interruption. Then to Andy, she said, "You don't have that kind of clearance." Averting her eyes, she took another long drink. "I can be your friend. I don't think I'll screw that up too bad."

"I can't see you screwing anything up."

She wanted to say, *yeah, well you just met me*. What she said was, "Good. I like it when people think well of me. I'll try to live up to that."

They sat in silence for a minute. "You seem sad, Sky."

Skylar looked upward. It was worse when there was a witness. Someone who actually noticed.

"It bothers me." His calloused hand covered hers again.

She felt her chin quiver. "Sorry, I can't do this." She fled, slapping some money down in front of the waitress who stood near the cash register. "I have to go. This should cover it."

"Don't you want change?"

"Keep it." Skylar hurried to her truck and drove around the block. She'd have gone further but her vision blurred when her eyes flooded. After a few minutes, she calmed and headed to the pet store. While she scanned the boxes she'd delivered, she asked, "Do you carry cat treats?"

"Sure do. Second shelf from the top in that aisle there." The man pointed.

She grabbed a bag and took it to the counter. "How much?"

"It's on the house." He smiled and handed it to her.

"Thanks." On the way to her truck, her cell signaled a text. It was her dad inviting her over for a barbeque. She hadn't let him in on her new life. And no one was better at eliciting information than Arturo Biondi, especially when one was in the same room with him. Skylar sent a polite brush-off.

CHAPTER TWELVE

ENRIQUE WAS SAYING GOODBYE to a customer when Andy called his name. "What?" He went to the shop door.

Andy had a bike on a lift. "I'm too greasy to come up front. I need you to tape up the box. The label's on the printer."

"Okay." While he did so, Enrique pondered the change in Andy. He was fine when he left for lunch. But all afternoon he'd muttered to himself instead of whistling that little tune of his or listening to music. And he hadn't scheduled his work around the delivery driver. Enrique went to his side. "What's eating you?"

Andy ignored him.

Enrique bumped his shoulder.

"She's not into me."

"Who?"

"You know who." Andy dropped a wrench. "Damn it." He picked it up.

"How do you know?"

Andy tightened a bolt. "We had lunch today."

Ah. He knew Andy had asked her straight out. Like always. "Well, now you won't have to shave every morning."

"Shut up." Andy glanced toward the bay door. "I think she's here. She's having a rough day so be nice."

"I'm always nice."

"Right." Andy rolled his eyes.

Enrique got the box ready and she rushed inside. "Where's Andy? I'm in a hurry."

"He's tied up. This is ready to go."

Her face fell. "Oh." She leaned down, came back up with the cat in her arms. "Have you picked a name yet?"

She wasn't too busy to hug the cat. He stifled a pang of jealousy. "I never agreed to that."

She smirked. "But you're coming around. I posted it on a few neighborhood sites, so you might get some new people in." She whispered something in the cat's ear and passed him a treat. As he chewed, the cat purred his thanks.

"You're corrupting him."

One brow shot up. "It was your idea. Is that ready?"

"I already said so." They did their scan and sign thing and she jogged toward the door, the heavy box under one arm like it weighed nothing. He pretended to read a piece of mail when he was really enjoying the sway of her hips. So she'd gone to lunch with Andy? Why did that bother him? And why couldn't he conjure any real pity that his ace mechanic—and good friend—had struck out?

She parked in the driveway at Smile & Relax. After another speedy entrance, she emerged from the building a moment later. Instead of rushing off as he'd expected, she glanced around. Then she sprinted to a window off the driveway and knocked on it. After a few seconds of animated conversation with someone inside, she returned to her truck, shoulders sloped downward.

After work, Skylar sped from the parking lot. Mia's sweet face had stayed with her all afternoon. Such a beautiful girl. Striking green eyes surrounded by long lashes that shone against china-doll skin. And that long hair. When they talked at the window, she'd been unable to get more than a first name. Seemingly starved for conversation, Mia had gone on about reading *James and the Giant Peach* all the way through. Skylar stopped by home to shower and eat. She grabbed a cap and shoved a book into her backpack she thought Mia might like.

Her cell rang as she was straightening the kitchen. "Hey, Alex."

"What do you mean, *hey, Alex?* Skylar, you haven't answered my texts. And you promised to call." He sounded genuinely worried. And why shouldn't he be? The last time he'd seen her, she'd been a wreck. Completely unhinged.

"I'm sorry. I only have a minute. I'm on my way out." It wasn't right to keep blowing him off. But the idea of seeing him scared her to death. What if she let something slip? Never in her life had she needed to cover something up. She hated lying even more than she hated being lied to.

"Where are you headed?"

"Alex."

"I'm free, I'll go with you. Skylar, I have to see you. I don't want to hear, *I'm fine, Alex.* I want the truth."

The truth could very well end their relationship. "I can't meet you tonight. But I'm doing okay. I'm working five days a week. That's something, right?"

"I feel bad that you're all alone."

She touched her forehead. "How do you know I'm alone?" Had he figured out where she lived?

"Seriously?"

"Are you having me followed?" She faked a laugh, wondering if it were actually true. He certainly had the means. And she wouldn't have noticed. Keeping her head above water was sucking all her energy.

"Not yet." He blew out a breath. "Come on, Sky. I promised I'd be there for you—and you know I suck at that—but I'm following through."

"Fine."

"Fine?"

"Let's meet for coffee or something."

"I don't drink coffee at night."

"Then you can have herbal tea. I am not going to a bar or a restaurant with you. And you have to disguise yourself. I don't want to end up on Facebook or in a tabloid."

"Okay."

"I've got an hour between eight and nine." She told him about a coffee house where she thought they might have some privacy.

After picking up a German shepherd named Whisper, Skylar drove to Grady's, where she'd met Andy for lunch. She wanted to poke around Smile and Relax to see if she could learn anything about Mia. The lot was nearly full. Apparently, a lot of people liked Karaoke, which was good, because it gave her plenty of cover. She backed her car between two SUVs and swatted at the imagined picture of her father sitting on her shoulder, ready to bark out orders.

There was just enough light for photos, which would necessitate a conversation with her dad. But she'd have to deal with it. Before she reached the fence at The Bloody Knuckles Garage, she pulled out some dog treats. When she whistled, Monty bounded up barking loudly, hackles raised. Apparently, he didn't recognize her without her truck and her uniform. "Monty. Hey, buddy, it's me." He stopped barking and sniffed her hand through the fence. "Good boy. Monty, sit." He obeyed. She tossed a treat through the chain link. "Release." He came to his feet and snapped up the snack. "Good boy."

Whisper came over and the two dogs sniffed each other. A soft growl rolled from Monty's throat. "Shh." She handed him another treat. "This is Whisper. He's a friend." Monty gave a tentative wag of his nubby tail. "I have something to do. Monty, sit. Stay. No bark." She signaled with her hand. So far, so good. She'd only tried that last command a few times, tired of the cacophony when she came and went at the shop. Monty remained quiet and still. "Whisper, come."

The pair moved noiselessly along the fence line, Skylar doing her best to appear that she was out for a leisurely stroll, cap pulled low. Using her phone, she stopped near each vehicle parked across from Smile & Relax and snapped a photo of the license plate. There were two more across the street near the building. She was making her way north where she could sneak across the street when the front door opened, forcing her to duck between some cars.

Enrique wiped sweat from his forehead. The heat made him dream of swimming. Doing almost anything outside would be preferable to spending another beautiful summer evening at work. Andy had ruled out air, compression and fuel issues with this machine. It was a vintage cycle and the owner had a bottomless bank account to restore it but he wanted the mechanical issues fixed first. The sooner it was completed, the sooner Enrique would get a big check. He'd sent Andy home, promising to look into the spark.

His microwave dinner felt like a rock in his belly, making him feel grouchy. A text disrupted his concentration. Another message from Kendra. *Enrique, you HAVE to help me. There is no one else. I promise I'll pay you back.* As if her promises meant anything. He wiped his hands on a rag, trying to think of a response that would make her leave him alone but he wouldn't beat himself up for later.

Monty barked. Enrique peered out the open bay door. The barking cut off, which confused him, because there was someone right outside the fence with a huge German shepherd. *What?* Monty was lying down. He stood and ate something off the ground. The person—a woman wearing a cap and sunglasses—spoke to the dog. Enrique's jaw dropped when Monty calmly sniffed the other dog. Then she tossed something else inside the fence. Monty ate it and sat perfectly still.

"Qué diablos?" What the hell? Enrique studied her. He knew those legs, that curvy build. She moved along the fence, pausing a moment behind each car, the German shepherd stopping every time she did. Her shoulders were squared and every few seconds she glanced around. Next, she turned toward his lot. Enrique snagged his gun from under the counter. If she was casing the place, they were going to have a conversation. Up close and personal.

He entered the lot. Monty—the traitor—lay still, awaiting her next command. So her day job was just a cover for her night gig. And the whole pet-lover thing was a means to an end. She was good. Really good. Kendra with an evil twist.

He snapped his fingers. Monty spared him a glance but his gaze quickly returned to the direction Enrique had seen her headed a moment earlier. There was a noise across the street. Bailey exited Smile and Relax with a young girl in tow. She wasn't crying or pulling away, but something seemed off. Enrique hadn't taken Bailey for the fatherly type. He practically stuffed the girl in the passenger seat of his car and slammed the door. Once inside, he pulled out and headed toward Colfax Avenue.

The woman popped out from behind a car and sprinted away, the dog at her side.

CHAPTER THIRTEEN

THE MOMENT BAILEY PULLED out, Skylar bounded toward her car, but by the time she jetted onto Colfax, there was no sign of his vehicle. She blew past other drivers, darting between lanes like she was in a video game. The light ahead turned yellow, then red. At the last second, she slammed on her brakes, having spotted a police car nearby. A sick feeling filled her at the realization that she may have missed her only chance to help Mia. Why hadn't she pushed harder for answers instead of allowing a young child to direct the conversation that afternoon?

She picked up her cell to call her dad. But he would want answers to questions she hadn't asked. Then he'd lay into her for not getting them. Knowing she couldn't deal with that, she tossed the phone back on the seat. If she made a report, Social Services might do a welfare check. But it would probably take time. And what was the basis? A kid out of school?

When she arrived at Whisper's house, she leaned back against the headrest. "Get a grip, Sky. It might be nothing. Bad parents are everywhere." Whisper whined in the back. "Okay, buddy. Good job out there tonight."

Skylar got out and sagged against her car door. She thought about the time her dad had missed her seventh birthday party, citing work as an excuse. A big case. *We had to get the bad guy, Skylar. Not every little girl has a life like yours.* She'd hated him for saying that ... as if her life were so great. He and Georgie fought every moment they were in the same room together. At the time, Skylar had hoped other girls *didn't* have a life like hers. But now, in light of her concerns about Mia, she understood what he meant. After returning Whisper to his yard, she yanked off her cap and pulled the band from her hair.

Time to meet Alex. Though her heart wildly objected, Skylar made herself drive the three and a half blocks. A horde of butterflies swarmed her gut as she parked on the street. She turned off the motor and stared at the building. A large maroon awning shaded the top of the front window. People chatted at the tables inside. Suddenly, a man stepped into her view, giving her a start. Alex stood outside her door wearing western boots, jeans and a cowboy hat. She laughed, opened her door. "What is this?"

"Hey, little lady." He drawled, tipping the brim of his hat with his hand that had been bronzed by so many days in the sun. "Come on in and I'll git you a sasparilla."

Skylar climbed out.

Alex wrapped her in hug. "I've missed you, Sky." He held on longer than she expected, but it felt so wonderful to be touched by another human that she didn't pull away.

When they parted, Skylar waved a hand in front of him in an up and down motion. "This isn't going to work. The idea was for you to be inconspicuous. We're not in Cheyenne."

"What difference does it make if you're seen with me?" His brown eyes surveyed her. "Are you ashamed?"

"Finally, you get it." She leaned against the car.

He laughed and moved next to her, one arm draped loosely over her shoulders. "You look good."

Skylar swallowed. "Please don't lie to me, Alex. We both know I'm a wreck. I don't remember the last time I put on makeup or wore something nice." She grimaced. "So now you've seen for yourself: Skylar Undone." She made an arc with her hand, as though the words were printed on a banner for all to see. "But I'm still breathing, still getting up every morning."

"And you're not drinking every night. I can tell. That's what I meant when I said you look good. Besides, you don't need makeup." He gave her a squeeze. "How did you stop? Drinking, I mean."

It had been less than two months and she didn't feel confident she wouldn't go back. "Do you mind if we skip that?"

"No." He chinned toward the coffee house. He was clean shaved, a stark change from the long beard he'd had the last time she'd seen him. "You wanna get some tea?"

She glanced over. The place was brimming with people. "Not really. I'm serious about staying below the radar. Are those boots comfortable enough to walk in?"

"Yeah."

"Good. Come this way." Skylar led him toward the sidewalk. The sun had just drifted behind the mountains, leaving the sky awash in pink streaks that bled to shades of gray in the east. "Just a few blocks. I'm exhausted. Tell me about your season. I know the stats and the scores. Give me the other stuff." She focused her gaze on the uneven sidewalk as they moved along. Washington Park was one of Denver's classic neighborhoods. Old flagstone sidewalks bulged upward from tree roots and many of the curbs weren't cement, but hewn rectangles of rock. They ambled along, him talking baseball, her mostly listening, asking the occasional question, not knowing until this moment how much she missed being inside the world of baseball.

A surge of desperation gnawed at her gut. What did one do when life took a sudden turn and the music stopped? When the dock suddenly ended and you found yourself in water that was over your head? It was as though she'd shed her skin and the new Skylar was as yet unformed, though completely exposed. She wished there were some way to know how long the process would take—assuming there would be an end to it—and how much pain to expect along the way. It was like emotional chemotherapy. Would she survive? If so, would she be more than a shadow of her former self?

"Where'd you go?" Alex moved his arm around her shoulders, drawing her out of the swamp.

"Sorry. Sometimes I get lost in my own head." Though she wanted to, she didn't dare put her arm around him. After what happened in June, she no longer trusted herself.

He sighed. "It's okay."

As they approached the second corner, she turned them around, walking back in uneasy silence. They'd covered all the safe topics. What remained were all the things they couldn't say. Subjects they couldn't raise for fear one or both of them might capsize. They crossed Ohio Avenue and arrived at her car. "So, are you seeing anyone, Alex? Or still playing the field?"

He elbowed her. "You are the only woman—no, the only *human*—who gets away with crap like that."

Knowing it was true, she couldn't help smiling. "That's because I knew you before you were Mr. Baseball." He'd been dubbed that by the press years before and it had stuck.

"Lots of people knew me then. None of them talk to me the way you do."

"Well, that's too bad. I think you need it."

Alex faced her, gently grasping her shoulders. "You're right, Sky. I do need it. You keep me honest." He looked like he wanted to kiss her. His hazel eyes, cloaked by dark lashes, gazed at her mouth.

Skylar put her palm on his chest. "Alex, don't."

"Don't what?"

"Look at me like that. We can't go there. It will just make things worse."

He whipped off his hat and ran a hand through his hair. Just like she remembered. "Skylar." It came out ragged. "There hasn't been anyone else. Not since …" He trailed off.

She clamped her eyes shut, thinking of her own indiscretion. Whether there had or hadn't been women in his life these past months made no difference to her—she was in no position to judge. And she didn't get why he said it. Had what happened made him regret his lifestyle choices? Skylar pulled her keys from her purse. "I should go. I hope you'll keep this between us. I'm not ready to face anyone else."

"I will. Thanks for meeting me." He pulled her close and she returned his hug, feeling guilty that she relished his touch. But it had been months since she'd walled herself off, the only affection being what she got or gave to the dogs she walked. He released her. "Tell me where you live. Please." Alex gave her a pleading look that matched his desperate tone.

Skylar sighed, looked away. "I'm embarrassed."

"What? Why?"

She blew out a breath. "It's a dive. A cave. A cheap apartment in a bad part of town."

Alex gave an incredulous look. "And you think I'm too—that I'll make some kind of judgment?" He stepped back. "God, Skylar."

She chewed her cheek, relieved to have the solid surface of her car door behind her.

"Are you punishing yourself? Why would you do that?"

Part of her wanted to tell him, if only to get if off her chest. But the objectivity he boasted of would melt like butter in the summer sun. She swallowed. "I better go."

Alex came close. Cupped her face in his hands. "I have to know where you're living. I promise I won't share it. And I won't bother you."

She pulled his hands away, determined not to give in to her need for connection. "You get chatty when you drink."

"Then I won't drink. I've been meaning to stop."

And I'll stop crying every night. "If this gets out …" Skylar dug a pen and a scrap of paper from her purse and scribbled it down. "Do not come over without checking with me."

"I won't." Alex carefully tucked the paper in his wallet. He kissed her forehead. "Love you."

What? But she left it alone. It could mean anything coming from him.

CHAPTER FOURTEEN

THE FOLLOWING DAY, SKYLAR braced before entering Smile &
Relax. Despite knowing Bailey hadn't seen her the night before, every
nerve danced like a live wire. Before opening the door, she paused and
took a deep breath. When she went in, he glanced over, the phone to
his ear. Skylar brought the box to the counter and scanned it. When
she held out the scanner, he put up a finger. She smiled and
meandered to the end of the counter, casually peering at the door Mia
had opened the other day.

Her heart beat faster when she spotted a deadbolt above the knob.
Had it been there the day before and she hadn't noticed? The keyhole
was on the outside and from where she stood she couldn't tell if the
lock was engaged. With a door so close to the reception area, there
could be many reasons for a deadbolt. Especially in a place like this.
For all she knew, every door had one. *Nothing here indicates a crime.* That
thought came in her dad's reasoned voice. And he'd taught her only
criminal matters elicited a police response. She tried to calm down.

"Sorry for the wait." Bailey's voice made her startle.

Skylar turned to face him. "No worries. How's your day going?" She
strung the words out, well aware her cadence usually sped up when she
was nervous or upset.

"Pretty good." He stood and stretched. "It's been hotter than hell
this week and the AC's out. The guy's fixing it right now. I'm hoping
he has it done before noon. We've got a lot of clients booked today."

Ick. "Who was that cute little girl here yesterday?"

Bailey scowled. "What?"

Skylar realized he had no idea she'd seen Mia, much less spoken to
her. "One of the ladies introduced us. She told me about a book she

was reading." She tried to sound low-key and resisted the urge to wipe sweat from her forehead.

"Oh." His eyes flicked away briefly. "Uh … she's my niece. My sister's out of town this week, so she's staying with me. I promised her we'd do something fun this weekend if she behaved during work."

"And she's not in school?"

"Well, today she is, but I didn't take her yesterday. It was too much to do before work. Mia's a genius. Always reading and telling me about things I've never heard of. Like kale. I never knew it existed. I looked online. It's really good for you. She eats it with her eggs. For breakfast." Color crept up his neck.

Over-sharing. A classic tell for lying. Another thing her dad told her that made her eyes roll at the time. Skylar saw a shadow move under the door. "Yeah, kale is really good for you." She knew her smile was too bright. A big fat lie. If her stomach tossed any worse, she might just get sick. "Well, I gotta run. Any pickups today?"

"No." He looked as relieved as she felt at the news.

"Alright." She left at what she hoped was a normal pace, then quickly pulled her truck to the building next door. She'd never had a delivery or a pickup at the place, but Bailey probably wouldn't know that. She grabbed the book she'd brought for Mia last night and crept to the open window. The sill was shoulder height. Skylar paused to listen for people talking inside. Nothing. "Mia." She whispered.

Mia appeared, a big smile on her face. "Hi."

Skylar's shoulders relaxed when she saw the girl was unharmed. A finger in front of her lips, she whispered, "I brought you something." She held up the book. "Have you ever read the Narnia books?"

Mia shook her head, eyeing the book like she was hungry and it was a plate of food.

"I think you'll like this. It's part of a series."

Mia shot a worried look behind her. "Someone's coming."

"I'll leave it by the tree." Skylar streaked away, kicking herself for not asking the critical questions at the outset again. But her instincts and training weren't focused on mining for facts. She's been taught to build trust. Kids were her passion. That old dream of becoming a cop and making her dad proud—or perhaps just finally getting his attention—had died a long time ago. She wasn't cut out for that kind of work.

Mia leapt from the window and plopped down on the sofa, a strange mix of happiness and fear in her belly.

Bailey burst in, slamming the door behind him. "Mia?" He glanced around wildly.

"Bailey, what jail is my dad in? Can we visit him?" If she could distract him, maybe he wouldn't notice Skylar's truck leaving the driveway next door.

He pulled up his sagging pants and straightened his shirt. "I don't know, Mia. I'm working."

"Can I play outside?"

"You could get in trouble. You're supposed to be in school."

"I'll sweep the sidewalk for you." Mia sat up and gave her best smile. She'd heard Devlin order him to get it done today. And in the short time she'd known him, she'd learned Bailey was lazy. He pushed his lips out as if he were thinking it over. "I'm a good worker," Mia added. "I do all the cleaning at home." Another lie, but not a bad one, since she did most of it. And sweeping the sidewalk wouldn't be any harder than sweeping the floor.

"You have to be quick." Bailey winked. "The broom is in the closet near the front door. Don't talk to anyone."

Though she wanted to dance around, Mia only let herself smile. "Okay." She got the broom and went outside. The hot sun felt good on her skin. She began near the steps, working backward so she could keep an eye on the door. When she heard Glenda call Bailey to the back, like she had the day before, Mia raced to the tree. She snatched up the book. *The Lion, the Witch and the Wardrobe*, by C.S. Lewis. The cover had a picture of a lion. She closed her eyes and hugged it, then tucked it inside the back of her waistband, covering it with her shirt. She quickly finished her work, agonizing over what the story was about.

While he ate a microwaved meal at his desk, Enrique worked on accounting. The numbers seemed to dance around on the screen and gave him a headache. After the helpful tip about how to save money on shipping, he'd tallied the current balances on the debts Kendra had saddled him with. If he put the money he saved toward the total each month, he'd have it paid off in four months, instead of nine. Before winter set in, he'd be sleeping in a warm comfy bed in a modest apartment. He finished his food, frustrated by how horrid it tasted. Forget the bed, he was more excited about having a kitchen again.

Monty growled and barked outside. Same time as last night. "Now what?" Enrique went to the window and there she was again. A dark colored wig and different clothes, but he knew the way she moved. Smooth and fluid. Burglary in motion. "What are you up to?" Ever obedient, Monty sat quietly after she spoke and signaled with her hand.

She had a different dog with her tonight. This one was light brown and medium-sized. How many did she own? No cars were parked where she'd taken cover last night. She walked along the fence line, her head angled toward Smile & Relax. Before she got to the end of the lot, Enrique had slipped out the side door, his gun tucked in the back of his pants. He locked up and hung his helmet on the handle bar of his motorcycle before moving silently to the sliding gate in a tucked run.

She strode west to the corner. Enrique kept his distance so the dog wouldn't pick up his scent. After a brief pause and a three-sixty glance, she crossed to the other side and made her way toward Smile & Relax. She stopped when she neared it. The dog sat when she tugged the leash once. After a moment, they got moving again, her speaking quietly to the dog. Enrique trailed her on his side of the street, taking cover behind trees and random parked cars. It was just before sunset. She paused again, directly in front of the building.

After crossing the street with a labradoodle named Maggie, Skylar found it difficult to fill her lungs. Apparently, she hadn't gotten the right strands of her dad's DNA. The kind that made him run straight into danger without worrying how things would work out. Questions flooded her mind. What if something went wrong? What if her suspicions were correct? What if it were unclear? All she had was a gut feeling. Mia didn't have any visible bruises or appear to be malnourished or neglected in the legal sense. She just wasn't in school, though she clearly wanted to go.

Sadly, Bailey was enough of a loser for his lame excuse to be true. Perhaps he didn't have what it took to get a kid off to school in the morning. And missing one week of school didn't rise to the level of a social services claim. It just meant a bad attendance record and lots of homework.

Besides, if Skylar made a report, she may have to give her real name. If that were the case, it would probably be ten minutes before her dad learned she was mixed up in something. Even though he was working in the private sector, he still had friends in every department of local government. She sighed, used her shirtsleeve to wipe sweat from beneath the brim of her cap. Then she adjusted her sunglasses and tugged her wig tight. *What am I doing?* But she kept walking, letting Maggie explore everything her heart desired.

She was thrilled when the dog took a long break in front of Smile & Relax. There must be all kinds of weird smells. That thought turned her stomach. Maggie peed at the base of the sign and Skylar allowed her to do the same at every bush. The retractable leash enabled Skylar to remain where she had a clear line of sight into the reception area. Several women dressed in skimpy clothing meandered in the room. Devlin chatted with them, laughing loudly at his own jokes.

His cell phone rang and he moved out of view, going in the direction of the room where Mia was kept. Skylar circled behind the building next door. "Maggie, sit." She obeyed. "Stay. No bark." Skylar peered around the corner and saw the lights had gone on in the room. She jetted across the driveway and crept along the side of the building, stopping below the open window.

"Glenda tells me you had that girl here again." Devlin paused. "And Sydney says you don't have a niece. I'm done being lied to." He ground out each word. "Be here with the girl at ten in the morning. I want the truth. And we're gonna deal with the problem of the money you owe me."

Skylar sagged against the wall. What kind of business was this? And why did Bailey owe Devlin money? It was time to set aside her issues and talk to her dad. As she backed away from the window, her foot caught on something. She crashed in the driveway, grunting in pain. Devlin's profile filled the window. "Hey!" Loud footsteps sounded inside and Skylar surged to her feet.

CHAPTER FIFTEEN

THE WOMAN SLIPPED BEHIND the business next door to Smile & Relax and Enrique pulled out his cell to call the police. She was casing the whole neighborhood. He was about to press Send when she reappeared. No dog this time. He stared, trying to piece it together. She sneaked along the side of the building and stopped below the same window she had before. He crept across the street, eyeing her through the window of a parked car. This time, instead of talking to someone inside, she stilled beneath the window, every muscle taut. When she backed away after a minute, she tripped and crashed to the ground. Enrique heard Devlin holler at her and she scrambled back where she'd come from.

Even if she were up to no good, Enrique wouldn't let her fall into Devlin's hands. Not with the way he treated women. Let the cops handle it. Devlin shot out the front door and slid something from his pocket.

"Hey, Dev!" Enrique shoved his cell in his back pocket and jogged toward him. "I'm glad you're still here. I locked myself out. Do you mind if I use your phone to call Andy?" He strained to see what Devlin held in his hand.

Devlin stopped briefly. "Sure. The phone's on the desk. Any of the girls can help you." He hurried off in the same direction the woman had fled.

"Everything okay?"

Devlin waved him off and sprinted toward the rear of the adjacent building. Enrique nearly choked when he saw her coming back around with the dog. She tottered as if she'd been drinking. As if by magic, she held an empty bottle of Jack Daniels in her hand. "Got 'er." She jerked the dog's collar. "You run off again and yer goin' to the pound. Stupid mutt." Her words were slurred.

Devlin slipped a gun into his waistband, his eyes toggling between her and the dog.

She gestured sloppily toward Enrique. "You work with him?"

Devlin cocked his head to one side and thumbed behind him. "No. This is my place."

She pushed her sunglasses higher up on her nose and glanced at the sign. Frowned. "Hmm. Yer not smilin'. And you don't seem very relaxed." She jiggled the bottle and eyed it a moment. "I'm out. Gotta go." Her wrist swiped across her mouth in an exaggerated manner and she stopped as she passed Enrique. "Yer a cutie," she whispered over-loud, the way drunk people did. She flashed a wicked grin and gave his bicep a squeeze. "Come by sometime. Third trailer on the left with a silver Toyota up on blocks."

He forced back a laugh. "I don't think you're my type."

"You never can tell." She waved like an actress on the red carpet. Took mincing steps toward the trailer park, barely keeping hold of the dog.

Devlin shook his head. "What a whacko. Come on in." He led Enrique inside where he pretended to call Andy.

Then Devlin left, heading away from the trailer park.

Enrique hurried back to the shop, grabbed his helmet and watched for her. Fifteen minutes later, she jogged up the street with the dog on its leash. He waited until she was inside her car before starting his bike. They ended up near Washington Park in front of a small bungalow. Enrique pulled behind a large SUV a few houses away and cut the engine. He eyed her through the windows of the SUV.

No longer wearing the wig and the ball cap, she hopped out and opened the door for the dog. After letting him inside a yard, she hung the leash over the fence and returned to her car. *Paseadora de perros?* She was a dog walker? Didn't she get enough exercise during the day?

His curiosity piqued, Enrique followed at a good distance. Her journey ended at a run-down apartment building. He cut his motor and rolled to a stop. She walked slowly to a set of steps that led to a garden-level unit. Enrique rolled his bike onto the kickstand and sneaked around the back of the building. Seeing lights go on inside, he drove back to the shop, unable to stop playing the scenes of the last several days in his head.

In his thirty years, he had never wanted to be further from or closer to a woman.

Skylar paced her living room, cell phone in hand. Three times, she'd dialed her father, disconnecting before it rang. She was itching to get her gun back. But he'd expect some sort of proof she was stable. Always with the questions. No doubt he'd want to stop by and see her in person. As soon as he realized the decisions she'd made about her job and where she lived, he'd laugh at the idea of returning her gun.

In his twenty-five years as a cop and the past several as a PI, Art Biondi had never cracked. No case had caused him to tilt off his axis. This situation had Skylar tied up in knots and she didn't even know the facts yet. She dragged a hand through her hair. This was about Mia. She had to set her fears aside. What if she texted him? Yes. And she wouldn't bring up the gun. Before she lost her nerve, she sent the photos and asked him to run them, not giving him any details. Maybe he wouldn't ask questions. A girl could dream.

While she waited, the sad ache returned. The one that had sucked her under in June. She considered a quick run to the liquor store. Wondered where the closest one was. She hadn't messed up once since the move. She crumpled onto the sofa, hugging a throw pillow to her chest. *Just one sip.* Which would become one glass. One bottle. "Stop it." She got to her feet again, wanting to grab her keys. Instead, she did what she'd promised to do and texted Mike. The only friend she'd kept in touch with because he had no connection to the baseball world. Also because he'd seen her in the gutter and neither pitied nor judged her. It helped that he was a counselor.

I'm thinking about finding a liquor store.

He responded instantly. *Where are you?*

My apt.

Be right there. Wait for me.

Ok.

Skylar went to the kitchen and downed a large glass of water. Then she paced until she heard a knock on the door. When she peered through the peephole and saw him, a huge knot of tension left her body. "Thanks for coming," she said after letting him in.

Wearing a wrinkled T-shirt and basketball shorts, Mike gave her an assessing look. "Sure."

"Did I interrupt your game?" Skylar remembered he played on a recreational basketball league.

He gave a reassuring smile. "We just finished. I'm glad you texted."

"Can I get you something?"

"I could use some water."

Skylar refilled her glass and got another for Mike. She gestured toward the table and they sat across from each other.

Mike glanced around. "I forgot your place was so nice." He smirked.

Skylar rolled her eyes. "I'm sorry to—"

He lifted a hand. "I'm not here for apologies. What's up?"

Skylar told him what happened. Unburdening herself settled her nerves and the need for a drink ebbed away.

"Maybe your dad could help you look into it." Mike rubbed condensation from the side of his glass.

"I already sent him photos of the plates." She checked her phone. "He hasn't replied. Which means he's working for a client or on his way to my old place. I didn't tell him I moved." She put her head in her hands. "I don't think I can handle an inquisition."

"If he crosses a line, stand up to him."

She lifted her head. "You make it sound easy. You don't know how he gets."

"I know it's not easy. But it is possible. And once you've done it, it's not quite so scary. My mom's the same way."

Skylar stared. "What?" Mike was the most stable guy she'd ever known. And he and his wife had an enviable balance in their relationship.

"She's a tyrant." He grinned. "Janie keeps joking about moving to Alaska."

"You guys can joke about it?"

"Most of the time." He tipped his chair back slightly. Like Joe had always done when he'd finished a meal. She pushed that thought away.

"I'm glad you reached out, Sky. It's progress … on several levels. You're opening up and you're not hurting yourself."

His words went down like homemade chicken soup, bringing a surprising measure of comfort. Progress. She stared at nothing for a moment. "How long until my heart doesn't feel like broken glass when I think of Joe?"

Mike gave a sad smile. "I wish I knew. There's not a road map for what you're going through."

She sighed. "Every little thing feels so huge. I want to get past my own problems."

"Seems like you are, Sky. You're trying to help that little girl. I'll bet there are plenty of people who've had questions or concerns and looked the other way."

"It could be nothing."

"But you won't let it go until you know." He smiled. "I admire that about you."

Skylar soaked that in, surprised at the warm glow it ignited inside. In that moment, she realized the wall she'd erected when she walked away from her life didn't just keep out the pain. It also kept out the good. Like being with people she cared about. It was too late to fix things with Joe. But not with her father. Despite all the years of hurt and frustration, she desperately wanted to find some way to connect with him. Especially now that she was alone. Her mother was another matter, all the way in San Diego in a new marriage to a golf course designer with OCOPD—obsessive controlling other people disorder. A title Skylar made up. Every little thing had to be done his way. On his schedule. Georgie and her new husband would have to wait. "So how do you keep from being steamrolled? By your mom, I mean."

"Bear in mind, our situations are different. Her tactics are subtle, harder to pin down. I think your dad needs to know how he affects you. He's probably not even aware of it. He probably assumes you're like him."

"Stainless steel?"

"Exactly. It's up to you to tell him how to treat you. If something is hurtful or offends you, you need to be clear about it. But you don't have to be abrasive. He also needs to know what you appreciate and respect about him. From what you've told me, it's possible he just gave up after the war between him and your mom."

"You're probably right." Granted, her father had been unfaithful. But her mother had been a shrew—even before the affair. Skylar asked about Mike's family and he filled her in.

When Mike got up to leave, he paused near the door. "Between work and walking the dogs, it sounds like you're not leaving yourself any time with your own thoughts."

She nodded. "That's the idea. Things didn't work out very well when I was alone with my thoughts."

"That's okay for a little while, but you'll only heal if you deal with reality. Take little steps and you may be surprised at how it adds up over time."

Tears sprang to her eyes. She blinked to clear them. "I'm so pissed at God. I feel guilty and angry and … some days I want to put my fist through the wall." She gave a humorless laugh. "How's that for dealing?"

"Not bad." He shrugged. "It's a place to start. And a lot better than some of the other ideas you've entertained."

She wiped her eyes.

"God hasn't abandoned you. Hang in there. You'll get through this. Tonight was a big step in the right direction."

Skylar let him out and got ready for bed. Mia's sweet face, so full of hope and determination, was never far from her mind. Before drifting to sleep, she wondered if Mia had gotten the book.

It was strange how you could dream and *know* you were dreaming.

May, senior year of high school

Skylar and Joe lay in her backyard studying for finals. When the weather was nice, outside was where both of them wanted to be.

"I aced my math final. I'm gonna get a B." Joe moved their books aside and pulled her close. "You saved me." As always, his kisses flooded her with warmth.

"You're welcome." Skylar smiled and ran her hands through his hair, hoping her mom wasn't looking. "Is there anything else I can do?"

He laughed and rolled them so he lay on top of her, his elbows taking most of his weight. "Seriously, Sky. I would have failed without your help. And I would have lost my spot on the roster." He brushed her bangs from her forehead. The soft, comforting gesture made her eyes close. He kissed a line down her neck.

The back door slammed and Skylar pushed Joe away.

"Skylar." Her father's voice boomed. So did his footsteps as he crossed the deck.

She bolted upright, shielding her eyes from the sun. "Dad? What are you doing here?" He'd missed their father/daughter time both of the previous weeks. Another big case. It couldn't be helped. Blah, blah, blah. But today was Tuesday, not Wednesday. Skylar struggled to make sense of his intrusion.

"Who are you?" Art skewered Joe with his eyes, which were darker than she'd ever seen them.

Joe stood, helped Skylar up. "I'm Joe Thomas." Totally calm, he reached out a hand and Skylar was shocked that her dad actually shook it.

"I haven't heard anything from Skylar about a boyfriend. You two dating?" He eyed them like they were a couple of felons.

"No." Skylar said, searching the house for her traitorous mother. It seemed that when Georgie's scheme to keep Skylar and Joe apart hadn't worked, she'd brought in the big guns. Or gun, as it were. Although one Arturo Biondi probably equaled four other men.

"Yes." Joe said, in the same moment she said no. He threw Skylar a questioning look. "Nice to meet you, Mr. Biondi. I may be seeing a lot of you."

"Is that so?" Art slacked one hip.

"It is. As soon as she'll say yes, I want to marry your daughter." Joe put his arm around her, which helped quell a tremble that was picking up steam in her middle.

Her dad laughed derisively. "Before or after you get her knocked up?"

Skylar's face heated. She wanted to scream, to punch him. But she stood mute, cringing inside.

"I don't plan to get her knocked up, sir."

"Yeah, that's not usually what any of us plan." Art turned to Skylar. "Let's go get some dinner. We need to talk."

I hate you. After she screamed it with her eyes, Skylar marched into the house and locked herself in her room. Despite her mother's cajoling that morphed into quiet threats, she remained there. After a loud rant from Georgie about Art's failings as a husband, ex-husband and father, he finally left.

Later that night, Joe knocked on her window. She slid it up, wishing the screen weren't between them. Every other guy would have texted a break-up. But Joe was there. Undaunted. Unruffled.

"Can you talk?"

"I'll be out in a minute." She stalked past her mother who sat at the dining room table working on a kitchen design for a client, and went out on the deck. Joe reached out and she put her hand in his. "Joey, I'm so sorry. I had no idea he was coming over. I can't believe he—" she choked off.

He led her to the steps and they sat. "He's your dad, Sky. He saw us kissing. I mean, I was on top of you." He rubbed her back. "It was totally my fault. I'm sorry."

"He has no right to preach to you about knocking me up. He didn't marry Mom until she was pregnant with me." Not to mention the fact that she and Joe hadn't had sex and didn't plan to anytime soon.

"Well, we both know that's not gonna happen, so it doesn't matter what he thinks." Joe twined their fingers.

"I hate him." She leaned into him.

He kissed her temple. "No, you don't."

Somehow Joe knew her better than she knew herself. How was it possible to love and hate her father at once? After a long moment, she gazed up at him. "I love you, Joey." She'd been meaning to tell him, but let fear hold her back. Seemed like he was brave enough for both of them.

He sighed. Kissed her. "Took you long enough."

Skylar woke up, grabbed a tissue from the nightstand and dabbed her eyes. Five tissues later, her alarm went off.

CHAPTER SIXTEEN

MIA LAY IN BAILEY'S bed worrying about the phone call. She'd heard every word Dev said because he was yelling. What did he want with her? Bailey peeked in. "Lights out, Mia." His hand rested on the switch.

"Bailey?" She got up on her elbow. "I need to find out what jail my daddy's in. I want to see him. I know they let people visit. You said—"

"Maybe tomorrow. After we see Devlin." He turned off the light and went out.

Maybe tomorrow. Maybe this, maybe that. Mia listened for the shower. The moment the water turned on, she jumped out of bed and got dressed. She grabbed her backpack and tiptoed from the room. When she got to the front door, she reached to unlock it. The little nob that turned was missing. Thinking it had fallen off, she felt around on the floor. When she didn't find it, her heart began to beat like a drum in her ears. She crept to the sliding door. The lock made a soft click when she pushed it up. The door didn't budge so she pushed it again.

Suddenly, music played loudly. Mia emitted a little yelp. Someone was calling Bailey's cell phone. She grabbed it from the coffee table and shoved it under the sofa cushion. Then she froze, wondering if she should run back to her room in case Bailey heard it. She reminded herself that if she were going to be a doctor, she had to learn to stay calm when things went wrong. Lives would depend on it.

Mia's memory kicked in and she got to her knees and pulled out the stick wedged in the bottom of the door. Now it opened easily and she stepped out in the dark, breathing cool air. A peek over the railing brought a sick feeling to her stomach. She slipped off her backpack and went inside. Maybe she could tie sheets together like they did in the movies. They were in a closet at the end of the hall, so she moved that direction and realized the shower had stopped. She swallowed.

Bailey's footsteps came down the hall. With no time to close the balcony door, Mia crouched near the TV. He rounded the corner and aimed for the sofa. "What the hell?" He ran to the balcony, snatched up her backpack and leaned over the railing. "Mia!" He paced, looking down. She wanted to sneak back to bed, but her legs wouldn't work.

He rushed back inside and stopped when he spotted her. "What do you think you're doing?" Bailey jerked her up by the arm but she crumpled to the floor like a wet rag. He turned on a lamp and his hands went to his hips. The angry look on his face cooled the room.

Bailey owed Dev money. And she knew by how he acted when Dev came around that Bailey was under his thumb. Her dad had explained what that meant after she'd seen the phrase in a book. Dev had power over Bailey so he would do what he was told. Her dad said he used to be under someone's thumb when he was in a gang and to never let that happen. No matter what. Mia gathered her courage. "I don't want to stay here anymore."

"Who else is gonna take you in, Mia?" He flicked on another light. "You're a lot of trouble and your dad's in jail. Nobody's gonna want you."

His words made her angry. It didn't seem like he was going to hurt her anymore, but she still needed to get out. "What's wrong with the lock?" She looked over at it. *What?* With the lights on, she saw it wasn't broken at all. The slot for the key was on the inside now. Which meant anyone outside could get in. "Why did you make it so someone outside could unlock it?"

His eyes darted away and he rubbed his neck. "The other lock broke, so I installed a new one. It takes a key on both sides."

Mia hated him for his lies. So he'd locked her in. Just like at work. But she knew that sometimes it was better to let a liar think you believed him. "After we meet with Devlin, will you help me find out where my dad is?"

"Sure."

Mia tried to think what to do. A million times, her dad had warned her not to go with a stranger. So had teachers at school. But she'd had no choice about going with Mrs. Dresden and that had been horrible.

How were you supposed to tell who was good and who was bad? She got her backpack and went back to bed, crying for a long time before falling asleep.

CHAPTER SEVENTEEN

AS SKYLAR CROSSED PATHS with Porter the following morning, she averted her gaze. Being assertive had failed so she'd try being passive. But he turned and followed as she headed toward the break room to buy a bottle of Gatorade from the vending machine. What if no one else was in there? She slowed, unwilling to find out how far he would take his stupid crusade.

"Are you ready to quit?" He sounded close. "I hear you were way over yesterday."

Skylar clenched her jaw. Fifteen more yards.

"My wife's pregnant," he hissed. "We need those benefits."

Four more steps.

"Hey. I'm talking to you." His hand gripped her shoulder.

Game over. Skylar grabbed his wrist and pivoted, spinning him toward the wall. Then a hard shove. According to her dad, the first strike was critical because it set the bar. Air whooshed from his lungs. He pushed back and she drilled an elbow into his spine and jerked up on his hand. Porter grunted in pain as she pressed his face to the wall.

"This is assault," he muttered.

Skylar set her feet and leaned close to his ear. "If you don't like it, you know how to avoid it." She ground her elbow deeper, making him writhe. "Say whatever you want if it makes you feel powerful. But if you ever put a hand on me again, you won't need to worry about having more kids." She released him and stepped clear.

He turned and stared, his jaw muscle tensing and relaxing.

"Stay. Away." She punctuated each word with a finger jab aimed at his face. Then, foregoing the Gatorade, she returned to the bay, hardly believing what she'd just done. Her body trilled with adrenaline.

Mia sat in the room near the driveway at Smile & Relax. The voices in the next room were so loud, she didn't need to stand by the door to hear what was said.

"Braden tells me you contacted him directly. You think you can go around me?" A loud noise made Mia jump. Tears burned her eyes. What was happening?

"I just wanted to pay you back and have something left over. I didn't think you'd be back so soon and I didn't want to take care of a kid for that long." Feet scuffled on the wood floor and there was a thud on the wall. Bailey grunted.

"Don't you try to cut me out again," growled Devlin.

Bailey wheezed. "Okay. Okay." He coughed.

Devlin's footsteps sounded. "I don't care if you found her. Braden's my contact and this is my deal. It'll pay off your debt and you'll be able to pocket the cash on the ones after her. You're good at this. She listens to you. Now go get those photos. I want to overnight them this afternoon."

Mia trembled when she heard the key in the lock.

CHAPTER EIGHTEEN

"ANDY, I'LL TAKE CARE of the shipping today." Enrique leaned back in his chair, exhausted from being up late the past two nights.

"Uh huh." Andy's smug look suggested he knew Enrique had more than shipping on his mind.

"You need to get that Goldwing done. Carl's a new customer and he has a lot of friends who ride."

"Convenient timing." Andy lifted a brow.

Enrique worked to keep a straight face. "I admit I also need a word with Miss Brown."

"I can't believe you didn't bother to remember her name. That's totally lame." Andy sauntered into the shop.

Enrique released a slow breath. He could always count on Andy to smack him upside the head with the truth. Maybe she'd warm up to him if he addressed her in a personal manner. He thought back to when Bill had introduced them that first day, trying to remember her name. *Diablos.* "What is it? What's her name?" he called to Andy.

"Forget it. You can apologize and ask her yourself. That's what she deserves." Andy hollered, his voice laden with disgust.

Enrique kept checking his watch to find it was only a little later than the last time he'd looked. She usually arrived mid-morning and it was only nine. He paced near the doors. The cat stared from his perch across the room, silently reminding Enrique that he'd treated an animal better than a fellow human being. He stopped moving and tidied the counter. How many times had she waited when Andy was slow getting a package together? Bill would have left and picked it up the next day. And she'd told him how to save all that money, unaware of the huge difference it would make in his personal situation. Her name-my-cat contest had brought in a surge of new business, not to mention goodwill.

After using the restroom, Enrique gave himself a once-over in the mirror. He should shave. He'd showered at the Y, but he'd gotten up late and let shaving go in favor of opening the shop on time. He did it now. After he wiped up the mess around the sink, he inspected his clothes. Sloppy. He went to his room and unzipped his duffel, pulling out one wrinkled shirt after another. Finally, he found one he'd folded. The phone rang and he remembered he was expecting an important call. He tugged off the shirt he was wearing and tossed it on his cot. He'd come get the other one as soon as he hung up. But the phone kept ringing.

Enrique was discussing something with a potential new customer when the front door opened. He glanced up. The delivery driver came in and scanned a box. He finished his call. "Sorry. Busy morning."

She laughed. "I guess. No time to get dressed? Or are you just showing off?"

His shirt! Enrique jumped up. "Uh, I was dressed. Before. Then …" The connection between his tongue and his brain shorted out.

"Then you thought better of it?" She passed him the scanner and he signed it. "Do I need to worry about whether you'll be wearing any pants when I come back later?"

He gave her a droll look. "Stay here. I'll be right back." He hustled to his room and slipped his shirt over his head, tugging it straight as he came back down the hall.

"Is dark horse your biker name?"

So she'd seen his tattoo. "I don't have a biker name." Enrique wasn't sure what else to say. Although he wanted to thaw the ice between them, it wasn't something he talked about outside his army unit. Not even Manny knew the story behind it.

"Never mind." She shrugged and petted the cat. "Sorry, kitty, no time for treats today. Any pickups today?"

"Yeah." The cat followed her to the door and she was careful not to let him escape when she left. Enrique mentally kicked himself. So much for asking her questions. Maybe if he was in when she came back.

"Enrique, I need those parts."

He carried the box to Andy and returned to the front to find a short woman with spiky red hair standing at the counter.

"What can I do for you?" Enrique noticed a Mercedes parked out front and wondered if she was lost.

The woman had a bright smile and expressive blue eyes. "I'm looking for the cat with no name." She laughed. "My friend told me about your contest. Made me think of the song."

"The song?"

"*A Horse With No Name.* Don't you know it?"

He chuckled. "Oh, yeah."

As if he understood he was the subject of their conversation, the cat strode toward the woman.

"Oh! You're so cute." She leaned down to pet him. He began purring, and she smiled broadly. "He's so sweet!" She pulled a note from the basket. "I have the perfect name." She scribbled and folded the note, placing it in the jar. "Do you have a brochure with your prices? We have two Harleys that will need to be serviced when the season ends."

"I do." With all the new traffic the contest was drawing in, Enrique had thought about that and put something together. "Here you go." He passed her one.

"Do you mind giving me several? We're in a motorcycle club and we're meeting tonight."

"Not at all." He handed her a stack.

"Thank you." She waved as she left.

Now he felt even more guilty for not thanking the delivery driver. He'd been so flustered about being half-dressed that his whole plan had derailed. Her comment about him showing off had made him feel like a lovesick teenager.

He pulled the note from the jar. *Muffin.* He laughed. "C'mere cat." The feline stared imperiously from across the room. "Muffin. Come here, Muffin." The cat meandered over, made a full twirl around his legs. Enrique petted him. "Should I warm you up and spread some butter on you?"

"Meow."

Andy laughed from the doorway. "She's got you talking to the cat now?"

Enrique turned to face him. "Just trying out the names. I figure that's the least I can do."

"You've been doing the least you can do since the day you met her. And despite that, she's done a hell of a lot to help you out. Bill never waited when we weren't ready."

Andy didn't know the half of it. "Tell me her name." Enrique resented the desperation in his tone.

"No," Andy said firmly.

Skylar pulled across to Smile & Relax, still amused over Enrique's reaction to being caught half naked. He was a living, breathing work of art. She'd have a difficult time putting the picture from her mind for the next millennium. It struck her as odd that he'd have qualms about being seen shirtless since he was a customer here.

Her stomach lurched when she spotted the black Mustang she thought belonged to Devlin. She gave herself a hard look in the rear view and quickly took off her cap. Hopefully he wasn't a leg man, because she'd worn shorts the night before and there was nothing she could do to disguise her legs. Although, work boots and brown socks were a far cry from running shoes. Sometimes context was everything. At least she hoped so.

No one was in the waiting area and she hefted the box onto the counter, catching her breath as she scanned the label. Still, no one appeared so Skylar crept toward that first door, scanning for any sign of Mia. She jumped away when she heard footsteps coming down the hall.

"Hi." Glenda hurried in. "Sorry. Dev told me to watch the front but I had to use the ladies room."

Skylar smiled, hoping her face didn't reflect the nervous knots in her belly. "No problem. Hey, where's the little girl who was here the other day?"

Glenda frowned. "Why?" Her wide eyes searched Skylar's face.

Skylar pulled a bookmark from her breast pocket. "I like to leave things for kids along my route. I understand she likes to read."

Glenda's features softened but she didn't answer.

"Is she your daughter?" Skylar asked casually as she passed her the scanner.

Glenda signed. "I don't have kids." She glanced away and Skylar moved to go. But then Glenda said, "She's Bailey's niece. She was just visiting. She won't be here anymore."

Interesting, since Bailey had implied she'd be there all week. He'd said something about taking Mia somewhere fun over the weekend if she behaved. Skylar nodded and opened the door. "Oh, okay."

A male voice—the same one from last night—said, "Hold on. Come here a second."

Skylar turned, every muscle twanging with tension. "Me?"

"Yeah." Devlin waved her back and preceded her down the hall.

When she passed Glenda, Skylar tried to affect an air of calm. As she moved into the hall, she mapped every door and peered into open rooms for windows she could fit through. Devlin stepped into a room in the back and she pulled her hand from her throat. "Have a seat."

Skylar swallowed. Had she done a poor job of disguising her voice the evening before and he was bringing her back here for ... for what? Devlin probably outweighed her by a hundred pounds. Hovering in the doorway, she scanned him for signs of a weapon. "I don't have time. What is it you need?"

He grabbed a large envelope from a shelf. Her gaze caught the muzzle of a gun jutting out from behind some books. She blinked, wishing she could telepathically summon her father. "I need to overnight this today."

Skylar filled her lungs, resisting the urge to touch her roiling stomach. "I pick up in the afternoon. Have it ready before three." She took a step back. "I'll run out and get what you need." And she wanted to run. But somehow she managed a measured pace all the way to her truck. After pausing a moment to recalibrate, she grabbed several envelopes and packing slips. Suddenly the truck shifted. Skylar gasped when Devlin's large frame filled the gap between the shelves.

"I'll need extra." There was a glint in his eyes she was unable to read. Lust? Something darker? Had he put things together and come to mete out her punishment where no one would see?

Her heart in her throat, Skylar touched her pocket, feeling the knife. Had he grabbed that gun from the shelf? "You can't be in here. I could get fired." Totally true. In defiance of her good sense, she moved toward him, hoping he'd back away.

"Well, I sure don't wanna get you in trouble," he drawled in what he probably thought was a sexy voice. His eyes groped her body and he took a step forward.

Terrified by her miscalculation, Skylar shoved the supplies into his hands and pulled out her knife. "Get out of my truck."

Devlin stepped back. "I'm just having a little fun." He chinned behind her. "Looks like you've got room for a party back there. I'll get the drinks. You've got everything else we need."

"I'm on the clock." Skylar tried to figure out how to cut him without getting hurt. Or caught by those powerful arms. *Strike fast and hard.* A guy as muscled as Devlin wouldn't be fazed unless she got a vein or an artery. Did she have what it took to do that to another person?

"Who's gonna know?" He reached for her and she jerked away.

"Get. Out. Unless you want to spring for a lawyer and bail." *And some reconstructive surgery.* Skylar extended the blade of her knife. She would go for his face. His hands would follow the knife and she could use her knee on his groin and head for the bulkhead door in the back.

CHAPTER NINETEEN

ENRIQUE WATCHED IN ALARM as Devlin followed the woman to her truck and glanced around before climbing in. "Mr. Jorgenson, I've got a situation. I'll call you back." Enrique slammed the phone down. "Andy, get the phone if it rings." He snatched some paperwork off the counter and ran.

Andy appeared in the doorway as Enrique jerked the front door open. "What's wrong?"

"Devlin's inside her truck." Enrique sprinted across the street. He paused near the open door, listening for signs of a struggle. For all he knew, she'd invited the man inside. But that wasn't what it looked like. The conversation got loud and he knew he was right.

"Hey, you shorted me. I need one more box," Enrique leaned in, waving papers that had nothing to do with shipping.

Devlin strode from the rear, his face set in hard lines. "Don't step in the truck, man." He stomped out and headed back to work.

She appeared, eyes wild, a utility knife in her hand. After wiping her forehead, she slumped in her seat.

"You okay?"

A deep breath. "I shorted you?" After sheathing the blade, the knife went in her pocket. Her hands shook as she picked up the scanner to check.

Enrique wanted to hold her. "No. I just saw him get in here. Thought maybe you needed some help."

"Oh." She took her keys from her pocket. "I'm fine."

"What's going on?"

Staring at the front door of Smile & Relax, she started the motor. "How would I know? I'm only here for a few minutes each day."

"You were here for a lot longer than that the past two nights."

That got him a glare. "I wouldn't need to poke around if somebody in the neighborhood was paying attention. You work right across the street and you're a customer here. You should know." She glanced at her watch. "I'm late."

Enrique stared as she drove toward Colfax. The truck stopped for a long time at the corner before making the turn, telling him she was anything but fine.

Andy came outside when Enrique returned. "Is everything okay?"

"I don't know. She wouldn't tell me anything." He shrugged. "She left. Said she was late." He turned her other words over in his mind. What had he missed?

Andy told him about the GPS system in her truck and how every second at every stop was tracked by the company.

"I couldn't work like that." Enrique dragged a hand over his chin.

"That's what I said." As they went back inside, Andy used a rag to clean grease off his fingers.

"She thinks I'm a customer there." Why did that bother him so much?

"You're not?"

Enrique glowered.

"What? I've seen you go over there more than once."

"I was helping Glenda with her car."

"I'm not a mind reader. I just call it like I see it. You've been out of circulation for a long time." Andy headed into the shop. "No calls."

"Okay." She was right. As a shop owner, he should have a better handle on what went down in the area than a delivery driver who flitted in and out for minutes each day. He wished she'd had time to share her concerns. But why would she? Especially with him? He slumped in his chair.

Skylar finished her morning deliveries on time. As she parked at a restaurant for lunch, she went over what had happened at Smile & Relax. It was good she hadn't said more to Enrique because she had no idea where his loyalties lay. He'd appeared at just the right moment last night. And he'd obviously been worried about her today. Her gut said he was concerned for her safety but it would be foolish to trust him until she was certain. Paying customers in that sort of establishment might not want their identities known.

This job was turning out to be more trouble than it was worth. Skylar sat in a back corner at the restaurant. After she ordered, she pulled out her phone and saw she'd missed a call from her dad. She called him back. "Hi, Dad. Do you have time to talk?"

"What's going on? I got all those photos of plates."

"Did you run them?"

"Not yet. I've been buried this week. I wanted to talk to you and find out what's up."

Her stomach churned. Where should she start? "There's a little girl on my route. I'm concerned about her situation."

"Your route?"

"Yeah. I'm working for—"

"Did you quit teaching?"

"I took a leave of absence." Skylar took a slow breath. This was exactly why she hadn't told him. Art Biondi was the only person who never screwed up. In *his* mind, anyway. "Do you have time to run the plates?"

"Will your job still be waiting for you?" He'd always been lauded for his interrogation techniques. She was his practice dummy.

"Dad." Skylar wadded her napkin and threw it at the wall. "I just need to know if—"

"This is why you've been ignoring my calls and not wanting to get together. Isn't it?"

A stony silence filled the line. Finally, Skylar spoke. "If my job isn't there, I'll find another one. I couldn't—"

"Are you staying sober?"

There it was. "Dad. Please." Her nose stung. She blinked quickly, avoiding the concerned gaze of the server when he brought her food. "I'm on my lunch break. I just need to know if you can help me out."

"What the hell are you doing? You have a masters degree."

Anger spiked. "Which I paid for with no help from you." Skylar slid out of the booth. "Never mind." She hung up and fled to the restroom, where she hid in the stall until she'd collected herself. When she returned to her table, the server was beginning to clear it. "Wait. I'm sorry," she said.

"Oh. I thought you left." He set down her plate. "No problem. Let me know if you need anything."

Skylar's cell buzzed. A text from her dad. *Sorry. I was an ass. Will run the plates and get back to you.* She took a bite of her sandwich and tried to remember if he'd every apologized before. Mike's advice came to mind. Small steps. There was no easy way to get out of this hole. Drinking sure hadn't helped. She texted back. *Thanks for running the plates. Dad, I want you to stop rolling over me.*

While she ate, Skylar visited the Colorado Secretary of State website. Smile & Relax Therapy was owned by a corporation. It was probably buried in a maze of dummy corporations and she didn't have time to dig deeper. The Bloody Knuckles Garage was an LLC with Enrique Avalos listed as the owner. Neither business had any complaints on record and both were up to date with their annual report to the state.

Skylar stirred her drink with her straw and stared out the window. Where was Mia? And what was her story?

Later that day, Skylar pulled up to Smile & Relax, elated that Devlin's car was nowhere in sight. The memory of him in her truck brought a chill to her spine.

"I've got the package right here." Bailey held up an envelope. "I just need you to check that I filled it out right."

As she perused it, she saw something move in her peripheral vision. He nudged a pink backpack out of her view with his foot. "Looks good," she said.

The music was louder than usual. Bailey turned it down when the phone rang. Skylar was halfway to the door when she heard a whimper from the other room. Her heart flooded with rage. But she kept walking.

Andy lifted a hand in greeting when she entered The Bloody Knuckles Garage. "Are you okay, Sky? Enrique told me what happened with Devlin."

She quickly scanned his box and set it on the dolly. "Is he here?"

"He's doing errands. He should be—"

"Good. Andy, do you have an extra set of coveralls? Sometimes you wear a cap. I need that, too."

"Why?"

She grasped his arm. "Answer me."

He gaped at her. "No. My other ones are at home. My hat is in the shop."

"Come here." She sized him up. "Are you dressed under these?"

He nodded.

"I need to borrow them. And your cap. I won't be long."

"What's going on?"

"There's no time." She glanced across the street. "I have to move my truck. Go take these off and find your hat. Open the back door for me when I knock."

"Sky."

"Andy, please. It's important." She gripped his arm again.

"Okay."

Skylar circled the block and sped down the alley, slamming to a stop behind the garage. She locked her truck and raced to the door. *Unemployment, here I come.*

Andy opened the moment she knocked. He passed her his sweaty clothes and his cap as she stepped inside. "Skylar, tell me what's up."

"I can't." He'd pass it on to his boss. Plus, she had no way of knowing if Andy also had an affinity for the business across the street. She untied her boots and kicked out of them. "Don't tell Enrique."

"Don't tell Enrique what?" Enrique rounded the corner, his countenance darker than ever. His hands went to his hips. "Get lost, Andy."

Andy vanished like a shadow in the face of the sun.

"What the hell do you think you're doing?"

Skylar backed away and pulled the coveralls up. "Borrowing Andy's clothes." She undid the knot in her hair and reworked it into a low ponytail which she stuffed inside the back of the clothing.

"Like hell you are."

"Stop swearing at me." She tugged on a boot and worked the lace. "What side are you on, Enrique?"

"De que me estas hablando." He rolled his eyes, as though he'd hadn't meant to speak Spanish. "What do you mean? What war are we talking

about?"

She tied her other boot and stood up. "Good versus evil. Are you a bad guy or a good guy?" She placed the cap on her head. Too big. She whipped it off and adjusted it.

"Depends on who's asking."

"Are you blind? I'm asking." She tried the cap again. Snugged it down low over her eyes. "Something is going on over there that doesn't involve consenting adults. I don't care if you're a customer. That's your business. But I can't look the other way." She yanked the door open.

He grasped her shoulder, his eyes filled with concern. "I don't remember your name."

"I don't have time to discuss your lousy manners." She wrenched free and sprinted down the alley.

CHAPTER TWENTY

ENRIQUE STARED DUMBLY AS the nameless woman slipped out the back door like a special ops pro. Then he ran and got his gun. Again. He hadn't handled a weapon this much since his tour.

"What is she doing?" Andy ventured out of the shop.

"Tell me her name," Enrique ground out.

"Skylar."

Por fin. Finally. "She thinks they're doing something illegal over there." Enrique pointed at Smile & Relax.

"Is she an undercover cop?" Andy stared out the window.

"No idea." Enrique patted his pockets to check for his cell. "But I'm gonna give her some backup."

"I'll be right out," Andy said.

"She's wearing your clothes. You might give her away."

Andy groaned. "Shit."

"Keep an eye out. If this blows up, it might not matter." Enrique went out in the yard and pretended to check a machine near the front gate. He got to one knee and watched for her across the street. Skylar shot from the alley, darting to the same window as before. She spoke to someone inside. Then she moved her hands along the window frame and tried to pry off the screen.

Devlin came out the front door with a bag of trash and headed her direction.

"Hi, Dev." Enrique called loudly, hoping she'd hear. He strode to the gate and fiddled with the lock, trying to look like he had a reason to be outside.

Devlin slowed briefly, lifting a hand to block the sun from his eyes. "Hey. Did you find your keys?"

"Yep."

Devlin turned the corner and passed by the window. Skylar had flattened herself on the far side of the big tree near the driveway. Devlin returned a moment later, paused in front of the tree and slipped something from his pocket.

Enrique exhaled when Devlin put his cell to his ear and kept walking. Skylar glanced over and Enrique held up a hand, telling her to wait. When the front door banged shut, she was already gone. Enrique sagged against the seat of an ATV. *Híjole.* Unbelievable. He headed inside and followed Andy down the hall. A minute later, she knocked. Andy let her in and she hurriedly unbuttoned the coveralls. She was panting and glistened with sweat.

"Are you okay?" Andy asked.

"Fine." Next, she untied her boots and yanked them off.

"What did you find out?" Enrique asked.

She slid out of the coveralls, not bothering to tie her boots when she shoved her feet back in. "I have to go."

"She's like a ghost," said Enrique as she sprinted to her truck.

Andy stared with worshipful eyes. "Yeah."

Mia slapped at Bailey as he tried to pull a frilly dress over her head. "No! I don't like it."

"I don't care if you like it." He twisted her wrist until she stopped fighting him. He tugged the dress down and she stuck her arms in the sleeves. "It's just for a few minutes, Mia. Your photos were great. Now we need some video. Don't you want to be in the movies?"

Mia rubbed her sore wrist and dashed tears from her cheeks. "I don't care about movies. I'm going to be a doctor." When he picked up the shoes, she jammed her feet between the sofa cushions.

"Do you want me to get Glenda?"

Mia looked worriedly at the door. "No." Glenda knew how to pinch. Hard. In places where the bruise wouldn't show. That was how they'd finally gotten her to cooperate for the camera.

Bailey zipped the dress and grabbed one of her feet. "Medical school is expensive and people make a lot of money in the movies."

Once the shoes were on, he began brushing the tangles from her hair.

So he thought she was stupid? These were not the kind of movies where people got paid. "What about my dad? You told me we could call—"

He squeezed her chin and brought his face close to hers. "Food costs money, Mia. So does water, electricity and rent. You need to do your part." He went about setting up a camera on a three-legged stand. "Okay, when you see the green light go on, the camera is recording. I want you to look right here and answer the questions I ask." He pointed to the round glass piece on the front of the camera.

Forget what her dad said about putting your whole self into something. Bailey was bigger and stronger than her so she had to do what he wanted. Not caring what happened, she lied in all of her answers. It was none of his business how old she was or where she was born. When they were done, he let her change back into her regular clothes. Mia curled up on the sofa and imagined finding a closet that would take her to Narnia.

Skylar parked in front of her father's new house with its nice landscaping and a late model Honda parked in the drive. She moved up the walk and knocked on the door, fighting anxiety that made her want to run the other way. There was more at stake than her own concerns.

Art Biondi did a decent job of masking his surprise when he opened the door. The only tell was a brief spark in his dark eyes. "Sky?" He glanced about, as though she'd materialized out of thin air and he was afraid of what might happen next. "What brings you here?" He moved back and ushered her in.

"I need to borrow some equipment."

Art tucked his hands in his pockets. "Do you accept my apology?"

"I replied."

"Not about that." He regarded her a moment. "Are we good then?"

One apology and they'd be good? After a decade and a half of being unavailable? Then being an impatient jerk when he did make the time? Skylar ran a hand through her hair. Mike had been talking to her about emotional honesty. It sounded so simple when they were eating scrambled eggs and hash browns at the diner where they met for breakfast every other week. But Art was trying, owning up. At least it was something. "No, Dad, we're not good. But I accept your apology. For today, I mean." Skylar braced for his reply.

Art gave a slow nod, his jaw jutting forward the tiniest bit. "I suppose I deserve that. I'll work on the rest." He ran a hand through his thick wavy hair and she realized she'd gotten the gesture from him. Art looked ten years younger than his current age of forty-eight. And he was what her mom called a *real looker*. That was probably how he'd landed his beautiful wife. Elana was seven years his junior.

A ruckus erupted at the back of the house and quickly made its way to the front. Her two half-brothers, Evan and Roan, rolled in like a couple of tumbleweeds, arguing over who broke a toy.

"Boys." Art took their shoulders, stopping their forward progress. "Your sister is here. Stop and say hello."

They both hugged her around the waist. "Hi, Sky!" they said in unison. Her throat tightened and she couldn't respond, so she bent and gave them a hug. They each kissed her cheek and then they were off. She went to the window to regain her composure. Not coming to the barbeque had been the right choice. Several hours of being around the children Art Biondi wasn't blind to and she'd have gone on a bender. This envy was wrong. Toxic. She took a deep breath.

Art came next to her. "So, what is it you need?"

Skylar faced him. "Do you have a video camera available? Something motion activated?"

"Something you can mount above a door?" He thrust his hands in his pockets.

She hadn't thought about the details. "I don't know how to do that." A photo of her father's new family hung by the stairs, next to a collage from his wedding eight years earlier. She felt a painful twinge inside when she noticed there weren't any photos of her. She was twenty-seven years old. Why did it matter so much?

"I have one that looks like a rock. You just set it on the ground facing the area you want to record."

Skylar reminded herself she'd come here for Mia. "That should work." She followed him to his office.

"I ran those plates. Nothing popped." He passed her some papers.

Skylar scanned them. Devlin Grant and Glenda Zuckerman were the only names she recognized. "Okay. Thanks for trying."

"You mentioned a little girl." He propped one hip on his desk.

"Her name is Mia. Is there any way to look her up without a last name?"

"No. And that's probably a nickname. It can be Italian or Spanish. Anything, really. I'd need a date of birth, social security number and full name to really get somewhere." Art went to a closet. "What else can you tell me about her?"

"She has long brown hair, green eyes. Caucasian, or maybe half Latina? I think she's about nine. She's not in school."

He thrummed his fingers on the closet door as he held it ajar. "That's not necessarily against the law. She might be home-schooled."

"I know. But she seems upset not to be in school. Like it's not normal for her. And if she is home-schooled, it's not happening this week. She's in a room all by herself."

"Where did you contact her?"

She filled him in.

He pulled a box from the closet and set it on his desk. After rummaging through it, he pulled out something that looked like a rock with a tiny black lens on one side. "You want me to help you set this stuff up?"

Skylar chewed her lip. "No, thanks."

"Okay." He explained how to use the camera, then passed her a teddy bear. "This is a nanny cam. If you can get it inside, you'll get video and sound. It's motion activated."

Skylar examined it. "I hope she's not too old for this."

He shrugged. "No harm trying."

As they passed through the hall on their way out, he stopped her. "I didn't forget you, honey." An array of photos of her and the two of them together—many of which she'd never seen—dotted the wall. Why hadn't she noticed them on the way in? "Between work and the war with your mom ... I felt like it would just make things worse if I pushed for more time with you. My schedule didn't fit with the custody agreement. She wasn't willing to work around things." He sighed heavily.

Skylar scanned the pictures, surprised to see them doing things she didn't recall. Fishing? When had they gone fishing? She looked to be about nine. And sledding. He'd taken a photo right as she'd lifted her head from the snow after a crash. Her smile beamed like a laser. A string of her mother's common complaints registered in her mind, like a TV commercial she'd seen a thousand times and could quote after hearing the first few words. Skylar stood stupefied. Georgie had successfully vilified Art in Skylar's mind. "Dad, I—I'm sorry." She choked off.

"I know what she did, Sky, the things she said." His hand moved softly over the small of her back. "But some of it was my fault. We all know how I can get sometimes."

Seeming to understand that her throat was not going to let her answer, he patted her shoulder and got her moving again.

They walked to the entryway just as her stepmother came down the stairs. "Skylar! So good to see you." Elana smiled and wrapped her in a hug.

"Hi." It came out sounding strangled. Despite her own struggles and her mother's vile words, she'd always liked Elana. The affair that ended her parents' marriage had happened years before her father met Elana.

"How are you, sweetheart?" Elana cupped Skylar's shoulders and gave her a long look.

"I'm doing okay." There was still a lot to do this evening. "Sorry, but I have to get going." Skylar took the box from her father. "I'll get this back to you as soon as I can."

"No hurry." Art kissed her cheek. Then his arm went around his wife, who smiled warmly.

On her way home, Skylar stopped at a bookstore to buy *Prince Caspian* for Mia. When she got to her apartment complex, she parked and grabbed the box from the backseat. She stopped cold when she spotted Enrique standing next to a motorcycle not far away. With her finger poised over the panic button on her key fob, she took a step back. "What are you doing here?"

"I want to talk to you." His face was impassive.

She shoved the box back in her car and locked it. "About what?" The words came out breathy, as if she'd been caught doing something wrong.

"What do you think?" He stayed where he was. Which was good, because she didn't have any means of defending herself. The guy was built like a tank. Big and muscled. Not an ounce of fat anywhere. Not twenty-four hours ago, she'd seen his powerful torso for herself.

"Did Devlin send you?"

He looked confused. "I sent myself." He crossed his arms over his chest. "I'd like to know why you feel free to do what you did today, giving orders to Andy, using my shop like it's your own private dressing room."

Skylar glanced around. A couple observed them from a balcony. "Will you keep your voice down? I'm sorry." She raked her hair back. "It was all that came to me in the moment." A man parked nearby and glanced over as he passed through the lot. "We can't talk out here."

"Let's go inside." He waved a hand toward her door. Which meant he knew exactly where she lived. *Oh, God.*

"You're not coming in my apartment," she hissed.

"You name the place." He remained where he was, making her question again whether he was a threat.

"How do you know where I live?"

"I followed you home last night. After you cased the neighborhood."

Skylar narrowed her eyes. "I was not casing the neighborhood."

"What were you doing, then? And what was all that today?"

She made a frustrated noise in her throat. "I don't have time tonight. Tomorrow—"

"Forget it." He took a step toward her. Lowered his voice. "Look. I could've taken you down today. Or called the cops. I gave you some latitude because it seems like you're worried. Talk to me."

Skylar sighed. Leaned against her car.

"Are you an undercover cop?"

Her stomach sent up a flare, reminding her she was very late for dinner. Or warning her to keep her distance from this man. "You know who I work for."

"Bill never showed up at night wearing a wig."

"Are you here because you're worried you might be listed in some kind of black book? That's not what this is about. I don't care if you're a customer there. I don't even care if you're a john."

"A john? Did you really just say that?" His eyes widened and he came a step closer. "I've never spent a dime in that place." He sliced the air with his hand.

"You just get the friendly neighbor discount?"

"What the hell are you talking about?"

Skylar sidestepped him and snugged her purse to her shoulder. "I told you not to swear at me. I saw you come out of there just the other day."

"Glenda needed help with her car."

Skylar thought about that. She also thought about how he'd helped her, not once, but twice. A sliding door opened nearby. Another neighbor stared from another balcony. She groaned. "Are you armed?"

"Of course. Aren't you?"

"No." She sighed. "I guess I can't blame you. You first." She ushered him down the steps to her door, careful to stay back far enough that he couldn't grab her.

"Do you wanna give me a pat down?" He flashed a wicked grin, easing the tension between them.

"Thanks, but I'll pass." She worked to contain a smile.

"I'm gonna give you my gun." He surprised her with that.

"Okay." She checked that the safety was on and placed it in her purse.

"Pull your shirt tight and give me a full turn." She made a circle with her finger.

He did. Nice and slow. No visible weapons. No threatening body language. He'd been surly, but she'd never felt the need to be careful around him like she did Devlin and Bailey. "Can I trust you?" *Said the mouse to the cat.*

"I've got a few letters of recommendation in my back pocket. Just reach in—"

"Shut up." If her father could see her now, he'd strangle her himself.

CHAPTER TWENTY-ONE

ENRIQUE STOOD ON THE tiny linoleum entry in Skylar's apartment. A large leather sofa banked by end tables took up the right wall in the living room. A matching leather chair with an ottoman crowded around a coffee table opposite the sofa. It was as if the place had shrunk after she furnished it. He frowned.

"What?"

He waved a hand. "None of this fits here."

"So you want me to talk to you and the first thing you do is insult me?" Skylar pulled the gun from her purse and ejected the mag before setting both on the counter. Then she racked the slide, checking for a round in the chamber. Her movements were practiced, giving him pause.

"I didn't mean it as an insult." He shrugged. "It just seems like it came from somewhere else."

He knew he'd hit the mark when she glanced away. The furniture wasn't just big. It was the finest quality he'd ever seen. And ... her place was neat. Not a speck of dust or dirt, nothing left out. It didn't match up with the crummy apartment.

"Have a seat." She pointed to the huge sofa. "And stay there."

"*Tendre recompensa si la obedecer.*" She shot him a questioning look and he realized he'd spoken in Spanish. "Do I get a treat if I obey?" He pictured the lot dog doing her bidding as if in a trance.

"Sure." She tossed him a bag from the kitchen counter. "See if you like them."

He grinned and set it on the coffee table. A crack in the ice.

"I don't keep any adult beverages here and I don't drink soda. Would you like a glass of water?" She turned on a window AC unit.

"Sure."

"Ice?"

"Please."

"So you *do* have manners. You have an excellent cloaking device." After bringing him a glass, she moved back to the counter. Not far from the gun. And a block of knives. Her shoulders were squared, back straight. She watched like a hawk as he took a long drink.

"Do you still have a job?" he asked.

A shrug. "So far. My over-under was screwed today. Yesterday, too. I'll probably hear about it."

"Andy told me about that." He set his glass on a woven coaster on the coffee table. "So, what were you doing today?"

"I hope I'm not going to regret this." She expelled a breath, rested a hip on a stool. "There's a little girl at Smile & Relax. She just showed up out of the blue. Her name is Mia. I think she was locked in a room today. "

Enrique raised a brow. "Maybe they locked the door to keep her safe from the creeps coming and going."

"Maybe. But what is she doing there? She should be in school."

"Does she belong to Bailey? I saw him leave with a little girl the other night."

"Bailey and Glenda say she's his niece but I don't believe them. I wanted to get more intel when I talked to her but she was telling me about the book. Then we got interrupted when Devlin came out."

"What book?"

Skylar explained and showed him the next book she had purchased.

So she wasn't just thoughtful toward him. "Why haven't you called the police?"

"There's no evidence of a crime. I need more information." She slid off the stool, anxiety playing in her eyes. "Smile & Relax is on my route. I don't want to get fired or have a guy like Devlin angry at me for no good reason."

"So you're really not an undercover cop or something?"

She showed him her work ID. "My dad was a cop. I know just enough to be dangerous. Or stupid."

"Skylar Biondi." He read it aloud.

"That's all I have so far. And ... I have something to do."

Enrique regarded her.

She rested a hand on her stomach, a question in her gaze. "Thank you for running interference yesterday. And today, too. I mean, that *is* what you were doing, right? Or are you friends with Devlin?"

"I was backing you up. I know Dev, but we're not friends." He'd never met anyone so jumpy. At least outside the war.

She pulled her hair back and used the band on her wrist to make a ponytail. "I'm sorry for crossing the line at your shop. It won't happen again. I'll apologize to Andy for commandeering his clothes."

Enrique laughed. "Don't. He'll be disappointed. It put him in a dream-like state and doubled his output this afternoon."

Skylar laughed. But her smile quickly disappeared when her gaze went to something in the hallway. He couldn't see what it was from where he was sitting. She refocused on him. "Anything else?"

"What's in the box you locked in your car?"

"That's classified. If I told you ..." She swiped her index finger across her neck.

"Am I allowed to stand up now?" he asked.

She snapped her fingers. "Release."

"What?"

"That's the command. You're no longer in a stay." Her lips rolled inward and her eyes sparkled with humor.

Enrique stood. "You're whacked." The sparkle fell away and he immediately regretted his words. Skylar was kind and thoughtful. Willing to put herself in harm's way for a stranger. Why did he treat her this way?

Skylar led him to the door and handed him his gun and the magazine. "Here you go."

"I guess I'll see you tomorrow."

"Yeah." She averted her eyes.

Ijo, otra vez. Not again with the creeping around at night. One more unanswered question popped into his head. "Hey, where'd you get that bottle of Jack? The other night?"

"It was behind the building where I left the dog. It gave me the idea to fake being drunk so I didn't have to try and outrun Devlin. I figured if he bought it, I'd probably be safer. I just hope he doesn't recognize me. I know he keeps a gun in his office."

Enrique shook his head. She might look like Kendra, but the two couldn't be more different. So many things he wished he could take back. "You were convincing."

"I've had lots of practice."

"Acting?"

"Drinking." Skylar gave an embarrassed shrug. "Not something I'm proud of."

He stuffed his mag in a pocket and tucked the gun in the back of his waistband. "I hope you get some sleep tonight."

CHAPTER TWENTY-TWO

LATE THAT NIGHT, ENRIQUE chuckled to himself as he watched the familiar silhouette come down the walk. It was later than last night, but he'd waited up, certain the box Skylar had stuffed in her car would translate into something interesting.

With the box in hand, Skylar stopped halfway down the block and eyed her destination. He checked the safety on his gun and snugged it in the holster. Then he made his way toward her so they could talk before she created another emergency situation. "Skylar," he whispered. "It's Enrique." He quickly closed the gap, making sure she could see his hands were empty and not any threat.

Skylar jolted, nearly losing her grip on the crate. Her eyes widened and she backed away. She glanced behind her, then pivoted and sprinted toward the trailer park, the contents of the box rattling around as she went.

She had a good set of legs and she knew how to use them. Not knowing if it would make things better or worse, Enrique pursued. He quickly caught up, but thought better of touching her. She'd probably scream. He ran alongside her, his breath coming heavy. *"Estoy consado."* It took a second to realize he'd spoken in Spanish. Why did he do that so often with her? "Hey, would you stop? I'm tired." This was the third night she'd cost him sleep.

She stopped in front of a green trailer, dropping the box on the ground between them. "What are you doing? Why are you following me?" She held a small knife in her hand, knees slightly bent, like she was ready to defend her life. It was the same knife he'd seen the day Devlin got in her truck.

Enrique stepped away, hands in the air. "I figured you'd be back." If she weren't so terrified, he would have laughed. That little blade wouldn't do her much good against someone with his training and experience. "I thought maybe you'd like some help."

Breathing hard from her sprint, Skylar searched his face. The knife lowered a bit. "Help with what?" Her voice carried a slight tremor. She increased the distance between them, but her eyes kept flitting to the box.

"Skylar, will you listen to me?" Enrique remained where he was. "Two times I've been caught off guard by your creeping around. I think things might work out better if we make some sort of plan. It's dangerous for you to be out here alone in the dark."

"I know." The knife lowered completely but she didn't sheath the blade. "But this is the last time." Skylar cast another furtive look at the box. Like she wanted it but was afraid to get close to him.

"What did you bring?" He picked it up. If he was going to get any sleep at all, it was time to get this thing moving.

"Leave that alone." Skylar moved closer.

He pulled out an object that looked like a rock but weighed hardly anything. Something glinted in the streetlight. He turned it and saw the small lens. "Cool. I should get one of these for my secure lot." He put it back and pulled out a teddy bear. "Is this for Mia?" He began walking toward Smile & Relax. Skylar came alongside. Just like he figured she would. Sometimes people needed to refocus and, for whatever reason, they couldn't do it themselves. She couldn't know she'd done that for him with her teasing and that silly contest.

"Give me that." She pulled at the box, but he kept hold.

"Just a second." Enrique stopped and faced her. Risked touching her shoulder. "You're all keyed up." She moved away from his touch but she didn't argue. If he could just get her listen … He caught her gaze. "This isn't a game, Skylar. If you're right, you could get caught in the net of some really bad people. Don't be a fool and do this alone." Enrique handed her the box.

Her shoulders lowered. She closed the knife and slipped it in her pocket. "Okay." She stared down the street, chewing her lip. "Do you have your gun?"

"Yes."

She grasped his arm suddenly. "Wait. Enrique, what I'm doing isn't exactly legal. I'm not a licensed PI. I don't want to get you in trouble. You have too much to lose." She pointed at his shop.

"And you don't?" He gaped at her.

"No." She said it so quietly, it barely registered.

"What about your life?"

She shrugged, started walking. "Maybe we should talk over there, away from the streetlight."

Enrique followed, curious about the low value she placed on herself. Here she was risking her safety for someone she didn't know and she was more concerned about the implications to him. They crouched near some bushes on the side of a building. In hushed tones, Skylar explained what each item was and what she planned to do with them.

"Shouldn't take long. Do you want me to place the rock cam and you can take care of the things you brought for Mia?"

"No." Skylar stood. Crossed her arms. "Enrique, I think I should do this alone. I don't want it to be another thing you resent me for. A bad outcome on this could cost a lot more than a free oil change. I mean … I know I sometimes go off half-cocked. I should have asked if the cat-naming-thing was okay with you. But you would've said no. Or maybe you wouldn't have answered at all. You're always so …" Her jaw worked. "Look, I know I can make people crazy with my—"

Enrique moved in and shut her up with a kiss. He hadn't planned it. Wasn't even sure why he did it. But he enjoyed it. Her lips were softer than he had imagined. After momentarily widening in surprise, her eyes drifted shut and she kissed him back. Heaven on earth. But after a moment, she pulled back.

"What is this? What are we doing?" She searched his face, gripping his shirt in her fists.

"I don't resent you." He caressed her shoulders, hoping she wasn't going to run. Or slap him. "I've wanted to kiss you since I laid eyes on you."

Her breath warmed his chest. "You did? You have?" Her hands moved over his ribs, sending a shock wave of pleasure through him. "But you've always acted like …" She blinked.

Enrique released a long breath. This was not the best prelude for war games. Before he could form an answer, she got to her toes and pulled him down again. Her arms encircled his neck, one hand cupping the back of his head. They delved in each other's mouths and he molded her to him. When they parted, tears streaked her cheeks. "Skylar, I'm sorry. I should have—"

"No. It's not you." Skylar dried her cheeks with her hands. More tears came and she rubbed them away. "I shouldn't … I can't do this. It's not right."

A cold feeling snaked into his heart, coiled down his spine. "Are you saying you feel guilty?"

"Yes. I'm sorry. I won't do that again." She stepped away, straightening her cap and her wig. After the most awkward silence he'd ever experienced, she said. "Let's get this done." She picked up the book and the teddy bear.

"Okay." Setting aside his need for answers, Enrique took the camera and positioned it so it pointed toward the front door.

They met on the far side of the building next door. "All set?" she asked.

He nodded. "I put a few twigs around it so it would look more natural."

"Okay. I should get going." Skylar gazed at him. "Are you angry with me?"

Enrique ran a hand through his hair. He was the one who'd started it. Without asking. Or thinking. He'd just grabbed her and taken what he wanted. And her response spoke of hunger. Unquenched desire. But she was obviously married. Or something. "I'm not angry." *With you.* He'd have to untangle it later. "I'll walk you to your car."

"No thanks." She hurried off, shoulders hunched.

CHAPTER TWENTY-THREE

SKYLAR'S GUT CHURNED AS she jogged toward the trailer park. It was stupid to go alone at this time of night, but Enrique was obviously upset and he wasn't going to level with her. How many times had he made her feel this way? And why had she kissed him like that? She groaned. It was a long road ahead. She'd focus on work and on taking those small steps. Mike was probably right. After more time passed, she would look back and see progress. In fact, just today, it had happened with her dad. For the first time, she felt hopeful that they could forge a relationship.

Skylar was so lost in thought, she hadn't noticed the car heading toward her. Just before she was caught in the headlights, she dove behind a pickup parked at the curb. Her head slammed into something that protruded from the bumper. Fiery pain made her crumple. She moaned and got to her knees, gingerly feeling her forehead. There was already a lump and she felt blood oozing from it. "Crap." She scowled at the offending instrument. A trailer hitch. Her head threatened to explode. She moved to get up but the sound of hurried footsteps made her freeze.

"Skylar? Are you okay?" Enrique rounded the pickup. He saw her injury before she could replace her cap. "You're hurt. Let me see." He helped her up.

She wobbled a little. "I need to sit."

"I've got you." He picked her up, kicked the empty box under the bed of the truck and carried her across the street.

"I need to get home."

"You will."

"Slow down. You're making it worse." She struggled to free herself.

He slowed. "Sorry."

"Do you even have anything clean at the shop?"

He laughed, but she'd been completely serious. They got to the door and Enrique set her down, one hand around her waist, probably to keep her from falling. He fished his keys from his pocket. "Are you doing okay?"

Her head was spinning. She swiped blood away so it wouldn't drip in her eyes. "Maybe I should go to the ER."

"Let me get a look first." When the door opened, she stumbled inside. He quickly locked it and lifted her again.

Skylar couldn't remember feeling so inept. "I think I can walk," she lied.

But he carried her to a back room, flicked on the light and set her on a cot. "Lay down if you get dizzy."

She glanced around. Next to the wall, a large duffel bag overflowed with clothes. His clothes. She recognized a shirt. A single burner sat on top of a metal file cabinet. Nearby was a shaving kit, a toothbrush and toothpaste sticking out of the top. "Do you live here?"

"I do." Enrique squeezed some liquid from a bottle onto a piece of gauze. "This is going to hurt."

Skylar's eyes watered when he cleaned off the blood. "Why?"

"Why what?"

"Why do you live here?"

He placed a large dry piece of gauze over her lump and pressed her hand to it. "Hold that. I can use butterfly closures or liquid bandage. Do you care which one?"

"Butterfly sounds fine." Skylar leaned so she could see the bag he kept delving into. "What is all that?"

"My med bag."

"Med bag? You're a mechanic." She gawked at him. "Or ... I know you own this shop. How do you—wait, is that an IV?" She spotted a plastic tube that led to a clear bag among his supplies.

"It is. I was a medic in the army."

"Seriously?" Keeping hold of the gauze, she leaned over to peek. "Wow. All I keep at home is hydrogen peroxide and a box of bandages. The little ones with—" Black spots filled her eyes so she laid down. "When were you in the army?"

"For someone with a head injury, you sure ask a lot of questions." He checked her pupils.

"When were you in the army?"

He shook his head. "I enlisted when I was nineteen. Stayed in for seven years."

"But you didn't want to be a medic anymore?"

A shadow settled on his features. "I'd seen enough blood."

"In Afghanistan?"

He nodded.

"That must have been hard. I can't imagine." She got up on one elbow. "Why are you doing this? If you've had enough? You could have dropped me at the ER."

He shrugged. "I have everything here. The ER takes forever."

Enrique put on the butterfly bandages and helped Skylar sit up. "Hang tight a minute, then we'll get your feet under you and see how you feel."

But she got right to her feet. "I need to get going."

He caught up with her, supporting her elbow. "Is it hurting a lot?"

"Let's just say I won't forget to look the next time I dive behind a truck." Skylar made her way toward the front, her hand trailing the wall as if she didn't feel balanced.

Enrique stayed alongside until they got to the door. "Do you think you're up for driving home?"

She shrugged. "I have to work in the morning. I need to get some sleep."

"You should probably take the day off."

A whole day with nothing to do? "I can't." She waited while he unlocked the front door. "Thank you for fixing me up."

"Will you let me drop you at your car? I really don't think you should walk." Enrique wanted to touch her. To hold her. But not if she wasn't free to do so. He would never do to someone else what Kendra had done to him.

She slumped on a chair in the waiting area. "I guess it would be better than walking, but I've never been on a motorcycle."

"Would you rather I go get your car?" he offered.

She exhaled and pushed off the chair. "No. Just go slow." He locked up and they made their way to his motorcycle.

Enrique glanced at her head. "I think a helmet will hurt. Do you mind going without one?" She shook her head. The short drive to her car was excruciating, being so close to her, feeling her hands on his waist. He kept reminding himself she was off limits. After she dismounted, Enrique cut the motor and engaged the kickstand. He kept his hand at the small of her back as they went to her car. It felt like there was a wall between them. Worse than before. And entirely his fault. She'd gone there with one thing in mind. And it wasn't to make out with him. "I'm sorry for kissing you like that. I just assumed … I should have asked."

Skylar turned her cap over in her hands. It was too dark for him to see her expression. "You couldn't have known."

His heart felt heavy. "What's your cell number?" She told him and he programmed it into his phone. She did the same with his. "Call me if you need anything."

"Okay." She unlocked her car and opened the door.

"Mia. Wake up." Someone was shaking her. She opened her eyes to see Bailey kneeling beside the bed. He'd finally come into her room during the night.

She scrambled away. "No!"

He went after her. "Mia, you have to get up." He plucked her out of the bed.

She kicked and scratched. "Leave me alone."

"Calm down." Pinning her arms to her sides, he hauled her to the bathroom where he stripped off her clothes and threw them in the hall. "I want you to take a shower. Put those on when you're done." He pointed to a neatly folded pile of new clothes near the sink. Just like that, he was gone. Mia stood there shivering. Then she did as he said because she was hungry. After she'd been so difficult during the video taping, Bailey had gotten angry and taken to giving her food only if she followed his orders.

Once she was dressed, she went to the kitchen. The clock on the stove read four in the morning. Bailey set his bowl near the sink and strode to the door. "We have to go."

"But I'm hungry. I did what you said."

He came over and raised his hand.

"Okay." Mia thrust her arm up to protect herself and hurried toward the door. When she saw it was unlocked, she jerked it open and ran, taking the stairs two at a time.

"Get back here!" Bailey's footsteps thudded in the darkness behind her, muttering threats her daddy would kill him for when he got out of jail.

She raced down the last flight and sped toward the parking lot. The night air was warm. If she could find someplace to hide, she'd be okay till the sun came up. "Mia, don't you want your backpack?"

Mia kept going. He could have her dumb backpack. She scrambled between the rows of cars with her head down, zig-zagging in an unpredictable pattern. Then she ran along a line of bushes on the outer edge of the lot. His footsteps got further away. When her lungs burned too bad to keep running, she stopped, unsure where she was in the maze of cars and buildings. She worked not to make so much noise when she breathed, but then tiny lights flashed in the backs of her eyes. Mia opened her mouth and sucked in more air.

When she felt better, she peeked through a car window trying to spot him. His car hadn't started so he must still be searching. She flattened herself against the cold metal door and listened. Crickets chirped merrily, as if all was right with the world.

If she were outside the apartment near the Smiley Branch Library, she would have ten good hiding places. She'd walked down the alleys and streets, memorizing every detail. Because of her dad's frequent warnings, she'd often imagined where she would hide if anyone came after her. Whenever she'd thought about it, she'd gotten goose-bumps. Why didn't she have them now? When it was real? Nothing made sense anymore. Her daddy was gone and she'd gotten herself into trouble too big to get out of.

Mia's eyes stung. Then her nose. She no longer cared about being a doctor. She just wanted food. And a safe place. Once she started crying, she couldn't stop. And she couldn't be quiet. Her legs gave out and she slid to the ground.

Suddenly Bailey was there. He picked her up and pulled her to his chest. Still she cried. Even though she should fight. "Hey, Mia, don't cry. It's okay. We're going to meet Braden. He's waiting just for you. You're gonna be his special girl."

Even though it was still dark, they drove to Smile and Relax and went inside. The lights were on and Devlin was there. "You're late."

Bailey glared at Mia. "We had a little problem."

Devlin grasped her shoulders. "Are you giving him trouble, Mia? Your clothes are all dirty." Without waiting for her to answer, he let go. "Hurry up. We need to have her ready by five. Braden's gonna take a test drive. If he's happy, he'll wire the funds. Once they're verified, he'll come pick her up. Should take about twenty-four hours. Then you find us another one. Your money problems will be solved before long." Devlin herded her into the room where they always kept her.

No longer caring what happened since she couldn't do anything about it, Mia curled up in a ball on the couch. While Devlin was setting up the video camera, Bailey brought in a teddy bear and a book, which he practically threw at her. "These must have fallen out of your backpack." She only shrugged and turned away. He yanked her by the arm and she yelped at the pain. "Mia, Braden is here. If you want something to eat, you need to do what he says." As he had in the bathroom, he stripped off her clothes and put on some clean ones from a bag in the closet, grumbling about how much trouble she was.

Something told Mia that what she was in for with Braden would be worse than what happened with Camden. Instead of crying or screaming, she shut herself off. In her mind, Mia went to the tide pools in San Diego. Her daddy was there. Then they went to the zoo. It was the best one. You could walk in a clear tunnel under the sharks. Daddy said people came there from all over the world.

CHAPTER TWENTY-FOUR

IT WAS NEARLY TWO in the morning when Skylar drove home from the trailer park. Her cell phone buzzed and she checked it at a stoplight.

Enrique had texted. *Make sure you're not followed. Text when you're home safe.*

She touched her lips, recalling the warmth of his kisses, the pleasure of being desired by him. It was pure bliss. Until guilt plowed her under. And Enrique once again turned to ice.

When she arrived at her place and was safely inside, she texted him back. *Home safe.*

Thx.

Determined to clean off the layers of sweat and grime, Skylar used clear packing tape and a folded paper towel to create a waterproof cover for the cut on her head. After a shower, she dried her hair and crawled into bed, practically begging Joe to show up in her dreams.

High school graduation

"Joe's gonna drive me home, Mom." Skylar twirled the tassel on her graduation cap. They'd all posed for pictures in front of the school.

"Okay, but don't be long. Your father will be over in an hour."

"We'll be there on time," Joe assured Georgie. He turned to Skylar. "You ready to go?"

"Mmm hmm." She cradled her diploma to her chest as they walked toward the parking lot. "Can you believe we're done with high school?"

He put an arm around her waist. "Not really." His melancholy tone took her aback.

They got to his car and shed their caps and gowns, tossing them in the back seat. Instead of starting the car, Joe removed his tie and unbuttoned his collar. Then he stared out the windshield. Skylar eyed him, not sure what to make of it. No jokes. No kisses. She moistened her lips. "What's wrong?"

Joe turned toward her, a pensive look on his face. Skylar sucked in a breath. She hadn't seen this coming. Today of all days. Things had been going so well. She'd said those three little words that were not little at all. More than once. He picked up her hand, looking at it instead of at her. *Oh, God.* Why had she ever agreed to this? She could have looked back on their friendship with fondness. Now ...

"I signed with Cal-Poly last night."

Her mouth was too dry to speak. She stared, waiting for more.

"UC Irvine is ranked higher, but I changed my mind."

"Why?" It came out as a whisper.

"San Luis Obispo is awesome. And they're both Division One schools." He gazed at her now. "I know you'd like it there. I want you to come ... I'm asking you to come with me."

Skylar's hand went to her throat. Her mind tried to shift into reverse.

Joe smiled apologetically. "I'll be super busy. I checked the workout schedule and it's abusive. There's also a required weekly study time with the team. And I have to workout for an hour on my own three days a week, in addition to the team workouts." He cupped her face. "I don't think I can go without you, Skylar. I'm not saying I'll break up if you say no. But ... I need you there. We'll have to be apart a lot during the season but I want to be with you as much as I can." He waited. Smoothed his thumbs over her cheeks. "Say something."

She laughed. Hugged him in that awkward way you had to in the front seat of a car. "I thought you were dumping me."

His eyes widened. "On graduation day? Really?"

"It's just ... you had that look on your face. All serious. And you were so quiet. You're never quiet." She laced their fingers. "You totally freaked me out."

"Babe, how long is it gonna take for you to trust me?"

"Joey, I'm sorry. I don't know what's wrong with me." As she ran her finger along the edge of the seat, Skylar saw the hurt in his eyes. "I get these thoughts. And … I let them carry me off." She was quiet for a moment. She had to stop doing this. Stop thinking this way. It would destroy them. "I think about slapping Missy Brunswick at least once a week."

"You do?" Joe laughed, looking confused.

"And her evil twin, Monique."

"You lost me."

"But I never do it. I don't even say it. Well, except right now. To you. But I'd never tell anyone else. And God knows I'd never follow through."

"Sky." He waved a hand in front of her face. "Where are you?"

"I'm not going to do that again. I'm going to ignore them."

"Missy and Monique?" He frowned.

"No. The lying thoughts." She raised his hand to her lips. "You've been my best friend since fourth grade. You've screwed up occasionally but you've never hurt me on purpose. I let my mom brainwash me. I have no right to lay my dad's failings on you. I'm sorry, Joey. I love you." It all gushed out, a river of words.

He caressed her shoulder. "Are you finished?"

"Maybe. If you forgive me."

A laugh rolled from his chest. "Done." He kissed her and started the car.

After going to Skylar's, they went to Joe's, then stopped in at a few other parties. When he took her home that night, he led her out to the deck instead of heading back to his car. "I got you something."

Skylar felt bad. "Oh, I didn't even think about that."

"Quit. It's not for graduation." He pulled a small velvet box from his pocket. "I know you want to wait till we're older to get married. You have your whole *plan*." He grinned. "But I want you to have this. No matter what you decide about Cali."

Skylar opened the lid and found a gold necklace with a teardrop-shaped pendant, a sparkling stone suspended in the middle. She gasped. "Joey, is this a diamond?"

He nodded, gave a half-smile. "Do you like it?"

"It's beautiful." She threw her arms around him. "Thank you."

"Can I put it on you?" Skylar turned and gathered her hair. After he finished, he spun her around. "Have you made your decision or do you need more time?."

Fingering the pendant, she gazed up at him. All day, she'd been going over things in her head. "My mom's gonna freak, but I'm thinking I could work for a year and then I'd get in-state tuition. If I go to summer school, we might be able to finish at the same time."

His eyes softened and a wide smile bloomed. "You would do that?"

"I cry every time I think about saying goodbye." Her throat tightened and she took a moment to collect herself. "I want to be with you, Joey. Forever."

Skylar woke after a few hours of sleep to find her pillowcase wet and her eyes puffy. In the bathroom, she ran cold water over a washcloth and wrung it out, holding it to her eyes till it warmed. There was no time to wallow. When she arrived at work, she pulled her brown cap low so it covered the gash in her forehead. She'd loosened it, but it still made her head throb. It would come off the moment she left.

Someone rapped on her dash while she was checking her load. "Knock, knock." The truck shifted and she glanced toward the front. Wyatt, her manager, peeked around the corner.

"Hey, what's up?" Her stomach did an unhappy flip.

"I'd like a word in my office." He hopped out and she followed, making a conscious effort to relax her shoulders and keep her hand off her roiling gut. He closed the door behind them and offered her a seat. Her hat was sending pain messages to her brain. The red-alert kind. Skylar breathed deeply to keep her nausea at bay.

Wyatt stared wistfully through the window that looked out on the warehouse. "I'll make this quick so you can get on the road. It's come to my attention that Porter Glass has been hassling you. I need to know what's going on. The die-hard union guys don't like it when a street hire gets through but we didn't break any rules bringing you on."

Skylar wished the floor would swallow her up. "I've taken … evasive action. I think it's under control." She loosened her grip on the armrests of her chair.

Wyatt leaned against his desk and gave her a probing glance. "What has he done?"

Skylar sighed. Nobody liked a rat. "I'm already on the hate list."

"I heard he's made sexual slurs toward you. We don't tolerate that."

Though he was far and away the worst, Porter wasn't the only one. And it wasn't sexual at its root. He just wanted her job. "I think it's behind us now." Besides, if she ratted on Porter, he would definitely bring up the knife incident. And the slamming him into the wall and threatening his manhood thing.

"So that's how you want to play it?"

"It is." Skylar rose to her feet. "I should get going."

Wyatt stood. "I'll give you a few days to change your story. No questions asked. This conversation never happened."

Skylar eyed him. "Why would you do that?"

He sighed. "I'd been working here for a few years when I decided to come out. It was ... rough."

"Oh." Skylar had no idea how to respond. Wyatt was one of the guys who'd treated her with respect. But he was her manager and she didn't want to belittle him by saying the wrong thing.

"Surprise," he said wryly.

Skylar realized she was chewing her lip and made herself stop. "Wyatt, I don't know what to say."

"Clearly." He regarded her. "But this isn't about me. This is your shot, Sky. These things have to be documented to be pursued legally. I'm trying to help you out here."

"I know. And I appreciate it."

"Think it over. It's your decision. You're the one who has to live with what comes after. No one knows that better than I do."

"Okay. Thanks." As she hurried out, she saw Porter staring from his truck, arms crossed, face impassive.

Mia hovered in Skylar's mind all morning. As if a pounding headache wasn't enough, she got behind schedule waiting for a train, stuck behind a car wreck and had to answer several long-winded questions for a new customer. Finally, she turned off Colfax and headed for the shop.

Enrique met her at the door and held it open. "How are you feeling?" He eyed her forehead.

"Do you have any Tylenol?" She hauled the dolly toward the counter.

"Yep. Be right back."

He returned and handed her a glass of water and two pills. "Are you dizzy?" He gazed at her pupils.

"Is my color off or are you talking about me being so blond that I crashed into a parked car?" She flashed a teasing smile.

His gaze softened. "You know what I mean."

"Where's Andy?" Skylar scanned the packages and had him sign for them.

"Test driving a bike he's working on to make sure it's fixed." He placed his hands on her upper arms. "Stop avoiding my question. Tell me how you're doing."

"I'm fine. I mean, I have a horrible headache, I'm a bundle of nerves, and I'm running behind. And before I headed out on my route, my boss asked if I want to report a guy who's been harassing me. But it's all good." She pasted on a smile and stepped out of his reach. The ice man had a warm touch.

His brow furrowed. "What's going on with the guy at work?"

She shrugged. "Union crap. I'm beginning to wonder if this job is worth it. How are you? How are things here? Have you named the cat yet?"

"What has he been doing to you?" He was a hound on a scent.

Skylar slid the box off the dolly. "Threatening me. Following me around. Lurking when I come out of the restroom." Why was she telling him all this? Had her tongue been loosened when she hit her head?

Enrique gaped at her. "What's your boss going to do?"

"Nothing."

"What?"

"It was my call. I think it will work against me to do anything. I'm running late."

"Sorry. You came here first. Anything you need?"

"A shot of courage?"

"And maybe some recon training." Enrique smiled grimly.

Skylar backed toward the door, the dolly in tow. "If Mia's there, I'm not leaving until I get some real information. No matter what happens."

Enrique's eyes sparked with concern. "Do you want some help?"

"What could you do?"

"Glenda's battery came in. I'll take it over. Hang on a sec." He went and got it. They went out at the same time. "Give me a head start. I'll see if I can get some of them outside." He tugged his shirt over the gun in his waistband. "I should put in for combat pay."

Skylar stopped short. "Enrique, you don't have to do this."

"Bueno pero no te enojes."

Skylar shot him an annoyed look. "English."

"Don't be angry." He waved her off, a broad grin on his face.

CHAPTER TWENTY-FIVE

SKYLAR WATCHED ENRIQUE SET the battery near a car on the east side of Smile & Relax and jog to the door. She decided that if Mia was inside, she would call 911 and make up a lie to get the cops there. If she lost her job or the cops got mad or Devlin held a grudge, so be it. Her father could dispatch Devlin easily enough. The rest didn't matter. She checked that her cell and her knife were in her pockets. Enrique and Devlin came through the front door and down the stairs. The sight of Devlin gave her a chill. His short spiky hair was an accurate representation of his personality. He was a handsome bully. She pulled across the street and backed in closer than usual so the rear of her truck was close to the window and would give her some cover.

Devlin waved. "Be there in a minute."

"No hurry," she said. "My load is light today." *Let the lying commence.* Once inside the building, Skylar sagged with relief when she saw the reception area was empty. She shoved the box on the counter and raced to the door where Mia was kept. She knocked firmly. "Mia, it's Skylar. Are you in there?" Something rubbed against the door. *Dear God.* "Mia? Is that you?" The sound came again. Why couldn't Mia talk? Skylar's heart skittered. "I'm going to the window."

On the way out, Skylar leaned over the desk and dialed 911 on the office phone. The address should show up on the dispatcher's screen, so it was better than using her cell.

"911, do you have an emergency?"

A door opened in the hall. She heard a man and woman in quiet conversation. Bodies rustled against the wall and the woman laughed. "I need the police," Skylar whispered into the phone.

"What is your emergency?" the dispatcher asked.

"I gotta go, baby," the man in the hall was approaching. "Don't wanna get fired."

Skylar set the phone down, knowing the open line would be interpreted as a red flag. Hopefully, they would act on it. Skylar schooled her features and scanned the package as the pair emerged from the hallway.

Skylar tried to sound casual. "Hey, Glenda, do you mind signing for this?"

"No problem." Glenda did so and Skylar slipped outside.

Enrique glanced up from Glenda's car when Skylar went outside. She gave a quick nod and hurried toward her truck.

Devlin followed. "Hey, I'll have a pickup later today."

"Okay." She stopped, unwilling to open the door with him nearby.

"I've got her hooked up, Dev. Get in and see if she starts." Enrique trailed Devlin, one hand behind him, likely on his gun. His steady gaze reassured her she wasn't alone.

Devlin turned away and Skylar unlocked her door, climbing inside.

"Man, I gotta get me some of that," Devlin crowed, like a prize-winning rooster—like she would be lucky to give him *some of that*. She spun toward him.

Enrique cleared his throat. "Come on. I've got paying work to do." Enrique's gaze darkened. He widened his stance, hands on his hips.

"Fine." Devlin returned to Glenda's car.

The moment he turned away, Skylar flew to the window, finding it closed. "Mia." She knocked on the frame. "Can you come to the window?" No response. Had Glenda gone in? Skylar's breath hitched, keeping pace with her heart. She clamped her eyes shut so she could think. Then she crept to the corner of the building. Devlin had gotten out of the car again. Enrique spotted her and signaled for her to wait. Skylar pulled back, feeling like she might explode from the pressure building inside her. Enrique had Devlin get a tool and do something under the hood. He motioned behind his back and she rushed and got back in the truck, closing the door as quietly as she could.

Skylar yanked the dolly toward the bulkhead door in the rear. An oblong box protruding from the shelf stopped her progress. She yanked it off, leaned it in the aisle and got going again. Beads of sweat wreathed her face. Devlin was probably wondering why she wasn't leaving. She pressed forward, dolly in tow. She released the lock and slid the bulkhead door up, cringing at the squeak she'd never noticed before. She hopped out, hauling the dolly across the driveway without letting the wheels touch the ground, straining from the effort.

She set it beneath the window, placing the handle with its two crossbars against the building like a ladder. Then she grabbed the sill and climbed up. The dolly rolled and she hopped off, scanning the ground for something to brace it. One of the bricks used for edging the landscaping jutted up on one end. That was probably what she'd tripped over the other night. She knelt and clawed at the dirt. It was packed tight. She whipped out her knife, using the blade to slash at the ground. Her pulse rushed in her ears like a river at flood stage. Every few seconds she stole a glance toward the front, certain Devlin would round the corner and discover her. Finally the brick came free.

Skylar wedged it in front of the wheel and tried her weight again. The dolly held firm. She took a big gulp of air and climbed up, holding onto the sill with one hand, using her knife to slice the screen with the other. Once she made a good cut, she sheathed the blade, jammed the knife in her breast pocket and tore the screen apart. The window was closed but not locked. She rubbed her hands on her shorts and placed them on the glass, fingers splayed. Bracing her knees and the toes of her boots against the building, she pushed up slowly. The window squeaked as it lifted, threatening to stop her thundering heart. Once it was open a few inches, she stuck her palm underneath and shoved it up all the way.

"Mia?" Skylar peered in.

Mia was bound to a rolling chair with duct tape, a big silver strip covered her mouth. She looked at Skylar, tears flowing from her eyes.

A shot of adrenaline dumped into Skylar's gut, followed by a rage chaser. "It's okay, honey. I'm going to get you out of here."

Mia nodded. Her eyes flicked to the door.

"I am *not* going to let them hurt you anymore." Skylar thrust her upper body inside and shimmied her hips through. She brought in one leg, touched the tip of her boot to the floor, then the other leg. With a finger to her lips, she tiptoed across the hardwood toward Mia. "We need to be quiet." Mia's eyes widened when Skylar opened her knife. "I won't hurt you. I have to cut the tape." Mia nodded. "Honey, it's going to be really hard, but I need you to be quiet until we're out and I get us away from here. Can you do that?"

Another nod.

Skylar smiled. "Good girl." She took a steadying breath as she placed the tip of the knife near Mia's small wrist. "Don't move." Once she'd cut a small slit, she pulled Mia's wrist up to complete the tear. "See? It won't hurt." Mia gave her a pleading look. "I need to get you off this chair first, then I'll take care of your mouth."

Mia began working the tape on her mouth with her free hand.

"Good thinking. Take it slow. It might hurt." Skylar focused on Mia's other wrist. Once it was freed, she worked on her foot. One foot was free when someone slid a key into the deadbolt. Mia gasped and Skylar sprang to her feet. She rolled the chair around the corner so Mia couldn't be seen from the doorway. The knob turned. Skylar bent her knees and raised her hands, knife poised to strike. Someone stepped inside. A fresh punch of adrenaline shot into her belly.

"Mia?" It was Glenda. "How did you ..."

Mia jolted in the chair, terror-filled eyes directed toward the voice. Skylar put her finger to her lips and shook her head. She'd never cut anyone before. Never even been in a fight. Everything her father had taught her had been theory until she'd slammed Porter against the wall the other day. *God, help me.*

Glenda rounded the corner and Skylar grabbed her by the hair and shoved her to the floor, face down. A key fell from Glenda's outstretched hand and Skylar snatched it up. Barely able to reach with her leg outstretched, she gently toed the door shut. If she got up to lock it, Glenda would be free to move. But if she didn't ...

Pressure built in Skylar's chest and she commanded herself to think. She jerked Glenda's shoes off her feet and pressed the side of the blade to the shocked woman's throat. "It seems you're not a good witch after all, Glenda," she said in a low growl. "This is your femoral artery. Maybe you learned about it in massage school. If you even went to massage school. It takes about one minute to bleed out once it's cut and I'm guessing an ambulance wouldn't get here in time. I just replaced my blade this morning," she lied.

Glenda whimpered.

"No. Noise."

Glenda nodded.

"Turn over and take off your leggings." Skylar removed her knee from Glenda's back.

Glenda complied, eyes wide with fear.

"What the hell's wrong with you people?" Skylar spat. "She's a child, for God's sake."

Glenda was smart enough not to answer, keeping Skylar from committing cold-blooded murder in front of Mia.

"Get in there." She wagged the knife toward the closet. In the back were packages of toilet paper and paper towels. After Glenda obeyed, Skylar ripped open a roll of paper towels and tore off a few. She wadded them and crammed them in Glenda's mouth. "On your stomach." Glenda turned over and Skylar used the leggings to bind her hands and feet behind her.

Skylar quickly locked the hall door and went back to Mia.

"Glenda, the battery's installed." Devlin's voice boomed. Heavy footsteps pounded their direction. Mia and Skylar sucked in twin breaths.

Skylar sliced the tape and freed Mia's other foot. "We gotta get out of here. I have to lower you through the window. My cart is right there. If you can't reach it, you'll have to drop. I don't think you'll get hurt." Mia whimpered. Her whole body quivered. Skylar took Mia's face in her hands. "It's going to be okay." She kissed her forehead. "I'll protect you."

Devlin rattled the doorknob. "Glenda, where are you?"

Skylar pointed the blade of her knife at Glenda, who nodded again. Then she gathered Mia and lowered her out the window. Her feet barely reached the dolly. "Get in my truck. The back door is open. Find somewhere to hide."

"Glenda! Open up." Devlin hammered the door.

Skylar was kicking her legs through the window as the door blasted open. Devlin pulled his gun when he spotted her.

CHAPTER TWENTY-SIX

SKYLAR DROPPED TO THE ground and found Mia curled up next to the dolly. "I've got you, honey." She scooped her up, sprinted to the truck and set her on the floor. Just then, a loud boom sounded. A bullet whizzed past her head, finding purchase in a box. Skylar jolted. "Go go go." She shoved Mia toward the front of the truck and leapt inside. Mia didn't move. Didn't speak. Skylar grabbed for the handle and yanked the bulkhead door down, latching it as more bullets hammered the metal.

She leapt over Mia, grabbed under her arms and towed her toward the front. She placed Mia's hands on the pole that supported the divider between the front and the back and slid onto her seat. "Mia, hold on tight. And keep your head down." The bullets stopped. Which probably meant Devlin was headed outside. "We're gonna go fast." She jammed the key in and turned it. The motor roared to life and she stomped on the gas.

Confirming her fears, Devlin rushed out the front door. A bullet burst through the window of the right side door, spraying glass everywhere. It whizzed past Skylar's nose, exiting through the windshield as the truck careened into the street. Boxes shifted in back. More bullets came, pinging off metal. "Mia stay down! Watch out for the boxes." At the corner, Skylar didn't bother to stop, laying on the horn as she cut off a vehicle on Colfax. A cardboard avalanche sounded behind her, pushing Skylar to the brink of utter panic. "Mia, are you okay? I'm sorry. I had to get us off that street." A horn blared behind them. Ignoring it, she pulled out her cell and dialed 911.

"911. Do you—"

"I just rescued a kidnapped child. I have her in my delivery truck. A man shot at us and may be in pursuit."

Fingers clicked furiously on a keyboard. "What's your location?" Skylar answered, her words clipped. The dispatcher got the particulars on Skylar and her truck. "I've got officers headed your way. I need you to stop at—"

"No way. I'm not stopping until I see cops with guns. I'm unarmed and I don't know if he's following."

"I understand. Give me a description of the suspect."

Skylar gave her that and his name.

"And you're sure he has a gun?"

"I've got bullet holes all over my truck. Look, I can't hold my phone. I'll put it on speaker." Skylar stuffed her phone in her breast pocket. "Mia? Are you okay?" No answer. Had she been injured? Shot? Skylar checked her side mirrors. Traffic was light and she was flying. No other vehicles appeared to be following. She quickly switched lanes in case Devlin was on her bumper. Nothing. Maybe Enrique had dealt with him. She suddenly worried about having dragged him into this mess. What if he were hurt?

A motorcycle approached on the left. Enrique gave a thumbs-up and moved in front of her. Skylar slowed, relieved he was safe, and followed him into a parking lot. Sirens blared and lights flashed a few blocks away. She gave the dispatcher her location and raced to the back, unable to breathe when she didn't spot Mia. "Mia? Honey?" Relieved that she didn't see any blood on the floor, Skylar carefully moved boxes aside. Had she made things worse for the poor girl? Everything was a jumbled mess. "Mia. We're safe now. Where are you? Are you hurt?" A whimper came from the back on the left side. Skylar scrambled over a mass of boxes and found Mia curled up in the corner.

"Oh, baby. Are you hurt?" Skylar's eyes pricked with tears. She scanned Mia for injuries, seeing none that weren't there before. "Come here." Mia let Skylar pick her up, loud sobs erupting from her small body.

"Skylar?" Enrique's voice came through the broken window in the side door. "Do you want me to come in and help?"

"No. And tell the police to give me a few minutes. Mia's not hurt." *On the outside.*

"Okay."

Mia gripped Skylar's neck and buried her head in her shoulder. Skylar rocked slowly and Mia's sobs ebbed to soft cries. "It's okay, honey. You're safe now." Sirens whined to a stop. Skylar heard car doors slam outside, people talking, radio chatter. Several minutes went by.

Mia shuddered against her, the way one did after a hard cry. She pulled back, sniffed, sad green eyes looking up. "I—" She gulped. "I knew you would come." Her head fell against Skylar's shoulder.

Skylar melted. "You did?"

Mia nodded. Shuddered again.

Skylar leaned against the bulkhead door and rubbed Mia's back. "Enrique?"

"Yeah?"

"We need a female officer. Even if we have to wait. And I need you to call my dad."

"Okay. Hang on."

CHAPTER TWENTY-SEVEN

AFTER PASSING ON SKYLAR'S request to police, Enrique paced near the passenger door of her truck. "Skylar?"

"Yeah?"

"They've got a female officer on the way. Should only be a few minutes."

"Okay." She gave him her father's number. "Find out if he can come over."

He heard shuffling inside the truck. "Honey, I need to get this tape off. Hold still for me."

Tape? Enrique sagged against the truck and dialed. "Mr. Biondi?"

"Who's calling?"

"My name in Enrique Avalos. Skylar asked me to call."

He heard a quick intake of breath. "Is she okay?"

"Yes." Enrique explained what had happened.

"I'm on my way." A car door slammed and a motor roared to life just before they clicked off.

Enrique returned to the door. "Your dad is on the way, Sky. Does Mia need medical attention?"

"No."

Mia began sobbing again.

Dios mío. My God. Enrique sat on the step of the truck and raked his hands through his hair. Skylar's words about him not knowing what was going on right across the street plagued him. She'd been right. He flashed on her coming in and taking Andy's clothes despite his objections. What if she'd capitulated to him? Using only that little utility knife, she'd rescued a child and taken fire. After a blow to the head and only a few hours of sleep.

"It's okay, sweetheart. You're safe now." She spoke tenderly.

"That man. He hurt me." More sobs.

"Devlin?"

"No. The other man ... he did ... bad things."

Enrique tipped his head back in anguish. The brilliant blue sky with a few wispy clouds was a stark contrast to the evil that existed beneath it.

"Are you talking about Bailey?" Skylar said.

"Braden."

Skylar exhaled heavily. "Mia, we need to catch all of them and send them to jail. Will you help us do that?"

Mia sniffed. "Okay."

"First we need to talk to the police so they—"

"No!"

Enrique stood, fighting the urge to go in.

"Hey, what's wrong?" Skylar asked.

"The last time, after the police came, they put me with Mrs. D and Camden came in my room. That's why I took the other bus."

Skylar was quiet a long moment. "My dad used to be a policeman. You can trust him. He's helped a lot of kids just like you. He's on his way here. If he promises to stay with you the whole time, will you go with the police?"

"I want my daddy."

"Where is he? Can I call him?"

"He's lost. He didn't come home from work."

"Mia, listen, when did Braden hurt you? How long ago?"

"I don't know. I can't keep track." Mia sniffed.

"We'll figure it out. Can I take you outside now?"

"Okay. But I'm hungry."

"I'll get you something to eat."

Enrique heard Skylar kick boxes aside as they came toward the front. He moved away to give them some space. She made her way down the steps with Mia clinging to her, her face face nestled against Skylar's neck.

A female officer approached. "I'm officer Christie."

Skylar shook her hand. "Christie, this is Mia. She's hungry. Does anyone have something in their patrol car?"

"Probably. I'll be right back." The officer hurried off, returning a minute later with an apple and a sandwich. "Do you like peanut butter and jelly?"

Mia lifted her head from Skylar's shoulder and nodded. Enrique's heart went to his throat. She was a beautiful girl. Luminous green eyes looked around fearfully and remnants of duct tape marred her small wrists and her mouth. He went to the back of the truck and collapsed on the bumper. *Dios mío.* Had she been locked in that room when he came and went helping Glenda? He didn't get time to ponder the question. A man pulled up in a Honda sedan and he immediately saw the resemblance to Skylar. Art Biondi got out of his car and strode purposefully toward his daughter. Enrique followed.

Skylar calmed at the sight of her dad. She set Mia on her feet, keeping hold of her hand. "Mia, this is my dad."

Art took a knee. "Hi, Mia. I'm Arturo Biondi. You can call me Art."

Mia only nodded, clutching the sandwich to her breast.

Skylar crouched so they were all at eye level. "Let me help you with that." She opened the plastic bag and rolled it down so part of the sandwich protruded.

Mia took a big bite.

"Enrique, will you see about getting her something to drink?"

He nodded and disappeared.

Officer Christie had explained what would happen. It turned out Mia didn't need to face a police interview. There was a woman who would conduct a forensic interview. Someone who specialized in working with children. Skylar stepped away with Mia. "Mia, I'm sorry, but I can't go with you. I have to figure out what to do with my truck." She stroked the girl's shoulder. "Is your dad a good guy?"

"Yes." Mia's eyes teared up.

"So is mine. He can stay with you unless you don't want him to. He'll look after you."

Mia glanced at Art. "I do."

"Okay." Skylar took Mia back to the group.

Art took several minutes to get acquainted with Mia. He pulled out his wallet and showed her some photos of Skylar and his boys, eliciting a shy smile when he said Skylar called them the tumbleweeds.

Mia looked nervous and Skylar gave her a long hug.

As Mia, Art and the officer walked away, Skylar's hand went to her stomach. What had the child been through? Mia glanced over her shoulder and Skylar waved, barely keeping her emotions in check. She pulled out her cell and called Wyatt at the warehouse, explaining what happened and that she wouldn't be able to finish her route. After praising her for her quick thinking and bravery, he said he'd send someone over right away.

She spotted her father standing by the open door of his car and hurried over. Mia was buckled in the back seat. She'd finished the sandwich and was working on the apple. A bottle of water lay on the seat next to her. Skylar leaned close. "Dad, don't let her out of your sight. She had a bad experience she associated with the cops and she's terrified. It sounds like she was molested ... I think it was at a foster home. Make sure you find out what it was. I'll call when I'm free."

He nodded. Gave her a long look. "You did good, Sky." His eyes glistened. "I named you right."

"What?"

"Your mom wanted Skylar. But I chose your middle name. Alessa means defender of mankind." He wrapped her in a hug and kissed her cheek. "You okay?"

She nodded, not trusting her voice. The smell of his aftershave conjured a memory. He'd arrived late for her play during middle school. He'd been working a case, helping some other kid. And she'd been crestfallen that she always had to share him when all of her friends' fathers were present and accounted for. Now here he was, having dropped everything without a single complaint. Skylar was certain he'd see it through. Even though there wasn't a paycheck involved.

Officer Christie waved and got in her vehicle. Art held Skylar at arm's length, a question in his gaze. "Gotta go."

"I'll be okay. Thanks for coming, Dad." Skylar went to her truck and dropped next to Enrique on the bumper.

He stared at the ground. "I can't believe that was going on right under my nose."

She put a hand on his arm. "She's safe now." Suddenly, the flood she'd held back made its way to her eyes. Enrique put his arm over her shoulders. "She was duct-taped to a chair. How could anyone …" Sobs broke like a torrent.

Enrique stood, drawing her to him.

Skylar eschewed her embarrassment and held on. When she'd spent herself, she pulled away. "I got your shirt all wet."

"It'll wash out." He pointed at a brown truck as it approached. "Looks like your sub is here."

She mopped her face with her hands and dried them on her shorts. "I'm a mess."

"I'll handle it. Go wait by my bike."

"Everything should be on my scanner. The truck is a disaster. I threw my load. Maybe I should go over and help."

He gripped her shoulders. "None of that matters. You did what you had to do to save Mia's life." His hands moved lightly along her arms, giving much needed comfort. "Do you need anything from the truck?"

"My backpack." She was glad he thought of it because her brain was not functioning at full capacity.

Enrique strode away and Skylar went to his motorcycle. She traced the edge of the seat and stared at the mountains. Guilt stabbed over not sticking with Mia. But she'd known it wouldn't help if she crumbled during the ensuing legal hoops. How her father handled stuff like this was incomprehensible. Skylar was surprised she'd held herself together until after Mia left.

Several minutes later, Enrique's footsteps sounded behind her. "Should I take you home?"

Not having thought about what to do next, Skylar eyed the guys who'd come to clean up her mess. They'd brought a replacement truck. One of them must be headed back to the warehouse.

She held the back of her hand to her forehead, fearful of being alone when the next wave of emotion hit. As it surely would. If recent history had taught her anything, it was to expect the unexpected. To plan for the worst because it sometimes happened. "My car is at work. I guess I should ask that guy for a ride."

"Let me take you." Enrique put a hand at the small of her back.

"Don't you need to get back to the shop?" She turned, searched his face.

"This is more important." His eyes seemed to say *you're more important.*

Skylar inhaled. It was the better of the two options. "Okay."

Enrique tucked her backpack in a black leather saddle bag with silver studs along the top. He climbed on first, rolling the bike forward off the kickstand. Then he stood, balancing the bike while she slung her leg over. The motor rumbled to life, making a sound she decided she liked very much. "I need you to lean with me on the turns this time." A half-smile flashed on his face.

"Okay." The ride gave her time to gather herself. When they arrived at the warehouse, she climbed off. "Thank you."

"Sure." He parked and retrieved her backpack.

"You don't need to wait."

"I'm waiting. I'll come in if you want." The protective gleam in his eye reminded her she'd told him about Porter.

"That's not necessary. Everyone's out on their routes." She slung her backpack over her shoulder and headed inside.

Outside the warehouse, Enrique waited for Skylar. Despite her obvious discomfort with him hovering, thoughts of the guy harassing her made him stay. As did his concerns about her tumultuous emotions. She'd been steady and strong through so much, then after Mia left, it was as if a dam had burst. But he knew as well as anyone that it was impossible to know how you would deal with a trauma until after the fact. His cell phone buzzed.

"Enrique?"

"Yeah."

"Art Biondi. I've only got a minute." His words were clipped.

"What's up?"

"I'm gonna be tied up with Mia for a while. It may be a few days till we get things sorted out. How's Skylar doing?"

Enrique paced near his motorcycle. "She's pretty torn up about what Mia went through."

"I don't want her left alone. Can you stay with her?"

"Uh. I guess so." He wondered how Skylar would feel about that, but this phone call confirmed his concerns. Something told him Art wouldn't ask unless he felt it was necessary.

"I need to know for sure. If you can't, I'll find someone else. She's been through hell and I don't know—" Art cleared his throat. "I don't know how she's going to deal with this. I understand if you have other commitments. I'm not even sure how you know Skylar, but it's clear that she trusts you. And that doesn't come easy with her."

Skylar exited the building and headed toward him, her face a question. In place of her boxy brown uniform, she had on a pair of denim shorts and a light yellow T-shirt. Neither was tight but both accentuated her figure. "I can clear my schedule," he said, trying to affect a casual air as she neared.

"Okay. I want you to call me if anything changes and I'll make other arrangements. I can't let anything happen to her." The urgency in his tone—a stark contrast to his cool demeanor earlier—caused Enrique's stomach to tighten.

"Will do." Enrique hung up.

Skylar closed the gap between them. Her blond hair fell in soft waves past her shoulders. He realized this was the first time he'd seen it loose. She'd been attractive in the uniform with her hair pulled back. But seeing her like this ... Something caught in his throat and he was glad she spoke first.

"Is everything okay at the shop? You look upset."

Enrique wasn't sure if he should tell her the truth, but not doing so felt wrong. She wasn't a child. "That was your dad."

She gripped his arm. "Is Mia okay?"

"He was calling about you."

Skylar quickly released him and turned away. "Did he tell you?"

"He asked if I'd stay with you. Said you've been through a lot and shouldn't be alone."

Her shoulders rose and fell as she took a few slow breaths. "You don't have to do that. I can call Mike."

"Mike?"

She faced him. "He's a friend."

Which implied that she didn't regard Enrique as such. Her father was right about trust not coming easy. Though their rocky beginning was completely on him. "So, call him." He remembered their stalemate the other night when she wielded that puny knife. How he'd redirected and things had worked out.

Sparks shone in her eyes and he figured that meant she still had some fight in her. Which was good, because it seemed she was going to need it. "I'm not going to call him right this second."

He'd have to be smart. "Suit yourself. What kind of food do you like?"

Her scowl quickly melted to confusion. "What do you mean?"

"It's plain English. What kind of food do you like? What do you eat for lunch and dinner?"

"I don't really cook these days. I just eat … whatever." She lifted a hand.

For some reason, he loved throwing this woman off balance. Maybe it was the fact that she always had something to say. Was always so confident. For Pete's sake, she'd set up a contest at his business without even asking. Skylar was an odd blend of selfless and self-centered. No … self-assured. "Okay." Enrique started his bike. Skylar shook her head and strode off, that lovely hair rippling down her back. Her gait matched her father's, with the added action of her hips. He noted the contour of her calves, how they narrowed at her ankles. That particular curve was usually hidden by boots and dark socks.

Enrique arrived at work a short time later. He went straight to his desk and picked up the phone.

Andy blew in from the shop. "I'm fine. Thanks for asking,"

Enrique quelled a chuckle. *"Bueno pero no te enojes."*

"Too late. I'm already pissed."

Enrique raised a brow. "Is it safe to assume you weren't cuffed and Mirandized?" About thirty seconds after Skylar sped away with Mia, Andy had driven up on the customer's cycle he'd been test driving. Enrique had left him holding his gun on Devlin till the cops showed so he could go after Skylar.

"They made me get down on the ground." Andy slashed a hand toward the floor.

Enrique laughed.

"You think it's funny? Well, they confiscated your gun." Andy tucked a rag in his pocket.

"Shit."

"Just to check that ballistics match my story. They said you can have it back in a week or two if everything checks out."

"Well, hopefully we cleared the neighborhood of the cockroaches and I won't need it."

"We?"

"I took him down. We can share the credit."

Finally, Andy grinned. He threw out a fist which Enrique bumped with his own. "Just like old times. Only the gun was a lot smaller."

"Thanks for helping out, *camarada*." Enrique sat on the rolling chair. "Hey, I need you to manage the shop for a few days. I'm not exactly sure how long."

"You finally taking a vacay?"

Enrique shook his head. "Sky's dad asked me to look after her."

"She's not a kid." A jealous gleam shone in Andy's gaze. "I should do it. I know her better than you do."

"I gave him my word." Enrique went into his room and gathered things he would need.

Andy appeared in the doorway. "How is she doing?"

"I'm not sure. Devlin shot up her truck and she's pretty messed up over what that little girl went through. Her dad says she's been through hell. I got the impression he's worried she might hurt herself." He shrugged. "But he didn't give me any details."

"She *does* seem sad. I asked her about it at lunch and she wouldn't get into it. She got upset and walked out." Andy toed the floor mat.

"But she's always joking around." Enrique began putting clothes in his spare duffel bag.

"Are you blind? You gotta look past that and see what's in her eyes. Especially when she doesn't know you're looking. She's got a wicked deflector shield."

"No kidding."

Andy straightened. "Seriously, maybe I should go."

"I think I can figure it out. Besides, she might not take to the idea at all. I could be back here in an hour." He returned to his desk and phoned his mom.

"*Mijo*, how are you?"

"Fine, *Mami*."

"When are you going to come home for dinner? We miss you."

"Sorry, I don't have time to chat. I need some help." Enrique explained.

"I'll get Manny to help." Olivia's words were succinct, as though she'd received orders for her first combat mission. "And Jasmine can handle the phones while Edgar's in school."

After they finalized the details, Enrique headed to the grocery store, then the *carniceria*—the Mexican grocery. He hoped Skylar was up for this because the idea of a home cooked meal in a real kitchen made his mouth water. And doing something with her—or at least *for* her—might shrink the iceberg that floated between them. And salve his guilty conscience.

CHAPTER TWENTY-EIGHT

SOMEONE KNOCKED ON THE door and Skylar peered through the peephole. Enrique stood at the base of the steps, his arms loaded with grocery bags. She opened the door, glad she'd showered and put herself together rather than following her first inclination of crawling into bed. He wore a nice pair of jeans, black leather boots and a white button-down shirt with a subtle pattern. "I said I'd call Mike."

"What did he say?"

Her jaw clenched. She wanted to lie. "He hasn't gotten back to me."

"I'm here to borrow your kitchen." He lifted the bags. "May I come in?"

"At your service." Skylar waved a hand and made a low bow. "Be right back." She hurried to the hall, snatched the picture of her and Joe off the wall and crammed it on a shelf in her closet. When she returned, the kitchen counter was littered with bags and Enrique was staring into her fridge. "Well, make yourself at home."

"Are you on a hunger strike?" His gaze went from the fridge to her. One brow raised high.

"I said I don't cook." She peeked in a sack. Not that she couldn't. She just didn't. Lately. Except for breakfast. She'd managed to start with that, planning to work her way up to dinner at some point.

"Looks like you don't refrigerate, either."

She bristled. "I don't need to defend my culinary habits to you."

"Culinary?" He began filling the fridge with items from the bags. "It's good I went shopping. All you have is ketchup. And ranch dressing that looks—" He pulled it out and examined the label. "This expired nine months ago." He had the audacity to toss it in the trash.

"At least the fridge is clean."

He gave her a thousand watt smile. "There is that."

Skylar sat on a stool near the counter outside the kitchen. This was a new side of Enrique. Even the shirt. He almost always wore dark T-shirts at the shop. Which made sense, given the kind of work he did. But it was shocking how this one set off his obsidian eyes and olive skin.

He caught her staring. "What?"

She rolled her eyes. He knew exactly what. "Are you going to cook?"

"I am." Enrique rifled through cupboards and drawers. Clearly, he'd taken her comment to make himself at home quite literally. He pulled out a cast iron skillet that was covered with a red glaze. Part of a set she and Joe had purchased together. He turned it over and looked at the bottom. "*Le Cruset*. I was right."

The sight of the pan brought an ache to her heart. But Enrique looked like a kid in an ice cream shop. She thought of his spartan quarters at work and couldn't refuse him. "Right about what?"

"After seeing your furniture, I figured you'd have some cookware that was worthy."

"Worthy?" She laughed. Which made her head throb. She winced and touched the lump.

"Is that hurting?" He came over to look.

"Yes." She averted her eyes when he took her chin in his calloused hand, turning her head one way, then the other. His touch was gentle, his breath warm and good-smelling. "No sign of infection. The bandages are holding well. How did you keep it dry when you showered?" He released her.

She explained her tape and paper towel covering.

"Very inventive." He gave her an appreciative glance. "You look nice."

She'd put on a colorful floor-length summer dress. The fabric was stretchy, making it comfortable, her top priority when it came to clothes. "Thank you. The uniform gets old." She wanted to return the compliment because she'd never been in such close proximity to such a handsome man. But she barely knew him. And he was here in her private enclave where no man had trod. Except Mike, and that was a therapy emergency.

Embarrassment washed over her. This near-stranger who harbored some strange antipathy toward her had carried her in his arms, bandaged her head, held her during her melt-down. Then there were the motorcycle rides, clearly the world's most intimate form of transportation, with the possible exception of riding tandem on a horse with no saddle. The kisses they'd shared were like none she'd experienced, even with Joe. The sum total left her feeling off-balance, uncertain where to venture and where to stay away from. That new problem of keeping secrets. Her headache intensified. "I need to lie down." She made a beeline for the sofa. The moment she got comfortable, sleep grabbed hold.

Skylar awoke to mouthwatering smells. She opened her eyes and raised on one elbow. A soft blanket covered her. A thoughtful gesture that made her wonder again about the man in her kitchen. Steam rose from the stovetop. Something sizzled.

Without warning, the picture of Mia bound to a chair flashed in her mind, her frightened eyes begging for help. Their narrow escape while Devlin fired real bullets that could have killed them both, the choking worry as boxes toppled behind her, possibly hurting Mia even more. Feeling as though she were there, she sank down again, tugged the blanket to her chin and struggled to find the stop button. Her heart raced and sweat beaded on her forehead. She rolled toward the back of the couch.

A few minutes later, the anxiety ebbed, along with the scenes in her head. She wiped her face with the blanket and sat up. Enrique could probably use some help.

"Hungry?" Enrique moved efficiently in the small space.

"Starving." Skylar ran her hands through her hair, which probably looked ridiculous. "How can I help?" She pulled the blanket aside.

"It's done. Stay there and I'll fix you a plate." A minute later, he brought her a plate loaded with guacamole, fresh salsa, sour cream, corn tortillas, some kind of ground meat and a mound of crumbly white cheese. Then he set utensils, two glasses of water and several napkins on the coffee table.

Skylar took a whiff of the food and groaned with pleasure. "Okay, you get to say culinary when you talk about your kitchen habits."

He sat across from her on what was once Joe's favorite chair, a full plate on his lap. "I hope you like it."

Skylar watched him place a mixture of the food on double-stacked tortillas and followed suit. "What kind of meat is this?"

"*Chorizo.* Mexican sausage." He took a big bite. Then he sighed in that way people did when no words could express the pleasure they felt. "I can't wait to have a kitchen again."

Skylar tried it. "This is amazing. You can use my kitchen whenever you want. I'll buy the food." With each bite, her headache diminished. The water helped, too. She'd probably gotten dehydrated from all the exertion in the August heat. "Thank you." She moved to collect their plates.

"You're welcome." Enrique put up a hand. "But I'll get the dishes. You should rest."

"Forever?" She lay back and smiled dreamily.

He laughed. "Until your headache is gone when you move around or sit up."

"If you insist." Skylar put a hand on her satisfied belly. "You cook and clean up. I'll lay here and get fat." She'd never known such enjoyment from a plate of food. The euphoric feeling was sucked away suddenly when she thought of what she'd done to Glenda. The officer who'd taken the report hadn't said anything, but she knew these things sometimes grew legs of their own. She smacked the sofa and sat up. "I might get arrested."

Enrique turned off the faucet. "What?"

"I tied Glenda up and left her in the closet. I'm sure that's against the law. False imprisonment or something."

"Seriously? You tied her up?" He flipped the dishtowel over his shoulder and came near the sofa.

Skylar nodded. "And I threatened to cut her femoral artery with my knife. That's felony menacing." She bit her lip, then quickly came to her own defense. "She interrupted me when I went to get Mia. I needed her quiet and out of the way." She pointed at Enrique as if to convince him of her next thought. "But she deserved it. She was in on the whole thing."

Enrique's eyes were plates. "What did you use to tie her up?"

"Her leggings."

"No shit?" His eyes sparked with regret. "Sorry. I forgot you don't like that."

Skylar liked that he seemed proud of what she'd done, because she felt a sense of pride about it, rather than remorse—which any judge would certainly look for if she were charged.

"God, Sky. Have you ever water-boarded anybody?"

She gave him a hard look. "I think I might be able to do that to Devlin and Bailey. And whoever that Braden guy is."

He released a quick breath. "There's a lot more to you than meets the eye."

If he only knew. "I suppose that's true for most of us."

"I'll clean up my mess." Enrique went into the kitchen. "Do you have any containers I can use for the leftovers?" She heard him opening drawers and cabinets.

"Um. Just a few. Bottom right cupboard past the stove. There are Zip-locks in the pantry."

He glanced over, a bemused look on his face. "If I hadn't seen you attack that food, I'd think you were anorexic."

Skylar gave a weak laugh and lay down again. "Eating is one thing I do very well."

"Is your bathroom this way?" He pointed down the hall.

"Yes. On the left." He headed that way.

A minute later, she heard the door open, but he didn't appear. "Is this you … and your mom?" He must be looking at the photos in the hall.

Skylar cringed, her heart kicking into high gear. Good thing she'd thought to take down the picture. "Uh, yeah. High school and college graduation."

"You look a lot like her." A pause. "I guess it's just the hair and the eyes. You have your dad's features."

"I know."

He came to her side and tucked the blanket under her feet. "Thank you." She worked to keep her eyes open.

"Don't fight it. You should sleep."

"Sorry." Skylar shifted so she lay on her side. Closed her eyes.

CHAPTER TWENTY-NINE

SKYLAR AWOKE ON THE sofa and rubbed her eyes. She accidentally touched the sore spot on her forehead and made a small gasp.

A sigh came from nearby and she startled. Then she spotted Enrique crashed out on Joe's chair, his legs stretched over the ottoman, shoes off. She sat up, assessing her balance. It seemed okay, so she tiptoed toward the bathroom. When she returned, he stirred and opened his eyes.

"Sorry. You can go back to sleep."

He rubbed his hands over his face. "You've been keeping me up late this week." His voice was lower and a bit rough. She loved the sound even more than the rumble of his motorcycle.

"True. I suppose I should say I'm sorry for that, too." She sat on the couch and pulled her legs up, snuggling under the blanket again.

"How are you feeling?" Enrique stretched, his arms a big V.

Skylar remembered how it felt to be held by them. The warm feeling was quickly eclipsed by guilt. "My headache is gone."

"Good."

Suddenly uncomfortable with him in her living room, she went to the kitchen. From the moment they'd met, she'd been attracted to him. And he'd said the same about her the other night. But she was entangled. And he was … unpredictable. "I'm getting hungry. Should I reheat some food? Do you want something to eat? Or do you need to get going? Have I totally screwed up your schedule?"

He laughed. "Slow down."

"Sorry. Software glitch." Joe had coined that phrase for her propensity for shooting out a string of questions or comments without giving him a chance to respond. Her heart stung. How long would she think of everything in reference to Joe?

Enrique padded over in his bare feet. "Do you mind if I cook something else? I'm so happy to have access to a kitchen."

Skylar realized she was staring and shifted her gaze. He'd asked her a question. Oh, yes, he wanted to cook. "I'll help you this time."

He opened the fridge. "Cilantro. Love it or hate it?"

"Love it."

"Good, because it makes this dish." One at a time, he passed her fresh cilantro, a bulb of garlic, several tomatoes, a package of chicken and a container of chicken broth, which she placed on the counter. "Okay, we need …" He reached in a cabinet and pulled out olive oil, cumin, salt and pepper. "Where's the rice?"

She got it from the pantry.

"And we need one onion and the *pico de gallo.*"

"What are we making?"

"Arroz con pollo y frijoles." It rolled off his tongue like a sonnet. "Rice with chicken and beans."

Skylar risked a glance. Something had come to life in his eyes. Passion. *For food*, she reminded herself. He'd been living without a kitchen for six months. When Enrique spoke Spanish, something shifted. Skylar wasn't sure if it was in her or in him, or maybe the air? But it drew her in, making her want something she wasn't sure how to name. He seemed so … grounded. Like he knew who he was and didn't question it. It had been a long time since she'd felt that way. Perhaps he'd rub off on her.

"Is Spanish your first language?"

He paused and gazed at her. *"Sí."* Forget the stovetop, he could sear the food with a look. "But my parents are fluent in English as well. They thought it was important to know both."

Skylar felt like a teenager, fighting that fluttery feeling inside. If she weren't so moon-eyed, she might believe he was moved by her question. After a moment, he went to the sink and washed his hands, prompting her to do the same. Their elbows brushed lightly, sending a quiver of warmth into the far reaches of her body. Once more, guilt quickly vaporized the feeling. "So, how can I help?"

Enrique dug out a cutting board. "Pass me that knife on the top right."

Skylar pulled it from the block, enjoying that he was comfortable enough to commandeer her kitchen and tell her what to do. She didn't sense a power trip, just an easy confidence. A man comfortable in his own skin.

He cut off both ends of an onion and sliced it in quarters, disposing of the dry outer layers. "Start with the tip of your knife on the board and bring this end down." Enrique demonstrated, quickly slicing one section of the onion. "You do the rest. Make it all the same size."

Skylar had seen chefs on TV do this sort of thing and was surprised at how much more efficient it was.

Enrique came alongside and turned the tips of her fingers under. "It's safer if you keep your fingertips rounded."

His closeness turned her legs to rubber. "So, in addition to being a medic and a motorcycle mechanic, you're also a chef?" She kept her eyes on what she was doing.

"Self taught." He propped a hip against the counter and she felt his gaze. "And my mom's a great cook. She taught me a lot."

"A renaissance man. What size pan do we need for the rice?" She opened a cabinet, putting a little distance between them.

"Medium." Enrique faced her. The fire in his eyes made her wonder if he was feeling the same way she was.

She swallowed, suddenly fearful she'd act on her feelings. Then he might go cold again. But even if he didn't, the guilt that plagued her would eat her alive. "I think this will work." She set a pan on the counter and backed between him and the refrigerator, thumbing over her shoulder. "I need to get a tablecloth."

He gave a half-smile, those dark eyes regarding her under thick, long lashes. A few more seconds and he'd have to mop her up off the floor. The kitchen was too small for the energy that arced between them. The tablecloths were in the pantry, three feet from where he stood. But Skylar escaped down the hall and hid in her closet. She pulled out the picture she'd hidden and held it to her breast. This was no good being stuck between worlds. She shoved it back on the shelf and put a T-shirt on top of it.

When she returned, Enrique was stirring something on the stove. "I forgot ... they're in here." Her voice was unsteady and she wanted to kick herself. She pulled the pantry door open and grabbed the first tablecloth she saw. "I haven't used them since I moved in." Finally, the truth. The task of setting the table allowed her stomach to settle.

She couldn't go back in there and help him. If she loosened one brick in the wall she'd erected, the whole thing might come crashing down. "Do you mind if I take a break?" Skylar moved to the sofa, the farthest point from Enrique without leaving the room again, which would be rude.

"No. I'll let you know when it's ready." Enrique eyed her, concern etching his features.

"I'm okay. Just tired." With a sigh, she pulled the blanket up to her neck. Perhaps if she took her focus off herself ... "Andy said you inherited the shop from your uncle."

"Yeah. He passed away early this year."

"I'm sorry. Were the two of you close?"

He nodded. While he finished cooking, he told her about the financial challenges it presented. Then he invited her to the small dining area off the kitchen. "I'd have closed it and sold the building, but my family is counting on me to give them some work."

"How big is your family?" Skylar got up and filled two glasses with water, adding ice to his.

"Big. Like a town. Cousins are the same as siblings in my family. I stopped trying to count them when I was about ten."

"Where are you from?"

"Federal Heights. You?"

"Denver."

"All your life?"

"Mmm hmm. Except, I lived in California during college. I went to Cal-Poly. San Luis Obispo is beautiful." Memories flooded in, making her throat ache. She was saved by wonderful food and light conversation.

After cleaning the kitchen together, Skylar said, "Enrique, thank you for doing all of this. I'm sure you're exhausted. I should let you go so you can get some sleep." The thought of him sleeping on that cot in the windowless room made her sad. Even though he did it for the sake of his family.

Enrique turned to her, a serious look on his face. "Do you want me to sleep on the sofa tonight? I came prepared." His fingertips skimmed her shoulder.

Yes. Knowing he was there might be enough. But she'd been a huge burden all week. And now that she understood more about his life, she didn't feel right adding herself to his list of responsibilities. "No, thanks."

"Then I should call your dad. I told him I wouldn't leave you alone."

"What exactly did he tell you?" Her heart rate spiked.

"That you've been through hell and it wouldn't be good for you to be alone after what happened today."

"That's all?" The tremor in her voice was humiliating.

He nodded. Skylar eyed him. Saw no signs of deception.

He pulled on his boots and she walked him to the door. She touched his arm. "I don't know what would have happened if you hadn't been there today. I could have been killed. And Mia ... she might still be ..." A lump formed in her throat. The events of the day flashed again, more intense than before. A surge of emotion barreled over her. Skylar swallowed. Closed her eyes.

Enrique pulled her to him, rubbing her back. "I'm going to stay. You have a lot to deal with on top of whatever else has been going on."

Skylar's shoulders quaked as, once again, painful sobs wrenched from her throat. Her whole body trembled. He guided her to the sofa. "I'm sorry," she said. Like a child, she buried her face in a pillow, completely embarrassed by her inability to remain in control.

CHAPTER THIRTY

"IT'S OKAY." ENRIQUE COVERED Skylar with the blanket and grabbed a box of tissues from the bathroom. He took a seat near her head, wishing he could magically make it all go away. But he knew better. After his tour, in addition to PTSD symptoms, he'd had the issues with Kendra. There was no easy way to get through stuff like this. And he still had no clue what else she was facing.

Calmer now, Skylar shifted to her back. She sniffed and dried her eyes with a tissue. "I'm sure you have work to do. Maybe I can go over to Mike and Janie's."

"Work's covered. But if you'd rather be with your friends, I understand."

She sighed. Moved to get up.

Enrique put a hand on her shoulder. "What do you need?"

"I'd like something to drink."

"I can make you some tea. It might help. Do you have something without caffeine?"

"Yes. I keep it in the pantry." She sat up. Wiped her eyes. "I don't know where that came from. You must think I'm a head case."

He opened the pantry door and pulled out a basket filled with various teas. After putting the kettle on to heat, he returned. "I don't think you're a head case. I think you're the bravest civilian I've met in my life. This is just your body and your mind trying to heal. It sucks, but it's normal."

She eyed him warily. "So you're not wishing you'd never met me?"

He exhaled. "Actually, I'm wishing I'd met you about five years ago."

Her brow creased. "What happened five years ago?"

"I met my wife."

Her eyes widened. "You're married?"

"Not anymore."

"Oh." She absently rubbed the ring finger on her left hand.

"Sky, are you married?"

She blinked. Swallowed. "No."

It didn't ring true. If she weren't so traumatized, he'd have pressed her. Maybe she was in the middle of a divorce and didn't want to talk about it. That would explain the nice furniture in the low-budget apartment. "How long have you lived here?"

"I moved in July first."

"Where did you move from?"

"Wash Park."

"Is that how you met the dog owners? When you lived there?" He wanted to know everything about her. What made her tick. What made her happy. What turned her on. He'd have to save that last one until she was on better footing. The kisses they'd shared the other night were never far from his mind. But her hesitation when he'd asked if she was married was cause for concern.

She nodded. "Tell me more about your family. I always wanted a big family. It was just me and my parents till they got divorced. Then it was just me and my mom. Most of the time, anyway. Dad was always busy with work."

"I have three younger sisters. Bianca, Jasmine and Reyna." Enrique told her about each of them until the kettle whistled. Then he prepared two mugs and carried them to the living room.

"Thank you." She blew on her tea.

"My cousins are endless, but I'm closest to Manny. We're the same age. He's a first cousin, but he's more like a brother."

"Do you all get together for holidays and birthdays?"

"We do. Although I've missed most of them since I started running the shop. My mom's not happy about that."

"What's her name?"

"Olivia. She's five-foot nothing and she runs the neighborhood. And the church. Father Francis thinks he does, but it's really her."

Skylar laughed.

He sank into the comfortable couch. "It's Olivia Avalos who makes sure shut-ins get meals and people get prayed for. She was Facebook before there was Facebook."

Skylar eyed him over the rim of her mug. "You're not so grumpy anymore."

Enrique grimaced. "I'm sorry about that."

"What did I do?" The pain in her gaze cut him.

"Nothing. You resemble Kendra."

"Your ex-wife?"

He nodded, turning to face her. "I was trying to protect myself. I made assumptions." Regret swarmed his gut. "I heard you ask Andy about it." He traced the handle of his mug with his thumb. "I'm sorry I treated you that way, Skylar. You didn't deserve it."

Skylar shrugged. "It's okay."

Enrique squirmed inside. "It's not okay. But I hope you'll forgive me."

"Do I make you think of her?"

He gave a humorless laugh. "Not anymore."

"Well, I guess that's something." They were both quiet while they sipped their tea. Skylar set her mug on the coffee table. "Are you sure you can stay? You never said how you're making this work."

"My mom sent reinforcements to help at the shop." He carried their mugs to the kitchen and put them in the dishwasher. Then he went and sat next to her. "Your name-my-cat contest has brought in a lot of new business. I've been meaning to thank you."

"I probably should have asked, but … I like to mess with people when they're cocky. I can't seem to stop myself."

He elbowed her lightly. "You think I'm cocky?"

She snorted. "You're totally cocky."

He laughed.

"But so am I," she confessed with no remorse whatsoever. Then she smiled up at him. "I'm glad it helped."

"You're very thoughtful. I didn't give you any reason to be nice."

She waved a hand. "So are you. I've been a real pain the last few days and you're here acting like an indentured servant." Skylar looked at him like she really saw him. She lifted her hand as though she were going to touch him. The look in her eyes said she wanted to. But she didn't. And her hand drifted back to her thigh. She was quiet a moment. "I don't think I'm going to stay at my job."

"Because that guy's harassing you?" Enrique felt a surge of anger when he thought of the faceless man who'd followed and threatened her.

"It's not just that." Skylar ran her hand along the satin edge of the blanket. "It was never going to be a long-term thing. I'm not using my degree."

"What's your degree?"

"My bachelors is in math. I've been teaching high school math the past few years."

"Really? What are you doing driving that truck?"

"It's … complicated." Her eyes flitted away, but not before he saw the sad shadows Andy had mentioned. "And you're not the only one with questions." Skylar got to her feet. "Well, I'm going to hide out in my room now. What do you need in the way of bedding?" She glanced at the sofa. "Is this even long enough for you?"

"It's fine." He stood. "It's a lot more comfortable than my cot."

"Come with me." She led him to a bedroom filled with stacks of plastic crates. "Let's see … I've got pillows in this one. Blankets in here." She pointed.

He chuckled. "There's already a blanket out there."

"Right." She indicated a crate on top of a tall stack. "Can you get that one down?"

He did and she took out some sheets. "I don't need sheets."

Skylar gave him a befuddled look. "You're my guest." After he chose a pillow, they went out and she made up the sofa like a bed. "I don't have any chocolates for your pillow, but I'll turn down the sheets for free." With a smile, she pulled the top sheet and the blanket down in a triangle, smoothing it with her hand. "There. I hope you'll be comfortable."

Enrique sat and patted the cushions. "It's perfect."

"It's not commensurate with all you did for me this week." It seemed like she wanted to hug him, but she only shrugged awkwardly. "Goodnight."

San Luis Obispo, Joe's freshman year

Skylar scrubbed the counter at the bistro one last time before tossing the rag into the cleaning cart. She wheeled it to the kitchen, opening the swinging door slowly in case anyone was coming the other way. "I'm out of here, Wayne. See you tomorrow."

"Good job today, Sky. Have a good night."

"You, too." She went out front to unlock her bike.

"Hey, baby."

Skylar spun. "Joe?" He stood there with a big grin on his face. She got on her toes and kissed him. "What are you doing here? Are you okay? Did you get hurt?" She ran her hands over his shoulders, down his arms.

He smiled. "I'm fine. I'm all caught up on my homework. How was your shift?"

She pulled the band from her hair and let it fall. "My feet are killing me and I smell like food. But it was really busy and I made good tips."

"Good." Joe held her, stroking her back. "I have a surprise."

"Does it involve exercise?" she asked wearily. Most of their alone time was spent working out so Joe could fulfill his requirement to do that on his own three times a week.

"Not unless you count this." He gave her a lingering kiss.

"What about my bike?"

"We'll come get it on the way home. We won't have room in the car until then."

Skylar eyed him suspiciously. "Why not?" She walked over and spotted pillows and a blanket on the backseat. "Joe Thomas, we are not having sex in your car." She stalked away, arms crossed.

He caught up with her and spun her around. "Settle down. That's not the plan. We're going on a date. An old fashioned one. You're gonna love it." They got in the car.

"Sunset Drive-In." Skylar read the sign aloud. Joe pulled into what looked like a large parking lot with a weird series of bumps. Cars were parked randomly along each of them, front wheels on top of the bump. They'd made a stop on the way and a hot pizza now sat on the backseat next to the blanket. "I had no idea drive-ins still existed."

Joe maneuvered between rows of parked cars in search of an open space. The smell of popcorn wafted in the air, along with low conversations from open car windows. "Neither did I. I looked online and found a whole list of cool stuff we can do." He grabbed her hand and gave it a squeeze. "We're not gonna be like people who live in New York and never go to Ellis Island or Central Park. We're going to live in the moment." Sometime in the last month he'd taken to saying *we* all the time. A seriousness had settled over him with regard to their future and he'd talked again of getting married. The sooner, the better. But she wanted to wait until they'd finished school, though she couldn't articulate her reasons, even to herself.

Skylar put down her window. "What's playing?"

Joe pulled into a spot and the car tilted back as the front wheels went up a tiny hill. He hung a speaker box inside the half-open window. "Who cares? We'll be busy making out."

She smacked his leg.

"A chick flick. You know I'm no good with titles."

"Oh, there's the marquee. I've been wanting to see this. You're taking me to a chick flick? Are the pillows here so you can sleep while I watch the movie?"

Joe caught her chin and kissed her. "Just so we can get comfortable. I'm gonna be wide awake the whole time." When the movie started, he held her hand.

Touched by his thoughtfulness, Skylar brought his hand to her lips. He'd been run ragged with training, baseball practice and school, often coming to her place for small snatches of time after her shifts at the restaurant.

Near the end of the movie, his eyes drifted shut. Skylar smiled and kissed his cheek.

"Love you, baby," he whispered.

"Me, too."

Skylar woke up and felt beside her. Joe wasn't there. Where was he now? What was he doing at this very moment? Was there even a chance he was thinking of her? The questions summoned sobs, each one wracking her body and breaking her heart, like huge waves crashing on shore.

After the movie at the drive-in, she'd switched places with him and driven to get her bike while he dozed beside her. Then she'd dropped him on campus and ridden home in the cool darkness, the breeze carrying the scent of the ocean.

Living in the moment.

But that moment was gone. They all were.

A soft knock sounded and her bedroom door opened. "Skylar?"

Skylar quickly mopped her face with the sheet, having completely forgotten Enrique was there.

He took tentative steps toward her bed. "I heard you crying."

"Oh. Sorry." An involuntary shudder shook her body. She scooted back against the headboard and pulled a tissue from the box on the nightstand. "I'm … okay." She wiped her nose, drew her knees to her chest.

Enrique sat near her feet. "Did you have a bad dream?"

How should she answer? It was a lovely dream. A beautiful memory. It was waking that tore her apart. She hadn't spoken to anyone about the dreams, this reliving her past while she slept. Part of her enjoyed it, taking comfort in what once was. But they always ended in this altered reality. Joe was gone. And nothing she did would bring him back.

Enrique picked up her hand. "Hey."

She cleared her throat, glad he couldn't see her well in the dimness, all puffy and red-eyed. Light spilled from the hall, gilding his frame, making him appear like an angel. And that's what he was. A warrior angel. Like Michael. "I did have a dream," she ventured. "But it wasn't a nightmare. And it wasn't about what happened today."

"Do you want to talk about it?" His fingers gently massaged her hand. Warm human contact.

It felt good. So good. Skylar wanted to pull him in bed with her. Just to hold him so she wasn't alone. Instead, she used every ounce of willpower and withdrew her hand. The last thing she needed was more regrets. "I … no. I don't think it will help. Sorry I woke you. God. How many times am I going to have to apologize to you?"

"I'm not keeping track."

CHAPTER THIRTY-ONE

ENRIQUE LAY ON THE couch staring at the living room ceiling. It wasn't the memory of Skylar's sobs that kept him awake so much as the anguish in her voice when they'd spoken afterward. Even when she'd told him about finding Mia, there had been a measure of indignation in her tone. She'd been torn up, but there was a steel framework holding her together. This was different. As though her very soul had been stolen. It ate at him like battery acid. After a few hours of fitful sleep, he awoke and called Andy.

"How's Sky doing?" Andy asked.

"I'm not sure. She's really shaken up about what happened to Mia."

"The little girl?"

"Yeah." Enrique rested his hand on the linens he'd folded and placed on the couch. "And you're right about there being something else, but she's not ready to talk about it."

"It's a guy."

"She told you?" Enrique straightened.

Andy cleared his throat. "No. But only a man could do that to a woman."

Sometimes Andy surprised him. "You're probably right."

"Anyway, Jasmine and Manny are coming in today. We've got everything under control, so no worries."

"Thanks."

"Is Sky gonna go back to work?"

"I don't think so." He told Andy what Skylar had said about the guy who'd harassed her.

"I'd give him a proper beat-down if I knew who it was." Andy released a frustrated sigh. "Let me know if there's anything else I can do to help." They clicked off.

Since no sounds came from Skylar's room, Enrique took a shower, elated to use a spotless bathroom he didn't have to share with a bunch of other guys. Despite all she'd been through, she'd left him a clean, good-smelling over-sized bath towel, even doubling it over the towel bar the way they did at hotels. On the counter next to the sink was a basket filled with a variety of unopened shampoos, soaps and lotions that hadn't been there the night before. The special touches made him feel like an honored guest.

Accustomed to rising early and pushing hard all day—often late into the night—Enrique felt antsy. He stood and went to one of the bookshelves. Skylar owned all manner of books; one section contained college textbooks. There was also a wide range of fiction, from children's books to New York Times bestsellers in hardcover. He came to one shelf filled entirely with books about baseball. The rules of the game, the history, individual franchise histories, biographies and autobiographies of famous players. He slid out one about Jackie Robinson. The author had signed it: *For Joe. Best wishes for a great season and storied career.*

He replaced it and picked up a signed baseball, turning it over in his hands. The scrawl wasn't legible. He heard Skylar door open and placed the ball back on the shelf. When she went into the bathroom, he started some coffee, wondering what she usually ate for breakfast.

A few minutes later, she came down the hall. Her hair was pulled back in a knot and she wore blue shorts and an over-sized Cal-Poly sweat shirt. "Good morning." She covered a yawn. "Did you sleep okay? Were you comfortable?"

"Yes and yes."

"Sorry." She opened the fridge. "What do you like for breakfast?"

"I'm not picky. I usually heat up an egg burrito in the microwave."

"Yuck." She made a face. "Shoot. I should have gone shopping one of those nights when I was skulking on your street. I'm out of eggs. You didn't bring any, did you?" She moved things around in her search.

"No."

"If you don't mind waiting, I'll run out and get some. Cereal and toast don't get me through the morning." She drank a full glass of water and wiped her mouth with the back of her hand.

Enrique made a growling noise. "Such a cave woman."

"I know." Skylar grinned. Then her eyes sparked with awareness. "Hey, do you need to get going? I could make you some pancakes. Do you like pancakes? I don't know if I have any syrup. I could also make muffins ... wait, that would take eggs." She spun and opened the pantry.

He was getting used to her long strings of dialogue. "Actually, I was planning to hang with you today." He tried to gauge her reaction.

She came over to him. "Well, I'm not going to work, but what about you? Will the place fall apart?"

"Andy said everything is under control."

Skylar slumped on a stool by the counter. "I feel like you're my babysitter. You're probably wishing you'd said no to my dad."

Enrique had expected something like this. He'd have been embarrassed if she'd witnessed him losing it the year he returned from Afghanistan. She wasn't inept. Far from it. She worked hard every day and even kept busy at night. But it was clear she needed some TLC. "Do you want to go out for breakfast? Maybe we could go walk one of those dogs afterward, to get outside."

"Really?" Her face brightened.

"Sure. It would be a nice change. I hardly ever get out of the shop."

She gave him a once-over. "Do you have any shorts and comfortable shoes?"

Out of habit, he'd put on jeans and his boots. "I do."

"Okay. I should change, too. I'll just be a minute."

They ate at a restaurant near Wash Park, with Skylar telling him about her favorite haunts in the area. There were paddleboats in a lake at the park and lots of good restaurants. Enrique smiled. "You're so easy to talk to." He covered her hand with his. "I have a thousand questions, Skylar. I'd really like to get to know you better."

Her expression became pensive. "Like I told Andy, I'm digging my way out of a hole right now."

"I understand." He moved his hand.

"Enrique, don't take it as a brush-off. I'm not interested in Andy that way, but ... there's something about you." Her gaze captured his for a moment, as if she were having a debate in her head. He glimpsed pain. A deep well of sadness. She swallowed. "I'll answer your questions but I can't handle a thousand. How about if you throw out a few at a time?"

"Sure." Enrique was surprised at the relief he felt. "That makes me happy."

Trepidation shone in her eyes. "You should reserve judgment until you get your answers."

He wondered if she would expound on that. She did not.

The server brought the check and Skylar snagged it. "My treat." When they got to her car, she touched his arm. He liked how she did that. It was sort of a listen-to-what-I-have-to-say thing. Soft and unobtrusive. "Two stipulations on the questions."

"Shoot."

"Three a day. And you have to answer them, too."

He smiled down at her. "Fine. But not every question I ask counts as one of the three."

Skylar raised her brows. "What do you mean?" Her tone was sassy. He liked that, too.

"Like asking what you want for dinner wouldn't count. It's informational."

She grinned. "We'll see."

Enrique enjoyed the challenge she presented.

They picked up the large German shepherd. "This is Whisper." She patted his head. "He's my favorite."

Enrique reached out so the dog could sniff his hand. She passed him a treat to give to the dog and it earned him a happy wag.

The walk to Wash Park took only five minutes. They were on the west side near the middle. "Do you mind if we walk through the rose garden? They won't be in bloom much longer."

"That's fine."

They meandered through lush green grass between long narrow islands of roses. Just as it had been a few nights earlier, Whisper's attention was riveted on Skylar. He kept pace with her, stopping when she did without her having to do anything. He laughed to himself, thinking he was doing the same. The air was heavy with sweet scents from the various roses. "Isn't it beautiful?" Skylar stopped to smell a peach colored rose, caressing it tenderly.

"It is."

A jogger passed by on a path. "I used to run here," she said wistfully. Then she seemed to catch herself sliding backward. She pivoted and pointed to a large structure to the east. "That's the boathouse. It's a great venue for parties and ... big events. You can rent paddle boats and go out on the lake."

Enrique sensed she was struggling again and intervened. "Okay. Question number one."

Skylar clasped her hands behind her back. "Hit me."

"What's with the dog-walking? You aren't getting enough exercise hauling boxes and climbing in and out of that truck all day?"

She swallowed. "Something like that."

He nudged her shoulder. "You have to tell the truth or take a pass."

After a lengthy silence, she said, "I'm trying to get over a guy. I figure if I keep busy, that will help."

Enrique fingered the soft petals of a pink rose. "What happened? Did he leave you?"

She nodded, her eyes straight ahead. "It was ... unexpected."

"Had you known him long?"

"Since fourth grade."

"But you didn't get married?" He remembered the photos on her wall. There'd been the same guy in each one. Like they'd gone to both high school and college together. Why would she keep such a painful reminder where she'd see it so often?

Skylar took a long pull from her water bottle so she wouldn't cry. When her throat relaxed enough, she said, "You've exceeded your quota." She pointed. "Those are the paddle boats. They also have canoes and those things you stand up on. We'll have to come back without a dog and rent one sometime. If you like that sort of thing." She looked up in question.

Enrique put his hand on the small of her back. "I'd like to do it with you."

She smiled, reveling in the feel of his touch. "My turn. I already know why you keep so busy so I'm going to go with something else.

Hmm. I hope this isn't too personal. If it is, you can decline. Are you over your wife?"

He sighed, ran a hand through his hair. "I am. The only thing that bothers me is that I'm still paying off her debts."

"What?" She stopped in the middle of the sidewalk. Whisper did too.

"When I was in Afghanistan, I thought my paycheck was going into our savings for a deposit on a home. Kendra had a good-paying job. She said she opened an account at another bank and she'd send me listings of homes she was interested in." He jammed his hands in his pockets, stopped walking. "But I get back and there's no savings account. No money at all."

"None?" Skylar moved next to him.

"Zero. But there's a mountain of credit card debt and another guy in our bed." His features hardened. "So, while I was out on patrol dodging bullets and my best friend died in my arms, she was …" He kicked a rock into a bush. Skylar saw anger and pain flash in his eyes. In that moment, she understood why he'd been so cold. He'd been deeply wounded by a woman he trusted. One she had the misfortune to look like.

"Enrique, I'm sorry. That must have cut deep." She wanted to touch him, but in light of his revelations, she wasn't sure it would help.

He took a deep breath and they began walking again. "How it worked out is that the two of us had to split the debt down the middle, even though none of it's mine. That's another reason I'm living out of the shop. I'm trying to pay it down faster. I just want to put it behind me."

"And that's why you don't have a car?"

"Yeah. Plus, I told you about the mess the shop is in. I figure if I pay myself as little as possible, I'll get it turned around sooner." They rounded the lake and headed toward Whisper's house. "Last month, I dropped twenty-five grand on tools and equipment, including a trailer for picking up machines that aren't running."

"Why can't you drive the pick-up you pull the trailer with?"

"It's Andy's. I only use it for work stuff and I pay him for every mile."

Skylar ground to a stop and put her hands on her hips. "Hey! Is that the one I hit my head on? Should I file a claim against your insurance? Is that why you were so determined to get me fixed up? You wanted to save a few bucks?"

He laughed. "No. We keep ours in the secure lot."

She loved when he laughed. His eyes gleamed and crinkled in the corners. And that smile … It took her breath away. She remembered lying on his cot while he tended her. What must it be like to live in that small dank space? It probably made her apartment seem huge. "There's no shower at the shop is there?"

He glanced away. "I go to the Y."

"The what?" She trailed her hand along a bush as they passed.

"The YMCA." Enrique sounded ashamed. But to her he was a hero, sacrificing his most basic needs for the sake of his family.

"Oh."

"You get used to stuff like that in theater."

"You mean when you're deployed?"

"Yeah."

Skylar pressed the walk button on a traffic light. "I asked way more than three questions. I'm sorry if I overstepped."

"You didn't. It feels good to talk to someone sane about it."

As they crossed the street, she nudged him. "You're not at all like your first impression."

He groaned. "You're never gonna let that go, are you?"

"Probably not. I have an excellent memory." She tapped her head. "Like an elephant. I remember your tattoo." *And your gorgeous body.*

"And I remember you putting names in that jar." He nudged her with his elbow.

"No I didn't," she lied.

"Son of Grumpy? Handsome?"

"You should pick that one. It's perfect."

Another laugh rumbled from his chest. "I think I'm gonna go with Muffin. Shop Cat likes it the best."

Skylar laughed so hard, she couldn't keep walking. "Muffin. I can just hear you calling him." Whisper looked worriedly between her and Enrique. She patted the dog's head, nearly choking when she realized they were coming up on the two-story brick Craftsman style home. She'd always been alone and paid careful attention to whether anyone was there. The flowers glistened in the morning sun. Her hand went to her stomach.

"You like that one?" Enrique said softly.

"I do." Skylar blinked. Tried to shake the image of Joe on the front step, his duffel in one hand, tossing a baseball with the other—his perpetual motion.

"I love the big front porch. And the swing."

Skylar began to feel faint. Could a broken heart kill a person? Whisper started to prance, giving her a much-needed distraction. He lived a few doors down and Skylar headed that way. After she let him in the yard, she tugged Enrique's hand. "Come on." She meant to let go after she'd gotten him moving, but he held on, lacing their fingers, until they arrived at her car down the block.

Somehow, she drove to the grocery store without losing her grip. They wandered the aisles, filling the cart with real food that would make healthy, well-balanced meals—something she hadn't done in a long time. Eggs, cheese, yogurt, fresh fruits and vegetables, meats and whole grain bread. No frozen dinners or canned soup. Skylar felt grounded. If only she could hang out with Enrique every day, maybe there would be a way through this. An idea struck her. *No. Yes. Are you insane?* She made a frustrated noise in her throat.

"What?" Enrique shot her a puzzled look.

"Nothing." She headed to the checkout line.

"Tell me." He spoke in her ear, his breath warming the side of her neck.

She touched the spot. For the past year and a half, pleasure was always immediately quashed by sadness. Or guilt. Or they'd ganged up on her. This time, the good feeling lasted several seconds. "Do you enjoy cooking? I mean, you're really good at it. Crazy good. But … do you like it?"

He chuckled. Ran a hand down her arm. "Are you going somewhere with this?" Ten seconds of pleasure this time.

Wanting to see the truth in his eyes, she turned to face him. "Well, I was thinking, if you wanted to, you could come over and cook a few nights a week. Whenever it works for your schedule."

He looked as though he were weighing the idea.

"I'll buy the food. And I'll clean up. I could also make dessert."

Flattery followed by bribery. She'd never felt so desperate.

"Like a supper club?"

"Call it whatever you like." *A Skylar-won't-die-of-loneliness club.*

"I would love to. But you need more containers. For leftovers and stuff."

"I have a bunch in those crates in the bedroom." The checker totaled the bill. Skylar pulled out her wallet at the same time Enrique did. "You bought all that food yesterday. I can get this."

He shrugged. "Okay. But I'm not going to let you pay every time. Even if I cook."

They got back to her apartment and carried their purchases to the door. Skylar zinged with energy. The kind that could only be spent on a man. Only be caused by a man. Had ever only involved one man. Joe.

She had deceived Enrique.

CHAPTER THIRTY-TWO

ENRIQUE'S BRIEF, OFTEN HARRIED encounters with Skylar at the shop always left him wanting more. Now, after only one day with her, he was hooked. But he warned his heart not to leap. Though she'd said twice that she wasn't married, something seemed off. They descended the steps to her apartment, grocery bags in hand. His gut clenched when she faced him after letting him in. Something in her eyes gave him pause. As she put away the food, her movements were brisk, her breathing shallow and fast. Like she might start hyperventilating at any moment.

"Are you okay, Sky?"

Skylar faced him. Resignation weighing her features. "I lied to you."

He blinked. "About what?"

"I'm not trying to get over a guy. I mean, I am. But—" She dragged a hand through her hair. It got stuck and she yanked out the band and let her hair fall.

Enrique took a step back. "Tell me."

"I'm trying." She leaned forward, head over her knees.

"Do you need to sit down?"

"No." She groaned. Straightened. "I don't know where to start."

Enrique realized he'd stopped breathing and filled his lungs. "Skylar." He put his hands on his hips. "Are you married?"

"No." Her eyes filled. "I was going to be. We were engaged."

"You said he left."

"He did."

"Where's the lie?" Enrique rubbed the back of his neck.

"He didn't leave the way I implied." A long pause. "He died."

Enrique stilled. So many small things snapped into alignment. Her sadness, the way she avoided things in conversation and physical interactions he knew she wanted. "When? What happened?"

She turned away, bracing both hands on the counter. "March. Last year."

He went to her, lightly rubbing her arms, uncertain if she would want his touch. "I'm so sorry."

"That's why I'm here. And that's why I took that job." Her shoulders sagged. "I'm … hiding out." She inhaled a shaky breath. "He's the one I dream about at night. Why I go to work with my eyes all swollen. You probably haven't noticed because it's gone by the time I get to the shop. I'm sorry I lied to you. I couldn't—I haven't been able to talk about it. Except to Mike. And that took a long time."

Enrique's eyes glazed, blurring his vision. He kissed the top of her head and turned her toward him. "Oh, honey." He grasped her shoulders and looked in her eyes. Sadness in full bloom. "Can I hold you?"

"You want to? You're not angry? Did I hurt you?"

He pulled her close, smiling at the string of questions. "Yes. No. And no."

"Joe could never keep track." She sniffed. Grabbed a dish towel off the counter, dabbed her cheeks and blew her nose.

"You met in fourth grade?"

She nodded against him. "We were best friends until our senior year of high school."

He gave her a questioning look.

"Then he told me I was his girl."

Enrique ran his hands lightly over her back. "And you argued."

Skylar rolled her eyes.

"I knew it."

She poked him.

"You're just that way, Sky."

"Be quiet."

"Okay." He kissed her. Tasted tears on her lips.

Skylar linked her arms around his neck and responded like he imagined a Ferrari would if he stepped on the gas and popped the clutch. He shoved a bag aside and lifted her to the counter. She wrapped her legs around his hips, pulling him to her. Her mouth was all softness and fire. The fire quickly spread to his entire body. Enrique delved his hands into her silky hair. She did the same to him, making soft sounds that said more than words ever could.

He wanted to tell her he loved her. Because he did. With every fiber of his being. But the timing was wrong. Her heart was in pieces and it wouldn't be fair—to either of them.

When Skylar finally pulled away. They were both breathing heavily. "How can I want you so much when I'm … I don't know what I am." She leaned her forehead to his. "Your eyes. Your smile. Do you know that you light up a room when you smile?" Her thumbs grazed his cheeks. "You light *me* up when you smile."

"I guess. I can honestly say I've never been kissed like that." He pulled her close again, nestling his chin in her hair. "You're a six point three liter V-twelve with forty-eight valves. Seven hundred thirty-one horsepower."

"Translate." He heard a smile in her voice.

"Ferrari F12 Berlinetta."

"What color?"

"Red."

"Hmm. But I'm blond."

"Not here." He traced a finger along her lips. "Thank you for telling me. I know it wasn't easy."

Skylar rested her head on Enrique's shoulder. "I feel better. It's not like I'm trying to create a new identity, I just … there were so many people feeling sorry for me. Stopping by and reliving old memories near the anniversary of his death. It made it worse. I got stuck in a tailspin."

He smoothed her hair. "I'm sorry for your loss, Skylar."

Her throat was too tight to answer. His hands moved softly over her back and she began to relax. "I miss being touched." She glanced up. "But I'm a mess. It's like I'm swimming across an ocean and I haven't reached the other side yet."

"When were you supposed to get married?"

"The next weekend." Skylar pressed the paper towel to her cheeks again, then gave a small laugh through her tears. "Well. My dad finally did something right."

"What do you mean?"

"Asking you to stay with me." She pulled back and glanced up at him. "But I don't know what to think or how to act."

"What do you mean?"

"Will it bother you if I talk about things? About Joe?"

"Not at all."

"Even though I'm attracted to you? That seems weird. Like I'm crossing a line or using you or something."

"It's fine. But you need to work through this. You need to heal." He cupped her face. "I can comfort you, but no more Ferrari action." He set her to her feet. "I don't want to muddy the waters. Neither of us knows how you'll feel once you're through this."

"What planet are you from?" She leaned into him.

"I spent the last several years on Planet Stupid. And I don't want to go back."

She smiled. "Is hugging okay?"

"I think so."

"I'm sorry for your loss, too. For your marriage." She released him and filled two glasses with water.

His eyes filled with regret. "My parents have been married thirty-three years. And they still love each other. They're like two halves of the same whole." He took a long drink. "I never thought I'd get a divorce. If it had only been the money, I'd have tried to find a way." He expelled a long breath. "But I want a family. Under one roof."

Skylar chewed her lip. "I feel like I said too much. Like I dumped this huge burden on you and we've only just met. I hope I haven't scared you off."

Enrique came next to her and put an arm over her shoulder. "I'm actually relieved that you told me. Let's just keep being honest. I hate secrets."

She had plenty of those. "Do you need to know everything all at once?"

"What do you mean?" His brows drew together.

"I don't want to lose you."

"There's more?"

She nodded. Downed her water. "But that was the biggie. The rest is fallout."

He gazed at her a long moment. "Can you handle three questions a day?"

"Probably." Her cell buzzed and she dug in her purse. "So, is it safe to assume you're not seeing anyone?"

"Aside from a few boring first dates, you're the only woman I've been at close range with since Kendra."

"How long has it been?"

"The divorce was final nine months ago. But we separated two years ago."

"Wow." Skylar gazed at him. Those stunning dark eyes, skin the color most girls dreamed of having in summer. And his heart. The greatest gift. He'd let her in after being betrayed.

"It took me a long time to get my head straight. After what happened, I was gun shy." He quirked a brow, a slow smile taking over his face. "Now I'm glad I waited."

"Me, too." She read a text. "My dad needs to talk. Do you mind?"

"No. I'll get the rest of this put away."

She called her father. "Dad?"

"Sky. How ya doing?" He sounded tired.

"I'm okay. It turns out Enrique is a good babysitter."

Her father and Enrique both laughed. "I have good instincts. Hey." His tone became serious. "I got some bad news."

Skylar stiffened. "Is Mia alright?"

"She's doing well, happy to get back to school today." He stifled a yawn. "Sorry. I haven't gotten much sleep. The police just heard from the medical examiner. Turns out Mia's father died from a ruptured aneurysm while he was at work. He worked nights and wasn't found until the following morning. His employer didn't know he had a child and they didn't have his current address. They just connected the dots."

Skylar collapsed on the couch. "Oh, my God. Does she know?" Enrique came and sat next to her.

"Not yet. Skylar, I think she should hear it from you. But I didn't know if you'd be up to that."

She stared at the ceiling asking herself the same question. "I don't think I could go alone. Can you come get me?"

"Sure."

"I moved."

"You did?"

"I didn't tell you. But I didn't tell anyone."

A pause. "Text me the address." Skylar ended the call, grateful he hadn't ripped into her about not telling him where she was living.

"What's wrong?" Enrique took her hand, his face filled with concern.

"Mia's dad died. She thought he was just missing. It happened at work. My dad thinks I should be the one to tell her."

"He's picking you up?"

She nodded.

"Come here." He pulled her to his side. They sat without speaking until she heard a car door close outside.

"Do you want to go to the shop?" She looked up at him.

"I guess so. You probably have no idea when you'll be back."

"I'll text you when I get home."

He stood and helped her up. "Promise? I don't think you should be alone."

"Yes." She opened the door.

Art stepped inside, his eyes scanning the room the way someone in law enforcement was wont to do. "Nice digs," he said, with a wry smile.

"I knew you'd think so," Skylar replied. "I'll be out in a sec."

"Hi, Mr. Biondi," she heard Enrique say, as she went down the hall.

"Please, call me Art. Good to see you, Enrique. Thanks for taking care of my girl."

Skylar couldn't remember him calling her that since she was about ten. She used the bathroom and grabbed her purse. Enrique waited near the door with his duffel. "You're efficient," she said. The thought of being apart from him was a painful one.

Art seemed to pick up on the vibes and went outside. "I'll be in the car."

Enrique held her close. "I'm sorry for the reason we've been thrown together, but I love being with you." He kissed the top of her head.

"How do I tell Mia her father is dead? She was kidnapped and probably raped. Now this." She lifted a hand.

He cupped her shoulders and caught her gaze. "You do it gently. But she needs to know the truth. She has to trust you to tell her the truth."

Skylar inhaled deeply.

"You didn't like it when people pitied you. That's why you wanted to get away, right?"

She nodded.

"So don't do that to her. Tell her it'll hurt but she'll get through it. Lend her your strength."

"I'm not sure I have any."

"Sure you do. You're the strongest woman I know. And you can borrow from me if you need to. Time to go." He prodded her out the door. "I'll be over as soon as I hear from you."

CHAPTER THIRTY-THREE

SKYLAR THRUMMED HER FINGERS on the armrest in her dad's car. "Dad, can we stop by a book store so I can get something for Mia?"

"Sure." Art glanced over. "Skylar?"

She noticed he was white-knuckling the gear shift. "Yeah?"

"I need to know this isn't too much. I realize I've always pushed you too hard. Tried to mold you into another version of myself."

Her eyes glazed. "Dad, not now. Please. I'll crumble." She stared out the window, thinking about what Enrique had said. But she gave her father's hand a squeeze, hoping he'd know she appreciated his admission. "I'll get through this." Knowing Enrique would be coming over afterward gave her a shot of courage. They stopped in a bookstore and Skylar was pleased to find just what she was looking for.

When they arrived, Shirley, Mia's foster mom, led Mia into the front room. Mia stood still, hands clasped behind her back, small shoulders rigid. A trace of tape residue marred the skin near her mouth. Skylar wanted to make it disappear—along with the memories.

She felt her dad's fortifying grip on her shoulder. "Hi, Mia." She resisted the urge to pick her up and sat on the sofa instead. After what she'd been through, Skylar felt Mia should be in control of any physical contact. "Did you get your backpack back?"

Mia shook her head sadly.

"I thought that might be a problem so I stopped by the bookstore on my way here." Skylar set the bag on her lap and waited to see what Mia would do.

Mia's hands came out from behind her back. She stepped forward, knotting them nervously. "Why?"

"I thought you might like something to read." Skylar proffered the bag. "Take a look. I kept the receipt in case you want something else."

After tentatively parting the bag with her small fingers, Mia peeked inside. Her eyes widened. "Is that all of them?"

"It is." Skylar smiled.

Mia sat next to her. One at a time, she slid each book of *The Chronicles of Narnia* from the cardboard container, turning it slowly in her hands as though it were a priceless treasure. Skylar fought back a wave of emotion as Mia took time to inspect each one. She read the blurb on the back, seemed to memorize the front cover, tracing a finger over the title. Finally, she spoke, her green eyes lasered on Skylar's. "Did you read these when you were little?"

Skylar nodded. "I did. They were some of my favorites."

Mia gave a small smile and Skylar's breath came more easily. "Do you still like to read?" Mia asked.

Skylar nodded. "My bookshelves are overloaded with books. Sometimes I like to read the same book more than once."

"Me, too." Mia's eyes lit. "I read *James and the Giant Peach* twice in one week." Her face sagged.

Skylar's heart tore, certain Mia was thinking of the horrific things she endured during that week. She wanted to change the subject, but something told her not to. "That was a really hard week for you, Mia. You were very brave."

Mia's gaze moved to the book in her hand, the tiniest quiver in her chin.

"Sometimes a story can take us away when the place where we are is too painful." Though she wanted to scoop Mia up and hold her forever, Skylar forced her hands to remain in her lap. What was she supposed to do? How could she help? The question that burned a hole in her heart, though, was why anyone would hurt an innocent child. What kind of person could take a beautiful girl—*this* beautiful girl— and abuse her for their own twisted pleasure? Rather than focus on that rage-inciting thought, she asked what Mia had been up to. As Mia recounted her first day in a new school, Art and Shirley slipped from the room.

After they'd connected on a more intimate level, Skylar filled her lungs and willed her throat to stay open. "Mia, I have some sad news. Is it okay if I hold your hand?" Mia put her hand in the one Skylar held out and Skylar gently closed her fingers around it. She told Mia what had happened to Marcus, leaving out how he hadn't been found until the next day. Mia climbed into her lap and soaked her shoulder with tears. Skylar soothed her back until she calmed. "Mia?"

"What?" Her body shuddered. She wiped her eyes with the backs of her hands.

"Your heart is going to hurt for a while. But you're strong. You're going to get through this. I think your daddy would be proud of what a brave girl you are."

"Not as brave as you." Mia toyed with Skylar's bracelet.

"What do you mean?"

"You climbed through a window to get me."

Skylar smiled and moved a strand of hair from Mia's eyes.

"And you made Glenda take off her pants and get in the closet."

Skylar captured Mia's gaze. "I did that to save your life. You know that, right? I've never done anything like that before." She thought of the knife and her threats. "I'm sorry you had to see that. I don't like to treat people that way."

"I was glad. Glenda was mean to me."

"I know. That's why I did it. What those people did to you was wrong. You didn't deserve it." She cupped Mia's head to her breast and closed her eyes. For a long moment, the only sound was their breathing.

Mia pulled back, a worried look on her face. "Peter says he's trying to find my family in California so they can come get me."

Skylar straightened. "You're from California?" Peter Sedgwick was Mia's *Guardian Ad Litem*, a person appointed by the court to look out for Mia's interests until a long-term situation was worked out on her behalf.

Mia nodded. "Daddy brought me here when I was six."

"How old are you now?"

"Nine."

Skylar smiled. "I thought so."

Mia grasped Skylar's arms. "Could I live with you instead? Daddy said we should stay away from his family because of the gangs." Mia hugged Skylar as if she were a buoy in the ocean and Skylar felt as though a few pieces of her heart had been stitched back together.

The prospect was both exciting and terrifying. Was it possible? Could she take on the care of a child? "What about your mom?"

"She's in jail." Mia's eyes filled. "Bailey said my dad was in jail. I knew he was lying because daddy promised he'd never get in trouble again. He said he'd always be—" She began to cry.

Skylar wrapped her in a hug. *So many burdens for one so young.* "Oh, honey. I know he wanted to be there for you. He couldn't help what happened. He worked hard to take care of you." In the car on the way over, Art had mentioned Marcus having two gang-related arrests before Mia was born but nothing since. He was working nights as a janitor at the time of his death.

"Could I? Please?"

Skylar sighed. Her impulse was to say yes. But that would be foolish. The last thing Mia needed was more disappointment. "I don't know. Mia, I can't say yes until I know for sure."

"Why couldn't you?"

"There are a lot of rules. And I …" She wasn't sure what to say.

"You what?"

"I'll look into it, but I don't know if I can make that happen." She set Mia beside her and held her hand. "In the meantime, I'll find out if you and I can do things together. Maybe go to the park or the movies."

"We could go to the library!"

Skylar chuckled. "We could."

"The Smiley Branch. I went there every day last summer."

"You did?" Mia's exuberance reminded Skylar of herself.

"That's where I found out what I have to do to be a doctor."

"You're going to be a doctor?"

"Uh huh."

"That sounds exciting." Skylar sobered. Too many times, she'd let an opportunity slip away without asking Mia critical questions. "Mia, are things okay here? I know something bad happened at the other foster home." She kept her voice low. "You can tell me or my dad if you don't feel safe or if anyone hurts you."

"I like it here. Shirley is nice. I just miss my dad." Her eyes filled again at the mention of him.

Knowing how hard it was to adjust to that kind of painful truth, Skylar struggled for words that might begin to repair the hole in Mia's heart. "I'm glad you like it here. And I'm sorry about your dad." She reached into the bag once more. "Mia, I also got you a journal." She passed it to her. "It's a book for writing your private thoughts and feelings. Keep it somewhere safe, so no one can read it unless you want them to."

"It's pretty." Mia smoothed her hand over the sparkling pink cover and ran her fingers along the spiral wire binding. "Do you have one?"

"I do." Since Joe's death, she'd filled several. "I had someone close to me die, too. It helps sometimes to write down my feelings and my good memories."

Mia shifted, her gaze intent. "Who died?"

"His name was Joe. We were going to get married."

Mia blinked and hugged Skylar again. This time, Skylar was unable to fend off a few tears. How could a nine-year-old child overflow with such love and comfort? Especially when her own wounds were so fresh?

Before she left, Skylar made plans to take Mia to the Smiley Branch Library.

"Do you want to stop and get a cup of coffee?" Art asked her on the way home.

"That sounds good. I need to recover. But I think I'll have tea. Enrique suggested I avoid caffeine."

"How do you know him?"

"He owns a motorcycle repair shop across the street from where Mia was kept." She surprised herself by telling him about the cat naming contest and her budding relationship with Enrique.

They stopped at a light. He glanced over. "You want me to check him out?"

Skylar whipped her head toward him, then saw the telltale sparkle of humor in his gaze. "Funny."

He lifted a shoulder and grinned.

They pulled into a parking lot and made their way to a table in the back of a small coffee shop. "That might be the hardest thing you'll ever do, Sky. You're real good with her."

"So I did okay?"

"Oh yeah." He exhaled. "You could do a training at the PD."

"I was afraid I'd screw up. I've been a wreck the past few days."

Art frowned. "You said you were doing okay."

"I was. I am. It's relative, you know? Not everyone is as stalwart as you, Dad. We mortals have our ups and downs." Skylar stirred her tea. "I can't fathom how people can do things like that to innocent children. What on earth goes through their minds to justify that?"

He shook his head. "I'd like to reinstate the firing squad for perps like that."

"I keep having flashbacks of Mia taped to that chair. When I let her out through the window, I told her to hide in the truck, but I found her curled up in a ball next to the dolly. Devlin shot at us when I was dragging Mia inside the truck. It was …" She shuddered. "Both of us could have been killed."

"Damn." He shook his head. "All you had was that box cutter. And your wits."

Skylar caught his eye. "No. I had yours, too. I used to hate how you'd always tell me stuff. Where are the windows and doors? Keep track of the cars. Pay attention to what people are wearing."

He laughed. "I laid it on pretty thick. I'm just hardwired that way." She knew he didn't intend it as an apology. And for the first time in her life, she didn't want one.

She gripped his hand. "Mia is safe. And I think she's going to be okay. All because you're such a hard ass."

Art eyed her over the brim of his cup. "I'm glad you didn't become a cop."

Skylar scowled. "Geez, Dad. You're really throwing me off lately. It's like you got a prescription of nice-guy pills."

"You can thank Elana for that. She's been tanning my hide." He gave her a meaningful look. "I've been imagining you climbing in that window and confronting that woman with your little knife."

"I actually liked that part," she confessed. "I mean, I'm glad I didn't have to hurt her, but I admit I got a lot of satisfaction out of tying her up and telling her I'd slit her femoral artery if she caused any trouble."

"You said that?" He chuckled.

"I did. I told her she'd bleed out before help could arrive. I taunted her." Skylar shifted in her seat. "I'm not sure what it says about me that I liked it so much."

"It says you have a solid sense of justice." He cocked his head. "I heard what you said to Mia about that. But I think it was good for her to see that."

"Seriously?"

"Damn straight. She needs to know someone's gonna go to the line for her. That she's worth it." His cell buzzed and he read a text.

Skylar set her cup down, knowing he'd tell her it was time to go. Someone needed him. Client, wife, kids. And Arturo Biondi was hardwired to respond without counting the costs. "She *is* worth it."

"But you showed her." He pointed at her, eyes steely. "And she's not gonna forget it." He stood. "Let's get out of here. Elana's after me to get home. She says the two Indians are in need of a chief. I haven't seen them awake since this happened."

After her dad dropped her off, Skylar crawled into bed, staying awake only long enough to text Enrique. *Just got home. I'm gonna crash. Come by for dinner if you want.*

Be there at six.

She awoke at four-thirty. Just in time. She placed a call to Mia's social worker, explaining Mia's request.

"You're interested in taking this on? I understand you've just come through a big trauma yourself."

"I think I could help Mia. And … she'll probably help me, too. It's time to end my pity party."

They talked through the process. Background check, home visit, criminal history, finances. "I admire your spirit, Skylar. I'll email you the documents."

When they clicked off, Skylar felt as though she'd gotten on an escalator that was moving upward. One more phone call ended her employment. Wyatt was disappointed, but said he understood.

CHAPTER THIRTY-FOUR

JUST BEFORE SIX, ENRIQUE knocked on Skylar's door. The hours at work had been exceptionally draining. Jasmine wanted to help —he knew that—but she'd asked dozens of questions, making it impossible for him to figure out why the books were out of balance. Then there was Manny. He'd done a great job on some simple repairs, but Andy was bogged down teaching him how to diagnose more complicated issues on a couple of machines and neither had gotten much done. From a production standpoint, it was a net loss.

Despite all of that, the prospect of sharing a meal with Skylar and spending the night on her sofa, made his heart feel light. He hoped she was staying afloat after what must have been a rough conversation with Mia.

The door opened and Skylar crossed the threshold, wrapping him in a hug. "I heard you drive up." She pulled back and gave him an assessing look. "Are you okay?"

"Yeah. Just tired." Eyeing his backpack, she ushered him in. "I brought clothes in case you want me to stay."

"Alright. What's on the menu, Chef Avalos? Do they use first names or last names for chefs? Should I call you Chef Enrique?"

He released a weary laugh and tossed his pack on the floor. "I need to clear my head a minute. Do you mind if I sit?"

"Lie down, you look exhausted. I'll get you something to drink. Would you like water or iced tea?"

"Water." He shrugged out of his motorcycle jacket and lay down on the sofa, happy to be out of the sweltering heat. The cool leather felt good.

She set two glasses on the counter. "Ice?"

"Please."

She brought it over and plopped on the sofa near his feet. "Rough afternoon?"

"Accounting nightmares." He sat and took a long drink. "But let's talk about you. How did it go? You seem … lighter." Not at all what he expected.

"I am. It was hard. Super emotional. I felt so drained that I came home and took a nap." She turned her glass between her palms. "Mia asked about staying with me."

Enrique eyed her. "And?"

"I'm looking into it."

"Really?" Skylar never ceased to impress him.

"Her mom's in jail and she said her dad brought her out here from California a few years ago to make a clean break from his family. I guess they have gang ties. I'm not going to let her slip through the cracks. I'm sure to pass the background check. I just need to get my life more together, starting with my apartment." She got to her feet. "I'm hungry. Let me cook and you can chill."

"You're always hungry."

She laughed. "I know. It's a wonder I don't weigh two hundred pounds."

"You said you don't cook."

She waved a hand. "Well, not like you. And that had a lot to do with feeling depressed. But anyone can reheat. And I'll make something special for dessert. You won't lose those gorgeous abs if you eat dessert, will you?"

"I don't think so." Some time later, he woke to a soft touch on his shoulder.

"Wake up, sleepy head. The food is hot." Skylar stood next to him.

Enrique stretched and sat up. A fruity smell wafted from the oven, making his mouth water.

"You're so tired. I feel bad about keeping you up at night." She gave him an apologetic look.

"It's okay."

"I fixed you a plate."

"Be right there. I should wash up." In the bathroom, Enrique splashed his face with water. As he dried it with a clean, neatly folded hand towel, a longing he'd suppressed resurfaced again. Stronger than ever. He'd tolerated living out of a duffel bag, sleeping on a cot and having no kitchen. But this short time with Skylar had awakened his yearning for more. The small things were drawing him in; clean towels and bedding, home-cooked meals enjoyed in the company of a beautiful caring woman. Interesting conversations with a person, instead of monologues with a cat or a computer screen. When this crisis was over, he'd have to harden his shell and gut it out again. Thing was … he didn't think he had it in him.

The small table was covered with a fresh tablecloth. Skylar had set plates, folded cloth napkins, refilled his glass. Enrique took a seat. "I'm losing my edge."

"I like you without your edge." Skylar took a bite and motioned for him to do the same. "I know the guy who made this. It's really good."

Enrique obeyed. Like those dogs who did as she said for a token of food. He snorted at the absurdity, given that he'd made the food himself.

"What?"

"Nothing."

"You don't have to do as I say."

She was a good mind reader. "Yes I do."

"Do you mind telling me about your accounting woes? I'm a mathematical genius."

"Humble, too."

"Completely." She nudged him with her foot and he found himself confessing his inability to be proficient with numbers. She proceeded to ask a slurry of questions, many focused on when he was a child in school. "The interview's over," he finally said.

"Sorry." She brought him a slice of blueberry pie. "Do you like whipped cream?"

"You don't have any."

"We stopped by the store on the way home. How do you think I made the pie?" She went to the refrigerator and retrieved a metal bowl.

"Sure." He could tell by the flaky crust that she was telling the truth and had made the pie herself. It smelled heavenly. She put a large dollop of real whipped cream on top. He took a bite. Also from scratch. "You made this while I was sleeping?"

Skylar shrugged. "Pies are pretty easy."

"It's delicious. I might get fat after all."

"Be right back." She smiled and went to a bookshelf, returning with a few books.

He threw out a palm like a stop sign. "Stay back."

"I just need to look at some notes."

Enrique finished his pie and cleared their dishes. Then he went back to the table.

She thumbed through each book, taking time to read things on some of the pages. "Okay. This might sound weird, but I have a theory."

He groaned.

She passed him a book. "Read this paragraph out loud."

Shame reared its head. "Why?"

"Humor me."

He began reading. Stumbled. Kept going until he stumbled again.

"That's enough." She set the book down. "I think you may be dyslexic. Probably not very bad."

Not trusting himself to speak, he stalked to the window. If he were with anyone else, he would simply walk out. But it was Skylar. She had no way of knowing she'd touched a raw nerve. And the last thing he wanted was to hurt her. Throughout their conversation, he'd felt that old pressure building in his chest. How many times had he been ridiculed by classmates in school when he was called on to read something aloud?

When the principal had informed his parents that he wouldn't be moving on to fifth grade if he didn't learn how to read, his mother had stepped in. She read aloud and he memorized every word. When he had to give a speech or read a report to the class, he held up the paper and quoted from memory, only pretending to read. His teacher was proud, even giving him an award at the end of the year. But he'd thrown it away, not wanting to celebrate the lie. From then on, each day was an exhausting exercise in dodging situations that required him to read on the spot. Homework his friends finished in twenty minutes, took hours for him.

Skylar came to his side. "Dyslexia is when the brain doesn't interpret letters or numbers in the right order. It makes reading difficult and can affect math, too. From what you've told me and what I know of you, it may be worth looking into." There was neither disrespect nor pity in her tone.

Still, he bristled. "What do you mean, 'what you know of me?'"

"You're smart, good at learning in a hands-on environment. You're also very articulate, and I'm guessing you don't like to write."

All true. He eyed her suspiciously. "How do you know all that?"

Skylar shrugged. "I'm just observant. And I've had training so I can recognize this sort of thing." She went back to the kitchen and put the pie away.

"Training?" He swiveled to face her.

"Much of my masters work focused on learning disabilities. I'm fascinated by how the brain works."

She hadn't mentioned having a masters degree. He bristled at that, too. Though part of him wanted to go, he'd never given college serious thought. The idea of memorizing entire college textbooks was too much. And who would read it to him? "So you're saying I have a disability?" He leaned against the wall, crossed his arms over his chest.

"I'm saying you might. And I said learning disability. Not disability." She came close again. "I have one, too. It's nothing to be ashamed of."

Enrique shot her a dubious look.

Skylar gave an easy smile. "Mine is dysgraphia. It's a close cousin to dyslexia. I can read just fine, but I make mistakes when I write or type. I can easily spot them after the fact, but it's nearly impossible to prevent them, especially if I'm in a hurry. Or when I'm tired."

He exhaled. She wasn't goading him, but he did not appreciate her observations. Or their implications. "And you think this may affect the accounting?"

"It might."

He strode toward the sofa but didn't sit. "Well, what can I do? I can't afford to hire someone." This only frustrated him more. "So now I have an unsolvable problem?" He scrubbed his hands down his face and stalked to the counter. This place was too small.

"Come here." She led him to the sofa. "Lie down."

Her touch and calm tone comforted and irked him at the same time. But he grudgingly did as she said. "Are you a therapist, too?"

She poked his ribs. "I'm a lion tamer. If you snarl at me, I'll get a whip and a chair." She took a seat in the large chair opposite him. "Enrique, I think what you're doing is amazing."

"Laying here listening to you?"

She laughed. "The shop. Instead of selling the place, you're knocking yourself out to build something."

Knowing she meant every word softened the blow, if only a little. "Where did you get this sudden burst of energy?"

"I don't know. I've sucked plenty from you, so maybe I'm giving some back."

"I'm not sure I want it." He shoved a pillow under his head and stared at the ceiling.

"I have an idea. Actually, two. Please hear me out."

He circled his hand. "Go on."

"I quit my job today. If I get Mia, I'm not going to work for a while." Skylar propped her legs on the ottoman.

Enrique raised to one elbow and gawked at her. "Are you gonna go on welfare?"

"I don't need welfare. And if you interrupt me again, I'm going to come over there and sit on you."

He lay back and pictured that. "Scary."

"You have no idea. First, there are things that help with dyslexia. If you want, I can show them to you." She paused. "Second, I'll need something to do while Mia's in school. I can't be alone that much. I was thinking of volunteering somewhere but I could come help you at the shop. You don't need to pay me. You'd be doing me a favor. And it would give us time to get to know each other."

That idea had a lot of appeal. "You could be my shop girl. Who gets to name *you*? Maybe I'll have another contest. If I put up posters with your picture, I'd get a lot of guys to come in. If they knew you'd be there in person to sign autographs, they'd call all their friends."

A weight crushed his belly, thrusting air from his lungs. He opened his eyes to see Skylar sitting on top of him, like a chipmunk perched on a rock. "Off."

"Answer me." She folded her arms. Crossed her legs at the ankles. "Yes, no, or I'll think about it."

He almost said yes. But now that his mother had called in the cavalry, Enrique didn't know how to turn back the tide. Jasmine enjoyed getting out of the house. But it would take her all of two seconds to pick up on his feelings for Skylar. Who looked like Kendra. Who'd shafted her brother. His family didn't let things like that go, and they were never shy about sharing their opinions. The last thing Skylar needed was another wound. "I'll think about it."

"Okay." She stood just in time.

Enrique had come close to pulling her down and kissing her. But he may not have been able to stop there. And neither of them were in a good place for that. He didn't want a fling. More than that, he didn't want to hurt her when she was so vulnerable. He tried to wrap his mind around her sudden transformation. He'd come over expecting her to be completely wrung out. Somehow, the tables had turned. He gazed up at her. "Who are you and what did you do with Skylar?"

Skylar nudged his hip with her knee. "You've never known the real Skylar. I met you after I hit bottom. I'm just getting going." She bent and kissed his forehead. "And I have you to thank for helping me find my way again."

CHAPTER THIRTY-FIVE

SEVERAL DAYS LATER, SKYLAR stood in the spare bedroom overwhelmed by the task before her. The first step was to go through each crate and pull out things she needed to keep in the apartment. Then she'd somehow have to swap the crates with furniture from her storage unit. Impossible with her small car. Maybe she could rent a truck. But she'd still need someone to help load and unload the furniture. Enrique was overwhelmed at the shop, so she didn't feel right asking more of him. Her stomach rumbled, giving her a good excuse to put off solving the problem.

As she scooped a forkful of eggs into her mouth, her cell phone signaled a text. It was Alex. *Drop me a line. I'm getting worried.* Since she hadn't responded to his recent texts checking on her, she called him instead. "Sorry. Things have been crazy." She cleared the table and went to the sofa, laying with her legs draped over the armrest. "How are you?"

He sighed. "The season's over."

"I know. Are you depressed?" The Rockies had started off strong, but petered out toward the end with no hopes of the playoffs after a string of injuries.

"No. I just don't know what to do with myself. Especially now."

Skylar knew he meant, *now that Joe's gone.* The two of them had always spent loads of time together in the off-season. "Well ... Are you free today? I need help with something."

"I am. What do you need?" His voice perked.

"Do you still have that old truck?"

"I have a new one."

Of course he did. She explained what she needed to accomplish without mentioning Mia. "Let me buy you lunch first. And no cowboy garb. You need to blend."

"Let's just order in and you won't have to worry about being seen with me."

She kicked her feet. "That works. Pizza or Chinese?"

"Pizza. I know what you like. I'll pick it up on the way. And I'll bring some beer."

"No, Alex. No alcohol. I'll make iced tea or you can pick up some soda."

"Okay."

"I should be ready by noon. And remember what you said about not judging where I live."

"Sure. I can't wait to see you, Sky."

She wondered at his tone. Was it relief? It sounded like more.

Before she began the big project, she grabbed her purse and went to her car. She wanted to talk to Enrique. She hadn't seen or heard from him since the night he'd come to dinner, which left her feeling uneasy. At first, she figured he needed some time to think about her offer to help at the shop, so she'd given him some space. But now she worried she'd screwed up by talking to him about being dyslexic.

Why did she have to be so impulsive? Most of the time, it worked out. Like the cat-naming thing and rescuing Mia. But she didn't want to hurt him. And, though her motives had been good, whether or not he had a learning disability was really none of her business. Not everyone was comfortable discussing things like that. Her stomach knotted more tightly with each passing block.

Just in case there was anyone at Smile & Relax, Skylar parked behind The Bloody Knuckles Garage. She climbed out of her car and stared at the door, her feet cemented in place. What if Enrique was upset? She'd barely been able to handle his dark side in small doses before her heart was involved. She leaned against the car, fighting the urge to leave. *No.* If she had offended him, she needed to make it right. Never had she been more keenly aware that there wasn't always tomorrow. And that the little things were really the big things.

Taking a deep breath, she went to the door and knocked. "It's Skylar."

A moment later, Enrique appeared. "Hey, what are you doing here?" His smile was only a glimmer of it's usual wattage. Was he unhappy she'd come?

"Enrique, I need help with this invoice," a female voice called from the front.

His face clouded. "Just a minute." Rather than letting Skylar in, he slipped outside. "Let's talk out here."

Skylar's stomach dropped and she backed away. "I'm sorry. I should have called."

Enrique closed the distance between them. "No. It's okay. That's my sister, Jasmine. I don't know if you're ready to meet her."

Skylar blinked. After all she'd been through with Joe in those early years, here she was assuming the worst again. She struggled to right herself. "You never got back to me. Did I upset you the other night?"

Enrique smoothed his hands down her shoulders. The simple gesture did a great deal to calm her. "It was hard to hear. But I'm not angry if that's what you're thinking." He wrapped her in a hug.

Skylar nestled into him. "Has work been crazy?"

"Totally. I had some stuff to catch up on. And my family swooped in to help when I went to your place. I'm trying to figure out how to dial it back without causing a rift. They mean well, but they tend to take over and they need a lot of oversight." Enrique led her to a shady spot near her car. "Jasmine has thrown herself into doing the accounting. Sorry about not being in touch with you. I've been putting in some long hours." He forked a hand through his hair. "I'd love to have you here. But Jas would ask you a million questions. I didn't want to put you in that position."

"It's okay." Skylar toyed with her keys. "I've been busy, too. Mia's coming soon. I had to fill out a ton of paperwork and they need to do a home study. They're waiting for me to get her room put together. I need to get all those crates out and move some furniture in."

Enrique's brows lifted. "By yourself?"

"My friend, Alex, has a pickup. He's coming by this afternoon."

Enrique's gaze sharpened.

She put her hand on his arm. "Enrique, you've already done so much. Alex is an old friend. His schedule is wide open. Plus, he's been worried about me since I dropped off the radar."

He nodded understanding. "Do you feel ready to take care of Mia?" He pulled a leaf off the tree they were under and flattened it between his palms.

"As ready as I can be." Skylar smiled. "It's been good for me to get my mind off myself. I feel stronger. More balanced."

Enrique shook his head. Skylar wasn't kidding about bouncing back. And he'd been impressed by her at that low point. *"Te extraño."*

"What?" She gave him a curious look.

"I miss you." He linked his arm around her waist.

She did the same with her own, leaning into his side. *"Te extraño.* Is it the same if I say it to you?"

He smiled at her accent. "It is."

"I love when you speak Spanish." Her fingers traced his waistband. "But you better watch it." Her eyes flashed a warning. "I don't seem to have an off button with you."

He eyed her curiously. "What do you mean?"

"It's different." She lifted one shoulder. "With us. With you. I know we need to take things slow, but it's hard for me." She released a frustrated breath.

"Tu eres muy sexy," he said in a low, husky voice.

She took a step back. "Enrique."

"Bésame."

"No."

He laughed. "You know what that means?"

"No. I took French. I'm just saying no. To all of it."

"It means kiss me." Knowing full well what he was doing, he flashed a big smile.

"You're the one who put a moratorium on us kissing." Skylar gave him a scathing look. "Don't play games with me."

He sobered. "I'm sorry. I guess it's not fair to tease." He brought her hand to his lips. "I don't want to screw things up with you. It looks like you have something on your mind."

Skylar softened, moving close again. "I'm not sure what to do about *us.* Mia's going to need—well, I have no idea what she'll need. But she was abused by men, so I don't think it will be good for her if we spend time together when she's out of school. I want to talk to her therapist and find out the best way to handle it."

"Okay." Enrique caressed the curve of her waist. Mia was lucky to have Skylar in her life. He knew mothers who weren't as careful with their own daughters. "Hey, I did some research online. I think you're right about me being dyslexic."

She cast a worried look. "Did I cross a line? Sometimes I don't think things through. Or maybe I'm too direct."

"You're kind of growing on me." He squeezed her gently. "I like you just the way you are."

Skylar exhaled. Glanced up. "Tonight may be our last chance to have dinner for a while. Are you free?"

"I'll get free. Six o'clock?"

She nodded and gave him a quick hug before taking off.

When he returned to the front desk, Jasmine passed him the phone. "Hello."

"*Mijo*. Jasmine tells me you're backsliding." It was his mother. Using her commando voice. He didn't bother to respond because he knew she wouldn't listen. "Who is this Skylar? Jas says she's another Kendra. *Otra lagartona.*"

A bitch? Enrique's temper flared. "Don't you dare call her that."

"*Mijo*, you can't do this again."

Enrique glared at his sister while Olivia continued. It was just like Jasmine to spy on him. He must not have latched the door when he'd gone out to see Skylar, or he'd have heard Jasmine open it. When his mother finally took a breath, he said, "*Mami*, Skylar is nothing like Kendra. And if Jasmine had waited to meet her, she'd have figured that out in about two seconds. Skylar is grieving a huge loss. If you guys can't trust me and treat her with respect—even when she's not around—then we won't be seeing each other."

"Respect! Jasmine says she didn't even come introduce herself."

Kendra had treated his family like they were a lower class and he knew it had hurt them. His mother may have been justified calling *her* a bitch, but he'd chosen her, so the blame lay with him. "That was my call. Look, we all know I screwed up. And no one is paying a higher price for that than me. This is different. Skylar is different." Olivia began talking again, but he tuned her out. "I'll talk to you later." He hung up, feeling a twinge of guilt for having done so to his mother but there was no reasoning with her when she got like this. And he couldn't remember her ever using language like that. The fact that she'd referenced Skylar in that manner made his blood boil. He turned to his sister, who had one hand on her hip, a triumphant look on her face. "Thanks for the help, Jasmine. You can head home now. I've got it from here."

She lifted her chin. "I'm only trying to save you, Enrique. Kendra shredded your heart. You haven't been the same since. I don't want you to go through that again."

"I won't." He gave her a hug, but she remained stiff. He gathered her things and led her to the door. "Tell Benny I said hi and give Edgar a kiss for me."

"Enrique, don't be a fool." She pushed against him as he shepherded her to her car. Fortunately, she wasn't much taller than their mother. "You're blinded by pretty women. They eat you for lunch."

"You're a pretty woman, Jas. Does the same go for Benny?"

She slapped at him as he opened her car door. "Benny's not like that. And you know what I mean."

He extended his arm toward her seat and she climbed in with a huff. *"Adiós, carnala."* She was his sister. And even though she didn't deserve it right now, he would still be respectful.

Andy stood wide-eyed near the counter when Enrique got inside. "Did you get a spine implant?"

"Yup." He sat down and grabbed the stack of work orders awaiting parts. "I am not gonna screw this up."

"You're in love."

He wagged a finger Andy's direction. "Not one word to my family." He'd confided in Andy about Skylar's fiancé. "Skylar's been through enough."

CHAPTER THIRTY-SIX

WHEN SHE HEARD THE telltale rumble of a truck, Skylar opened her door. Alex saw her wave and backed in near her steps. Her stomach did an unpleasant flip. Could she trust him not to make a big deal about her living situation? She ascended the stairs and met him as he climbed out. As was everything Alex owned, the truck was shiny and bedecked with every possible accessory. Double tailpipes, fancy pinstripes along the sides, a huge metal thing on the front that could probably push cattle out of the way. And she doubted it had ever seen a dirt road.

"Do you want me to carry something?" she asked.

"Yeah. Hang on." Alex leaned in and came out with a large bouquet of yellow roses. "These are for you." He kissed her cheek, his several-day stubble brushing her lightly. Perhaps he was growing a beard again. He lacked his typical baseball hat today and his brown hair was still short. He and Joe usually let their hair grow longer in the off-season, but kept it short while they were playing.

"Oh, they're lovely. Thank you." While he got the pizza, she blinked and rubbed the sting from her nose. No matter where he was on her birthday, Joe always made sure she received a bouquet of roses from him—a combination of pink and peach because they were her favorites. She led Alex inside, fighting the onslaught of memories, dreading losing control with him there to witness. "Let me get a vase." Skylar headed down the hall, thinking it odd that she hadn't been emotional when she and Enrique walked through the rose garden in Wash Park. This probably had something to do with their shared history with Joe. Sometimes grief still surprised her, sneaking up out of nowhere and piercing her heart. Searching for a vase in the extra bedroom helped her regain her equilibrium.

While she arranged the roses, Alex quietly surveyed her place, stopping at the shelf holding Joe's books. He picked up the baseball, rolling it in his hand like Joe always had. "It's still hard to believe …" he trailed off, set the ball down. His large shoulders rose and fell slowly several times before he turned to face her. "I'm glad you called." His sadness seemed to fade. He came over and opened the pizza box with a flourish. "I got your favorite—everything but anchovies." His thick eyebrows lifted when he smiled and she felt glad that he seemed happy.

Skylar finished with the flowers and washed her hands. "Awesome. Thanks for picking it up. Water or iced tea?" She picked up a slice and took a bite. "Mmm. It's still hot."

"Tea sounds good."

She poured two glasses and they sat on the stools, eating straight from the box while making light conversation about what he planned to do in the off-season. The shift helped allay her fears of plunging into an abyss of recollections of Joe. "How much do I owe you?" She picked up her purse.

He waved. "Don't worry about it."

Skylar pulled some bills from her wallet, folded them, and stuffed them in his pocket. "Let me get it. You're helping me do all this work. I'm not indigent." Then she laughed. "It only looks like it."

"Fine." He feigned offense. "So put me to work." He got to his feet and followed her into the spare bedroom, taking in the stacks of containers. "Is this all of them?"

"Yes. And we need to bring back a bed and a dresser. Maybe a few other things." She paused. "Do you have time to come back?"

"I've got all day." Warmth she didn't remember emanated from his smile. They worked together to empty the room and strap down the crates before heading across town to her storage unit. On the way there, he caught her up on the latest news about their mutual friends in baseball. Who might get traded, who may retire, who had a baby or one on the way. It wasn't as painful as she'd anticipated. Either no one had asked about her or he was sensitive enough not to mention it.

They arrived at the storage center. "I really appreciate you helping me out, Alex."

"No problem." Alex parked near her unit and they climbed out.

After removing the lock, Skylar stiffened, unable to make herself open the door.

Alex's hands came to her shoulders, grounding her like weights on a hot air balloon that threatened to fly away in a strong gust of wind. "Is this the first time you've been here?" he asked.

She nodded. Took a deep breath. Mike and some of his friends had moved her things here.

"Do you want me to do this? You can wait in the truck." He rubbed lightly.

Skylar leaned her head on the door. "I'm just afraid. I'm not even sure why. But I can't let it stand in my way anymore." Slowly she lifted the door. Light filtered in, illuminating neat stacks of boxes and furniture covered with moving blankets. Dust motes danced in a swath of sunlight. She ran a hand along the box that must contain the TV, given its long, thin shape. The thing was a beast. Way too big for her tiny apartment.

"Are you sure about this?" Alex asked.

Mia was counting on her. This would probably be the first of many things she would need to get past. It was time to beat back the darkness. "Yes. We need to find a single bed and a dresser. I'd also like to get a small bookshelf if we have room in the truck." They made the exchange of items, using a few of the moving blankets to keep the furniture from getting scratched.

Alex tied it all down. "All set?" He came beside her as she stared into the unit.

She nodded. Glanced up. "Thank you. I don't think I could have come here alone."

"I was surprised you actually asked for help." He smiled down at her.

They drove back to her place. After setting up Mia's furniture, they went to the front room. Skylar collapsed on the chair and Alex slumped on the sofa. "Did you take the day off?" he asked.

"I quit my job."

His eyes glimmered with curiosity. "Why?"

"It's a long story." Skylar got up and refilled their drinks.

"I'm not in a hurry." He gulped some tea.

Skylar went to the window and gazed at the mountains.

"Come on." He appeared beside her, turning her toward him. "Sky, it's just me you're talking to. I haven't said a word to anyone."

The tenderness in his gaze brought a quiver of discomfort. They'd never been especially close. Alex wasn't the kind of guy who let people in. Very different from Joe in that regard. But she supposed they'd both been changed by what happened. Death had a way of getting your attention, rearranging your priorities. She pulled her work ID from her purse. "Here's my mug shot. I had a truck and a route."

"Seriously?" Alex's eyes widened. "Why did you take a job like that?"

"I was doing okay. Hanging on. But when the anniversary of Joe's death rolled around—" Skylar swallowed, leaned both elbows on the window sill, unable to look him in the eye. "It was too much. Everyone coming by or calling to talk about him. It tore the wound open. I fell apart. I don't think I'd really dealt with it. I just tried to power through. That's when I started drinking. It got bad. Well, you know that. I suppose everyone does. I lost the whole month of June. I can't remember anything." She wasn't going to mention the few exceptions to him.

"I don't see how that relates to your job."

"I had to stop. Had to have something to do. I thought maybe if I was working hard, doing something physical, living in a different environment …" She lifted a palm. "Anyway, I'm sober. So I guess it worked."

"Then why did you quit?" He looked worried.

She wouldn't drag Mia into this. Alex was as public a figure as one could be. If he let anything slip, Mia's privacy would be history. "A man was harassing me. I finally decided it wasn't worth the trouble."

Alex spun her toward him. "Harassing you how?"

"It's behind me now." Skylar smiled.

"Who is he?" Alex's gaze hardened. "What did he do?"

She rolled her eyes. "What are you gonna do? Go over there with your bat?"

"Sure. And half the team would come with me."

"That's sweet, but I'll pass. The job served its purpose."

That seemed to satisfy him because he took his glass to the kitchen.

"Well, I guess I should get going." Skylar saw him to the door. He eyed her, serious all the sudden. These shifts in him were a new thing and she wasn't sure what to make of them. "So you really lost the whole month of June?"

She grimaced. "I did."

"Any memory of dinner at Ellynton's?"

She frowned. "What?"

"It was late. On a Friday."

Skylar's heart skittered. "You mean with you? Just the two of us?" She thought back. The name sounded familiar but nothing came to her.

He nodded.

As though it could jumpstart her brain, her palm went to her forehead. "Alex, I'm sorry." She glanced away. "I'm so embarrassed. I hope I didn't make a fool of myself. Or you. I was ..." *Shattered.*

Alex dragged a hand through his hair, an inscrutable look on his face. "I'm in no position to judge." The pain in his gaze belied his words. She'd hurt him. Then or now, she wasn't sure. Which was worse —completely forgetting or going out with him and blowing him off afterward? Seeming to bounce back, he gave her a hug. "Take care. It was great hanging out. I'll sleep better knowing you're doing so well."

"It was good to see you, too. Thanks again for the help."

He started up the steps, then paused and turned. "Are you busy tomorrow?"

She took a moment to think. Enrique hadn't gotten back to her about helping at the shop. Now she was ready for Mia, but someone from Human Services had to stop in and check out her place before things were finalized.

"I could use your help with something," he added.

"If late morning would work, I could spare a few hours." It would be good to have something to do.

"I'll pick you up at ten." He took the steps two at a time.

Skylar laughed. "Hey. What are we going to do?" She couldn't imagine Alex needing any of her talents.

"Wear clothes you don't mind getting dirty. We'll be outside."

CHAPTER THIRTY-SEVEN

WHILE SHE WAITED FOR Enrique to arrive for dinner, Skylar hung the photo of her and Joe on the wall. Minutes later, she took it down again. Every few minutes, she did one or the other. Her feelings for Enrique had burgeoned way beyond friendship. It wouldn't be right to keep him in the dark any longer. She took the photo down again. "Joe, I don't know what to do." But it wasn't true. Enrique had been betrayed by his wife's duplicity. She wouldn't hurt him that way. She hung it one last time and busied herself making up Mia's bed and fluffing the pillows.

A knot formed in her stomach at the knock on the door. She opened it. "Hey." Her eyes took in the man on the landing. Warm smile. Broad chest. Those dark eyes crinkling in the corners made her melt. The skin on his face glistened and she knew he'd just shaved. He was the most handsome man she'd ever seen. Bar none.

"Are you gonna let me in?"

She laughed nervously. "Yes. Come in. Sorry. I was … you look …" She glanced down at her T-shirt and shorts. "Oh. I completely forgot to change. I was moving stuff all day and—" *Freaking out again.*

"Bésame."

"But you said—"

"I can't wait." He closed the door with his foot and pulled her into his arms, kissing her deeply. His leather jacket creaked when he moved and felt cool on her skin. "You look—" He kissed down her neck. "Perfect."

Skylar sensed where things might end up and wanted to keep going. But that wouldn't be right. She splayed her hands on his chest. "Enrique, we have to slow down."

"Okay." But he swooped in again and she got caught up, taking, giving. His hands worked magic as they moved over her, eliciting feelings and sensations she'd forgotten, or perhaps never felt so intensely. Were they more potent because of her long months of loneliness? Or was it him? Them? It didn't matter. Skylar pulled back, cupped his face with her hands. "Time out." It took all of her will. He eyed her crazily, like he'd taken a drug. "Enrique, I want you. But we can't do this now."

His eyes cleared and he seemed to come back to himself. "*Lo siento.* I mean—I'm sorry." He pulled her into an embrace. His hands soothing her back. "You do things to me. I've never felt like this before."

"It's okay. And I feel the same way." She gazed up at him. "But you have to know me ... my whole story. Before we dive in."

Enrique leaned against Skylar's front door and collected himself. She had a dazed look on her face and he felt bad. "Do you want me to go?"

"Of course not." She smiled warmly. "But you came here for dinner. I'd like to talk. I'm not sure when we'll get the chance again."

"Okay." He rolled his shoulders. "I'm sorry—"

She touched his mouth with one finger. "No more apologies. I love kissing you. I'm going to go change. Do you want to get some food started?"

"Sure." He watched her move down the hall, thinking she looked fine. No ... *hermosa.* Beautiful. Every curve cast a spell. He released a ragged breath and went to the kitchen.

When Skylar returned a short while later, he had chicken, garlic, onion and bell pepper cooking in one pan and penne pasta boiling in another. "Mmm. That smells great." She peeked. "This doesn't look too complicated. Tell me how to make it."

"It's not." He explained what he was doing, sneaking glances at the dress she wore. It was purple with white flowers. Narrow straps over her silky shoulders. "You sure know how to torture a guy."

Skylar glanced down. "Should I put on some baggy jeans and a sweat shirt?"

He chuckled. "No." She'd put on light makeup and the fabric of the dress clung to her curves. He liked that she was comfortable without makeup and nice clothes but he also appreciated that she'd gone to the effort because she looked lovely.

She set the table, placing a candle in the center. "Should I have called before showing up today?" Her voice was thin, as though it were difficult for her to ask.

Enrique turned. "You don't need to call. It's just that sometimes I'm out doing errands."

She took a sip from a glass on the table. Paused a few beats. "When you opened the door, you had a look. I wasn't sure what it meant. What you were thinking."

He thought back. "Seeing you made me remember my time here with you. It makes me miss things."

"What do you mean?"

He grabbed the colander and drained the pasta. "All the little things that make a place home. Stuff I used to take for granted. Clean towels in a clean bathroom. Having a tablecloth and a real table." He waved toward the stove. "All of this."

She smiled and came near.

"I've gotten used to living like a vagrant. But I don't like it."

"Are you gonna morph into a wild man again if I touch you?"

"Go easy." He meant it. The cliff was inches away.

"I really admire what you're doing, but it makes me sad that you live that way. You deserve so much more." Despite his warning, she grabbed hold of him, leaning her head on his chest, her arms clinging tightly around him. An embrace so full of longing and tenderness, it touched a place so deep inside him, he didn't know it existed.

He held on, savoring the moment, the woman in his arms. More than he'd ever wanted anything, Enrique wanted to love her and make her his own.

After a moment, she pulled back. "Let's fix our plates." During their meal, Skylar asked all about him, how he was doing, things at the shop, always attentive as he answered. He'd never been with a woman so interested in the details of his life. The flickering candlelight highlighted her eyes and the line of her jaw, the soft rounds of her cheeks. She refilled their glasses, then took her seat again. "Okay. Question time. Don't worry about how many."

Enrique wiped his mouth. She'd made it clear it might be a long time before they got to do this again and he'd had several questions swirling around in his head these past days. "Okay. I guess I'll dive right in. I'd like to know how you feel about me, Skylar."

"I'm not exactly sure." She chased a piece of pasta around the plate with her fork. "If I weren't grieving, it would be clear."

"What do you mean?"

She met his gaze. "I think I love you. But I don't completely trust myself. I feel guilty, like I'm being disloyal to Joe if I go on with my life. And I feel guilty for telling you because I don't want to hurt you or put a burden on you that belongs to me." Her eyes glazed, filled with uncertainty. "You said you wanted honest answers."

He took her hand. "I do. And I'm not hurt." He knew all about survivor's guilt. It was insidious, cutting both ways. "That night you pretended to be drunk, you said something about having a lot of practice."

"That wasn't a question." She squirmed in her chair.

"You also mentioned not keeping adult beverages here."

Shallow breaths.

"Do you have a problem with alcohol?"

She held his gaze. "Not right now."

"But you did."

Skylar looked at her hands. This was clearly a painful topic. Why had she offered to do this? She kicked off her sandals, folded one leg beneath her. "After Joe died, I took a few weeks off work. Then I went back, even taught summer school. Near the anniversary of his death, people started calling and showing up again, wanting to relive the memories. It was too much." She looked at the ceiling. "I couldn't sleep one night. So ... I went to a bar." She was quiet a moment.

"Skylar, you don't have to—"

"Yes. Yes I do. You have to know the real me or I'll second-guess everything. And I won't deceive you." He knew the rest; *like Kendra did.* She picked up her drink and moved to the stool at the counter. "I got smashed. Ten sheets to the wind. I might have a glass of wine with dinner or a beer during a game, but getting totally wasted is not something I do." Another pause. "The next day, I quit teaching. Although, technically I'm on a leave of absence." Skylar planted an elbow on the counter, supporting her chin with her hand.

Her gaze remained on him, as though trying to read his reaction. "It got worse and worse. I spent the whole month of June in various stages of inebriation. I wanted to die. And what better way? If I was wasted, I wouldn't feel anything when I hit a tree or drove into the side of a mountain … or off a cliff. Shooting myself was off the table since my dad confiscated my gun the minute he found out what happened to Joe." Her jaw worked. "Anyway, I came up with a different plan every night. But I couldn't get up the courage." The glass shook in her hand. She noticed and set it down.

Enrique found it almost impossible to stay in his seat. He wanted to stop this but that wasn't what she needed. Guilt and shame oozed from her every pore. Familiar with this brand of self-torture, he fisted his hands in his lap and kept his mouth shut.

"One morning—" she choked off. Took a deep breath. "I woke up in a suite on the top floor of The Brown Palace hotel. I still don't know how I got there or who was taking a shower in the bathroom when I left." Her chin quivered. "It's like I forgot who I was."

Enrique kept breathing. In. Out. The pain on her face made him crazy.

"And today I found out that somewhere in all of that, Alex and I went to dinner. I can't conjure a single memory of it. I don't even recall the restaurant he mentioned. We've been friends for thirteen years. He was hurting, too. I can't imagine how it made him feel that I just blanked it out." Skylar looked at Enrique as though he could explain.

He kept his expression neutral. Something told him she wasn't done yet.

Skylar stood and turned toward the sofa, hugging herself. "The last morning in June, I woke up in my car. I had missed the driveway and was parked in the grass. The window was down and my face was all wet. I think the sprinkler woke me up." She faced him. "This is why I told you to reserve judgment. To get your questions answered before you jumped to any good conclusions about me."

Enrique got to his feet. "Skylar, I get why you feel bad about all of that. But I don't understand why you're being so hard on yourself."

"That's because I'm not done." This came out hard. Pure self-loathing. "Joe was killed by a drunk driver." She fled down the hall.

CHAPTER THIRTY-EIGHT

ENRIQUE SLUMPED ONTO SKYLAR'S sofa, trying to figure out what to do. She'd tortured herself with alcohol, then punished herself for having done so. There was no rushing this journey. That truth pricked his heart because he would do anything to end her torment, to throw her a life line and pull her to safety. If it were only that simple.

Instead, he cleaned up the kitchen and pulled a book from her shelf. It had been a long time since he'd done any reading. He placed a piece of paper beneath the line of text—something he'd learned could be helpful for people with dyslexia—and found that it did make the words easier to decipher.

When it was almost eleven and his eyes would no longer stay open, he made sure the front door was locked and slipped into her room. He paused just inside, waiting to see if she'd stir. He didn't want to wake her, but he wouldn't leave her to face her demons alone. And they seemed to come out at night. He removed his boots and his jeans and slid beneath the covers. She lay on her side, facing away. He moved close, curving around her, one arm circling her waist. She murmured, nestled into him.

Probably remembering Joe.

Eighteen months earlier …

Skylar rushed into the kitchen where Joe sat eating breakfast. "My car won't start."

"Are you out of gas again? This wedding stuff has you all stressed out." He smiled sympathetically.

"I'll check." Skylar made a noise that sounded like a growl. "I hate being late." She'd spent the night at his place so they could finalize their honeymoon plans—a month-long road trip to their favorite places. It would have to wait until school let out, but they were excited about having four uninterrupted weeks together. She headed back out to see if gas would fix the problem, glad Joe always kept a full can in the garage.

Before she got to her car, Joe jogged outside, passed her his keys. "I'll deal with it. Take my car. The weather's great. I was thinking of walking today." He coached at South High School, a few blocks away.

"Are you sure? I have a meeting after school. I won't be back until five or six."

He smiled. "Of course." He kissed her, giving her backside a squeeze. "One more week, Sky. Finally."

"I know." She smiled, warm with anticipation. "I can't wait." She jangled his keys. "Thanks."

Late that morning, Skylar sat at her desk grading papers. Someone knocked and opened the door.

The principal entered. "Skylar?" He was flanked by a police officer and another man with a white square in the middle of his black collar. Her dad had told her about death notifications. Always a uniform and a chaplain, if one was available. She surged to her feet. Had her father been shot? Had something happened to her mom in San Diego?

"What? What is it?" Her hand went to her throat.

"Ms. Biondi. I'm Officer Collins. This is—"

"Just tell me. Please. Is it my dad?" She moved toward them, searching their faces.

The two men shared a pained look. The principal hovered behind them, hands thrust in his pockets.

"No." The officer and chaplain strode over to her. "I'm sorry. It's Joe. Joe Thomas. He was hit by a car near the high school." The men caught her when her knees gave way.

Someone was beside Skylar, holding her when the wave hit. "Joe." *Joe?* She turned, clinging to him. "Oh, Joe ... You're here. I thought you were gone." Just a dream? All of it?

"Skylar." Joe pulled back. No ... That wasn't his voice. "It's Enrique. I'm here, honey. I'm right here." He brushed the hair from her face. "Joe's gone. *Siento escucharlo.*" He pressed a kiss to her forehead. "I'm so sorry, Sky."

She froze. "Enrique?" Her hands went to his face. "Oh, no. I'm—I thought—" The truth crashed down on her and she moved away from him. "I didn't mean to—"

"Shh. It's okay." His voice was gentle. "Come here. You don't have to face this alone." He drew her to him.

Skylar tried to wrap her mind around Enrique comforting her when she'd just called him Joe. Moonlight seeped through the window, revealing the beautiful symmetry of his face. She ran her hands down his chest. He still wore his shirt but she felt every muscle. The ache in her heart threatened to kill her. "Make love to me." She fought to get out of her dress.

He caught her hands. "Skylar, no. I can't do that."

She began to cry. "We might not get the chance." She struggled against him. "I can't wait. I can't."

CHAPTER THIRTY-NINE

TAKING A SLOW SHUDDERY breath, Enrique moved so he was sitting against the headboard. *"Quiero hacerte el amor."* He gathered Skylar in his arms, cradling her head to his chest. Then he said it in English. "I want to make love to you. But it's not what you need."

"It is." A soft whimper. She grasped his shirt.

He caressed her cheek. "No. Not like this. I love you too much."

She stilled. "The real me? The big mess?"

"Yes."

A pause. "Even after I called you Joe?"

"Yes." He smoothed the hair from her face.

She began to cry again and he tucked her head beneath his chin and let it play out. After several minutes, her tears abated. "It was my fault he died," she whispered, the words holding a world of pain.

His throat constricted and he took a slow breath. "Why do you say that?"

"My car wouldn't start. He let me borrow his." She choked off. "I'm the reason he walked that day. And he was hit crossing the street."

Enrique tipped his head back. *Dio, give me the words.* "Sky, I think you know that's not true. But you have to forgive yourself. You won't be free until you do."

"That's what Mike says."

"He knows what he's talking about."

"How do you know?"

Enrique drew a ragged breath. "Do you remember when I said my best friend died in my arms?"

She nodded.

"We were out on patrol. Medics are targets over there. If insurgents kill a medic, they get money and notoriety. They know the whole unit will be more cautious if there's no medic along to help if someone gets hurt.

She gasped. Her fingers traced his shoulder. The gentle touch made it easier to continue.

"Rawlins took a bullet. My medical pack was made up of different sections that came apart, so I could take just what I needed. Some of the pouches could fit in my jacket. That made it safer—it was harder for the enemy to tell who the medics were because we looked like we were just carrying extra ammo. Anyway, Rawlins was worse than I thought and I needed more gear. But I was pinching his artery so he wouldn't bleed out. Swan ran to get my pack. We were taking fire and he got hit on the way back. The others guys covered me while I took care of Rawlins." He saw it all again as if he were there. "One of the other guys tried to help out but by the time Rawlins was stable, it was too late for Swan. I did everything I could, but it wasn't enough."

"There was only one medic?" Her voice was filled with compassion.

Porque no pude ayudarte mas. Why couldn't he have done more? Enrique nodded, his heart breaking all over again. "Swan and I went to basic together. Then we got the same tour and ended up in the same unit."

"I'm sorry." Skylar touched his face, a soft caress.

Enrique exhaled, feeling wrung out. "The finality is the hardest. All the never-agains." He laughed, in spite of the burden he felt. "Swan was the funniest guy I ever knew. No matter how dark things got, he'd say something that made us all laugh. And for a minute we'd forget where we were."

"Thank you for sharing that with me. It helps to know I'm not alone." Fresh tears sprang from her eyes and she dashed them away. "And thank you for what you did over there." Skylar wound her arm around his neck, threading her fingers into his hair.

"Kendra said she didn't want to know any details."

"But how could you ever be close? I want to hear as much as you're willing to tell me. That's the only way I can really know you. Besides, you've listened to my story."

"Mi vida. Gracias." He kissed her forehead. Let her settle into him, loving the way she felt in his arms. She was his life. His new life.

"Let's lay down." He released her and they snuggled together, him curving around her once more. "Tell me about your dream."

She did.

Enrique's gut wrenched. "I wish I knew what to say, Sky. How to help you."

She turned toward him. "There isn't anything to say. And you are helping. You're here, listening. Even though I've interrupted your sleep for the hundredth time." She rose on an elbow, wending her fingers through his hair again. Soothing. Calming. "I know I have a ways to go before I get past this, but I don't take time for granted anymore." She pressed a soft kiss to his cheek. "I love you, Enrique. I want you to know." Once more, she turned over, her warm softness resting against him.

Amid strands of moonlight that filtered through the blinds, Enrique struggled to grasp how the depths of pain and the height of comfort could coexist the way they did in that moment. If he hadn't experienced it, he'd never have believed his heart could be both torn and mended at once. Grieving and loving with no gap between. He felt a deep sorrow for Joe, having lost out on a lifetime of loving this woman. Then he vowed to love her enough for both of them.

In the morning, Enrique awoke to a delicious blend of smells that roused his hunger. How Skylar had gotten up without waking him was a mystery. He pushed the covers aside and set his feet on the floor. Found his jeans folded beside the bed, next to his boots, his socks slung neatly over the tops. She'd done that. The simple kindness touched him deeply. He tugged on his pants, picked up the boots, and headed to the bathroom. After a quick shower, he dressed and made his way toward the kitchen.

As he went down the hall, he realized there was a photo in the spot that had been empty a few days before. He stopped. It was a close-up of Skylar and Joe. Not just any Joe. Joe Thomas. He stared. Recalled the baseball books, the signed ball. And finally, the news reports of his tragic death. He ran a hand down his face.

Skylar came next to him, a tremulous look on her face. "Do you still feel the same way you did in the dark?"

He slung an arm over her shoulders. "I do."

She sighed and he felt her back muscles relax. "I was worried. That's why I took this down the other day. I mean, there's nothing wrong with me and Joe. But some people are so weird about the whole star thing. He was the most down to earth guy you'd ever meet. He wasn't even taking a check from South High. Just wanted to coach while he finished his degree."

"Do you think I can live up to him?"

Skylar turned him so they faced each other. "Joe had a special talent and he worked hard to perfect it. How are you any different?"

He exhaled. "I feel pretty different."

She captured his gaze. "Enrique, it wasn't money or baseball that drew me to him. It was the kind of person he was. He was devoted to me. He helped me through some difficult things. Way before he had a big paycheck."

"I can't share you with him." Enrique knew about the dreams. And her reaction to them revealed the depths of her love. How did a woman move on from that? A woman like Skylar, who held nothing back?

"I know." Her hands went to his hips, giving a gentle squeeze.

"Do you think you'll be able to let him go?" Joe Thomas was larger than life. An icon. Enrique owned an ailing motorcycle repair shop and had no place to call home.

"I have to." She gazed up at him, a promise in her eyes. "It wouldn't be fair to either of us if I didn't."

Enrique nodded toward the kitchen. "Smells good."

She pulled him along. "I'm not bad with breakfast."

He smiled, glanced around. "Wow. Real food." He loaded a plate with pancakes, fried potatoes and scrambled eggs. "Thank you."

"You're welcome." Skylar kissed his cheek. "Thank you for letting me know you. The real you." Her hand came to rest over his heart.

Enrique set their plates down and put his arms around her. "I feel safe with you. Like I could tell you anything and you'd stick by me. And this—" He indicated the food. "You have no idea what it means to me."

"I think maybe I do." Her hands moved softly along his sides.

He cupped her face. "I'm going to kiss you."

"And I'm going to like it." She smiled. "But I'm not ready to go beyond that, so don't start if you won't be able to stop."

Enrique covered her lips with his own, searching. What he found was a tenderness and fire uniquely Skylar. Their tongues did an intimate dance and her hands mapped the contours of his body, satisfying one ache while creating another. He finally managed to pull away.

"I love kissing you in the morning." Skylar ran her hands over his stubble, a murmur of pleasure. "You're so …" She eyed him as she searched for words. "You're like a living, breathing sculpture by Michelangelo."

He smiled. Though he wanted to take her back to her bed, he picked up his plate. "We better eat." They carried their food to the table. Time to get his mind on other things. "When will Mia get here?"

"It's not confirmed yet. Maybe today after school." Skylar sipped coffee. "But it may get pushed back till tomorrow."

"Do you want to come to the shop today?"

"What about your sister?"

"I took care of that. But when we're at work, I'd like to keep us just between us. Till we're—" He wasn't sure how to say it. "Until you're on the other side of this." He sipped his coffee.

"Okay."

"But Andy's already figured it out."

"He's funny. So perceptive, but so … not."

Enrique laughed. "I know. He blurted out yesterday that I'm in love."

"Is he upset?" She gave a worried look.

"He's not like that."

"Okay. I could come by in the afternoon. I have plans with Alex at ten."

Enrique shifted in his seat. "What are you doing?" This was new territory. While he knew Skylar better than he'd known any woman, he didn't know her friends, or her life. Not the real one, anyway. The gaps were worrisome. He wasn't keen on the woman he loved hanging out with other guys. What man with a pulse could be *just friends* with Skylar?

"He wouldn't say. He just asked for my help and told me to wear clothes I don't mind getting dirty." Skylar shrugged. "He helped me get all that stuff moved on the spur of the moment. I want to return the favor."

Despite feeling uneasy, Enrique nodded. They'd have to take things one step at a time.

"Back to keeping us between us at the shop. I can do that." Skylar chinned toward him. "What about you? You're all over the place. We're kissing, we're not kissing …"

"I'll do my best." He grinned. "By the way, I got rid of that calendar you hate."

She nearly choked on a bite of pancake. "What?"

"I saw your reaction that first day."

She waved her fork in the air. "What is it with guys and pictures of naked women? I mean, they're perfect strangers. And they've been waxed and airbrushed and photo-shopped. I'll bet most of them have after-market parts. Real women don't look like that."

Enrique laughed. "After-market parts."

"It's true." Skylar's eyes sparked with fire.

He eyed her breasts. "So … you're all you? No upgrades?"

She threw her napkin at him and picked up her glass, looking like she might dump it on his head.

"I'm kidding." He put up his hands. "It was my uncle's and I just kept it. I've been kinda busy." She shot him a droll look, which made him feel guilty, so he added, "I'm the one who put the post-it note on there."

"Yay for you."

CHAPTER FORTY

SKYLAR OPENED THE DOOR after Alex knocked. He greeted her with another extended hug and a kiss on the forehead. She felt a prick of guilt when she thought of Enrique, knowing he would be crushed if he'd seen it. Before their time ended, she would set Alex straight. "I'm all ready." She slung her purse over her shoulder. "Where are we going?"

"You'll see." His eyes glinted mysteriously.

After locking the door Skylar followed him to his truck, her curiosity piqued. He held the door while she got in. "Hmm. You brought the truck. What does that mean?"

He went around and climbed in, keeping his eyes straight ahead. "You've never been good at waiting."

She laughed. "You're worse than me. Joe ratted you out a hundred times." But she drummed her fingers on the armrest, trying to guess his plan as he drove through Denver. They ended up at a garden center. "What are we doing here?"

"I want you to show me how to plant flowers. Whatever grows in the fall." Alex glanced over as he took the keys out of the ignition. "I've never taken the time, but I always liked how Joe's place looked with the flowers out front."

Skylar smiled, happy he was taking a new direction. Perhaps he would settle down and create a real life for himself. "Do you have any containers?"

"Nope. I'm starting from scratch."

They spent a full hour meandering along crushed stone pathways choosing an assortment of mums, heliopsis and sedum. Skylar added some vinca minor with small purple flowers that would spill over the sides of the containers. The sun warmed and the air cooled, as it always did in late September. Next, they chose pots in a range of sizes and colors. When they finished, each of them hauled an overloaded cart to the checkout. An employee helped them heft bags of potting mix and peat into the back end of the truck bed. Finally, Skylar hopped up and Alex passed her the plants, which she tucked behind the cab so the wind wouldn't destroy them.

They stopped at a restaurant and got food to go. When he pulled into his driveway, she stared at the sprawling, two-story home with its six-car garage. "I forgot how big your house is. I don't think we got enough containers to make an impression."

"We could always get more tomorrow." Alex cut the engine and took out the key.

"I don't think I'll have time."

"Well, thanks for doing this with me."

"Are you kidding?" Skylar opened her door and gathered the food and her purse. "This is one of my favorite things to do. I feel a bit selfish." She eyed him, looking for evidence that he'd really done this for her benefit. The idea of Alex planting flowers was still throwing her off. "I have another commitment this afternoon, so I can get you started, but you'll have to finish on your own."

"No problem."

She glanced around. "This is going to look great."

They ate outside at a stone table beneath a large tree. Afterward, Alex collected the trash and tossed it in the garbage.

"Come here." Skylar preceded him to the front porch. "Do you want them out front?"

He shrugged. "No idea."

"Where do you spend the most time? I like to plant flowers where I'll see them the most. But maybe you want them to dress up the front. Whatever you prefer. You can always move them with a dolly or a wheel barrow if you change your mind. The main thing is that you don't forget to water them. Out of sight—" She rolled her eyes in embarrassment at the amused look on his face.

"That's the Sky I remember." He grabbed her hand.

She pulled away. "Alex, you need to know I'm seeing someone."

"You are?" That sadness she'd seen the day before returned to his gaze.

Skylar couldn't make sense of it. "Yes."

"I thought you were still trying to get over Joe."

"I am. We just met. And we're taking things slow. I still have a lot to work through."

"So, it's not serious?" He sounded hopeful.

Skylar exhaled. "It is. I mean …" She was not about to bare her soul to Joe's best friend. "Alex, you know I don't play around with things like this." The dots suddenly connected. At least she thought they did. "It that what this is about? You and me?"

For the first time since she'd known him, Alex looked embarrassed. "Kind of." He shifted his feet. "I need to change. I don't like who I am."

Knowing how hard it was to pull off his mask, she wanted to hug him. But that would send the wrong message. Instead, she said, "Let's sit." She went to the table where they'd eaten lunch. He sat opposite her and Skylar waved at the collection of flowers and pots, "Not that I'm any expert, but this seems like a good step. Doing something real, that feeds your soul."

He regarded her quietly. "*You* feed my soul."

Skylar couldn't figure out where this was coming from. "Alex, I don't understand. We've been friends for—"

"I want more than that, Skylar. I'll give you all the time you need. There hasn't been anyone else since June. You know that's not normal for me. And it hasn't been difficult. Except for not seeing you and worrying whether you were alright." His eyes pleaded with her to understand. To believe him.

What? She racked her brain to recall any details from their dinner together, but nothing surfaced. "You said something about us going to dinner. Did I say or do something that made you think—" Suddenly, she feared there was more she had to forgive herself for. Why else would she have blocked it out? She felt the sting of tears and was unable to stop them. "What did I do?"

Alex took a knee in front of her chair. "Baby, it's okay." He cupped her face, wiping her tears with his thumbs.

Panic rose up and dark spots swam in her eyes.

"Oh, God. Sky, what's wrong?"

CHAPTER FORTY-ONE

AGAINST HER BETTER JUDGMENT, Skylar allowed Alex to help her into his house. It was either that or pass out in the yard.

His face full of worry, he guided her to a sofa in the front room. "I'm sorry. I didn't mean to upset you." He shoved a coffee table out of the way and knelt next to her. "Do you want a glass of water?"

Skylar eyed him, unable to see anything in his manner that was cause for alarm. She stifled a groan. "Please." He left for a moment and she gathered herself. When he returned, she sat up. "Thank you." After a long drink, she bolstered herself with a deep breath. "Alex, tell me what happened between us."

Alex ran his hands through his hair. "We had dinner together."

"You said that before. It had to be more than dinner. You're calling me baby. Telling me there's been no one else." It killed her to sit there when she wanted to pace. But with the way she was feeling, sitting was the safer option.

"I thought it might come back to you if we spent some time together."

Her jaw tightened. "Alex, please. What happened? What did I do?"

"I stopped by your place. You were upset and I thought maybe a night out would do you some good. We went to Ellyngton's."

"I don't know that place."

"Inside The Brown Palace."

"The Brown Palace?" Her hand flew to her mouth. "That was you?" Skylar wanted to run. Forever.

He nodded, looking confused. "I'll be right back." After leaving the room for a half-minute, he returned with something shiny in his hand. "I was wearing my Rolex. You said you liked it and I gave it to you.

But I found it on my pillow after you left." He passed her a watch. Gold, with a crown where the number twelve should be. She'd seen it in her mind a thousand times. But just that once on her wrist. Skylar clamped her eyes shut.

Alex sat beside her. "Do you need to lie down?"

"No." She rubbed her thumb around the bezel, feeling each diamond.

"Alex, I don't know what to say. I'm so humiliated. So ... sorry. But I'm not even sure what for. Using you? Hurting you?"

He touched her arm. "It wasn't like that. We were both lost in our grief. It was a comfort."

Skylar's fingers fluttered to her breast. "Why can't I remember?" She looked up at him. "Was I wasted?"

"We shared a bottle of wine. But I've never seen you drunk, so I don't really know."

She swallowed. "That's worse."

"Why?" He caressed her hand.

"Did my brain just ... shut off? God. What else did I do that month?" She looked at him, fearing what she'd see in his eyes, but needing to know just the same.

He smiled sadly. "It's okay."

"No, it's not. I've never slept with anyone but Joe." She sighed. That was no longer true.

He gazed at her steadily. "You changed me, Sky. One night with you changed me forever. Made me want more. It wasn't just the sex. We talked on a level ... " He lifted both palms. "I've never known anyone like you. I totally get why Joe was hooked. I don't know why I never saw it before."

Skylar left that alone and lifted the watch. "I do remember this. I woke up with it on. I didn't know where I was. I heard—well, it must have been you in the shower—but I couldn't remember a thing. I freaked. I got dressed and ran out with my shoes in my hand when you turned off the water." She wiped her eyes. "I didn't know it was you, Alex. I'm so sorry." She scanned his face, wanting him to hate her as much as she hated herself.

"Please don't tell me you're sorry again. It kills me that you can't remember." A heavy silence descended between them.

Skylar placed the watch on the arm of the sofa, not wanting to touch it anymore. She needed to go. But he'd driven her here, so she couldn't just leave. A hundred apologies lodged in her throat, but Alex didn't want to hear how much she regretted what they'd done. She supposed she'd feel the same way if the tables were turned.

He went to the window, shoulders stiff. Blew out a long breath. "It's kind of ironic."

"What?"

"I have no idea how many women I've done this to."

CHAPTER FORTY-TWO

STILL REELING FROM ALEX'S revelation hours before, Skylar paced her living room. She'd been unable to go to the shop because someone from Social Services called, asking to see the apartment. Everything was a go and Mia would arrive after school the following day. But she had to talk to Enrique. Though she feared what it would do to his heart, she'd never be able to live with herself if she didn't tell him. Her stomach felt sick so she trudged to the kitchen and started water for tea.

After creating and deleting six different texts before sending them, she settled on, *please call me as soon as you're free.* A short time later, her cell rang. "Hey," she said, her voice barely audible.

"What's up?" Worry laced his words.

"I need to see you. It's important." She dropped to the sofa. "Mia's coming tomorrow after school. She should get here around four. Do you have any time before then? I can come by the shop if that will help."

"Uh …" He paused. She heard papers rustling.

Skylar's stomach felt like she'd lit it on fire. "You can call me back when you're not busy."

"Do you have time to make dinner? I could stop by around six. I've got a whole evening of work ahead of me."

"Sure. Okay. Thanks." She sounded like a fourteen-year-old. A cup of chamomile tea did little to calm her nerves, but it did settle her stomach. It had been a long time since she'd cracked open a cookbook, but she thumbed through her favorite one trying to find a recipe simple enough to do right the first time. Shepherd's pie. Classic comfort food. Once it was in the oven, the minutes dragged, her mind useless in coming up with any way of sharing the truth that might cause less damage. Finally, she heard Enrique's motorcycle outside. She stood in her doorway and watched him park and take off his helmet. She waved and attempted a smile as he strode toward her.

He shrugged out of his jacket on the way down the stairs. "What's the matter?" Concern etched his features.

"I know you're in a hurry. Let me get your food first. I made shepherd's pie."

"Sounds good." He set his helmet and jacket on the sofa and sat on a stool near the counter.

Skylar passed him a full plate. "Water or iced tea?"

"Water's fine." He took a bite. "Thank you. This is good." He smiled and she hoped that was a good sign.

"I need to tell you something."

"Shoot."

"I mentioned helping Alex with a project at his place today."

He nodded.

"We planted some flowers." Skylar filled a bowl with salad and set a few bottles of dressing within his reach. "He was Joe's best friend."

Enrique stopped eating. "Are you talking about Alex Kelly?"

She swallowed. "Yes. We all went to high school together." She fixed herself a plate, then went to sit next to him. "I need you to let me tell you everything. I know you were hurt by lies and I don't want there to be any secrets between us."

He stared at his plate.

"Remember when I told you about what happened in June? How I woke up in a hotel?"

"The Brown Palace." He met her gaze. "It was him?"

"Yes." Skylar left nothing out.

Though he didn't interrupt, when she was done his lips made a thin line. He blinked slowly. "How do you feel about him?"

"He's a friend. I care about him getting past Joe's death but we've never had any emotional ties. Alex is ... well, he's not the kind of man I'm drawn to. He—"

"He's in love with you, Skylar." Enrique set his fork on the counter.

"He didn't say that."

"He said you feed his soul. He could have any woman he wants and he hasn't been with anyone since he was with you."

"I don't intend to pursue a relationship with Alex. He knows that."

Enrique dragged his hands down his face. A muscle pulsed in his jaw. Finally, he looked at her. "Sky, I respect you for being honest with me." He slipped off the stool. "I have to get back."

Skylar's heart sank. "Enrique, Joe and I were apart a lot and I never even looked at another guy." She'd known this could backfire. But she'd clung to the hope that he could look past it if she told him the truth. She almost apologized. But she hadn't done anything wrong. Not to him. In this case, it was Alex she'd wounded. Not to mention, herself. Why did life have to be so complicated? "So where does this leave us?"

"I'm not sure. I don't trust my own thoughts right now. I only know I can't deal with another ..." He trailed off.

She followed him to the door, moved in front of him. "I know that. I do. But that's not what this is. Enrique, you're free to walk away. But if you do, it won't be because I'm deceptive or unfaithful. I'm neither of those things." She filled her lungs. "Do you have any idea how hard it was to tell you the truth knowing what you went through before?"

Enrique stared past her. "*Sabes me tengo que ir.* I gotta go." He grabbed his helmet and jacket.

Skylar risked touching his arm and he bristled. "I love you. I'm willing to give you some time. But you have to decide if you can give all of yourself to me, because I won't accept anything less. I'm going to get out of this pit and move on with my life. I want to do that with you."

CHAPTER FORTY-THREE

ENRIQUE SKIMMED BETWEEN CARS on the way back to the shop, ignoring drivers who honked when he blew around them, nearly clipping their bumpers. Andy's truck was still parked outside. He considered hiding out until Andy left, but he didn't have the luxury. Going to Skylar's meant he'd be working past midnight. And when his head finally hit the pillow, he'd lie awake. Thinking of her. He slammed the door as he entered.

Andy popped his head up from behind a four-wheeler he had on a lift. "Looks like things didn't go well." He pushed a shock of sandy hair from his glistening forehead. "What happened?"

Enrique stalked through the door that led to the office, slamming that one too. What the hell was he doing? Why did he work so damn hard? And why did he love her so much? Eight months ago, none of these questions existed. Then *Tio* Armando died unexpectedly. Of course Enrique would take the helm. It was a simple business. People bring in their broken machines. You fix them. You get paid. What a fool he'd been. He'd worked there for a long time. How had he been so clueless about what it would take?

Then ... when he was flat broke—no, when he was completely sideways—he'd foolishly opened his heart again. What did he have to offer Skylar? Living on love was a fantasy. *She* was a fantasy. It was only a matter of time before she'd tire of the blue-collar life and drift back to Alex. Or someone like him. She was the kind of woman one would expect to see on the arm of a pro athlete. Not a mechanic.

He stalked to the bathroom and turned the faucet on full. Leaning down, he directed the cool flow over his face, his head, his neck. Avoiding his own gaze in the mirror, he turned off the water and toweled off. This was his life. And he hated it. So would she. Skylar would resent him when they didn't have money for expensive vacations and nice cars. *Diablos.* He was thirty years old and didn't even own a car.

This one-way diatribe was getting him nowhere.

Andy glanced up when Enrique returned to the shop.

He picked up the clipboard of work orders. "Where are we?"

Andy twisted some wires together and grabbed a wire nut. "I should be done with this soon. I got those finished." He pointed to twin Harley Davidsons near the overhead door.

"Already?" Enrique raised his brows.

"Yep." Andy looked pleased with himself. Warranty work paid by the job, not the hour. He was more motivated by the flat-rate work, knowing he'd net more per hour if he finished under the time the manufacturer allotted for a given repair. It worked out for Enrique as well, because it meant more machines got out the door faster.

"I don't have money for overtime. You can head out when this one's done." Enrique chinned toward the four-wheeler Andy was working on.

"No can do." Andy twisted the wire nut onto the wires. "You need to get out of here. I'm gonna stay and finish them all." There was steel in his voice and Enrique knew it would be pointless to argue. "Does she love you?"

"That's what she says." Enrique heard the doubt in his words and guilt swept over him. Skylar had shown him in myriad ways she was nothing like Kendra. *Maldita sea. Dammit.*

Andy shook his head. "You told me you weren't gonna screw this up. Do what you gotta do to get your head straight."

"I've got work to do." Enrique flipped through the paperwork.

"Don't be a moron."

Enrique escaped to the front desk and sagged in his chair.

Andy pursued. "Go tell her you were a jerk and you're sorry."

He glared at Andy. "Would you leave me alone?"

Andy threw a rag on the counter. "You're already alone. You've got a chance to change that with the most good hearted, beautiful woman either of us has ever known. What the hell's wrong with you?"

Enrique crossed his arms. "Alex Kelly is in love with her. Alex Kelly.

He's a gazillionaire. I'll never be enough."

"Skylar's not like that."

"How the hell do you know so much about her?"

"I talked to her every day. And, unlike you, I paid attention." Andy shook his head. "But for some reason, she chose the ox. The blind man. The—"

Enrique pointed a warning finger. "I get it."

"The oaf."

"And now she can move on."

"Sure, because she's that shallow." Andy pointed toward the building across the street. "Just like she ignored the plight of that little girl because she might put herself in danger or lose her job. Are you telling me you can't see who she is?"

Enrique heaved a sigh. He saw exactly who she was. And it terrified him.

"I looked online. She and Joe met in fourth grade. Skylar couldn't have known he'd become a major league baseball player."

Enrique raked his hands through his hair and tipped his chair back.

"Skylar was lucky. Then she was unlucky … in a really big way. And then she met you. It's up to you if that works out in her favor." Andy paced in front of the counter. "I'd have given half my paycheck to have her in our unit in Afghanistan. She's a damn superhero."

"Exactly."

Andy balled his fists. "How many times have you prayed for a miracle? You meet her and somehow she drags you out of your cave. Then she falls for you and wants to start over with you." Now it was Andy who wagged a finger Enrique's direction. "If you walk away from her, don't you go asking God for anything else. He's given you *more* than you asked for and you're too proud to take it. Or too scared." The shop door slammed when Andy disappeared. It opened again a half minute later. Andy calmly placed his gun on the counter. "Put this away so I don't shoot you in the head." He returned to the shop.

Enrique went to the window. The sign at Smile & Relax had been covered over with a *for lease* sign. A new business would move in and life would go on. Just not *his* life. He kicked the wall, thought about throwing a chair through the window. Why did Andy have to be so damn ... right?

He couldn't live like this anymore. It was one thing when you were at war. But living like a vagabond by choice? It was true; he'd begged for a lifeboat. Some way to stay afloat. Skylar showed up and everything changed. From the new business she'd brought in with that contest, to her offer to help him for free. Never mind the warmth of her smile, the strength of her resolve to come back from a tragedy without making excuses ... she was a godsend. His heart felt alive when he was with her. He supposed he couldn't blame Alex for feeling the same way. After one day with her, Enrique had been permanently altered as well.

He snatched the keys and the gun from the counter and entered the shop the way he'd entered buildings during the war. Slow, careful, looking for threats. Andy ignored him. He went over and passed Andy the keys and the gun. "You mind locking up?"

"Nope." Andy's gaze flickered briefly on Enrique. "And you better do the right thing or I'm quitting. I can't take working for stupid. Down-on-his-luck was okay. But not stupid."

Enrique kept his mouth shut and got on his cycle, watching for cops because it was easier than watching his speed. Andy's question had to be answered. What was wrong with him? Why would he push Skylar away?

He went to a gas station and filled his tank, then headed west on I-70 toward the mountains, not caring that only a few hours of daylight remained. Rather than enjoying the scenery as he usually did, he thought about Kendra. How he'd come home after a year in the desert and found some other guy's clothes in his dresser. How she'd acted like it was his fault—that he had no right to expect her fidelity if he left her alone. On top of everything from his tour, it nearly killed him. Then in the ensuing weeks, her lies about money had come to light. A great web that left him with a mountain of debt and no hope for the future. After all he had sacrificed, after all he had suffered, they were broke and their marriage was over.

Rather than deal with his pain, he'd pushed it aside and looked for a job. That didn't pan out. Looking back, it was likely people could see he was a ticking bomb and were fearful to take him on. Too proud to move in with his parents, he'd spent a week or two on the sofas of various friends. That was when he asked Uncle Armando for work. His uncle was happy to help and Enrique threw himself into it, most of his low hourly wage going to pay his divorce attorney. After Uncle A passed, he clung to the notion that if he could save the shop, he'd have something to be proud of and his family would respect him. Maybe he would, too.

That was the root. As though he were nothing but a used car, he'd been easily replaced by another man. That spoke to his value. His worth. As a medic, Enrique was an invaluable asset, trusted and respected by every soldier in his unit. Everyone got a nickname in the army. His was Dark Horse. A winner unexpected, the one who came from behind and snatched life from death's hand. The kid who couldn't read had become a medic that every soldier, regardless of rank, wanted to stand next to when he was in harm's way. Over and over during the war, he'd done things no one—even Enrique himself —thought he could do. And a lot of guys went home alive.

But Swan's death had taken him under. They were just days from the end of their tour and Enrique had gone home alone. Boxing Swan's dog tags and other personal effects for Swan's mother was the hardest thing he'd ever done. In that moment, he'd sworn off the name, wishing it weren't tattooed on his chest. What difference did all of it make if his best friend was the patient he lost?

With the help of Andy and others, he'd slowly worked through the worst of his guilt. But he'd never again thought of himself as Dark Horse. To top off his failure as a medic, Enrique the man wasn't enough to keep Kendra from straying.

As dusk drew the sun westward, he exited the freeway near Genesee. He parked in an empty lot with a breathtaking view of the mountains. A hawk cried overhead, the melancholy tone echoing through the valley. A gentle breeze whispered in the tops of the trees. He sent up a prayer. Not the rote kind he'd memorized as a kid. A plea for help. Direction. He closed his eyes and listened for a voice bigger than his own. Wiser. More powerful.

As the sky darkened, it came to him that as much as Skylar needed to forgive herself and let go of Joe, he needed to break free from his bitterness toward Kendra. It had infiltrated his heart like a cancer, threatening to poison his future. He recalled his dad saying that forgiveness didn't let her off God's hook, just his. After the fog of war, he was no longer sure about God the way he had been before. The lines had blurred. But he still held that there was right and there was wrong. Good and evil. And what he felt toward Kendra was not good.

Putting a new twist on something the leader of a support group had taught him, he mentally walked through each moment that haunted him, letting himself feel every emotion, every pain, remembering each vile thought and the words they had conjured. Connecting with that injured part of himself, he asked for healing. Then ... he released her. Wished her well. Closed the door.

It was full dark, a canopy of stars overhead sent a silent message of hope.

CHAPTER FORTY-FOUR

FOR THE FIRST TIME since she'd moved into her dumpy apartment, Skylar wished for a TV. There was nothing else to distract her from this new pain. Reading was out of the question. And one could only reorganize a mostly empty room so many times before going mad. She'd moved Mia's furniture around several times, trying every imaginable arrangement, finally settling on the way it had been in the first place.

She meandered outside, taking a seat at the top of her steps. A light chill breathed on the evening air and stars began peeping from the darkening sky. Joe's death was the worst thing she'd ever endured, but the threat of losing Enrique elicited a whole new kind of heartache. He hadn't said it was over between them, but the stiffness in his gait as he'd left had shaken her to the core. As did the vacant look in his eyes. Like she'd smothered his soul.

Leaving was probably better than spewing whatever had filled his head at that moment, but it hurt nonetheless. Even now, looking back on it, she was glad she'd told him everything. At least her conscience was clear. Besides, honesty was the only basis she would accept in a relationship with any man. It was the reason she and Joe had been so close. It was also the reason losing him hurt her so deeply. Neither had held anything back.

Life was too short for regrets that could be avoided with something so simple as a direct conversation. In spite of that truth, the thought of not having Enrique in her life stole her breath away. A man who put others before himself was a rare find. That heart in such a spellbinding package, even more so.

Except for low-level traffic noise drifting from the freeway, the night was quiet. She lay back on the sidewalk, cushioning her head with her hands. She'd made space for him, not just in her heart, but her life. The simple chore of preparing a meal had become so much more—an amorous dance that hinted at what might come later. Shopping for food was no longer mundane because there was the promise of spending time with Enrique, then a mouth-watering meal accompanied by meaningful conversation.

What would she do without him? The answer was simple: she would go on. She was stronger now, no longer afraid of harming herself in an effort to numb her pain. In good part, she had him to thank for that.

Skylar's head began to throb from resting on the hard surface. Tiny rocks on the concrete had embedded themselves in the tops of her hands. She stood and moved slowly down the stairs. There was Mia to think about now. A forward momentum that would give Skylar a reason to get up every day. It struck her that merely thinking about the sweet, sometimes quirky, little girl made her heart ache with love and a fierce need to protect her. They'd only had a few brief interactions before the rescue. Their subsequent visits, though a bit stilted at the outset, had left Skylar with a longing to be more than a mentor or friend. The trip to the library had been wonderful. Deeply moving, in fact. Every person who worked there knew and adored Mia and her spirits had been lifted, renewing her dream of becoming a doctor, despite what she'd been through.

There was still no word from Peter about Mia's extended family. Skylar understood it was usually in the child's best interests to live with blood relatives but something inside her rebelled. She and Mia shared a connection unlike any other Skylar had experienced. Was it selfish to want to be a mother to Mia? A fool's dream?

Knowing sleep would evade her, Skylar grabbed a book and got ready for bed. She was turning a page when she heard a familiar rumble in the parking lot. The motor cut out and a single headlight turned off. Skylar threw her book on the floor and shoved the covers aside. She lifted the blinds and spotted Enrique removing his helmet. It was too dark to read his expression. Unable to wait, she raced and opened the door.

Her feet felt leaden. Should she run up the stairs and throw her arms around him? Or had he come to officially end things? She decided it didn't matter. If this was the last time she got to hold him, she was going to do it.

He was halfway to the stairs when she cleared them, his eyes focused on the sidewalk, shoulders drooping. Skylar's steps faltered and she suddenly wished she hadn't been so impulsive. Their gazes connected. What was probably half a second dragged on forever. In the dim light, she worked to parse the emotions that played on his face.

Then he surged forward, pulling her against him. *"Lo siento."* His voice broke. "I'm sorry. I should never have walked out like that." His kisses were somehow both tender and fierce.

Skylar gave as good as she got, wrapping her arms about his neck. His helmet thudded to the ground and both arms came around her. Their tears mingled as their faces nestled against each other. "You came back," she whispered, hardly able to believe her good fortune.

His hands moved over her, reaching the hem of the T-shirt she'd worn to bed. "You're not dressed." He chuckled.

"It's late. I was in bed. Be quiet." She covered his mouth with hers. His hands went to her bottom and lifted. Skylar hopped up, winding her legs around his hips, connecting them at her ankles. "That's better." She got down to business again, every taste making her want more. His scent filled her nostrils and she tipped her head back and groaned. "You smell good. Like the wind."

"I've been out for a while." He glanced around. "Let's go inside."

"Okay." She slid down his body, picking up his helmet and snaking an arm around his waist. They headed toward the stairs, where light spilled out through the open door. There wasn't room to walk abreast, so she went in front. Once inside, she locked the door and leaned against it. "Sorry."

He gave a slow smile. So alluring she thought she might die of wanting him. He brushed her cheeks with the backs of his curled fingers. "You surprised me. I wasn't sure you'd open your door."

Opening her door was just the beginning. "I said I was willing to wait." She glanced at her watch. "You had three more minutes."

He shook his head. "I guess I cut it close."

Unexpected tears burned her eyes. "Please don't ever do that again.

Not without telling me when you'll be back."

He pulled her to him. "I won't. I promise. I'm sorry." His voice was ragged, his hands moved softly over her, quelling the ache that was strangely worse now that he was here.

Skylar bit her lower lip and tried to make sense of it. Enrique made her want things she thought she'd never want again. She hadn't believed there would be life after Joe. Certainly not like this. She'd hoped for something akin to a black and white movie. This felt like The Wizard of Oz after the tornado was over. But they had things to sort out. And Mia was coming. "I'll be right back." She went to her closet and pulled on some jeans. Then she returned and nestled at his side. "I don't want to lose you, Enrique. Tell me what you need."

He kissed the top of her head. "First, I need to know you forgive me."

Skylar rested a hand on his thigh, glanced up. "Of course I do. I've asked a lot of you. My life isn't usually so dramatic. *I'm* not usually so dramatic. It's kind of embarrassing. No, it's totally embarrassing. Especially what I found out today."

"I won't hold that against you."

"Do you trust me? About Alex?"

"I do. That wasn't really the problem."

"What was it?"

Enrique paused a few beats, cleared his throat. "I told you that before we could move forward, you had to let go of Joe." He glanced away briefly. "But I wasn't being fair. I realized after I left here that my resentment toward Kendra seeped into things with you. It discolored everything."

"What do you mean?"

He took a deep breath before answering, his jaw muscle tense. His gaze met hers. "I was replaced by another man. And she acted like it was no big deal. Like one was as good as another so long as she had a man in her bed. It really messed me up." His voice was rough.

She squeezed his hand. "What she did doesn't reflect on you. At least not in my eyes."

"When you told me what happened with Alex, it brought all of that back. I need to know I'm enough for you, Skylar. Even if I can make a go of things at the shop, I'll never be able to give you what Alex could." The words were drenched with self-doubt. Enrique gave her a searching look.

Skylar turned toward him, caressing his face. "Enrique, you have it backwards. Alex could never give me what you can. He lacks your heart. Your character. No amount of money can buy those things." She let those words hang in the air, hoping he'd soak them in. Then she added, "I'm going to say this once. Then I need you to trust me."

"Okay."

"You are more than enough for me. But I need all of you. And you'll get all of me. That's the only way it will work."

"I'm ready now."

CHAPTER FORTY-FIVE

EVERY FEW MINUTES, MIA glanced at the clock in her classroom. Would this day ever end? She hadn't been able to pay attention to anything. Even during silent reading time, the words swam around like guppies on the page. There were two hours left. Beneath the desk, her foot tapped a fast rhythm. That morning, she'd packed all her things and her foster mom promised to take her to Skylar's right after school. *Tick. Tick. Tick.* The second hand seemed to drag around the face of the clock, like it was stopping to say hello to each number. She put her head in her hands, elbows on her desk.

After what felt like a year, the final bell rang.

Mia grabbed her new backpack and raced outside, straining to see over the heads of the other kids at the pick-up point. The moment she saw her foster mom's car, she leapt inside.

"Hey, sugar," Shirley said cheerily.

"Hi." Mia felt a tiny bit guilty that she wanted to leave and be with Skylar because Shirley was nice. But Skylar was ... well, she didn't know exactly. All she knew was that she felt like there was a magnet inside her that drew her to Skylar. They'd been learning about magnets in science. She hoped there was one inside Skylar, too.

"Guess I don't need to ask if you're ready." Shirley chuckled.

Mia wondered how she could be excited and scared to death at the same time.

When they arrived, Skylar was standing outside, a big smile on her face. She wore a red dress, a denim jacket and black leggings with shoes that looked like boots cut off at the ankle. As pretty as someone in a magazine. Mia ran to meet her and Skylar gave her the best hug ever. She smelled like flowers and was softer than Daddy. That thought made a little pain in her heart.

"Hey, Mia." Skylar's voice was airy and she kissed Mia's cheek. "I'm so happy you're here." She held Mia away, running her eyes over her. They were shiny, like she might cry. "How are you?"

"I'm good." Mia felt like she might burst from happiness and she hugged Skylar again. "I mean, well. I'm doing well." Her teacher had corrected her twice that week. Mia hated when she had to be reminded of things.

Skylar laughed and pulled Mia close again, rubbing her back. She remembered the feel of it from Skylar's truck. Skylar straightened. "I'm glad."

Mia took Skylar's outstretched hand, hoping she'd never have to let go. This must be what having a mommy felt like. A good mommy. She'd only ever seen her mother in jail. And even though her mom could have hugged her or held her hand when they met in the big room with the tables, she never did. She just sat there with an angry face, hating it when Mia tried to talk to her or gave her a picture she'd colored. Mia was relieved when her daddy finally stopped taking her there. "You look pretty. I like your dress," she said to Skylar.

"You do?" Skylar sounded surprised. "Thank you." She glanced down, smoothing a hand over the fabric. "I haven't worn this in a long time."

Mia did a little skip. "Did you drive your truck today?"

"No. I'm not doing that anymore. Hey, we should get your things and thank Shirley for taking such good care of you. We can talk more after we get inside."

Shirley, who was leaning on her car door, straightened and shook Skylar's hand. "You're looking well." They chatted for a few minutes. Mia tuned out their words, choosing to bask in the good feelings that came from being where somebody really wanted her. If her daddy was here, he'd take a picture with his phone. He always said how important it was to remember the good times. Even though her heart hurt at the thought of him, it didn't suck out the happy feelings she got from being with Skylar.

She'd been writing every good memory of him in the journal Skylar had given her. And Skylar was right. It did help. Sometimes, instead of writing, she went back and read them. Shirley had some colored pencils and Mia would use them to draw little flowers in the margins. So far, she'd kept it to herself. Tonight, she would write about this. She secretly hoped her daddy could read her journal from heaven so he wouldn't be sad. Sometimes when she said her prayers at night, she asked God for that.

The two women hugged. "Mia's a joy. And smart. Whooee! That girl's gonna keep you on your toes." The way Shirley said whooee always made Mia laugh. Even though she wasn't very good at drawing people, she'd drawn a picture of Shirley saying whooee in her journal. She tried to make her lean back just a little and made a big smile on her dark face. Now she wouldn't forget.

Mia gave Shirley a hug. "Thank you for taking care of me. I liked staying at your house."

"Oh, you are so welcome, honey." Shirley patted Mia's shoulder.

As the three of them hauled Mia's things from the car, Skylar asked Shirley about school; things like when Mia had to be there and when it let out. Then they all said goodbye. Mia loved the way Skylar's shoes clicked on the sidewalk with each step. When they got inside, Skylar showed her around. It wasn't big, but everything was nice and very clean. The kitchen tablecloth had colored leaves and pumpkins on it. Sort of like the decorations in the hallways at school. There was even a candle in the middle. It was lit and the room smelled like pumpkin pie. That made Mia smile.

Skylar gestured toward the sofa. "The furniture is kind of big, but it's really comfy for reading." They went down a hall and Skylar opened a door. "This is your room. Let me know if there's anything you need."

Mia peeked in. "A bookshelf!" She looked up at Skylar. "Are those all for me?"

Skylar smiled. "They are. I put a variety in here since you're at a higher reading level. I have lots more where these came from. Go take a look. And you can unpack your things if you want, or I can help you do it later. I'm going to start dinner. Do you like spaghetti and meatballs?"

"Who doesn't? But we need vegetables, too. Do you have salad? Or broccoli? Or Kale?"

Skylar chuckled. "I have salad. I'll come get you when it's ready. But you can feel free to come and go whenever you want."

Mia didn't know what was funny about vegetables but she didn't care. This was like a dream. A shelf full of books in her very own bedroom. She pulled the set Skylar had given her from a box she'd packed that morning and placed them on the shelf that had the most room.

When she went to get something else, Skylar sat on the bed and patted the spot next to her. "Actually, before I make dinner, let's chat for a sec."

Mia sat, loving the feel of Skylar's arm around her shoulders.

"Mia, I want you to know something." Skylar's eyes got shiny again and Mia's stomach felt a little pang. "I know you've been through a lot lately. And it seems like you're doing really well. But if you're ever feeling upset or scared or anything at all, you can talk to me about it. I'll do everything I can to help you."

Mia chewed her cheek so the tears wouldn't come. "Is it alright if I unpack my other things now?"

"Of course." Skylar smiled and her warm hand left Mia's shoulder.

"Dad?" Skylar hid in the kitchen, eyeing the hall in case Mia appeared.

"Hey, Sky."

"Mia's here." For the fourth time, Skylar used a dishtowel to polish the already sparkling kitchen faucet.

"That's great. How's she doing?"

"She's fine." Skylar leaned against the refrigerator.

"What's wrong?"

"I don't know what I'm doing."

"Sure you do. You're used to a roomful of teenagers. This'll be easy."

"That was teaching. It was a job. There were rules and a chain of command with someone else at the top. Plus, the kids were practically grown. What if I screw up? She's been through so much. And shouldn't I have a TV? Is she going to hate me?"

"Where's your TV?"

"In storage. It's way too big for this place."

He paused and she imagined him giving her a long-suffering look. "Skylar."

"What?"

"Take a deep breath."

She did. "It didn't help."

Art chuckled. "Mia adores you. She'll give you a month of mistakes before she gets riled. Maybe a year."

"So you don't think I'm crazy?"

"I didn't say that."

They both laughed. Skylar couldn't remember the last time they'd done that. She'd spent her best years resenting him. In that moment it felt as though a wall between them had crumbled.

"You'll be fine. And don't worry about screwing up. It's guaranteed. You're human, just like the rest of us. Might even humble you out a bit."

"Skylar?" Mia came out of her room.

"She's calling me. Gotta go. Thanks." Skylar ended the call.

CHAPTER FORTY-SIX

SEVERAL WEEKS LATER, ENRIQUE returned to the shop in the late morning after picking up a snow mobile. "Andy, do you mind unloading that?" Skylar hadn't come in at her usual time, so he'd missed seeing her before he went out.

"No prob." Andy headed outside.

"Skylar?" Enrique didn't spot her in front. She'd been coming in about five hours each weekday and created systems so they could easily track everything. Parts were ordered the same day he gave her a list and his bottom line was looking better all the time.

They often went to lunch together. Skylar had told him of her parents' divorce and all that came after. And he'd shared myriad stories about his antics with Manny. The two had looked like twins during their middle school years. Sometimes Manny would take tests for Enrique so he could eke out a passing grade in a class. They'd switch clothes in the bathroom and that was all it took. All the worrisome gaps between him and Skylar were closing.

"I'm back here." He found her in his room. The floor sparkled and his cot was made up with a set of clean sheets he'd never seen before. There was now a dresser where he'd kept his duffel and a plush area rug near his cot. She turned. "I hope you don't mind. Andy helped me. I thought you might like it a little more civilized. You mentioned missing things like that."

He closed the door and went to her. "Come here, Shop Girl." Breaking his own rule, he kissed her.

She pushed him away. "Hey. You said—"

"Andy's outside." He cupped the back of her head and took

possession of her mouth, revving the Ferarri that was Skylar when they kissed. She responded like gasoline that met a match, moving against him, lighting him on fire. He groaned. Captured her roving hands and pulled back. *"Tu me vuelves loco."*

"And you don't drive me crazy?" She broke free and held him close. "Enrique, you can't kiss me like that and then slam on the brakes. And you can't tell me one thing and then do another."

"You're right. I'm sorry. I don't know what to do." He rested his chin on her forehead. Waved at the cot. "This is a dump. It's not what I want."

"Well, what do you want?" She stepped back and his brain switched back on.

"I love you. I want …" He wasn't sure if he should voice his fervent wish. It might be too soon. Though she'd adjusted well to caring for Mia, for weeks she'd avoided the subject of Joe altogether. Was it because she was hurting or because she'd made progress?

"Marry me." Her eyes glistened with hope.

"But—"

She put one finger over his lips. "Joe wanted to get married a long time ago. I let my plans get in the way."

"What about Mia?" Enrique hadn't stepped foot inside Skylar's apartment since Mia's arrival.

"I spoke with her therapist last week. Then the three of us talked. Mia wants to meet you. She knows what you did to help her."

"Isn't she completely freaked out about men?"

Skylar leaned against the dresser. "You would think so. But she was raised by her dad. And he was a good man. A little rough around the edges, but totally solid. He left a gang to bring her out here and give her a chance at a better life. Aside from the short time with Shirley, I'm the first real mom she's ever had." Skylar came over to him. "Enrique, I need to know what I love you means to you. Those aren't words I throw around. If you need more time, or you don't want to get married again, you have to be straight with me. I won't get involved with you if that's not where we're headed."

"I lay here every night dreaming of what it would be like to be with you. Not just making love. Everything. Having a home, a family." He grazed her cheek with his thumb. "I would be honored to marry you.

But … I'm old-fashioned. I'd like to do the asking."

"Okay." She sighed, wrapping her arms around him. "Are you free sometime tomorrow?"

"What?" His voice rose an octave.

She laughed. "To meet Mia."

He gave her a squeeze. "I could break away in the afternoon."

"Okay. I have a plan."

He smiled down at her. "Does it involve a dog?"

She poked his ribcage. "Dogs are a great ice-breaker."

"Just so we're clear … In that future I imagine with you, I do not sit on command."

"Yes you do. And you roll over, play dead, fetch—"

"Get back to work, Shop Girl." He propelled her toward the door.

"And you stay." She said this over her shoulder as he guided her through the hall, his hand at the small of her back.

"Always." He patted her bottom.

"How long till we get there?" Mia strained to see through the front window of Skylar's car on Saturday afternoon.

"A few more minutes." Skylar patted Mia's leg.

"Now I know what it's like to have a mom." She couldn't stop grinning. "I wish I could stay with you forever."

"Maybe you should give me more time before you say that, Mia."

Suddenly feeling worried, she gave Skylar a look. "Why?"

"Because sometimes moms have to do things kids don't appreciate. It's not always fun."

"I like eating vegetables."

"You sure do, but there's a little more to it than that." Skylar laughed and switched on the thing that clicked before she turned.

"What is that called?" Mia pointed. She hated not knowing things. And cars were something she knew little about, since her dad couldn't afford one.

"This?" Skylar touched the knob.

"Mmm hmm."

"The blinker. It makes lights blink on the outside of the car so other drivers know I'm going to turn or switch lanes. It's also called a turn signal." They parked in front of a big house. "See." Skylar flipped it up again and a small light turned on and off in front of the steering wheel. "Climb out and go to the back. Look for the light."

Mia got out. Skylar did this all the time, teaching her about things in a way that was fun. She liked that a lot. Sometimes she wrote about it in her journal since she'd already written the good memories of her dad. "I see it."

"Now go look in front."

Mia ran to the front and saw the orange light turning on and off. "Cool." She beamed at Skylar.

Skylar turned off the car and got out. "Are you sure you're okay meeting Whisper? He's a big dog."

Mia nodded. But she wasn't sure at all.

"He's going to bark because he doesn't know you. But he won't hurt you."

"Okay." Mia's heart raced as they moved down the sidewalk. Though she'd never been around dogs, she felt embarrassed to say so. When Whisper ran up to the fence barking loudly, she stiffened and squeezed her eyes shut.

"Whisper, no bark." The dog got quiet and Skylar's arms came around her. Mia opened her eyes as Skylar soothed her back. "See, he listens to me. Whisper, this is Mia. She's a friend."

Mia peeked over and saw the big brown and black dog sitting quietly.

Skylar slipped something into her hand. "This is a dog treat. If you give it to him, he'll know he can trust you."

Keeping a tight hold on Skylar's hand, Mia leaned forward and tossed it through the gate. Whisper snapped it up and wagged his tail wildly. Skylar reached over and scratched his head. He seemed to like it.

"Good. Now put out your hand and let him sniff you. Most of the time, when a dog learns your scent, they stop barking when you show up."

Mia sucked in a breath. Then she slowly reached out, her hand shaking a tiny bit. The dog's breath felt warm and the long stiff hairs that grew near his nose tickled her palm. "What are those?"

"Whiskers." Skylar stroked Mia's hair.

"What are they for?"

"I have no idea. Maybe you can look it up online when we get home. Are you ready? Can I put him on the leash and let him out?"

"Okay." Mia wished she had the courage to say no. Skylar was brave about everything. Mia hated feeling afraid, but she didn't know what to do about it. Looking in a book wouldn't fix it.

"Okay. I'll keep him right next to my leg and you can walk on the other side."

Mia stepped away.

When Skylar attached the leash to his collar, Whisper got even more excited. "Here he comes." The dog stayed near Skylar just like she said.

Mia started breathing again and Skylar took her by the hand. Maybe this wasn't so bad.

"The park is this way." They'd talked in the car about Mia staying close to Skylar at the park. They also talked about how to read people. Mia thought you could only read things that were written, like books and signs. But Skylar told her how to look at what people did with their bodies and what it told you about them. She called it body language. Folded arms, something called body angle, how they used their eyes and where they put their feet. It all meant something. Unless they knew how to fake it, it told you the truth about them. Mia was glad she was so good at remembering because sometimes Skylar told her a lot of things at once.

It got Mia thinking. She told Skylar how Bailey always looked away when he lied. And how Glenda's eyes got smaller right before she pinched Mia. But even though she wanted to, she didn't say that sometimes when the day was going along just fine, a movie of the bad things that had happened after her dad disappeared would start playing in her head. Mia would forget what she was doing and feel like it was happening all over again. Even though Martha, her therapist, told Mia to let Skylar know when the flashbacks happened so Skylar could help, she couldn't make herself do it. Skylar would be disappointed in her. She wasn't afraid of anything. Not bullets. Or bad people. Or driving that big truck like it was a racecar.

Mia patted her pocket to make sure her new cell phone was there. They'd practiced how to use it in case she got lost or something went

wrong at school. Skylar's number was in there and so was Art's, along
with others Skylar thought were important, like her school and Martha
and Shirley. Mia knew to call 911 right away if there was an emergency.
Skylar even got Mia an extra charger and they found a small pocket in
her new backpack where Skylar told her to keep it. Always. *So if the
battery dies and you're not at home, you can find an outlet and charge it up.*
Skylar had smiled when she said it, but Mia saw something else in her
eyes which told her it was really important.

They came to a corner and there was no crossing light. "Mia, tell me
how to cross the street."

Mia scrunched up her face. "You know how to do it."

Skylar touched Mia's shoulder. "I want you to tell me as if I don't
know." Whisper pulled at the leash and Skylar gave it a tug. "Whisper,
sit." The dog sat.

Mia heaved a sigh. "Fine. If you're too dumb—"

Skylar's eyebrows went up. "Hey. It's not okay for you to talk to me
that way."

Mia folded her arms. "You're acting like I'm stupid."

Skylar got to one knee. "Mia, we're new to each other. I don't know
what you know. Crossing the street can be dangerous." She looked
away when the sadness came in her eyes. After a few seconds, she
faced Mia again. "Sometimes cars come really fast. I want you to be
able to do this alone, but first you need to show me that you're good at
it."

Mia felt a sting in her nose. "I'm sorry."

Skylar stood, gave her hand a gentle squeeze. "It's okay. Let's start
over. I'll tell you the things I want you to think about. Then we'll
practice when we go places." Skylar told her about making sure if
there was a car coming that the driver was looking at you or you
should wait. Even when you had a green light or a walk signal. Her
voice got quiet when she said that last part, like she ran out of air.

They got to the park and Mia looked around. "What does Enrique
look like?" She knew he was there the day Skylar had saved her, but
she couldn't remember him.

Skylar smiled. "He has light brown skin and short, dark hair, almost
black. And his eyes are really dark, too." Her voice sounded different
and Mia looked up. Skylar was happy again. More happy than ever

since Mia had come to stay with her. "He's tall and big. Not fat. Just muscular."

Mia scanned the park. "Where are the paddle boats?" That's where they were supposed to meet.

"Up that way. Past the rose garden. To the right."

"Come on! Let's run." Mia tugged Skylar's hand.

"Okay." They laughed as they ran. Whisper's ears moved back and forth and his head turned at every noise.

"There he is! I see him!" Mia sped up, pulling Skylar along. At the same moment she spotted him, he waved and got up off a bench. Mia sneaked a glance at Skylar and saw her big smile.

Skylar gave him a kiss and a hug. Then she turned to Mia. "Mia, this is Enrique Avalos."

"Hi, Mia. I'm glad to meet you. Skylar has told me all about you."

"Hi." Mia stared at his white teeth and dark eyes that got soft when he looked at Skylar. No wonder she was so happy to see him. Mia knew right away he was a good guy. Just like Skylar's dad. She wanted to hug him, but Skylar had told her not to touch people she didn't know well and that they shouldn't touch her.

"What should we do first?" Skylar asked. "Would you like me to push you on the swing?"

"Yeah." Mia wanted to skip, but she didn't since Enrique was there.

Enrique held Whisper while Skylar pushed Mia on the swing. Every time she swung close, Skylar tickled her legs above the knees. Mia laughed more than any time she could remember and Skylar did, too. She thought about what Skylar had said about things not always being fun with your mom. Mia didn't understand that at all. It had been weeks and Mia never wished for another mom. Whenever she daydreamed about being part of a family, she wanted Skylar to be the mother. Mia dragged her feet to stop the swing.

"All done?" Skylar reached for her hand.

Instead of taking it, Mia threw her arms around Skylar's waist. A gush of air escaped Skylar and she leaned down and hugged Mia. Not caring that other kids or Enrique were watching, Mia held tight. Finally, Skylar let go and kissed her cheek.

"Can we go in a boat now?" Mia asked.

Skylar glanced at Enrique. "How much time do you have?"

He looked at his watch. "A few hours."

She sighed, looking embarrassed. "Let's take Whisper home." He shrugged. "Mia, we'll come right back and go out in a boat, okay?" Skylar spoke quietly to Enrique as they walked. "Sorry. I didn't think it through. I'm not good at this yet."

He grabbed her hand. "It's fine."

CHAPTER FORTY-SEVEN

ENRIQUE SAW SKYLAR STIFFEN as they neared the corner on the way to Whisper's house.

"Okay, Mia, what do we do?"

"Look both ways," Mia said huffily. "And hold hands." They all did, Enrique on the right with the dog so Skylar could take Mia's hand on her left, because she'd told him to be sure not to touch Mia yet. They started into the street.

"*Todo va a estar bien.* It's gonna be okay, Sky." Enrique stroked Skylar's hand with his thumb, wondering how close they were to where Joe was killed. After they crossed, he put his arm around her and she leaned into him while Mia walked a little ahead.

"Enrique?" Skylar whispered.

"Yeah?"

"I need to tell you something. Do you want to talk now? Or maybe you could walk me back here when we leave and Mia can wait in the car."

"Are you okay?"

"Yeah." It came out more like a question.

His pulse kicked up a notch.

She put Whisper back in his yard and hung the leash on the fence. She stared at the home next door. He remembered her looking at it the first time they'd come here.

"Mia?" Enrique said.

"What?"

"I need to talk to Sky a minute. Do you mind having a seat in the grass by Whisper's yard?"

She shrugged and sat down.

"What is it?"

Skylar turned them both toward the two-story Craftsman style home with a large covered front porch. "It's not bad, it's just ..." She eyed the front door.

"You used to live here?"

She shook her head. "Joe did."

He slung an arm around her shoulders. Learning Skylar's story was like peeling an onion. Every time he thought he knew everything, there was another layer.

"We planted those roses." She swiped her cheeks. "If I can stop being so emotional, there's actually some good news here." She fanned her face. "It's mine. He bought it for me."

Enrique gaped at her. "You mean it's yours? Free and clear?"

Skylar nodded. "Joe knew a baseball career could be cut short. He wanted to have something paid off so we wouldn't have to worry." She looked up at him. "If things go well between you and Mia ... Well, I know you want to be the one to—" She clamped her eyes shut. "I'm screwing this up."

"No, you're not." He pushed away feelings of inadequacy. This could change things for them. Relieve some pressure. He eyed the black wrought iron fence that bordered the front yard. The back had a wooden privacy fence. The front porch was decorated for fall. "It looks occupied."

"I have tenants on a month-to-month lease. Mike's wife, Janie, handled it for me. She's already contacted them. I want Mia to have a house with a backyard. It's a beautiful home."

He followed the lines of the roof with his gaze. "It is. But are you sure you can live here, Sky?"

"I think so. I love this place. Joe had a lot of work done." She faced him. "But I wasn't sure how you would feel. If you'd be okay with living here. I'll be happy to sell it if you want a fresh start. It's your decision."

Enrique struggled to digest it all. "How about if we talk that through later? We should get going." He signaled to Mia that they were done and they headed back toward the park. Skylar held his hand and Mia skipped in front.

They rented a paddleboat and even though there were two rows of seats, Mia sat on Skylar's lap, taking turns on the pedals. Enrique sat on their left. When they tired of that, they walked around the lake. "I need to run to the restroom," said Skylar. "Mia, do you want to come with me?"

"I already went."

"Oh, that's right." Skylar leaned and whispered in her ear.

Mia flashed her eyes at Skylar. "It's fine." After Skylar was out of earshot, a shy smile came over Mia's face. "Enrique?"

"Yes?" Having her speak directly to him with it being just the two of them made his heart soar, but he tried to act cool.

She toyed with the end of her long braid. He was still struck by what a beautiful child she was, which immediately led to a sad pang. If she weren't so lovely, perhaps she wouldn't have been victimized. She cleared her throat. "Sky is looking after me, but I think someone needs to do that for her."

He raised a brow. "Why do you think that?"

"She told me she was going to get married but he died. His name was Joe. Sometimes, when she thinks I'm occupied, she gets a sad look. And she does this." Mia sighed.

A mix of fascination with Mia and compassion for Skylar filled him. He gave a half-smile. "Occupied? Is that a word you use a lot?"

She clasped her hands behind her back. Now her smile wasn't so shy. "I have a big vocabulary. I'm in third grade but I read at a ninth grade level."

He laughed, reminded of how Skylar had called herself a mathematical genius. Two peas in a pod. "Wow."

"I'm going to be a doctor." Mia dug the toe of her shoe in a crack on the sidewalk.

"I know a lot about emergency medicine."

"You do?" Her eyes widened.

He nodded. "I was a medic in the army."

"What's that?"

He told her about it and offered to teach her what he knew.

"Okay, but you never answered me about taking care of Skylar." Mia pointed, indicating she was on her way back.

"Mia, I think you're right. It's painful when we lose someone we love. I'll do all I can for her." He paused. "And if you think of any ideas, you be sure to let me know."

"I will," Mia said solemnly.

Skylar jogged back. "Are you two getting to know each other?" She eyed Mia as if gauging her reaction to being alone with him.

"Enrique's going to teach me about emergency medicine." Mia beamed. Then she became serious. "But I didn't touch him. And he didn't touch me."

"That's what I thought. I would never leave you with anyone I didn't completely trust." Skylar smiled and gave Mia's shoulder a squeeze. "Are you guys hungry? I think we have just enough time to get something to eat before Enrique has to head back to work."

That evening, Skylar sat on the sofa reading a book. Her cell buzzed. A text from Enrique. *Free to talk?* She couldn't help smiling. "Mia, I need to make a phone call. Do you need anything before I do that?" Mia didn't respond, so she surged to her feet and hurried down the hall. Already in her pajamas, Mia lay in bed, a book on her chest, eyes closed. It was only eight o'clock. Skylar brushed the hair from Mia's face.

"That feels good," Mia said in a breathy half-asleep tone.

Skylar kissed her cheek. "Good night, sweetheart."

Mia's eyelids fluttered and she pulled Skylar down for a hug. "I love you, Sky."

Skylar's heart overflowed. "I love you too, Mia." After turning off the light and closing the door, she practically floated to her room. She lay down on her bed and dialed Enrique. "Hey."

"Hi. I loved hanging out with you guys today."

"Me, too. Mia went on and on about you. All good."

He laughed. "I'm glad." He paused. "I'm staring at the ceiling thinking of you."

"I wish you were here." Skylar touched the place next to her, imagining him there.

"So do I. Hey, I've been thinking about the house. I'd like to go see it before I decide."

"Okay. I'll set something up." She grabbed a pillow from the other side of the bed and hugged it to her chest, pretending it was him. "You were great with Mia today. Thanks for making the time."

"She's a great kid." A pause. "Sky?"

"Yeah?"

"I'd like you to meet my family."

"Okay. But ..." She trailed off. Enrique had told her about the conflict having to do with her.

"But what?"

"What if they don't like me?"

"Then I'll miss them." He laughed.

"I'm serious."

"So am I. It's gonna be fine, *corazon*. I just talked to my dad."

Skylar loved when he called her his sweetheart. "Okay. Enrique?"

"Hmm?"

"Do they know what Mia's been through?"

"Yes."

Skylar sighed, feeling conflicted. If she and Enrique did marry, it was important for them to know, but she felt it was just as important to guard Mia's privacy. "Does the whole family know, or just your parents?"

"My parents. I made it clear that they need to keep it to themselves. Normally, that's a problem with my mom, but she promised."

A pressure lifted from her chest. "How did they take it?"

"Dad offered to send a bunch of my cousins after Devlin and Bailey. Mom cried."

She stared at the ceiling, trying to decide whether to voice her true thoughts.

"What's wrong?"

Skylar massaged the tight muscles in her jaw. "If they're going to meet her, they have to be ... I don't want her treated like a victim, but they need to understand that she might not want to be hugged or go off without me."

"I'll talk to them. But I don't think there's anything to worry about." His soothing tone helped quell her anxiety.

"I know I can't protect her from everything, but this is foreseeable."

"I feel the same way." They finished and clicked off.

CHAPTER FORTY-EIGHT

THE FOLLOWING WEEKEND, ENRIQUE held Skylar's hand as he drove to his parents' place. Despite his request to go out to dinner, Olivia had insisted they come to the house so she could cook. That meant there would be a big crowd. He'd done his best to prepare Skylar and Mia and hoped for no family drama.

"What did you tell your parents about Joe and me?" Skylar glanced back at Mia who was asleep, exhausted after spending the day at the park.

He stopped at a red light and moved his hand to the nape of her neck. He'd figured out she liked to be touched there, especially when she was anxious or upset. "Not a lot. That you were engaged and that you'd known each other since grade school."

"Did they make a big deal about it?"

"Not really. But they were surprised."

Her eyes sparked with anxiety. "And you're sure they'll be good to Mia?"

"If I wasn't, we wouldn't be going." He moved his fingers softly on her neck. "They can't wait to meet both of you."

Skylar's brow furrowed. "Am I a mess after being outside?" She pulled down the mirror in the visor and tugged a brush from her purse.

They'd spent the afternoon at Sloan's Lake Park. "You're beautiful." The light changed and he hit the gas.

"But am I a mess?"

"Just run the brush through your hair. You look great." He moved his hand out of the way.

"You always say that." She began brushing.

"We're talking in circles."

"I'm so nervous."

"No kidding."

"You're not helping."

"I guess I need some instructions."

"Just be quiet." The brush was shoved back in her purse.

"Yes, ma'am." Enrique turned right.

Skylar leaned her head on his shoulder and hugged his arm. "I'm sorry."

He kissed her forehead. "It's okay." He switched on the blinker. "I'm used to the cool, sassy Skylar."

"Me, too. I wish I knew where she was."

They pulled into the trailer park. When Enrique had told her about growing up there, she hadn't reacted negatively. Another marked difference between her and Kendra. When Enrique was young, his father installed flooring and his mother cleaned houses. Later, his father started his own installation company and his mom quit her job so she could manage the office. They could probably afford to live somewhere else, but they'd stayed.

Enrique parked in front of their home, a meticulously maintained double-wide, painted a soft yellow. As she did every fall, his mother had planted mums near the mailbox. The large ash tree that grew near the front was beginning to turn orangish pink. This was home. His stomach did a little flip at the thought of his mom meeting Skylar. After he'd explained what had happened to Mia and how Skylar had put her life on the line to save her, Olivia had gone quiet, no doubt feeling bad about the judgments she'd made, but too proud to acknowledge it. He turned toward Skylar, running his thumb down her cheek. "Thanks for letting me drive. I'm tired of the bike."

"I'm glad you did. I probably would have killed us. I was less freaked with bullets flying through the windshield of my work truck."

He laughed. "You do love being in control."

"I think it's genetic. Apparently, Elana is helping my dad with that. Maybe you can do the same for me." Skylar roused Mia and helped her out of the car.

When they got to the door, Skylar placed a hand on Mia's shoulder and leaned down. "Mia, the house is full of new people. You can tell me if you feel overwhelmed. Or if you're uncomfortable. And you can —"

Mia cupped Skylar's cheeks. "Enrique already told me. You need to chill out, Sky."

Skylar watched in amazement when Mia grabbed hold of Enrique's hand as he knocked on the door. He winked at Mia.

A crowd came to the door, sucking them in like the vortex of a tornado. Simultaneous exclamations in Spanish were followed by exuberant hugs. Enrique was the only recipient of said hugs since Skylar was cowering behind him and had Mia ensconced behind her. He turned to face her. Placing his hand at the small of her back, he drew her out of hiding with Mia in tow. "*Mami*, this is Skylar." The warmth in his gaze gave her courage.

"Skylar, it's so nice to meet you." A short woman with dark wavy hair and the same eyes as Enrique took Skylar's hand. She wore black slacks and a colorful sweater. "I'm Olivia. Welcome."

Skylar returned her greeting. "Olivia, this is Mia." Skylar smoothed her hand over Mia's back.

"Mia, I'm so glad you came. Did you have fun at the park today?" Olivia wrapped Mia in a hug.

Skylar froze, unsure how Mia would react to the display of affection. Hadn't Enrique spoken to them?

"Yes," Mia answered excitedly. "We played soccer. Enrique's really good. He can bounce the ball with his knees forever. Then we fed the ducks. They were so cute. The babies swam in a line behind their mommy." She peered behind Olivia at a little girl who was close to her age.

Olivia noticed and brought her forward. "Mia, this is Enrique's cousin, Carmen. She brought some toys if you'd like to go play."

Mia turned toward Skylar, who leaned down to tell her she didn't have to. But Mia whispered in Skylar's ear. "I'll come check on you in a little while."

Skylar's eyes widened and her jaw hung slack as Mia took the hand Carmen held out.

Enrique cut off the introductions. "We'll be right back." He took Skylar's cold hand in his warm one and led her down a hall and into a bathroom.

Skylar glanced around. "Um … Are we looking for something to medicate me?" She opened the vanity cabinet.

Enrique spun her toward him and wrapped her in his arms. "I want you to enjoy yourself." He kissed her forehead. "Mia's fine. Can you settle down?"

She clasped her arms around him, basking in his warmth. "I'll try. But maybe there's something in there that will help." She chinned toward the cabinet.

"I have something better." He cupped her face, then kissed her, teasing with his tongue until she opened to him.

Warmth exploded inside her and she slid her hands beneath his shirt, exploring his taut abs.

"Whoa." Enrique pulled away and captured her hands. "I just wanted to get you refocused."

"Well, you did," she hissed. "Thanks a lot. Now I won't be able to string a sentence together."

He grinned wickedly. "You're welcome. And you don't need to worry about talking because my mom and sisters will do it. Let's go." He led her back into the fray, where she met his father, Juan Pablo. Aside from his mother's eyes, this was where Enrique got his good looks. But where had he gotten his height? Though he had the same solid build, Juan Pablo was a good six inches shorter than his son.

Next, she met his three sisters and their respective husbands and children. Skylar shook each hand and immediately forgot every name but Juan Pablo. She cast a nervous glance at Enrique who gave her a smile that stoked her fire again. *Great.* When she narrowed her eyes at him in a silent threat, someone laughed nearby.

Skylar turned to see Olivia whispering to her husband behind her hand. Juan Pablo had the decency to go into the kitchen before he guffawed. She leaned close to Enrique and muttered, "I'm going to join Mia and Carmen. Even if I have to play dolls."

He hooked an arm around her waist and pulled her back against him. "They love you," he whispered. The feel of his breath on her neck brought a frisson of pleasure. Which threatened to shut down what was left of her brain.

"How do you know that? Maybe they're just being polite."

"Trust me. My mom does not hide her feelings. It's not in her DNA."

"I'm starving." She shrugged Enrique off like a coat.

"I can see why. You've burned a lot of nervous energy in the last hour."

As if on cue, Olivia waved an arm toward the kitchen. "Let's eat. The food's getting cold."

Everyone moved like a school of fish toward the counter that was laden with food. Mouthwatering smells wafted up from each dish and they began filling plates. Enrique told her what was what and she chose homemade tamales, refried beans and Mexican rice. There was also pulled pork that melted in her mouth.

Animated conversations swirled like so many dust devils. She quickly realized Enrique and Juan Pablo were the only calm members of his immediate family. When the women spoke, hands waved and eyes widened, expressing what words alone could not. She was grateful he stuck close the whole evening, often explaining in English what people were saying in Spanish. At one point, Skylar laughed.

"What?" he asked.

"It takes twice as long to say everything in English."

"I know." He pointed. "Look at Mia. It's like she's always been part of the family."

They eyed Mia, who sat with Carmen, the two of them talking excitedly. Skylar caught his gaze. "This is so good for her." Her eyes filmed over and he gave her a gentle squeeze.

"I think it's good for you, too."

She laced their fingers under the table.

When they finished eating, Skylar went toward the kitchen to help clean up.

Jasmine intercepted her. "We have to talk." They ended up in the bathroom, which—if today was any indicator—was the only sacrosanct room in the house, the place where every private meeting was held. Jasmine's eyes glistened with tears. "I owe you an apology."

"What?" Taken aback by the sudden confession, Skylar touched Jasmine's arm.

"*Mami* told me what you did for Mia. I wanted to—"

Skylar stiffened. "She told you what happened to Mia?"

"Yes." Jasmine's face fell. "She wasn't supposed to?"

Skylar grabbed hold of the doorknob.

"Wait. I need to tell you something."

Skylar blew out a breath and turned to face Jasmine.

"I misjudged you. I'm sorry for what I did, calling *Mami* behind Enrique's back."

"Thank you." Skylar felt like a pressure cooker about to blow. "Maybe we can talk more about that later."

"But, what's wrong?" Jasmine's question was left unanswered because Skylar was already moving through the hallway.

Olivia stood near the table talking to Enrique. He stopped mid-sentence when he saw Skylar's face. "What's wrong?"

"Can we talk?"

He ushered her toward the entryway. "What is it?"

The things Mia suffered flashed in her mind and her throat tightened painfully. She swiped at a tear.

"Honey, what's wrong?"

"Jasmine knows about Mia. I thought you talked to your parents."

"I did." He glanced in his mom's direction. "What happened?"

"Jasmine says Olivia told her everything." Her body began to shudder. "I have to go. I'm so upset. It's not fair to Mia—" she choked off. "She's not going to be nine years old forever and she'd be so hurt if …" Skylar sucked in a breath.

Enrique's jaw tightened and he looked at the ceiling. "I'm sorry. I thought I could trust her. I'll get Mia and meet you in the car."

Skylar was putting on her coat when Juan Pablo walked over. "Please accept my apologies." Color crept up his neck. "I'll make sure this doesn't go any further. It won't happen again." He seemed to be barely in control of his temper.

There was something akin to an electrical current in the house. The hum of conversation had come to a halt and Skylar felt everyone's eyes on her. She attempted a smile and shook his hand, clearing her throat. "It kills me that I wasn't able to keep those things from happening to Mia, but I hope you understand that I'm not going to allow her to be victimized again by letting people know what she went through when it's none of their business."

His face was solemn. "I understand."

She felt her chin quiver and her eyes filled. "Thank you for dinner."
She let herself out, taking lungfuls of cool night air, which did a great
deal to calm her. The door opened and she turned, expecting to see
Enrique.

Olivia stood on the mat. "I thought Jasmine should know. She won't
tell anyone else." An I-know-best voice.

"But that wasn't your decision to make. You gave Enrique your
word."

Olivia bristled, then seemed to soften. "Okay then." She waved a
hand.

Skylar could see that this was all she was going to get. Olivia Avalos
was a proud woman. But she'd raised Enrique. He'd told her about
their relationship in their days at the shop. His mother held a special
place in his heart. And she'd put on this huge meal to welcome Skylar
into her inner circle, despite her earlier judgments. "Olivia, I want Mia
to get past what happened to her. I don't think it's fair to her if anyone
knows about it that doesn't absolutely need to. It could come up later
and cause her a lot of pain."

Olivia's eyes watered. "I wish ..." Her hands fisted.

Skylar inhaled slowly so her throat wouldn't close. "So do I. But it
happened. If you want to be in Mia's life, I have to trust you. I
promised her I would never leave her with someone I don't trust
completely. And I'd really like to have your help." That last sentence
was merely an olive branch. One that nearly choked her. But it was Mia
that mattered. And Skylar believed that Olivia had a big heart to go
along with her big mouth. How else would Enrique have become who
he was?

"Well." Olivia lifted her chin.

Enrique came out with Mia. *"Adios, Mami."*

Avoiding his gaze, Olivia wrapped Mia in a hug. "Goodbye, *nena.*"

"Bye," Mia chirped.

They were quiet on the way home. After several minutes, Mia said,
"Are you guys in a fight?"

Skylar tipped her head back. She didn't know what they were in.
The only conflict had been with his mother.

"Not exactly," said Enrique.

"What does that mean? Either you are or you aren't."

Skylar turned to face Mia. "Mia, we're upset. But it's not something we're going to talk about with you."

"Or in front of me?" She sounded disappointed.

"That's right, because it doesn't concern you."

"Are you mad at Olivia?"

Enrique and Skylar shared a look. The child didn't miss a thing.

"Mia, it's not appropriate for you to keep asking about it. After the two of us talk, we'll let you in on anything we think you should know."

"Are you guys breaking up?" There was a tremor in her voice.

Enrique pulled the car over. He turned and put his hand on Mia's knee. "Mia, Skylar and I need to work through something. We're not angry at each other and we're not breaking up." He gave Skylar a questioning look.

"He's right. Don't worry, honey." Skylar held his hand the rest of the way, grateful he hadn't let his mother come between them.

"Okay." Mia stifled a yawn and lay down on the seat.

CHAPTER FORTY-NINE

ENRIQUE CARRIED MIA INTO Skylar's apartment and laid her gently in bed. She murmured something but her eyes remained closed. He touched her cheek. "Is it okay if I kiss her goodnight?" Skylar smiled and nodded. He bent and brushed a light kiss on her forehead.

"I'll be out in a few minutes," Skylar whispered.

He watched from the stool at the counter as she walked Mia, now in pajamas, to and from the bathroom like a zombie. When she came out, they both slumped on the sofa.

Skylar kicked off her shoes and snuggled close to him. "Are you upset with me? For leaving?"

He sighed. "I'm upset with my mom. I can't believe she did that. I was very clear."

"I know how much your family means to you. It was a wonderful evening until then."

"What exactly happened?"

"Jasmine pulled me into the bathroom to apologize for calling your mom that time at the shop. She started by telling me she knew what I'd done for Mia. I was so pissed that she knew, I walked out without letting her finish." Skylar looked up at him. "Imagine how Mia would feel if someone brought it up. Especially as she gets older." Her eyes glazed.

Enrique stroked her shoulder lightly. "I'm so sorry." His heart clenched at the thought of what Mia had been through. The last thing he wanted was to cause her more pain. "I've never been so angry at my mom. I wanted to throttle her."

"Me, too." Skylar's hand went to his thigh and gave a soft squeeze. "Thank you for standing by me."

He looked down at her. "I'll always stand by you. I love my mom but she's not going to come between us."

"Okay." Her shoulders relaxed and she leaned into him. "Sorry I got all freaky on the way over there."

He laughed. "I've never seen you like that."

"Neither have I." They both went quiet.

After a minute, Enrique tipped her chin up. "Are we okay?"

"We're great." But anxiety sparked in her eyes. "I feel so protective of Mia, it scares me sometimes. It's like I turn into a mama grizzly. I can't explain it. It still doesn't feel real what I did the day I got her out. And now I want to teach her everything I know so she can defend herself. I'm turning into my dad."

He smiled. Kissed her temple. "Well, it's not like you smother her. You're giving her the confidence to stand up for herself. She's lucky to have you in her life."

"She really likes your mom. And Carmen." Skylar sighed. "She didn't mind at all when your mom hugged her. I don't want to keep good things out of her life. She needs family. I feel like I don't know what I'm doing."

"Don't be so hard on yourself. My dad's probably flaying my mom right now. She should have asked our permission before she opened her mouth." He stretched, slouching lower on the sofa. "I like you, but I am in love with this couch."

She elbowed his ribs. "It cost big bucks."

"I'm afraid to ask how much."

"You don't want to know." Skylar pushed up and kissed his cheek.

He sighed. "Did you see Mia take my hand when we went to the door?"

She nodded. "I almost cried."

"And I finally got to hold her tonight." He glanced toward the hall. "I'm falling in love with her."

"Mia's so easy to love." Skylar shifted, resting her head on his shoulder. "The other night when I tucked her in bed, she told me she loved me."

Enrique put a hand over his heart. "Wow."

"I can't believe she's so full of life and hope after all she's been through."

"A lot of that is your doing, Sky. Most people would have called it good getting her out of that place. You've become a mother to her." He moved a tendril of hair behind her ear.

"I get more than I give." Her fingers moved softly over his forearm, a comfortable silence falling between them.

It was funny how her touch affected him, sometimes calming and soothing, other times igniting a fire.

Skylar covered a yawn. "I feel like I'm finding my way out of the dark." She drew his hand to her lips and kissed it, rubbing his knuckles against her soft cheek. "Thank you for not listening when I begged you to make love to me."

"It wasn't easy." He nuzzled her neck. "It still isn't. But you needed time."

"About that ... it's not very romantic but now that Mia's here, spontaneity is off the table. I feel ready now." She wended her fingers in his hair. "What about you?"

"I do, too. But the only time we're alone is when Andy has to test-drive a bike when we're both at the shop. And there's no way ..." He tipped his head back, releasing a frustrated sigh. "I never imagined anything like this."

"What do you mean?" Skylar shifted toward him.

"It's like planning an invasion. All the logistics."

"I know. It's complicated. But I'm committed to Mia. I need to know if that's a deal breaker for you."

"Please don't take it that way. I love kids. And Mia ... I'd do anything for her."

"What should we do? I wouldn't feel right having you sleep here. I feel like Mia needs a real family. Something solid. For that matter, so do I."

"We all do." Enrique knew what he needed to do. And it *was* logistics. But he supposed every parent had to coordinate stuff like this. They would just have to start early. "Did you set up a time for us to see the house?"

"Actually, the tenants' new house is done and they'll move out early if I prorate the rent. If you can get away, I'll take you over on Wednesday. Mia and I are going to move in next weekend."

That surprised him. She hadn't mentioned it since she'd told him it was his decision to live there or not. But he didn't want to bring it up on top of the conflict with his mom. "Do you need help?"

"I hired a moving company."

He eyed her. "Can you afford that now that you're not working?" Money was one thing they hadn't discussed in detail. For his part, it was because his situation carried so much shame. The shop was on a good track, but it bothered him deeply to be in such a huge hole. He resisted the urge to reignite his resentment toward Kendra, reminding himself they wouldn't have to worry about a house payment.

"I'll be right back." Skylar left the room, returning a minute later with some files, which she passed to him.

They were filled with financial statements. There were lots of zeros at the end of each number in the current balances. He gave her a questioning look.

"Joe's dad is a financial planner. He helped Joe set up a number of accounts. The taxes were all paid up front. Plus there was an insurance policy. I was the beneficiary." Her tone was maudlin.

Given her aptitude with numbers, it was odd how she'd fobbed the files off on him rather than reviewing them together. The statements made it clear she could live wherever she wanted. "Why did you move here, Skylar?"

She got up and went to the kitchen. "I think Alex nailed it. I was punishing myself."

Enrique set the papers aside and went to her. He took the teakettle out of her hands and placed it on the stove. "Are you done now?"

Tears streaked her cheeks. "I want to be. I'm moving out." She glanced at the papers. "But it feels like blood money. There's no pleasure in spending it."

"Oh, honey." Enrique opened his arms and she walked into his embrace. He moved his hands softly over her back. "Do you know what you want to do with it?"

She shook her head. "I've been avoiding it. The only thing I know for sure is that if we get married, I won't sign a pre-nup. So don't even go there."

He smiled into her hair. "I can't get over the irony. You are so not about money."

"I don't want it to come between us. If that happens, I'll give it all away. I have a masters degree. Once Mia is stable, I can go back to work. And you have the shop." She glanced up at him. "Does this change things for you?"

"Sure it does."

She stepped back. "What? How?"

"It makes me sure you're the one. You've got this big pile of money and you're not drooling over it." He gave a half-smile. "You're not planning cruises and buying nice cars."

Skylar batted at him. "Don't scare me like that."

Enrique filled the tea kettle. "How do you feel about this: we can create a budget together and live on your money until the shop can support us. You can go back to work if you want to, but I love having you at the shop. Or, if you need time to think about it, we can wait to to get married. Without a pre-nup, it's all community property after that. I want you to think it through."

"No. I told you … I waited before." Over a cup of hot tea, they sat at the table and discussed their priorities, finally coming around to the topic of children.

"What if things don't work out with Mia's family?"

"I hope they don't. Maybe it's selfish, but I want to adopt her. She's afraid to go back to California. How do you feel about having an instant family?"

"Good. Really good. But we need to figure out how to make it all work. How about we take off after Mia goes to school on Monday? We can take a drive in the mountains and work out the details." He stood and pulled her to her feet. "If I don't get going, I'll be too tired to drive."

"You're amazing." She held him. "I feel … blessed."

"Me, too."

CHAPTER FIFTY

AFTER DROPPING MIA AT school Monday morning, Skylar headed to the shop. A cooler full of food and drinks sat on the back seat. She thrummed with excitement at the idea of spending most of a day with Enrique away from her apartment and his shop. She parked and knocked on the back door.

Enrique opened it, looking ridiculously handsome in his best jeans and a new patterned button-down shirt with the cuffs turned up once. *"Mi tesoro."* Without waiting for her to respond, he pulled her inside and kissed her as though he were starved.

"What does that mean?" she asked as his lips moved softly over her neck.

"My treasure. I feel like a kid at Christmas. I woke up two hours early and couldn't get back to sleep," he whispered. The way his hands moved over her confirmed his longing and fanned her own.

Skylar moaned. "We have to go."

"Okay." But he cupped her face and kissed her one last time. Merciless.

"Are you trying to kill me?" Skylar opened the door and sucked in a breath of cool morning air while he locked up. "Do you have somewhere in mind? I think I packed enough food for two days."

"I have a plan. Do you mind if I drive?"

She passed him the keys. He drove to I-70 and headed west. "So where should we start?" She figured, the sooner they worked out the details of combining their lives, the sooner they could focus on enjoying each other. A clock in her head ticked down the minutes until Mia got out of school.

"Where we're going isn't far. How about we leave the serious talking for later?"

Disappointment weighed heavily, but she didn't complain. At least they were alone. She plugged her phone into the stereo and played some music. Soon after they got to the mountains, he slowed and took an exit. "Are we going to see the buffalo?" The city of Denver kept a herd nearby.

"Nope." He took a frontage road, then turned on a dirt driveway that wound up a hill. It was rutted and full of potholes.

"You're not gonna screw up my car are you?" Skylar braced on the armrest.

"I've been here before." He deftly avoided the potholes and ruts. Trees closed around them and the road ascended steeply. Finally, it leveled off and he parked in front of a small white cottage with blue shutters.

Skylar made a small gasp when she saw it.

"I'll get your door." He went around and opened it, helping her out.

Her hand went to her throat as she stared at the quaint structure. "It's beautiful." Three wide steps led to a porch supported by a stone foundation. An array of flowerpots graced the left side and two red lanterns stood sentry on either side at the top of the steps. A white wooden bench with ornate carvings on the back perched beneath a window that was flanked by blue shutters. Above the front door, the roofline formed an A. In the middle was a small balcony with blue railings.

"Would you like to see the inside?" He had a comical look on his face.

"Sorry. I'm stunned. I thought we were going to be outside." A nervous laugh escaped. "Yes. Show me." Skylar's heart turned to liquid. During their hours at the shop, she'd talked of her love of the mountains. "How did you get this on such short notice?"

"The owner's a friend." Enrique smiled and unlocked the door, waving her in with a flourish. Suddenly feeling shy, she tucked her hands in her pockets and moved through the small entry. A floral sofa and an area rug sat atop a knotty pine floor in front of a large stone fireplace. A small built-in bookshelf was home to a plethora of books. He came behind her and molded her to him. "We're going to save the planning for the ride home. Until then, this is about us. You and me."

Warm kisses trailed her neck. She tried to turn so she could get to him, but he held her fast. "I'm not done yet. Be patient."

A hot thrill shot through her. "I don't want to be patient."

Ignoring her complaint, his lips worked their way to the other side of her neck, setting her on fire.

"This isn't fair." She struggled and he quickly contained her again, binding her arms to her body while he pillaged every inch of exposed skin with his mouth. Desperate with yearning, she heard herself beg, "Enrique, please." Finally, he released her and she spun toward him. After several minutes of fervent kisses, she said, "Don't ever do that again."

Enrique flashed a grin. "Okay. But it was fun. You've got that whole control thing going on."

Skylar smacked his arm.

"Come with me." He took her hand and led her to … the kitchen? Then they kept going. Right out the back door.

Skylar glanced over to see a smug smile lighting his face. Her irritation mingled with curiosity. "What are we doing?"

"You told me you love to hike. And there's a trail right over there."

"After what you just started?" She skidded to a stop, both hands parked on her hips. "You are evil."

"Skylar, come." Laughter rumbled from his traitorous chest as he strode toward the base of a trail that appeared to go straight up the mountainside.

"Very funny." Nevertheless, she obeyed, unable to resist this new facet of him. But if he told her to heel, she might just strangle him. No, she definitely would.

He grabbed her hand and towed her along the trail at a good clip, letting go and preceding her when it narrowed. It zig-zagged up a steep hill that rendered her breathless. Which was good, because some of the things she considered saying to him about this cruel torment would not make fond memories.

They came to a natural landing, a small flat spot with a view of peaks to the west. "Isn't it beautiful?" His face was guileless and she relaxed, reminding herself that Enrique had been slaving indoors at the shop for the entire summer.

"It is. Have you been here before?"

Enrique nodded. "I did some work here. One of the odd jobs I had after my tour."

She snaked her arm around his waist. "What a great place to work. Did you have to drive up every day?"

He shook his head. "I stayed here. It was during my almost-homeless stint. Right after I filed for divorce. This place helped keep me sane. There was wood to chop when I needed to hit something. I hiked this at sunrise and sunset, no matter how tired I was." He cast a wistful glance around them.

"Well, if I have anything to say about it, you'll never be almost-homeless again." Skylar moved her hand over his back, as much for herself as for him. The thought of Enrique not having a place to call home ate at her. But he didn't want charity. After weeks of working with him at the shop, knowing he motorcycled to the Y for a shower each morning profoundly affected her. The weather was changing and he often returned shivering, his lips a purplish-blue. One day, she'd offered to drive him or let him borrow her car. He'd thanked her and asked her not to bring it up again.

The same fierce feeling of protectiveness she felt toward Mia manifested just as strongly with him. It wasn't as though he needed her protection in a physical sense. But she wished there were something more she could do, some way to demonstrate her feelings without making him feel weak or inadequate. Because neither was true.

"Hey." A soft nudge jarred her from her thoughts.

"Sorry. I was just thinking."

"About what?"

She kicked a stone and it rolled down the hill. "You."

Enrique took a small foil-wrapped square from his pocket. "I brought chocolate." He opened it and popped it in his mouth. "Didn't you say you like chocolate?"

"No." She pointedly drew out the word. "I said I *love* chocolate." Skylar waited for him to give one to her. But he didn't.

"Want some?" His husky tone told her he wasn't only talking about chocolate.

Skylar tilted her head, trying to adjust to this abrupt change in him. It seemed like he'd shed some invisible layer, a weight of some kind. "You know I do."

Enrique took another one from his pocket and unwrapped it, taking half of it into his mouth. "Come and get it."

Ignoring her pride, she moved toward him, her hand outstretched. He used her forward momentum to pull her to him. "No ... Like this." His breath smelled of chocolate. And him. One finger under her chin, he coaxed her lips open and kissed her, tasting and feeling so good that her knees actually went weak. She grabbed for his shoulders and his hands came to the small of her back. They didn't part until the chocolate was gone. Kissing Enrique was like diving in a pool on a hot summer day. Although, instead of cooling her off, it heated her up. "Come on. It gets better." He took her by the hand, tugging her up the path.

"What is this?" she groused. "Some new sort of cross-training? Or enhanced interrogation techniques you learned in the army?" Frustration and longing competed inside her.

"Quit whining. This is going to be worth it." Another laugh wrung from him. She loved the sound of it—pure joy. He'd definitely crossed over some precipice. Probably not unlike the corner she'd turned after being with him. They had hours in front of them, so there was no rush. Gratitude filled her and the frustration dissipated.

After several more minutes of the upward climb, they ascended a set of stone steps that led to a gazebo. Skylar's breath caught as she took in the panoramic view—mountains to the west and the entire Denver area to the east. She released a long breath.

"Tim calls this the eagle's nest." Once more, he wrapped her in a hug from behind and she didn't fight him this time. She felt treasured, desired, loved. And nothing stole the feelings away. "I thought you'd like it up here."

Another gasp of pleasure escaped her as he slowly turned them. The sky was a brilliant blue, the sun glinting off the tops of the trees. Only a few lazy clouds floated above. Her whole body calmed as the stress of her world fell away. "There are no words for this, Enrique." A cool breeze blended perfectly with warm rays of sunlight. She turned and held him. "You have no idea how much I needed to get away."

"We both did." He glanced down. "And I want us to do this kind of thing often. Just the two of us, when Mia's in school."

"Can you do that?" What she really meant was *would* he do that.

"I need to. I can't live like I have been anymore. No matter how busy life gets, we're going to take care of us. I don't feel so pressured now."

Hearing him say that without any prodding buoyed her heart. It was clear he wanted to provide for his family, that he'd continue to work hard to that end even though he didn't have to. It was a matter of pride for him, self-respect. And she loved him for that. But it lifted her knowing that she could play a role in easing his burden with the money she had. It took the edge off the pain she felt when she thought of it.

They sat on a bench near the railing, arms pretzeled around each other, listening to the subtle forest symphony; wind rustling in the trees, the occasional chattering squirrel, bird calls, and quiet. Blissful quiet.

After a time, Enrique shifted. "I stopped by your dad's house yesterday."

CHAPTER FIFTY-ONE

ENRIQUE ENJOYED THE MOMENTARY shock on Skylar's face when she learned he'd paid her father a visit. "I had a question to ask him."

Her breath became shallow.

"I love you," he said. "It started the moment I laid eyes on you. I fought it, but you lured me in with kindness. Even though I didn't deserve it." He got to one knee and held out the ring he'd purchased the day before. "There's no woman more lovely, more brave, and more trouble than you." That got him an eye roll. "Skylar, will you marry me?"

"*Sí*. I will. Yes." He lost track of how many times she said it. Skylar let him slip the ring on her finger, then she pulled him to his feet for a lingering kiss. "I thought I would never be happy again." She rested her head against his chest.

Enrique held her tighter. "I know we'll have good days and bad days. But I want us to turn toward each other when things are tough … never away."

"So do I."

The wind kicked up. "Let's get back down."

"Wait." She pulled out her cell phone and took a few photos of the two of them. Then some of the view. This moved him. Every moment was poignant, none taken for granted. Their combined pain lent them a depth of gratitude for each day, each new experience. They were careful with each other, Skylar so tender and he so attentive. Life's trials would surely work to erode this, but he would resist. He was certain she would as well.

He helped her down the stone steps, then went in front down the trail.

"How soon do you want to get married?" Skylar's fingers touched his side briefly as they scrambled down the uneven path.

He loved how she always connected. She often did that at work when no one was watching; a soft touch on his arm or his shoulder, a kind word when things went wrong. "It's up to you, Sky."

They got to the landing where they'd stopped on the way up. She tugged his arm. "Do you mean that? Could it be soon?"

Enrique shrugged. "Of course." He got her moving again. "What time do we need to leave if we go straight to get Mia from school?"

"Two thirty."

"Okay." He glanced at his watch. They had plenty of time.

She stopped to pick up a pinecone, smiling as she stuffed it in her coat pocket. "Something to remember this by." When they got to level ground, Skylar placed her hands on his shoulders. "Request permission to come aboard."

He chuckled. "Permission granted."

She hopped up and he caught her legs, carrying her piggy-back to the door. Before she dismounted, she nibbled his earlobe. "I'm hungry."

So was he. In more ways than one. "I'll get the cooler." When he returned, she dug out two apples, offering one to him. "What else is in here?" He rooted around, pulling out a carton of fresh strawberries. She'd washed and hulled them so they were ready to eat. "How about these?"

"Sure. Will you show me around?"

He passed her a few strawberries and led her to the stairs, indicating for her to go in front.

"You first." She lifted one brow and he knew it was not a request.

And so it begins. He smirked, guessing she was checking him out as they ascended the steep stairs.

"I'm not checking you out."

How did she do that? "Yes you are."

She laughed and pushed him up the rest of the way, stopping suddenly when her eyes took in the room. Or, more to the point, the bed he'd covered with rose petals. The loft's antique furniture and angled ceilings lent an intimate feel.

Enrique pulled her into his arms. "You said you were ready. I wanted it to be special. Something we'll never forget. But if this is too sudden—"

"No." Her gaze traveled the room. "Oh my gosh, when did you do this?" Color seeped into her cheeks. "You did do this right? I'd be so embarrassed if Tim did this for you. I'd never be able to—"

He shut her up with a kiss.

"What about birth control?" she murmured. "We didn't talk about —"

"I've got it covered." He tasted her skin as he peeled off her jacket.

A soft smile—one reserved only for him—crept over her face. *"Quiero ser tuya."*

She wanted to be his. *"Quiero que seas mío."* He wanted the same. The fact that she'd said it in Spanish touched a place in his heart that only she could. It was as though she got the essence of him. Wanted the man that he was, not some American remake. Other women always wanted to change him. The way he dressed, his hair or his job. He could sense it from a first date when they made subtle suggestions couched in a compliment. Skylar wanted to know him. And he loved her for that.

Skylar unbuttoned his shirt, smoothing her hands down his chest and over his stomach. Her eyes went to his tattoo and she gently traced it with a finger before pressing her lips there. "Dark Horse," she whispered almost reverently, not pressing him for a response.

They took turns removing the rest of their clothes. When Enrique finally gazed upon the woman he'd been dreaming about, he sucked in a breath. Loose blond waves trailed over her breasts, partially concealing them like a sheer curtain. His breath caught. Using both hands, he slowly traced the curve from her hips to where it narrowed at her waist in an exquisite line. "You … you're … *belleza*. So beautiful."

Her eyes sparkled. "So are you." She pulled him to her, roaming the contours of his shoulders and ribs with her soft touch. Her arms circled his neck and she kissed him before pulling him down on the bed.

Their first coupling was crazed, a mad dash to the finish. All their pent up desire exploding like fireworks. As she did in everything,

Skylar gave herself fully to loving him. He returned the favor, eager to learn what pleased her, teasing and coaxing until she was breathless from pleasure. After hours of loving, Skylar lay in the crook of his shoulder, her arm draped over his waist. "It breaks my heart that you sleep in that windowless room."

He stroked her hair. "Tell me what you want, Sky."

"Let's get married today."

Enrique thought about that, not even sure it was possible. "How do you think Mia would take it?"

She sighed. "I don't know. She might be sad."

He pulled the comforter over her shoulder. "I think you'd regret your parents not being there."

She pushed up and captured his gaze. "But it kills me to know how you live. And I want you to be with me. As my husband."

The truth of it shone in her eyes. It nearly undid him. "I'll be fine." He curled a strand of her hair around his finger. "It won't take long to plan a small wedding. In the meantime, how about I come over for dinner every night? That will give the three of us some time together."

"I would love that. Mia would, too." Skylar gave him a lingering kiss. "I'm starving. I'll go get us some food." She slipped out of the bed.

He eyed her as she ran her hands through her hair, straightening the tangles.

"What?"

"Get back in here. We're not done yet."

"In a minute." She put on his shirt, fastened one button, and disappeared down the stairs.

Aside from the time he'd stayed at her place, Enrique hadn't been in a real bed for nearly eight months. And this one was soft with a down comforter. He kept telling himself to go down and help her, but his body rebelled. The warm bed lulled him into unconsciousness.

He awoke to find Skylar propped against the headboard beside him, a pillow tucked behind her. She plucked a grape from a plate loaded with food and popped it in her mouth. "Hungry?"

"For you," he said sleepily.

"Sorry. I'm like a hummingbird. I have to eat a lot to maintain my pace."

"I've noticed that." He ran his hand up her thigh. Desire surged again.

She nudged him. "You don't want to get out of here, do you?"

"I think I'm gonna need a tow."

Skylar laughed. "Relax. We're not in a hurry. I brought you sustenance." She offered him a grape. He opened his mouth and she placed it on his tongue. Her fingers lightly combed through his hair. She probably had no idea how soothing it was.

"I love when you do that."

"Good. I can't keep my hands off you."

"You don't have to." He brought her hand to his lips.

Smiling, she stood and passed him the plate. "I want to gather these rose petals."

"There's a cleaning person. Tim rents this place out a lot."

"I want to save them." She began picking them up and placing them in a small paper bag she must have found in the kitchen.

After he finished eating, she climbed in and lay next to him. "If you're tired, I'll set the alarm on my phone and we can take a nap."

"I didn't come here to sleep." He unbuttoned the shirt she had on and helped her out of it.

CHAPTER FIFTY-TWO

THE FOLLOWING SUNDAY, ENRIQUE drove his motorcycle down the alley to Skylar's house, stopping behind the garage. The door was open and he saw her moving things around inside.

"Hey." She waved him in. "I cleared some space for your cycle."

He parked and set the kickstand.

She passed him a remote and a set of keys. "The remote will get you in here. The key with the green top is for the house. The blue one unlocks that door." She indicated a door that led to the backyard.

"Thanks. Tell me about this." He went to examine a vintage yellow sports car with a wide black stripe down the center of the hood.

Skylar forked a hand through her hair. "Oh … that's Joe's. I mean, it *was*. It's a seventy-seven Triumph Spitfire. I gave the tenants a break on the rent so I wouldn't have to move it."

"Does it run?" Enrique eyed the convertible. The paint looked original and was in excellent condition. A small British flag flanked each front fender.

"I'm not sure. He got it last year, but to my knowledge, he never drove it." Her arms wrapped around her mid-section. "I don't know what to do with it." Shadows had reappeared in her eyes, worse than any time since he'd known her. Accustomed to seeing her happy and energetic, this sudden shift was alarming.

He closed the gap between them. "Maybe Alex or Joe's father would want it."

"Do you think that would be okay? I feel like I'm sweeping Joe under the rug."

Wanting to reestablish their connection, Enrique touched the small of her back. They'd enjoyed making dinner together until she and Mia moved. Then they'd taken a few days off so they could get settled here. He regretted it now. "What stands out the most to you about Joe?"

Skylar met his gaze, her face a question. He lifted his chin, encouraging her to speak freely. "Joe was so funny. He'd tease my mom." A spark of happiness lit her face. "And *nobody* teases my mom. He was confident. Cocky, like you, but more outgoing. A total extrovert. And patient. Really patient. Especially with me. And he loved kids."

This was like covert ops. She needed to process, to feel safe talking about Joe. And he needed to know she was his, that they'd be able to forge a new life without Joe in the middle. Somehow, he'd have to help her without making things worse for either of them. He sent up a silent prayer asking for help. "So how does this car play into that for you?"

Skylar's face fell. "It makes me never want to come out here because it reminds me of all the things that will never be. The things I put off, thinking we had plenty of time."

Well, that didn't work. "How important do you think the car was to Joe?" He tried again.

A shrug. "Not very. He never had time to do anything with it. He bought it after his shoulder injury. I think it was a just-in-case thing; something to keep him busy during the interim. He'd had surgery on his rotator cuff. After physical therapy, he couldn't pitch anymore, but he could do stuff like this. Then the thing with South opened up and he did that instead."

"It sounds like the good things about Joe didn't have much to do with physical stuff. Like he was deeper than that." Enrique glanced toward the house. "I'm not surprised. For a major league baseball player, this house isn't what I would expect. I mean, it's nice, but this is a regular neighborhood. No gates or guards."

"That's who he was. A regular guy who knew he got lucky."

"Maybe you can find a way to continue his legacy without keeping things that make you feel sad. If Alex or Mr. Thomas don't want it, you could sell it and use the funds to support a little league team."

Skylar turned, clinging to him. "I had no idea how hard this would be. I thought I'd turned the corner."

"You did, Sky. I watched it happen. Maybe living here is too much."
It had only been forty-eight hours and it seemed to be crushing her.
Enrique wasn't sure what to do. She'd been clear about it being his
choice if they lived here, but then she'd set this in motion. With her
being so fragile, he wasn't going to call her on it.

"But I want Mia to have a real home. She's lived in apartments and
motels her whole life. And she loves it here." Skylar sagged against
him.

Enrique rubbed her back. The night he'd first kissed her, she'd
confessed to being impulsive. But it seemed to come from a generous
heart.

She released him and turned toward the car. "Alex might want it.
But I should check with Joe's dad first. I just don't know if I can have
that conversation."

"Let's go inside." When he guided her out by the small of her back,
he felt a slight tremor. It was only a matter of time before Skylar
crumbled. He had to find a way around it. "Give me their numbers
and I'll take care of it."

"Are you sure?" Skylar stopped near the back door.

He cupped her face. "I'm going to help you through this."

As the evening wore on, she seemed to cheer. They had a nice
dinner with Mia chatting happily. Then he and Mia sat down and she
read to him. He loved watching her expressions. Often, she would
look up to get his reaction and ask interesting questions about the
characters. When she finished and put in the bookmark, she glanced
up. "Can you stay longer tonight? Skylar knows how to make popcorn
in a pan. It's really good." Her luminous eyes shone with uncertainty.
This was the first thing she'd asked him to do. Usually it was Skylar
who planned their activities.

"Sure. Hop on." Mia clambered onto his back and he stood, helping
Skylar to her feet. When the popcorn was ready, they ate at the island
in the kitchen. Enrique showed Mia how to throw a piece in the air
and catch it in her mouth.

"I'm not good at it." Mia's small fist came down on the granite
counter.

"Well, you'll have to work on it then." He gave her a hug. "I better
go."

"Why?" Mia grasped his arm.

"I've got some work to do tonight."

"You always have work to do."

He picked her up. "Not for long. After we get married, I won't work so much. You'll probably get sick of me." Mia clung to him and he patted her shoulder. *Oh, cariño.* He couldn't say it aloud. Not knowing if he would be able to raise her, he held part of his heart in reserve, not wanting to make it harder for either of them if things didn't work out. "Do you want to walk me outside?"

"Okay."

Skylar gave him a kiss and took the pan to the sink. "I'm going to take care of the dishes. I'll see you tomorrow." But he knew she was only avoiding going in the garage.

"Hang on," Enrique told Mia, setting her down. He followed Skylar, reeling her in for an extended hug. "I'll make those phone calls about the car tonight."

Her eyes flitted away. "Okay."

Mia held his hand as they went outside. "Enrique, what's wrong with Skylar?"

"She's hurting right now."

"What can we do?"

It touched him that she'd asked, that she'd noticed, but he was conflicted about placing another burden on her. "I don't know for sure, but maybe the two of you could spend time together until it's time for bed. It might help her not to be alone."

His heart felt like a stone as he drove away.

CHAPTER FIFTY-THREE

THE FOLLOWING EVENING, SKYLAR sprinkled dried cranberries and feta cheese on top of a salad. Though her skills paled in comparison to Enrique's, some nights she did the cooking so he could spend time with Mia. At the moment, they were playing soccer in the backyard. Mia had taken to him as quickly as Skylar had, enjoying their physical play.

Her therapist was closely monitoring Mia's relationship with him for anything that would cause concern. She'd explained how reintegrating a positive male role model could help Mia heal so long as she had a strong sense of her personal boundaries and trusted that he wouldn't cross them. Enrique told Mia often that she had every right to say what she did and didn't want to happen between them with regard to their physical contact. He even said it was her responsibility to do so, so she would be able to do that with guys as she got older.

Music played on the wireless sound system in the kitchen. When one of Joe's favorite songs came on, Skylar stopped what she was doing. It conjured the memory of the two of them driving up the Pacific Coast Highway with the windows down. It was his junior year and they'd gone to Carmel to spend time together before his season started. Brushing tears from her eyes, she turned off the music.

Everyone said it would get easier as time passed. So, why was it more oppressive with each passing hour? She'd spent the entire school day at the shop so she wouldn't be alone in the house. This new trajectory was frightening. Mia needed her. So did Enrique. Her heart felt like cracked glass. What if it shattered? She held up her hands. The new tremor that began shortly after moving in had gotten worse.

The timer dinged. Skylar pulled a pan from the oven and went to the back door. "Dinner's ready."

"That was a terrible kick. You totally could have blocked it," Mia complained as they both came inside.

Enrique laughed. "It wasn't terrible ... just not very good." They entered the kitchen, him bouncing the ball from knee to knee.

"Don't treat me like a baby." Mia faced him, hands on her hips, elbows out.

"It won't happen again." But he was grinning, still bouncing the ball.

"Enrique, please don't do that in here. You might break something," said Skylar.

"Geez, you girls are ganging up on me." He put the ball down and gave Skylar a kiss.

Mia made a face. "Ew. You guys always kiss."

Enrique jostled Mia's shoulder. "You think it's bad now? Wait till I move in. If you don't want to watch, you can keep a bag over your head. This is what people do when they love each other."

"I would suffocate!" Mia rounded the corner to the hall and Skylar heard the bathroom door close.

"Come here, *corazon*." His embrace reminded Skylar she had a living, breathing man in her life.

She held on tight. "You feel so good."

He glanced down, his face a question.

Skylar knew better than to bring up her struggle. She'd made a mistake. A whopper. Now she had to figure out how to live with it. A quiver of fear streaked through her because she was beginning to question if it were possible.

His features softened. "Are you thinking about Joe?"

She flooded with guilt. "Yes. No. I mean, not just Joe. The way I'm dealing with it. Or not dealing with it." She attempted a smile. "But I'm sure you're hungry." They parted and carried food to the table. "Do you still have time to stay and talk after dinner?"

"I do." He gave her a meaningful look. "So she still won't talk about it?"

At work, she'd told him of Mia's refusal to talk to Skylar about her flashbacks. "I don't know what to do." She had to find some way to get her mind off herself. Mia was struggling and Skylar needed to help her. Mia returned and they sat, chatting amiably while they ate.

After they finished, Mia cleared her place. "I'm going out to the tree house." That was Mia's new favorite place in the world. Although the weather was turning, she'd layer on coats and hide out up there, reading with the aid of a portable lamp.

"Actually, we need to talk to you." Enrique's neutral tone made Skylar grateful he was there.

Mia stiffened.

"It's important." Enrique carried his dishes to the sink.

"I just remembered I have homework." She ran upstairs and they heard her door close.

Skylar placed her chin on her hand. "I don't get why she won't trust me."

Enrique came over, put his hands on her shoulders. "Is she doing well in school? Making friends?"

"Yes. And Martha told me that Mia has talked with her each time it's happened."

He moved her hair to one side and rubbed the tight muscles in her neck. "Maybe we should give her more time. She is getting help and that's a big step."

"I know." She gazed up at him. "I just want it to be me she turns to. She only sees Martha once a week, but I'm here every day."

"It will happen." He kissed the top of her head.

While the two relaxed on the sofa in the front room, Enrique mulled the situation with Mia. It came as no surprise that Skylar wanted to be a perfect mom. He hoped he could be an effective buffer or mediator … whatever was needed. That was something his father could help with so he made a mental note to call him about it. He was certain Juan Pablo had played a role in Olivia coming by the shop to apologize to Skylar earlier that week. Enrique was happy that Skylar had reciprocated by inviting Olivia to join her and Mia when they went shopping for a Halloween costume the following week.

The doorbell rang and they both went to answer it. "Peter, what a surprise. Come in." Skylar let a middle-aged man into the foyer and introduced them. He wore a rumpled brown suit and the top button of his dress shirt was undone.

"Nice to meet you, Enrique. I've heard wonderful things about you. Congratulations on your engagement." Peter smiled broadly, then looked embarrassed and fumbled with his shirt. "Sorry. I was on my way home and decided to stop on the spur of the moment. I have a habit of taking off my tie when I get in the car."

Skylar waved a hand. "Don't worry about it. What's up?"

He stilled, a sober look on his face. "I'm glad you're both here. Do you mind if we sit?" Peter chinned toward the front room.

"No. Is everything alright?" said Skylar.

But Enrique knew the answer. With the exception of one meeting at his office, he knew all of Skylar's previous contact with Peter had been over the phone or via email. As Mia's *Guardian Ad Litem*, Peter was the one conducting the research on Mia's family. The court would rely on him to determine who Mia should live with for the long term. Peter settled on a chair and Enrique sat next to Skylar on the sofa.

"Believe it or not, I do have good news. I'll get to that first. You know we prefer children live with blood relatives in cases like this."

They both nodded and Skylar grabbed Enrique's hand.

"Mia's mom is incarcerated. I found out her parental rights were terminated before Marcus brought Mia to Colorado. My subsequent diligence search ruled out everyone on both sides of Mia's extended family. So, pending the background and criminal checks on you, Enrique, the two of you will be clear to adopt Mia within several months." Peter's knee bobbed up and down.

"I don't expect any snags there." Enrique couldn't connect Peter's encouraging words with his body language. Skylar cast a glance that told him she was having the same problem. "What's the rest of the story?"

Peter sighed. He ran a hand through his wavy brown hair, adding to his disheveled look. "I had an unexpected visitor today. Mia's fraternal grandmother stopped by my office."

"All the way from California?" Skylar went rigid.

Peter glanced around. "Where is Mia?" he whispered.

"Upstairs." Enrique got up to make sure her door was still closed.

"Well, I just wanted to give you a heads-up. Grandma has a rap sheet a mile long and has no documented income, though she lives in a nice house in San Diego. Any idea what real estate costs in San Diego?" He shook his head. "She showed up demanding to see Mia."

Skylar tightened her grip on Enrique's hand. "Do we have to allow that? Mia's afraid of her father's family."

Peter put up a palm. "No. She could petition the court, but given her background, it's a non-starter."

"But you're here," Enrique said flatly.

"I am. Something didn't sit right. She didn't make any threats—I get the feeling she knows exactly where the line is when it comes to that kind of thing. But ..." He shrugged. "She pumped me for information about where Mia is."

"Did you tell her?" Skylar sounded panicked.

"No. But I sensed that she's not planning to leave town without Mia. I want to be clear—she didn't say as much. But I learned early on to go with my gut. That's why I decided to stop by. Forewarned is forearmed, as they say." He got to his feet.

Skylar stood, too. "Peter, what are you saying? How careful do we need to be?"

His jaw worked. "Look, this could be nothing. But when a kid's life is at stake, I don't screw around."

Skylar's hand went to her stomach.

Enrique got up and extended his hand. "Thank you for stopping by." He checked Mia's door again. "What does this woman look like and what's her name?"

Peter whipped out his phone. "I'll email you her mug shot right now."

"Was she alone?" asked Enrique.

Peter nodded. "But drugs are the family business. My money says she didn't come all the way from California alone."

While Enrique saw Peter out, Skylar fled to the study and closed the door. He knocked before turning the knob. "Sky?" She stood hugging herself in front of the window. In three strides, he had her in his arms. "It's gonna be okay."

She grabbed hold of him. "I couldn't bear it if—" her voice broke.

"You won't have to." He soothed her back. "Nothing's going to happen to Mia on my watch." His mind began forming a plan.

"We need to talk to her." She moved toward the door.

"Hold on." He caught her hand. "Let's make sure we're on the same page."

Trepidation filled her eyes. "Right. I don't want to frighten her, but she has to know enough to help keep herself safe. I don't want to disrupt her world again if we can avoid it."

Enrique's gut churned. They discussed their ideas and came up with a plan, but he realized he was the only one who viewed it as tentative. Skylar felt strongly that Mia needed to remain in school. But he knew that in any war, the best commanders knew when to pivot. Mia was a fighter and she had a big support system now. Another disruption was better than the potential alternative if Peter was right.

Skylar turned to him. "I know I'm strong and capable. But … I need you. It's like you're half of who I am now." She held him again and he sensed her desperation.

"I feel that way, too." Enrique tipped his head back, both liking the sentiment and worrying over how much more she could take. They had agreed that he would stay with them until the matter was resolved. "Let's talk to Mia, then I'll run to the shop for my things."

"Okay." Skylar exhaled wearily.

He kissed her forehead. "I'll go get her." Knots formed in his stomach as he climbed the stairs. "Mia, I need you to come out."

"I'm not done yet."

He opened the door and peered in. True to her word, she sat at her desk with a notebook open. "I'm sorry, but something's come up and we need to talk. You can finish this later. Do you want a piggy-back ride or ground transportation?"

"Can't you wait?" Mia tapped her pencil on a notebook in an exaggerated manner.

"Nope." He motioned with his index finger, mapping the path from her desk to the hall.

"Fine." She trudged over and accepted his offer of a ride down the stairs.

When they were settled on the sofa with her in the middle, Enrique explained that they were now officially free to adopt her.

Mia blinked. "Is it my choice?"

He flooded with uncertainty. "I thought this was what you wanted."

She stared at the coffee table. "Do you want to be my dad, or are you just going along with Skylar?"

An ache began in his heart. "I love you, Mia. I want to be your dad."

Mia's eyes glistened and she ran from the room. Again.

CHAPTER FIFTY-FOUR

MIA SLAMMED HER DOOR and ran to her dresser. She pulled out her dad's wallet and her journal and hid in the closet. The picture on his driver's license wasn't how she remembered him. But she slipped it out and moved her fingers over his face, trying to remember what it felt like to touch him. Wishing for the impossible. She remembered the sound of his voice, how he smelled good after he'd showered and shaved. How it felt when he held her and called her his baby doll.

Mia loved Enrique. Sometimes when she dreamed, Enrique was there and she called him daddy. When she woke up, she always felt bad. "Daddy," she whispered. Tears streaked her face as she slid down the wall. She rubbed them away with a shirt that hung from a hanger, but more took their place. Her throat hurt like it had when her cries had led Bailey to her. Except for when Skylar rescued her and she had flashbacks, she'd been able to keep from crying like that again. It was the worst feeling. If she hadn't given in to her stupid emotions, Bailey wouldn't have found her. And the bad things with Braden would never have happened.

There was a knock on the bedroom door. Mia froze, worried Enrique might spank her or take her by the chin like Bailey had done. He'd been so nice to her and she'd run off like a little baby. "Mia?" It was Skylar. Mia was too scared to answer. "We're coming in, honey."

Mia shoved some clothes in front of her.

The closet door opened. "Mia, we need to talk. Do you want to come out or should we come in here?"

Making no answer, she hugged her knees. Her heart thudded loudly.

Skylar sat on the floor. Mia spied her through a gap in the clothes. There was a rustling noise and Mia spotted Enrique sitting next to

Skylar.

"I didn't want you to be alone up here," he said calmly.

This wasn't how people acted when you were mean to them. Any minute, one of them would lose their temper.

"I see your toes." Skylar sounded amused.

Mia peeked and saw Skylar had a small smile. It made her heart slow down a little. Then she shifted so she could see Enrique.

He'd laid down on the floor, taking up almost all the space in the big closet. "You know, I kinda like it in here. I think maybe I'll move in here instead of into Skylar's room."

"Well, I'm not going to sleep alone so I'll have to move in here, too," Skylar said. "It's going to be crowded."

Mia pushed the clothes aside. "I shouldn't have slammed the door."

Skylar reached out her hand. "Come here, sweetheart."

Mia went and sat in her lap. "Do you like sitting in closets? It's kind of strange. Sometimes I wonder about you, Skylar. And you're being a bad influence on Enrique. Look at him." She loved the feel of Skylar's chin on the top of her head, the way her arms folded around her, pulling her close to her warm, soft body.

Skylar laughed and kissed Mia's forehead. "You're not the first person to wonder about me." She rocked slowly. Like she had in the truck. And when she'd come to tell Mia about her dad's death.

Mia felt a sting in her nose, then her eyes. She tried desperately to keep it inside but it didn't work this time. She threw her arms around Skylar's neck, crying like she had in the delivery truck. Suddenly, it was hard to breathe and the whole thing played out in her head. The sound of a bullet breaking the window and others hitting the metal wall. Skylar yelling for her to hold on. Boxes sliding and falling while she scrambled to find a safe place. The screech of tires as the truck made a turn. But this time was different. Somehow in all the noise, she knew Skylar was holding her, heard her speaking softly.

Another hand touched her back. A big one. Then it moved and two big arms circled both Mia and Skylar. The pictures in her head came to a stop. "Mia, we're right here," Enrique whispered.

"We're not going anywhere, honey." Something wet hit Mia's cheek. She glanced up to see Skylar's eyes full of tears.

Mia's sobs shuddered to a stop. "You're ... crying."

Skylar nodded.

Enrique let go.

Mia tried to make sense of it. "Why? You never get scared."

"Why do you say that?" Skylar eyed her strangely.

"You're like someone in a movie. You cut the screen and climbed in the window. Then you did that to Glenda. And even when Devlin shot at you, you didn't stop."

Skylar moved Mia's hair from her face. Every time Skylar touched her felt good. "You didn't see what happened later."

"What?"

"I fell apart. Enrique had to take care of me. Ask him how much I cried."

"Is that true?" Mia glanced over at him.

He gave a half-smile that was a little sad. "She cried rivers."

Mia wiped her eyes, feeling awkward. "No one could cry rivers. There's not enough water in the human body."

Skylar laughed.

"Who needs Google when we have you? Come here." Enrique pulled Mia onto his lap and she'd never felt so happy and safe.

"I need a tissue." Skylar scrambled out, returning with a box from Mia's desk. They each dabbed their cheeks.

"Why did you run away?" Enrique asked.

Mia's lip quivered. "I don't know what to do."

"About what?"

"I already have a daddy." She felt angry at herself because she began crying again.

"It's okay to cry, *nena*." Enrique pulled her close.

Skylar touched Mia's arm. "I think I might know a little about how you feel. Do you remember when I told you about Joe dying?"

Mia nodded.

"Later, when I met Enrique, I liked him. But I felt guilty because I also loved Joe. I felt like I was being disloyal."

"Do you still love Joe?"

"I do. But not in the same way. He's not here anymore. I'll always treasure my memories with him, but it wouldn't be fair to Enrique if I didn't let go of Joe in here." She touched near her heart. "It's different for you, Mia. We want to be your family but that doesn't mean you have to let go of your dad. It's not a romantic relationship. It's completely okay for you to love your dad and Enrique at the same time. You can talk about him whenever you want to and we can visit places you went together. Whatever will help you."

Mia glanced up at Enrique.

He smiled. "Mia, I never want you to forget your dad."

She reached for her journal. "I've been writing things about him in here. So I won't forget."

"That's good." Skylar squeezed her shoulder.

Enrique shifted Mia so they were eye to eye. "How about if you call me *Papa*? That's what Carmen calls her dad. It's Spanish."

"You speak Spanish?"

"*Sí.*"

She knew that meant yes. "Fast, like Carmen?" Mia loved the way it sounded and Carmen had promised to teach her.

"*Sí.*" He kissed her forehead.

"Okay." Mia clambered off his lap. "But I know you're not really going to live in here. You're way too big. You were just trying to get me to talk."

"Well, it worked, so I guess I know what I'm doing." He grinned. Got to his feet. "Sky, how about we go downstairs and let Mia finish her homework?"

"Sure." Skylar took hold of his hand and got up. "Come find us as soon as you're done. We have something else to talk about. No reading till bedtime."

Mia sighed. But she felt relieved. Like a huge load had been taken off of her. She would have a real family.

CHAPTER FIFTY-FIVE

"GOOD JOB, MIA. ONE more time. Try not to make any noise." Though her chest felt tight, Skylar tried to sound cheerful. Enrique had driven her car to the shop to get his things and she and Mia were practicing what to do if the worst happened. When Mia came down after completing her homework, Enrique had done most of the talking. To Skylar's relief, Mia remained calm and self-assured. When he said she could handle herself, Mia believed him. Now Skylar did too.

"I'm tired," Mia complained.

"You just want to get to your book. And you can do that as soon as we're done."

Mia rolled her eyes, but she followed Skylar from the backyard into the house.

"This time I want you to do it alone. Go put the flashlight on the step."

"It's creepy down there," Mia said when she returned.

"I know. Nobody likes basements in old houses. I'll replace that light bulb and vacuum the cobwebs tomorrow." Skylar went to the sofa and pretended to talk on her cell phone. "Houston? I've never been to Houston." That was the code word—something Skylar had learned from her dad as a young child. They'd watched *Apollo 13* and, though they'd never had to use it, Houston was their code word for needing emergency assistance if either was under duress. If Skylar or Enrique said the word Houston, Mia was supposed to get to safety and summon help, leaving the adults to deal with the threat.

Mia ran to the basement. This time, Skylar didn't hear her footsteps on the stairs. *Nice.* Skylar ran to the cellar door in the backyard. Five seconds later, it opened and Mia popped out. She closed it noiselessly and raced to the tree house ladder in the cool darkness. It took about ten seconds for her to scramble up. Then she pulled up the ladder and closed the wood panel.

"Good job. What would you do right now if it wasn't a drill?" Skylar's breath fogged the air in the light that spilled from the patio.

"Call 911. Then Enrique. Then Art." Mia opened the hatch and peeked out, a look of satisfaction on her face.

"Perfect." Skylar felt lighter. It wasn't likely they'd need this, but she was confident Mia wouldn't freeze up like she had at Smile & Relax. "It's cold out here. Let's go inside."

Mia came down. "Was I faster this time?"

"You were. And quieter, too." They held hands on the way to the door, Mia skipping the way she did when she was happy. "I'm proud of you, Mia."

"Thanks." They shrugged out of their jackets and stowed them in the closet. Mia ran upstairs and Skylar wandered the lower floor. Though it was more prevalent in certain rooms, no part of the house lacked remnants of Joe, each with its accompanying memories. The doorbell rang, interrupting her nosedive. Had Enrique forgotten his shop keys in the rush? She flicked on the outside light, surprised to see two young men on the front porch, one huge, the other about her size. Skylar's heart skipped a beat. They eyed her through the window in the upper part of the door. "What do you want?"

The big guy on the right smiled broadly, glanced down at a clipboard. His dark hair was buzzed short on the sides and longer on top. A thin mustache and precisely sculpted beard wreathed his mouth. "Are you Skylar?" He spoke loudly, thumbed over his shoulder. "The neighbor said you might be in need of someone to mow the lawn."

Skylar frowned. Who made sales calls after dark? And in a few weeks, no one would be cutting their lawn anymore. She looked past them and spotted a white Cadillac Escalade. There was no logo on the side and it was way too nice for landscape work. But it was a perfect vehicle for running drugs. And there was plenty of room to stuff Mia inside. Skylar swallowed, wishing she'd gotten her gun from her dad. "No."

The two men shared a look.

Mia's footsteps sounded on the stairs, sending a hot spike of adrenaline into Skylar's stomach. She skipped past, humming a happy tune. The smaller man's eyes widened when he spotted her and he whispered something to his cohort.

"Houston!"

Both men slammed their bodies against the door. Wood splintered and debris flew through the air.

Houston. Mia froze momentarily, but the loud crash brought her out of it. A man sprinted toward her and she lunged for the basement, locking the door behind her. He swore and jerked on the knob, making the whole thing rattle. She reached for the flashlight but her foot knocked it over. It tumbled off the stairs landing somewhere below. Mia flipped on the light and raced down the steps.

In addition to the man banging on the door to the basement, loud yells and thumping noises sounded on the wood floor upstairs. *Get to safety and call for help. That's your job.* Enrique had said it over and over. But she wanted to go help Skylar. *No matter what happens, that's what you do, Mia.* She'd promised him. He'd told her about her grandmother's visit with Peter and the risk she was in.

Mia felt around on the floor and located the flashlight. It was covered in cobwebs. She shuddered and pushed the button. The light didn't turn on. It must have broken when it fell. She flung it aside and hurried to the next room, throwing the door open. This was where the light bulb was out. A long cobweb clung to her face as she felt her way along the wall in the dark. She gasped and slapped it away. Arms outstretched, she took small, careful steps to keep from tripping. They'd cleared the path of boxes, but doing this in the dark was a lot scarier than it had been with the flashlight. Her heart galloped as her mind conjured spiders crawling where she couldn't see them.

A man yelled and hurried footsteps pounded above her. Mia stilled, her eyes clouding with tears. She crumpled to the floor. What was happening to Skylar? *Mia, you have two things going for you; you're smart and you're strong.* Enrique had said it. His steady gaze had told her he meant it. He'd explained how important muscle memory was when you were scared. That's how he was able to insert an IV on a patient when bullets were flying around him. He'd practiced so many times that his body took over when he was afraid for his life.

Mia wiped her eyes on her sleeve and crawled toward the stairs that lead to the backyard. Feeling the first one, she crawled up, the cold from the hard concrete seeping into her knees. She kept her head low, remembering how she'd bumped it the first time. Her fingers moved like antennae feeling for the lock. It didn't budge when she pushed it. Mia jerked it harder. Then she remembered it went the other way. She pulled to the right and it quickly slid free. He was right about muscle memory.

Skylar yelled and a loud thump sounded upstairs. Like a body falling to the floor. A sob broke from Mia's throat as she worked the handle. The door opened and a rush of cold air hit her face. Mia peeked out to make sure it was safe. Then she shoved the door up and climbed out, closing it quietly even though everything in her wanted to let it slam shut. In the darkness, she sprinted for the tree and scrambled up the ladder. Near the top, her foot slipped and she lost her balance, dangling at an odd angle by one arm.

CHAPTER FIFTY-SIX

ENRIQUE WAS NEARING SKYLAR'S neighborhood when his cell phone rang. The car was crammed full of his belongings. It had taken longer than he'd expected to get everything together. Then he'd gotten stuck behind an accident. Skylar was probably wondering what was taking so long. He picked up his phone and saw it was Mia calling. He frowned. "Hey, Mia."

She was panting. Or crying? "We need help."

His stomach caught fire. "Where are you?"

"In the tree house. Just like you said. They're here."

He floored the gas. "Where is Skylar?"

"Inside." Mia sobbed. "They're hurting her."

"Did you call 911?"

She gulped some air. "Yes." Sobs erupted.

The car shimmied when he slammed to a stop at a red light. Joe being killed crossing the street was never far from his mind. As much as he wanted to hurry, he knew he had to be careful. "Good job, Mia. Try to calm down. I need you to help me. What did you see?"

"A man. He tried to get me."

"But you said 'they're here.' Did you see more than one?" Enrique skidded around a corner and gunned it, going as fast as he dared.

A pause. "I only saw one. But it sounds like more."

"Okay, I'm almost there. Call Art right now. I want you to stay where you are until we come to get you. I need to hang up."

When the door flew inward, Skylar turned and ran toward the study, hoping to draw them away from Mia. Only the big one followed. As she sprinted through the hallway, she pushed a small antique table to the floor in her wake. He slowed going over it, giving her a slim lead. Worries about Mia crowded her mind, along with thoughts of how to overcome this large thug. On the far side of the house, the other guy was swearing and banging on the basement door. This gave her a small measure of relief because it told her Mia had successfully locked it, buying her some time.

Rounding the corner to the study, Skylar shot through the door and slammed it behind her. But the man had caught up and had hold of the knob, so the latch didn't catch. She jammed her foot against the base of the door and leaned away from his hand as it flailed about, trying to grab her. The pressure on her foot was fast becoming unbearable. She glanced around and spotted Joe's lucky bat propped in the corner. Too far away.

She grabbed a small metal lamp from a table nearby and hacked his arm with the base. He only grunted and the door pushed in further. Now his whole arm was inside. "You and me are gonna have some fun when I get in there." He had a thick Mexican accent.

Her foot now reaching its pain limit, Skylar grabbed a knife-shaped letter opener from the mail basket and jammed it into his bicep. "How's that for fun?" He howled and pulled his arm away. Skylar slammed and locked the door, knowing it would only give her a few seconds. She jetted across the room and picked up the bat, her mind calculating the best way to strike. He was big, so she'd have to go for his head or his groin. And he was probably armed, which meant she'd have to be fast. She said a quick prayer for Mia as the door flew in, splinters of wood flying every direction.

He barreled in like a linebacker after the snap. Having moved around the corner out of his view, Skylar spotted the muzzle of his gun before anything else. Rather than going for his head, she instinctively brought the bat down full force on his hand. The weapon flew from his grip, landing several feet away. "Bitch." With a growl, he lunged toward her. Skylar sliced with the bat, clearing a shelf, sending chards of glass from one of Joe's awards into his face. Some of the pieces dug into his skin, bringing droplets of blood to the surface.

"Ven ayudame," he yelled, using the back of his hand to sweep spikes

from his face.

"I'm coming," called a voice from the other side of the house. Heavy footsteps pounded their direction.

Skylar realized he'd called his accomplice and raised the bat, introducing the business end to his right temple at a speed that surprised even her. His eyes rolled back in his head and he went down like a boulder, blood from his head oozing onto the wood floor. She grabbed his gun and flung it under the desk, then hid around the corner just as the other guy came through the door.

His mind churning with potential scenarios and how he would deal with them, Enrique sped down Skylar's street. When he spotted a white SUV in front of the house, he braked hard, angling so his headlights illuminated it. A silhouette in the back seat could easily be Mia's grandmother. Praying he was right and that she wasn't armed, he parked inches away from the driver's side so they wouldn't be able to move the vehicle or open the door.

In one fluid movement he leapt out of the car, drew his gun, and slid across the hood. Standing next to the window, he flicked off the safety, racked the slide, and tapped the muzzle on the glass next to the woman's head. "Open up." She complied, emitting a surprised yelp when he yanked her out by the arm. "Shut the hell up." They moved toward the gate and she opened it without being told. His grip on her neck probably made that happen.

"How many guys?"

"Two. They're my nephews. Don't hurt them. Please." Her voice wavered.

He almost laughed at her pathetic act. She was a hardened criminal. "How many guns?" He dragged her up the sidewalk, then the front steps, her short legs struggling to keep up. This woman—a drug dealer —looked something like his mother. Same age and build. Same short, dark hair.

"They don't have guns."

"Right." The front door was ajar, the jam splintered from being kicked in. This caused his heart to pound even faster. He shoved it open with his boot, aiming his weapon in front. "Skylar!" He positioned the woman in front of him, the gun at her neck.

"I'm back here." Her voice sounded strong. But he knew better than to assume all was well.

He headed that way, keeping the woman in front, checking for threats over his shoulder every two seconds. They stepped over a table on its side in the hall. His mind conjured pictures of Skylar being chased down by thugs. The bottom fell out of his stomach when he saw the study door had also been kicked in. "Sky. Where are you?"

"On the left. We're playing a little baseball. One more strike and he's outta there." She said it like an announcer calling a game.

Enrique toed the door lightly and it swung in a few inches. He spotted a man lying on the floor and scanned him for weapons.

"Oh, Tiny." The woman struggled to free herself.

"Shut up." Enrique tightened his hold and shoved the door open the rest of the way. Tiny—who looked to weigh two-seventy-five—moaned, but made no attempt to get up. A large bloodstain surrounded his head. In the far corner, Skylar stood with Joe's bat in her hand, poised as if she were ready to swing at a pitch. Behind her were two handguns. *Qué diablos?* Andy was right—she *was* a superhero.

"Took you long enough," Skylar said, without looking up. "My arms are getting tired. I was about to knock him out so I could put this bat down, but I really don't want more blood to clean up." She had a cut on her chin, another under her nose, various minor cuts along her arms. A smaller guy cowered in front of her, hands over his head. Blood oozed from a large lump on his head and several large purple knots dotted his arms.

"Call the cops before she beats me to death," the guy wailed. As if he'd conjured them with his words, flashing lights appeared outside.

Not wanting to have a gun in his hand when the police burst in, Enrique shoved the woman to the floor next to Tiny. "Stay there." He crammed his weapon in the desk drawer and took over for Skylar. "Go get Mia. Take her upstairs. I don't want her to see them," he said in her ear.

"Police!"

Cops rushed through the front door as Skylar ran into the backyard. "Mia? It's safe to come out now." The trap door opened and Mia peeked out. It was too dark to see her expression. The ladder unraveled and she scrambled down. Skylar caught her in her arms before her feet touched the ground. Emotion clogged her throat. Mia's arms banded around her neck and she held on with her legs. Skylar leaned against the tree and rubbed Mia's back.

Mia wiped her eyes. "I thought you might be …" she trailed off.

"I know. It was scary for both of us. But I'm okay. It's cold out here. Let's get you inside." She set Mia to her feet and took her hand. "You did everything right. I'm so glad you're safe." Skylar opened the door and hurried Mia through the house, which was now a hive of blue uniforms.

"Skylar?" An officer tried to catch up with her.

"I'll be down in a bit."

"I want to ask Mia a few questions," he persisted.

"And I want to be taller." Skylar ushered Mia up the stairs. Enrique was right. Mia shouldn't see the men. She had enough nightmare fodder already.

Footsteps followed behind and Skylar turned at the landing, ready to shove whoever it was down the stairs.

"Skylar." Art pulled her into a fierce hug, somehow scooping up Mia at the same time. "Mia. You're okay." His arms banded around them like warm steel. "I got here as soon as I could." He was winded. The three of them huddled together for a minute.

Finally, Art pulled away, keeping Mia in his arms. He captured her gaze, caressing her cheek. "Good job, honey." To Skylar he said, "She called me and I stayed on the phone with her until you came out."

Mia glanced at Skylar. "I wanted to come help you, but he told me not to." Tears filled her eyes.

Skylar smiled, feeling pain on her chin. Her fingers probed and felt blood. "Oh, honey. I know you did. But Dad was right. That would have been dangerous."

Mia eyed Skylar's chin. "Does that hurt?"

"A little."

The police officer that had tried to stop Skylar waited at the bottom of the stairs. Art put up a finger. "Sky, he needs to talk to her."

Skylar clenched her jaw. "Dad, she's been through enough. And she didn't see anything. Enrique doesn't want her to see them."

"She won't. I'll handle it. Enrique's worried about you. Go find him." He looked at Mia. "We're going to go talk to that detective. I'll stay with you."

"Okay." Mia's chin trembled slightly.

Art cupped her head to his shoulder, pressed his lips to her hair. "It won't be like the other time, sweetheart. We'll be right downstairs and it won't take long at all."

Skylar watched him carry Mia downstairs, knowing he was doing the right thing, but hating that Mia had more trauma to deal with.

CHAPTER FIFTY-SEVEN

ENRIQUE WAITED AT THE bottom of the stairs so Art could have a private moment with Mia and Skylar. The two guys and their aunt had been cuffed and taken away, two of them in an ambulance. Still brimming with uniforms, the house looked like a war zone. A man and woman in CSI jackets lugged what looked like large tackle boxes into the house.

Art carried Mia downstairs. "We're going to take care of her statement. Maybe you can see to Skylar. She got banged up."

Enrique took the steps two at a time. "Are you okay?" He ran his hands down Skylar's arms, searching her face.

"Yes and no." She looked dazed.

"Start with yes." He led her to the bathroom and had her sit on the counter.

"I did what I needed to do and Mia is safe." She winced when he used a wet cloth to wipe blood from a small cut on the top of her hand. "I wasn't sure I could bring my A game but when they showed up, it all clicked."

Enrique rinsed the cloth and wrung it out. "Why weren't you sure?"

"When I'm with Mia, I'm not as aware of everything else. After Peter stopped by, I was worried I'd screw up if anything happened."

"You hardly screwed up, Sky. Every one of those cops wants you in the next police academy." He dabbed at the dried blood near the cut on her chin, careful not to touch the actual wound. "You could use a butterfly bandage on this one. My med bag's in the car."

Skylar didn't answer.

"What's wrong?" he asked.

She sighed heavily. "I'm just going to come right out and say it. I can't stay here. It feels like Joe is in every room." She met his gaze. "I'm sorry. I know I told you it was your decision, but when you're not here, I feel like I'm being sucked under. I'm afraid of what will happen to me if I stay. I feel like I'm falling apart."

"I wondered how this would go." Enrique stroked her cheek with his thumb. He'd get the bandage later. "Let's sit down." He led her to the love seat in the master bedroom and they collapsed together.

She leaned her head against his shoulder. "I was doing so well. I thought I was out of the woods. I did this for Mia. I wanted her to have—" her voice cut out.

Enrique rested a hand on her thigh. "And that's one of the reasons I love you. You have such a big heart. But you haven't been the same since you've been here. And it's only been a few days."

"It's like June all over again, only without the drinking. But I'm afraid I might start up again. I'm turning into emo-girl. I hate it. It's not normal for me."

Enrique sighed. "Skylar, it's okay about the house. I was leaning that direction anyway. But now that I see what it's doing to you, I know we can't stay." He put an arm around her, drawing her to his side. "But that's not the only problem."

"What are you saying?"

"When I got back from my tour, I kept waiting to get back to normal. Up here." He touched the side of his head. "It took a while—and some help from other people—but I finally figured out that what I went through changed me. I can't go back to who I was before. I always thought I'd pursue a medical career. But after the war I couldn't bring myself to apply for any of those jobs, even though they paid well and I was desperate for money. I'd seen enough trauma. And what happened with Swan made me lose my confidence. I had to do something different." He settled deeper into the sofa, bringing her with him. "I used to love going to things like concerts and games. But I can't stand it now."

"Why?"

"Part of it is the stress. When you're over there, you know you're a target. Every minute of every day, all you think about is how to avoid being killed. When you're out in the open, you calculate how many steps it is to the next cover. And you're constantly scanning for snipers or people who could be carrying a bomb in their clothing. Insurgents don't wear uniforms and they don't give a damn about the rules of warfare. So anyone—even a child—can be a tool of the enemy. It's gotten better but I still don't like crowds. It's impossible to relax."

"I never thought about that." She rested a hand on his thigh.

He picked it up, threading their fingers. "My point is, you probably shouldn't expect to be the same as you were before. Even if you're not living here. You've been through a personal tragedy. Why wouldn't it change you?"

Skylar groaned. "But what about Mia?"

"I think Mia cares more about having a family than where we live. Besides, kids are resilient. You said yourself she shouldn't be treated like a victim. Look how well she handled what happened tonight. All it took was a little coaching."

"But—"

Enrique shifted, cupped her face in his hands. "Skylar. You are the reason she's safe, maybe even alive. Taking care of yourself isn't selfish. If you fall apart, where will she be? And what will it do to you and me?"

After a long silence, she said, "You're right."

"I know."

She poked his ribs. "I have to go make a statement. If Mia's done, will you see if she wants any help getting ready for bed? I don't think she'll be able to go to sleep on her own. Maybe you guys can read or something. I don't want her downstairs until we get it cleaned up."

"Sure."

Skylar met Mia and Art on the landing midway up the stairs. She gave Mia a hug and a kiss. "Enrique's waiting to tuck you in. I'll come up in a bit."

She nodded, covering a yawn.

Art stooped to give Mia a hug. "Go get some sleep." To Skylar he said, "Your turn." He gestured toward the detective, who gave a slight nod.

Skylar signaled that she'd be a minute. "Dad, thank you for being here."

Art eyed her. "Of course."

"No, I don't just mean here. Tonight. I mean through this whole thing. I shut you out. And for a long time, I resented you."

"Honey. You don't need to—"

"I just want to tell you that it's going to be different. I mean, I want things to be different. Moving forward. I didn't have the chance to tell you ... we found out today that we're clear to adopt Mia. Well, there's Enrique's background check—"

"He's clear."

She smacked him on the arm. "Dad."

He lifted an unapologetic brow. "That's great news about Mia."

Skylar rolled her eyes. "I want Mia to know you. And Elana. And the boys."

His adams apple bobbed once. "I want that, too."

Skylar kissed his cheek and gave him a brief hug. "You're so gonna pay for checking him out."

He laughed and prodded her toward the detective.

When the house was finally quiet, Skylar pulled Enrique out of the study where he'd just finished scrubbing blood off the floor. The furniture was back in place and everything that had been broken had been thrown away, the mess swept or vacuumed. The only evidence of what happened was the missing trim on the doors. Art had called a friend who promised to take care of repairs the following day. The front door was being held shut with a sliding lock her father had found in the garage. "We should get some sleep."

He answered with a yawn, grabbed his duffel and followed her up the stairs. They got ready for bed like a couple of zombies. Too spent for anything else, they snuggled together and fell asleep.

Skylar awoke just after three in the morning. Enrique had turned to his other side and was sleeping soundly. Wide awake, she stared at the ceiling, knowing she wouldn't get back to sleep. After several minutes, she slipped out of bed and went downstairs. The only sound in the house was a low whir coming from the refrigerator.

She wandered the front room. Joe had brought in a wood worker who added a wall of built-in bookshelves that matched the smaller originals on the opposite side. It was impossible to look out the front windows without remembering the weekends they'd worked on the landscaping together. One day—the day they'd planted the roses— she'd thrown a dirt clod at Joe and they'd ended up slathered in mud, too dirty to go inside without hosing off first. All the memories conspired, bringing a crushing weight on her heart. This was their place. Where they'd planned to raise a family and grow old together.

The study drew her like a magnet and she sat at Joe's desk, running her hands over the smooth, cool surface. She opened a drawer and took out the photo of him in his pitching stance dressed in his Rockies uniform. He'd been so proud to play his last season in Denver. In spite of his career-ending shoulder injury that cut the season short, he was grateful to the hometown fans who cheered at each game. As she had so many times, Skylar traced the lines of his body. "I'm so sorry, Joe. I wish—" she choked off. "Please forgive me." She moved to the bookshelf, picking up his baseball, fingering the spines of his books. "I will always love you. Always."

Then she took a deep breath, knowing what she needed to do.

In the middle of the night, Enrique turned over and reached out for Skylar. Her side of the bed was empty. "Sky?" He sat up and listened, hearing nothing. The clock on the night table read three thirty-two. Had he slept through Mia waking with a nightmare? He tugged on his pants and headed down the hall. Mia's door was closed, so he stood and listened outside. Then he noticed a dim glow in the hallway downstairs. Maybe Skylar was hurting from being knocked around. He padded toward the kitchen, but didn't find her there. A noise drew him to the basement stairs. "Skylar?"

"I'm down here." Rustling noises drifted up.

He descended the steps. She was wrestling with a stack of flattened boxes in a corner. They seemed to be caught on something. He went to her. "What are you doing?"

"Packing Joe's things." She sniffed. "But I can't get these stupid boxes—" her voice cut out.

"Hey." He took a roll of packing tape from her hand and set it on a shelf. There was an overstuffed chair nearby. "Come here, *amorcito*." Enrique pried her hand off the boxes and led her to the chair, pulling her onto his lap. A torrent of tears burst forth, causing her body to quake. He held her until they subsided. "Were you in the study?"

She nodded.

He blew out a breath.

"What's wrong with me? Other people don't have to move when someone dies. They just ... go on."

"It doesn't matter what other people do."

"Why did Joe have to die?" Her tears started again. "And why did I insist on waiting to get married?"

Her fist landed softly on his chest, rending his heart. "Were you asking these questions before you moved in here?"

A pause. "Not anymore."

Seeing her like this terrified him. He realized it had been a mistake to bring up Mia and her family when she'd talked about getting married right away. Between waiting and her coming here, she was on a perilous ledge. "Come back to bed." Enrique took her by the hand and led her upstairs.

In bed, Skylar snuggled close to him.

"Sky, let's get married today. We'll do it after school or Mia can skip a day. Just the three of us."

"But—"

"We'll invite everyone to the adoption proceeding and we can have a big party afterward to celebrate our new family."

She was quiet a moment. "Don't we need an appointment with a judge?"

"If they don't have an opening, we'll do it ourselves. You can do that in Colorado. We already have our marriage license, so we just need to go to the clerk and recorder's office to make it official."

"Really?" A flicker of hope returned to her voice. She clung to him. "Are you sure?" He heard the doubt in her tone.

He turned, cupped her face with his hands. "I want nothing more than to be your husband. I'm sorry I asked you to wait. It wasn't what you needed."

Skylar sighed contentedly. "So in less than twenty-four hours, I'll be the wife of the hottest Latino on the face of the earth?"

Enrique laughed. "You'll be stuck with me. For life."

"There's no one I'd rather be stuck with."

"Sky, I'm going to take some time off work." He rolled so he was on top of her, supporting most of his weight with his elbows. "After we say our vows, we'll find a place to live. Something different so we can make our own memories."

"Okay."

Careful to avoid her various cuts, he feathered kisses on each cheek, then on her lips. Her hands moved softly over the small of his back. "Then we're going to get away—wherever you want. I'm sure my mom or Elana will take care of Mia. And on the weekend she can hang out with Carmen."

"Do you think Mia will be okay?"

"She's been worried about you. I think if she knows you've got your feet back under you, she'll be fine."

"What about the shop?" Her fingertips slid beneath his waistband, making it difficult for him to think.

"Andy and Manny will step up. So will Jasmine." Skylar parted her legs. Enrique nestled closer and gave a slow smile.

"I love you." Skylar smiled, too. In the lamplight, he saw that it reached her eyes. "And I need you. Right now." Her hands worked his briefs down several inches.

He thought about all she'd been through that night. "Aren't you tired?"

"Not yet."

"Then I better get busy."

I am grateful to those who helped with this story. Sergeant Ron "Doc" Johnson, NRP, FP-C, and Nathan Rudolph, who served as a medic with the first infantry division in Bosnia and Kosovo during his tenure in the army. Thank you both for your service and for your willingness to share your experiences on the front lines.

Others who helped are Troy Marx, Owner of The Bloody Knuckles Garage in Castle Rock, Colorado, Edward Leger, who answers every question I throw at him and always knows a guy (or gal) I can tap for more information, Denver Police Sergeant Daniel Steele, who supervises the FBI Rocky Mountain Innocence Lost Task Force, Jodi Byrnes, Forensic Interview Program Director with the Denver Children's Advocacy Center, Alyssa MacMahon, Matthew D. Garrett, Cardboard Placement Operative, Edgar Contreras, formerly of Mexico city, who painstakingly bridged my wide Spanish language gap, Daril Cinquanta, Barb Dyess, and Becky Clark.

Dear Reader,

Thank you for reading *Changing Sky*, Book One in the *Colorado Chronicles* series. If you would like to connect with me, visit www.TRFischer.com where you can sign up for my email list and find links to purchase all of my books. I use my list to notify readers of upcoming releases and run a quarterly contest to win a free copy of one of my books.

If you enjoyed this story, please share it with others you know and post a review on Amazon and any other review sites you like.

Happy Reading,

TR Fischer